THE DIVIDE

THE SOLDIERS OF THE EARTH BOOK ONE

ELLE NOLAN

DRAGON HOUSE
PUBLISHING

ONE

My father told me the day someone dies is the best time to escape. Somehow, it feels like no one ever dies here. Every illness and every ailment gets cured. There is no crime. We know as long as we follow the rules, we will live. And we will live in controlled comfort.

I look out across the grounds from a window I can't open. There is no latch. The glass is unbreakable. But it's not to prevent escape. We are useful, and they need us alive. We all get little homes with our own rooms and doors that cannot lock. Nothing sharp: no knives, no razors. We get work clothes, school uniforms, and pajamas. Everything is a riveting color palette of white and silver. Little luxuries to keep us compliant inside these walls.

People have too many theories for why the aliens came here. They wanted slaves. Resources. Since they controlled other planets in other galaxies, this was one more to add to their collection. Honestly, I stopped caring about the reasons a long time ago.

This is my life now. Every day is exactly the same. Every morning I wake up to white walls and silver furniture. To the smell of toast and eggs. I get ready to work at my assigned job and hope I have enough extra points to buy something fun at the end of the day. Stay in line and there will be no trouble. Do as you're told and the aliens won't hurt you.

Except, this day is different. This is my day to deviate. Today is the day I turn 18. That doesn't mean much here in the Reserve. I don't get the day off from working. I don't get extra food at lunch or points at the end of my shift. But there's a small change. All the white banners above the main buildings are purple today. A human has died on the day I'm celebrating my birth. I shouldn't be happy that someone died, and I'm lucky it's not someone I know. Still, it's hard not to contain my excitement. I've been dreaming of this day since I got here.

When my father left, my mother grieved for weeks. He could have been as good as dead for all we knew. Captured by the Emigres (the human nickname for these aliens who never tell us anything) and punished for attempting to leave. My mother called him foolish for believing in the rumors that there were rebels outside the walls. But my sisters and I secretly believed they were out there. And that he had joined them.

I remember waiting every night by the sewer drain my dad used to escape. When no guards were around, I would lift the cover. Looking down into the black abyss, I would check again and again for some sign that my dad was alive. I knew in his nature he would do anything to let us know and ease our minds. Two months later, I got my wish. A note taped to the underside of the cover. It addressed my family, and his distinct cursive handwriting told us that he was alive. And he made it to a rebel base.

That was my hope that I clung to, and I wanted to follow him that very day. If he could escape through the drains, any of us could. But my mother shot my plans down, forcing my sisters and me to stay quiet. No one else could know, and none of us could try. Stubborn as a mule, I often begged until she agreed to let me try about a year ago. I was nearly an adult, and the decision was up to me.

"You're late to work!" My neighbor's voice startles me as I leave the house. "Your mother left ages ago."

"Good morning, Mr. Nelson," I reply, attempting to smile at him. He's sitting on his usual folding chair outside his home, watching the world as he always does. In my experience, he's the only human who enjoys every aspect of living here, in alien captivity. With our homes built next to each other, we saw each other often. He spent every second of the first few months telling anyone that the "geniuses" cured his terminal cancer. I was lucky enough to be healthy as could be when I got here. In my mind, I didn't see the appeal of curing every ailment of each human to make them prison workers.

"My coffee is almost cold. Sleep in, did ya?" He points his cane at me, which serves no use to him anymore, but he carries it around anyway.

"Yeah," I lie. As nice as he could be, Mr. Nelson was another reminder that I couldn't tell anyone about my dad's escape route. The more people that knew leaving was possible, the quicker the Emigres would find out. And part of me felt like Mr. Nelson would rat me out if he knew.

"I heard the death was Mrs. Mabel," Mr. Nelson sighs. "Heart attack finally got her. They couldn't get to her in time."

"Sad to hear that," I say back. Never met Mrs. Mabel, but according to my dad, she'll grant me the opportunity to escape. Humans don't get gravestones here. We can't go to waste, so we get thrown into the sewers to feed the beastly creatures the Emigres brought here. When they're fed, they're distracted. And sleepy. I have a chance to make it through the sewers and get out alive.

"Rachel!" I hear my older sister, Mary, call from behind me. "You forgot your vitamins." She hands me the dark red container, a nervous smile on her lips. I scan the barcode on the bottle with my silver ID bracelet to open it, trying not to let Mr. Nelson see me blush. Clearly, I had too much on my mind today.

I take out one dissolvable yellow strip and place it on my tongue. As I taste lemon, the familiar but unnatural sense of calm washes over me. No human knows for sure what's in the vitamins. But a well-accepted theory is some kind of mood stabilizer or anti-anxiety drug. All the Emigres told us is that the vitamins keep us healthy. And it's mandatory that we take them.

"Thanks," I reply before lowering my voice. "Still on for tonight?"

"Of course," she nods, grabbing my hand and giving it an encouraging squeeze. "But if you want to wait, that's alright, too." She always picks up on my fear, even if I hide it. Before I can reply, she heads off to her job. She has the mind-numbing task of putting together the all-white uniforms each of us humans wear in this prison. My job at least let me move around.

I hold my bracelet up to the scanner by the door of the greenhouse, avoiding eye contact with the Emigre guard by the door. Technically, their species name is Kofali. From the planet Kofal. But calling them Emigres is what little control humans have left and they let us keep. With a beep, the door opens and I make my way inside. As the humidity level rises and the smell of vegetation hits me, I look for my mother. Spotting her familiar head of blonde hair, I make my way over and begin harvesting with her.

The Reserve has gotten a lot less strict in the past two years. We now can work with whoever else we want in the greenhouse and we can talk to each other, too. But I can't find any words today. My mind is too consumed with getting out. My mind thinks every Emigre guard is staring at me. Their violet eyes and sharp features always seem menacing to me, and now it's making my nerves climb. I can't help but feel as if they know I'm up to something.

"You're pale as a sheet today, Rachel," Tina says, blowing her auburn bangs out of her face. She harvests carrots next to me as she eyes me with concern. She's my only other friend in the Reserve. Part of the reason was that we both work in the greenhouse. No one else in this job is close to our age. "Are you sick?"

"She's tired," my mother interrupts, smiling at her. "Today is her birthday. She stayed up until midnight last night."

"Ah, how exciting!" Tina's face lights up. "I can't believe I forgot.

You're 18, right?" When I nod, she throws her arms around me in a hug. My heart falls. As much as this place feels like hell, she was one of the few things that made this new life easier. And I'm leaving her behind without even telling her why. "I've got enough points. I'll get you a chocolate bar! Unless you want a cookie?"

"Either is fine." I force myself to sound and look more positive.

"Are you getting your hair done again?" She asks, knowing I got my hair highlighted. One of the few nice things about the Reserve is the point system. You could save up points for some luxury things you enjoyed pre-invasion: massages, pedicures, and hair cuts and color. Before the invasion, I highlighted and straightened my hair a lot. Years of ballet and trying to fit in at school made me hate my dark, curly hair. But when the world went to hell, I didn't hate it anymore. Especially since it was a feature, I got from my dad, like his brown eyes and tan skin. But I liked the small sense of feeling like my life was normal, and there was something still within my control.

"Not this time. Can't afford it." I lie, shrugging. There would be no point. After today, I'd either be out in the real world, captured, or dead. A part of me wishes I could just leave right after my shift and get this over with. But I need to leave at dark like my father did. I try to pass the time by thinking about the escape plan I've obsessed over for a year and a half. Open the cover of the sewer closest to the wall that traps us here. Enter the sewer and put the cover back. Avoid the beasts everyone claims to hear rumbling through the tunnels. Walk about 10 minutes following the map from my dad and open the next cover. Climb out and enter what we call the Divide.

The Divide is the remnant of cities visible from the top floor of the registration center in the Reserve. The collapsed buildings cut us off from the rest of the world. Every single human here could see it when we received our silver ID bracelet. Emigre ships patrolling overhead added to the feeling of unease. It was a reminder of the destruction, pain, and death that surrounded us before. At least here we had a bit of a break.

It scared plenty of people into staying put and complying. Past the twenty-foot wall were Emigre guards and past the guards was the Divide. And rumors swirled about the Ruins beyond it. Food, medicine, and clean water were scarce. Violence was rampant. The Reserve had everything we could ever need, and all we had to do was work six hours a day.

But my dad was proof that people can get out alive. And the rebels exist. All I have to do is get out and stay alive until I find them.

TWO

"WHAT WOULD YOU LIKE, BIRTHDAY GIRL? CHOCOLATE BAR OR sugar cookie?" Tina asks me again. She scans her bracelet at the grocery shop door and her point balance flashes on the screen.

"Cookie!" My little sister Annie yells for me, hopping up and down as Tina laughs. I had just picked her up from school after my shift and whatever snacks they gave her had her bouncing off the walls. Placing a hand on her shoulder, I hushed her while looking at the Emigre guard. His violet eyes don't even glance at us, and I breathe a sigh of relief as we head inside. Whether the guards were strict or lenient depended on the day.

"You don't need any more sugar, little one," Tina grins at her. With a gentle touch, she braids Annie's blonde locks that had fallen through the day. "Besides, this is for Rachel's birthday!"

"Yeah," Annie huffs. "I made her a card." She hands me a folded piece of paper with a colorful drawing of two stick figures. My heart pangs, but I force a smile.

"This is so sweet, thank you," I hug her as we get in line. Sometimes I envy how young Annie is because life is so simple in her eyes still. A dead branch is the world's finest sword, a rock is the rarest gem, and our house was her castle. In her world, even with all the horror she'd seen, the aliens were standard villains who could be won over with love. If she was kind, she didn't think they would ever hurt her. I knew they would the first chance they got.

The first table we reach has the produce selection, and I grab a bag of potatoes and an apple per my mother's list. At the sweets table, I ask Tina for a cookie knowing I'll give it to Annie anyway. Tina is the kind of person that would spend the last of her points to get Annie a treat, too. But I knew she spent every bit on her younger brother, Ben. Ben was two years older than Annie. He used to come over daily and play with Annie, but now that he was 9, he felt he was too cool to hang out with little girls. I felt he was becoming a bit of a jerk, but Tina still spoiled him rotten.

She loved living here. Outside, before the invasion, her mom was addicted to drugs. They ended up on the streets. Food, shelter, and safety were already scarce for them. Inside these walls, she had everything she could ever dream of and more. And her mom was clean. Here, they could be a normal family. They could enjoy the things they never had before. Tina would never want to leave, so I kept my plans to myself.

I grab a small pound cake, my mother's selection to celebrate my birthday, and our last meal together. Out of the corner of my eye, I see Annie grab another cookie when she thinks no one is looking. I snatch it back from her and place it on the table.

"Annie!" I hiss under my breath. "You know better. We can't go above the daily limit."

"But I want a cookie," she whines, her green eyes filling with tears.

"You can have mine." I roll my eyes, but I'm thankful this quiets her. Our family has to follow stricter rules thanks to my dad running away. We have limits on food and breaks, we earn half the amount of points as others do, and we have to follow an earlier curfew. They monitor us more than other humans. But over the past year, the Emigres have gotten more lenient with the monitoring. I don't want to push them, not before I plan to escape. And not when we don't know what the punishments are: would we be beaten, thrown into the rumored prison, killed? I didn't want to chance it.

Most of the stories of people escaping are rumors. People notice when someone disappears, but don't always know why. Sometimes a family swears to the rest of us that their loved one escaped. The truth is they do not know if their family member made it out alive. Escaping became gossip instead of reality. Stories over the dinner table about a man who scaled the walls. Or a young kid sneaking onto an Emigre ship leaving the Reserve.

I was one of the lucky ones. When most people didn't know if someone made it out alive, I had proof from my dad that he had been successful. A part of me feels like that should give me confidence in my plan, but my nerves refuse to ease. The trauma of the invasion scarred us all even past the two-year mark.

Being on the run from the Emigres as the world fell under their control was one of the most terrifying moments of my life. A large group of them had stormed into the abandoned barn we had been seeking shelter in. They forced us against the wall with their guns before my father had time to reach for his own. With their violet eyes cold and calculating, they spoke perfectly in our language. They let us know we had a choice. We could either surrender and come with them, or we could resist and be killed on the spot.

If I left the Reserve, I would put myself back into that state of chaos. Looking over your shoulder for the enemy every second. Often wondering when you could find food and water. And begging the Universe to let you see another sunrise. Yet, staying here would mean staying in limbo. You do your assigned job. You take what they give and nothing more. And what you get is a life of comfort completely out of your control.

The urge to be free and the urge to fight back draws me to the rebels, like my father. They were the hope that no matter how bad things got, an army would be built and take the Earth back. No matter how many people said they were stupid or naïve, I couldn't wait to join them. Living each slow day in the Reserve just to die in captivity was not how I wanted my life to go.

Despite my mother's best attempts at a cheerful birthday dinner, the mood in the air is tense and grim. While the table is adorned with my favorite pasta and pieces of pound cake, I have to force myself to eat. If it was any other night, I'd let my anxiety take over and skip the meal. But if I make it out of here alive, it might be awhile before I find food. I stare at the tablecloth my mother always brings out for special occasions, focusing on the lace pattern woven with gold.

My family sings happy birthday before serving the cake, and my mind drifts back to happier times. Birthdays used to mean shopping for presents. New clothes, makeup, and books. My mom always wanted everything to be perfect, and she would decorate the house with whatever theme she had decided on that year. I would have a party with my friends. I got to see my extended family. But now, I had none of that. All those people are gone from my life and maybe gone from this world, too. The mall I loved to go to had already turned into a pile of rubble by the time my family was on the run from the Emigres.

Every memory of my past was slipping away like sand in an hourglass, faster and faster. I even suspected that the trauma of the invasion made it harder to recall things from before, even if the memories were good ones. Happy ones. It was getting harder to visualize everything. I knew our old house had white panels and dark green windowpanes. But when I tried to recall specific memories, some features would cause me to draw a blank.

"Did you enjoy your birthday?" My mom interrupts my thoughts, forcing a smile. Mary heads upstairs to get Annie ready for bed. The dining room falls silent.

"Of course, thank you," I reply, noticing her makeup. She always had lipstick, but the blush was new. My guess was she had borrowed makeup from Mary. That's what Mary spent all her points on. She would even work extra hours to get more. She loved whatever the

Emigres made. I convinced myself it was lazy crap they threw together to make us think they cared.

A knock on the door shifts our attention. My mother answers it, assuming someone is stopping by to wish me a happy birthday. I half expect to see Tina, but to my surprise, Ben is at the door with his mom. Their worried expressions cause me to stand.

"Did Tina come over?" Their mom says, peering into the door.

"Uh, no," I answer, walking up to them. "What's wrong?"

"She never came home from work. We thought she came to visit you, but it was getting late, so we thought we'd check. She always tells us when she'll be out. This isn't like her." Her mom's voice rises as her eyes dart to Ben. His pale skin reddens. "When did you last see her?"

"Um, the grocery. A few hours ago." I stammer, feeling my panic build. Tina wouldn't try to escape. She liked it here with all her family. If she was gone, it meant one thing. The rumors of Emigres taking people away were true. I feel the blood drain from my face as an all too familiar fear grips me.

Tina's family leaves, saying they will search for her. But we know the guards won't tell them anything. Their daughter is gone, and they will be expected to accept it and move on. I always thought the people who were disappearing were just people that tried to escape. I didn't believe the stories of Emigres kidnapping people. We were already here, following their rules. What more did they want?

"Tina would never leave without telling them," I mutter as if the Emigres were listening.

"I know," my mother whispers, her voice hollow.

"You should come with me," I look into her eyes, pleading. "You, Annie, Mary. We should all go. It's not safe here and you know it."

"We can't leave." She shakes her head. "Not all at once. It's too risky."

"Fine. But promise me you will leave. As soon as you can, you will leave." I can feel my eyes filling with tears. Her mouth hardens in a thin line. She hates promises now. The world has made them impossible to keep.

"Wash up and change. Don't leave this house looking like that in your work clothes." She sighs as she takes the dishes to the kitchen. There's my old mom. Strict and proper, not a hair out of place. She grew up doing ballet, teaching me as soon as I could walk. Her discipline thrived in this environment. But I knew that was her way of telling me I could still leave. She wouldn't try to argue with me to stay any longer.

THREE

When the sun dips below the horizon, I grab my white linen messenger bag filled with as much water and non-perishable food as I can comfortably carry. Which is unfortunately not a lot. If only the Reserve had issued us some regular, sturdy backpacks. Taking the chance to say goodbye to my mother and Annie for what could be forever, I bite my tongue to stop myself from crying. They don't need to be any more worried than they already are.

"Are you sure you want to do this?" Mary whispers to me as she glances out the window, waiting for the nightly guard to take his position outside our home. Her brown eyes are bloodshot even as she keeps her voice light.

"I'm sure," I reply. With a deep breath, Mary opens the door and begins chatting with the guard like she has every night for the past year. I watch as she twirls her chestnut hair and smiles at him. I can't help but envy how easily she can charm anyone here, even the alien guards. Her beauty and positive, outgoing nature drew everyone in; which was the complete opposite of me. When she lures him away just enough, I make my way out the door and toward the wall. I reach the sewer cover quickly, scanning around for any guards. I've made it to this place so many times, yet my escape tonight has my heart pounding so fast I feel it's the only thing I can hear.

Mary makes her way to me alone, silent as a mouse. She helps me lift the cover, and I climb in as quietly as I can while my body shakes. Once I am low enough, she starts to close the cover.

"I love you, Rachel," she whispers, locking eyes with me.

"I love you, too," I reply.

I grab the cover to help pull it down as Mary's eyes dart away as a voice yells. The muffled words of "curfew" and "get back here" are enough to confirm it's a guard. Under her breath, she snaps at me to go. I can't even argue before she takes off, but not toward our home. Toward the wall. I want to cry out to her. What is she doing? She's going to get caught!

My heart lurches, yet I can't speak. I have to run. If there's any chance of me getting out of here, I have to go now. I lower the cover without a sound. Climbing down the ladder as fast as my body will let me, I jump down from the last two rungs as my feet splash in the ankle-deep water. Running will make noise, but I have no time. I take off in the direction of the Divide.

A sudden clang forces my attention back toward where I entered. A figure with white Emigre armor lays crumpled on the floor. I freeze for a second, staring in confusion. The figure moves, slowly forcing their body up. A burgundy liquid spills from a small knife on their neck as their violet eyes lock onto mine. She tries to reach for her gun as she makes a horrible choking sound.

Not willing to risk it, I turn and run. The path to the Divide is straight, but I veer to the right to avoid her aim. A fizzling sound follows bright light, illuminating the tunnel. A minor explosion startles me, but at least the Emigre missed. There's no way for me to avoid making noise, but I have to hope whatever injury hinders the guard enough that I can escape. Mary must have injured her, but how? Knives are forbidden, especially in our family. How did she get one, and how did she manage to stab the guard and throw them down into the sewer? If I made it out alive, hopefully, one day I will see her again and ask her.

A low growl in the distance confirms my worst fear. Beasts really live in these tunnels. I pick up my pace and take another turn, away from where I think the creatures are. The water sloshes up into my eyes, making it even harder to tell where I'm going. My bag slams against my hip. But stopping even just to catch my breath means death.

Every second of running through the sewer has me paranoid that something is after me. I keep checking over my shoulder, getting no relief when I see nothing behind me. I try to turn toward where I think the Divide is, suddenly tripping over something. My knees and wrists hit the ground, the water softening the blow. A stench I recognize from before fills my nose. Death.

I can't bring myself to look at the body. It has to be the woman that passed away this morning. They tossed her body in these sewers for the beasts to feed on. Stifling a gag, I force myself up and continue to run. The further I go, the more I realize how lost I am. I feel like I'm going around in circles, but have yet to see the guard that was coming after me. The beasts have also gone silent. As much as it terrifies me, I grind to a halt to check the map my father drew and get my bearings.

My breathing still panicked and my mind still racing, I find it hard to make sense of the map. I try to go where I think I should, even though every part of the sewer looks the same. I nearly pass out in relief when I find the cover marked with an orange "X". The cover to the Divide. I finally pause for a second of rest and allow myself to only focus on my breath. If I let my mind drift, the worry I have for Mary will make me want to turn back. I have to keep going.

A low hum rumbles through the sewer, warning me of an Emigre ship overhead. My hands holding the ladder vibrate, increasing in intensity as the ship gets closer. I can't go up now or I'll get caught. At best, they'd take me and send me back. At worst, they'd shoot to kill.

My eyes shift to my bracelet, silently pleading that it won't give my location away just yet.

The sound of growls and snarls accumulate below me. It's the beasts, probably able to smell me, although I'm covered in sewer water. I try not to make a sound as I climb a little higher, keeping my eyes on the darkness below and waiting for the ship's rumbling to stop. But the sounds of the beasts get too close for my comfort. The glint of golden yellow eyes comes into view, making my heart drop.

I take a risk and hope the ship has passed. Climbing up and opening the cover ever so slightly, I'm greeted with the scent of burnt metal. The ship is far enough away that I hoist myself out of the sewer and quickly put the cover back on. As I work to calm my ragged breathing, I take in the run-down, abandoned buildings that give the Divide its name. Humans from the Ruins apparently have been sneaking in here to scavenge for food and supplies since the attacks started, but I doubt there was much left after all this time. The land is empty of life. Or at least seems to be. If my dad is right, some rebels are here.

Without warning, my silver bracelet lets out a shrill beep. A faint blue light flashes off and on from it. I can only guess the Emigres know I escaped and are tracking me. I'm running out of time to find these rebels. If I fail, everything Mary did to help get me out would be in vain. I dash into the new world and take in my surroundings.

Not seeing any other Émigré ships yet, I figure I could at least try to find something useful while I look for the rebels and take cover from the ships. Running down the street, I enter an abandoned convince store and can immediately tell that the rebels have been here. They've taken nearly everything inside. The shelves are completely ransacked, and all that's left are a few newspapers and some magazines.

These things seem so out of place to me, especially the magazines. People who used to be celebrities fill the once glossy covers, but now they are dead or just as equal as the rest of us. The newspapers seem just as strange, covered with photos and articles of the spaceships before anyone on Earth even knew what was going on. Not seeing anything good in the rest of the store, I turn to leave, only to see a figure standing in the doorway.

It looks like a young man, but my mind races, automatically thinking the worst and that I have run into an Émigré. I turn to run, but he is much quicker, grabbing me firmly by the arm. "Not so fast." He growls. Yanking me toward him, he uses his free hand to swiftly pull out a knife from the pocket of his pants and place it on my throat as he backs me up against the store wall.

Whoever this guy is, he's tall and well-built. I can't see the color of his eyes in the darkness. . . or much of anything other than the general outlines of his features. Is he human? Could he tell if I was human?

"Please let me go! I-I'm human!" I decide to weakly stammer in protest, swallowing hard. Without saying a word, he lets go of my wrist but keeps the knife at my throat. He then pulls something out of the backpack on his back, and suddenly, a bright light nearly blinds me.

"Weird." his lips curve up into the slightest smirk as he lowers the knife from my throat. "Should have known. No Émigré would walk around the Divide alone and without weapons."

"If it's so obvious that I'm human, why attack me?" I bite back. I observe from the light that his eyes seem to be brown and not violet. Dirt and grime covers his face, and his short brown hair sticks up in every direction. He must be a rebel.

"You move like they do. Like you've got a stick up your ass." His answer confuses me. I'd never noticed how the Emigres walk. But maybe, since I used to be a ballet dancer, he has a point? "Better safe than sorry, I'm sure you understand," He says with an annoyed sigh. "You're a much younger human than I expected. How old are you? 15?" Something about his tone and the way he looks at me irritates me.

"I'm 18," I tell him firmly.

"What the hell are you doing here?" He demands. "I take it the Reserve isn't letting people go exploring all of a sudden."

"I escaped so I can find my dad," I answer.

"You really should go back." He says, and his seriousness throws me off.

"Why should I go back?" I ask, baffled.

"It's a million times easier to survive in there than it is out here. I mean, your dad could be dead. And look at you. You won't make it-"

"I'm not going back." I stop him with a scowl. "I left to find my father. He's-"

I'm interrupted by the muted sound of an explosion. Both of us momentarily freeze in fear as we realize what that sound means. The Émigrés are nearby, and they were getting closer.

"We need to leave here. Now." Panic washes across his face as he quickly puts his flashlight back in his pocket and makes his way out the door. "Are you going back to the Reserve or what?"

"No, I need to go to the Ruins. And I need to get this bracelet off." I hurry to catch up to him.

He stops without warning and takes out a device I've never seen, seeming to know exactly what to do. Holding it up to the bracelet, I hear a crunch and feel a faint sensation of warmth. In a matter of seconds, it falls off my wrist, and he kicks it into the pile of magazines.

"How long-" I start.

"Ask questions later." He says with a roll of his eyes, grabbing my wrist and pulling me forward. Once out of the store, we spot a small Émigré ship to our right, firing light blue lasers at what appears to be another human. It looks like a scene that belongs in a sci-fi movie, but somehow, it's my current reality. "Okay, run as fast as you can and follow me." The boy instructs before letting go of my wrist and taking off into the chaos.

FOUR

No sooner have I started running after him when another small ship flies in from our left. It's sleek, silver, and about the size of a car. As soon as the pilot spots us, they fire. The lasers hit the buildings surrounding us, sending debris in all directions. Squeaking out in surprise and fear, I try to pick up speed. I will myself not to flinch as pieces of debris fly past my eyes and hit my cheeks, and urge myself not to slow down. Even as my messenger bag feels too heavy and my breathing gets out of control, I push my legs to go faster.

The boy looks like he had been through this many times before as he weaves in and out of buildings with ease in order to avoid the lasers and debris. We run in the front door of buildings and out the back door, sprinting through narrow alleyways covered in rubble and never running in a straight line. I'm running as fast as my legs can carry me, my heartbeat pounding in my ears, but I am losing ground on the boy.

He seems to sense this and calls out to me over his shoulder: "Come on! Just a little further! Once we're in the Ruins, they'll let us go!" I don't question him. Not wanting to die is more than enough motivation to keep me going.

Thankfully, he's right. A few moments later, our feet are pounding on grass rather than cracked pavement. The lasers stop and the hum of the ship's engine fades away. As soon as I think they are gone for good, I stop running and gasp for breath.

"Good job. I didn't think you were going to make it." The boy says as he slows down and turns to face me, looking the slightest bit impressed. I note jealously that he has already recovered from his run and his breathing has almost returned to normal.

"Thanks," I attempt to catch my breath, unable to think of anything else to say as I try to calm down. He slides off the backpack he's been carrying and pulls out a water bottle, taking a long swig before handing it to me. I shake my head, pulling out my own bottle and gulping water down so fast that I almost choke.

"I'm Tyler," He tells me as he puts his water bottle back in his backpack.

"Rachel," I manage to reply.

"Okay, Rachel, we've got a long walk ahead of us. Any questions you have, you might as well ask now. You ask me a question, I'll ask you a question." Tyler says as he immediately starts walking further into the Ruins. Taking a deep breath, I reluctantly urge my tired body to follow him.

"Why didn't the Émigrés follow us into the Ruins? I mean, they let us go when they could have easily followed us further." I ask my first question.

"I think it's because they don't think we'll survive out here. As long as we're in the Ruins, they won't waste their time. Shooting us down in the Divide is almost like a game to them." He responds.

"Aren't they—"

"Ah, no, it's my turn to ask a question." He interrupts me, ignoring the glare I shoot him in return. "You said you were looking for your father. Who is he? I might know him."

"His name is David Collins," I answer, hoping with all my heart that Tyler knows him and can tell me where he is. I feel a wave of relief as a flicker of recognition flashes across his face, and he smiles a small smile at me.

"I know a David. He's actually on a run for supplies just like I am, but he went with a group that's going in a different direction. They're going a lot further out than we did, but they should be back tomorrow. Could be your dad."

I'm so ecstatic and relieved at his words I could reach out and hug him. My father's alive! He was alive, and I was going to find him! And I found the rebels just like I needed to. How could some young, unarmed girl like me be lucky enough to make it through the Divide and just happen upon the rebels who knew my father? I can't help the huge grin on my face and the extra bounce in my step, but I compose myself enough to remember my other questions.

"Going back to my first question, shouldn't they be low on fuel by now too? How are their ships still running?"

"We don't know what the primary source of fuel they use for their ships, but it looks like all of them use solar power as a backup. All of their ships have solar panels on them." He rattles off his answer easily. "My next question is: why are you looking for your dad now? David's been here for a while."

"There're these alien monsters in the sewers."

"Oh, right. Better to wait until someone dies and they're fed. Your dad mentioned that."

"Plus, my mom didn't want me to leave until I was 18, and I agreed. It's hard enough at home without one family member. Did you know who that other person was in the Divide?"

"Yeah. That was Alfie. He and Rebecca should be meeting up with us any minute now." He tells me firmly. I can tell he's trying to sound confident, but his voice sounds just forced enough to show that he still had his doubts about whether his friends had made it. "Did you bring any weapons with you?" He continues.

"No," I answer, feeling my cheeks flush as he looks at me like I'm the biggest idiot he's ever seen. "There's nothing in the Reserve that you could use as a weapon. They wouldn't even let us have knives to cut our food." I quickly insist. "I mean, I guess you might use a fork as a weapon. . ." I trail off, wondering if that's how Mary stabbed the guard. "But I don't. . . you'd have to get really close, and. . ." Realizing I'm rambling, I shut my mouth and look away from him.

"Right. I forget how much they keep from you. How the hell were you planning on making it to the Ruins, then?"

"Running and hiding. I know it's not the best strategy, but it's all I've got."

"You realize that the Émigrés aren't the only danger out here, right? There are probably hundreds of crazy psychopaths out there in the world right now, and if you were in the wrong place at the wrong time, they wouldn't hesitate to kill you." He picks up the pace of his walk, and only now do I realize he had gotten his knife back out again. I hadn't even thought about people other than the rebels.

"Well then, good thing I found you." I sigh.

"Yeah, some Reserve girl tagging along with me is exactly what I need," He mutters. I don't let his bitter tone bother me. I know I'm an inconvenience to him, but at least he's helping me. "Do you know how to fight?" He continues.

"Not really," I admit, quickly wanting to change the subject. "What did you mean when you said that the Émigrés use the bracelets to track us? I thought they were just used to identify us as people of the Reserve. It never seemed like the Émigrés cared that much."

"I think they use trackers because they want you to stay in there. They need all of you. With the trackers, they can contact the other Émigrés in the Divide to either kill you or bring you back. That's what happened to one guy that was staying with us. He escaped from the Reserve and came across us.

"We had been living in the basements of buildings right next to the Divide back then. A bunch of Émigrés came and attacked our hiding spots, and they looked at his bracelet before taking him away. We could all tell they recognized him and had been looking for him.

Now we know the bracelets are trackers, and our hideout is much further out." His explanation causes me to feel like ice has just been pumped through my veins. That probably meant that they were on the lookout for my father, and as of now, they'd be looking for me, too.

"You said the Émigrés need us in the Reserve. Wh-"

"Shh!" Tyler interrupts suddenly, throwing his free hand over my mouth and glancing around wildly. "Do you hear that?" He asks. I pause, listening as intently as I can before finally being able to hear the low hum of an engine. I follow his gaze to see two headlights far off in the distance coming toward us from the direction of the Divide.

"Shit!" Tyler hisses, but to my surprise, he doesn't try to flee.

"Shouldn't we run?" I urge him, looking anywhere for a place to hide. Unfortunately, we're surrounded by fields of grass. There are no trees or buildings or anything to hide behind. I meet his eyes again, flashing him a panicked look. His face has lost all emotion as he looks back at me, his mouth hardening to a thin line.

"They've already spotted us. And we can't outrun whatever they're using."

"I thought you said they don't go into the Ruins," I snap.

"They don't. They must be looking to take you back." He puts his knife away and pulls out a small handgun from the pocket of his jacket.

"But I took the bracelet off!" I feel myself panicking even more. Tears are filling my eyes, and my voice is faltering.

"I know. I don't understand why they're coming out here, either." He moves to stand between me and the headlights that are coming closer every second.

"You should try to escape. They're only looking for me." I insist, feeling myself getting even more upset about the idea of him dying or getting captured because of me.

"Like I already said, they've probably spotted both of us. Even if I started running now, they'd still catch me."

"So, what do we do?"

"I haven't exactly come up with a plan, so we'll just have to wait and see." He replies in an oddly calm voice, aiming the gun at the oncoming headlights which appear to belong to two separate vehicles that look like high-tech Vespas.

"Are you going to shoot them?" I whisper, wondering why he was only just now getting out his gun. Better yet, how did he even find a gun and find ammo at a time like this?

"Maybe," Tyler murmurs in reply, his voice completely void of fear. "If anything, it'll show them that we're not going down without a fight. We won't surrender."

My breath catches in my throat as the vehicles pull up to a stop a few feet away, the faces of the Émigrés obscured by helmets with visors covering their eyes. Maybe Tyler would rather die than surrender, but to me, going back to the Reserve seemed a hell of a lot more appealing than dying.

But if I surrendered, what would happen when they realized I was the one who had escaped? Would they take me back and torture me? Would they do anything to my family? What did they do in these situations?

"Stay behind me." Tyler orders under his breath. As the two Émigrés approach us, I realize that I'm shaking. This was it. All of Tyler's years of being a rebel in the Ruins were over, and my journey to find my father was over. All I could hope for was that I wasn't about to die.

FIVE

"Stay back," Tyler warns the two Émigrés, pointing his gun at them and clicking the bullet into place as they slide off their vehicles. The Émigrés let out a chuckle, taking off their helmets and finally revealing their faces. It's a boy and a girl around our age, and they both look at Tyler and grin. To my complete surprise, Tyler lowers his gun and grins right back at them. "You assholes," He sighs with a shake of his head.

"We got you good!" the boy exclaims proudly, bursting into a fit of laughter.

"You should have seen the look on your face," the girl smirks, tossing her long blonde hair over her shoulder. Her gaze falls on me for the first time, and she shoots Tyler a curious look. "Ty, who's this?"

"This is Rachel." Tyler turns to face me and moves out of the way so that he's no longer standing in front of me. "She escaped from the Reserve."

"Nice job, Rachel," the boy comes toward me, extending his right hand. I shake it hesitantly, observing his blue eyes and freckle-covered face with the help of the headlights. "I'm Alfred Mallon, but you can call me Alfie. That girl over there is Rebecca Morgan. She doesn't like to be called Becca, so don't do it unless she pisses you off." He winks at the girl, who rolls her eyes at him before shaking my hand as well.

"You can call me Bec if you want. They sometimes do." She offers, her grass green eyes gazing curiously at me. "I escaped from the Reserve as well. Alfie and I left together about a year ago. You made the right choice by coming here."

"I can't believe you actually thought we were Émigrés," Alfie says to Tyler, chuckling again. "We're not even dressed in white!"

"Better safe than sorry," Tyler replies with a shrug. The second time I've heard him say that. He really treats everyone as a threat. Are all rebels like that? Is my dad like that? "Did you kill any Émigrés to get these?"

"Nope. We just found them next to a building. They must have left them there and gotten on the ships to come after us." Alfie answers.

"Did you disable the track-" Tyler starts before Alfie interrupts him.

"Yes, dad. We're not stupid. This is a good thing. We need more of these things."

"I know, I know," Tyler nods. "We should get going. The sun's coming up." He observes. Motioning for me to follow him, he grabs the helmet Alfie was holding and hands it to me before getting on Alfie's vehicle. Alfie gets on Rebecca's vehicle, and she takes a seat right behind him. "You coming?" Tyler looks back at me, patting the extra space behind him.

"Uh, yeah," I answer quietly, with a quick shake of my head. I slip on the helmet and slide onto the seat. The vehicle is sort of like a motorcycle. Even though I've never been on a motorcycle either, I find space to put my feet right behind his, feeling my cheeks flush as I wrap my arms around him so that I won't fall off.

"You remember how to ride one of these?" Alfie calls over the hum of the engine as he starts it up. Tyler starts our vehicle with the press of a button, causing it to vibrate to life. In a second, I feel the vehicle lift in the air. I notice with a bit of interest that there aren't any wheels on the bottom of the vehicle; it hovers off the ground and moves forward because of some kind of jet on the back. It takes Tyler a few seconds to make sure the vehicle isn't hovering too close to the ground, but after a few curse words and random button pressing, he gets us at the right height.

"Not really, but I'll figure it out," Tyler calls back, accelerating forward so quickly that I almost fall off, my small yelp of surprise lost in the wind. He sounded like he was joking, and I really hope he was.

Soon enough, the fields of grass surrounding us give way to a forest. Tyler slows the vehicle down a bit, but we're still weaving through the trees at a much faster speed than we probably should be going. Tree trunks whiz past my vision, and I wonder how he can even see where we are going. It's impossible for me to tell a difference between any of the trees as they all blur together to form a mass of brown and green.

After what seems like ages, he finally slows down as we approach a small building. Right next to it is a man pointing a gun at us. I tense automatically, but Tyler calmly waves. As soon as the man appears to recognize Tyler, he nods and waves us through.

Tyler stops the vehicle in front of a large house made of red bricks faded with age. After he shuts off the engine, I let him go immediately. He slides off the vehicle and makes his way up a small set of stairs toward the front door. I take off my helmet and have a look around as I get off as well. The sun is casting an orange glow over everything, and I can clearly see a wooden shed along with a field full of a plant that's beginning to sprout.

Further out is a field of cows grazing. I've never lived on a farm, but after living on the Reserve for nearly two years, this is the closest thing to my old home that I've ever seen. It makes me feel safe, nostalgic, and also sad all at once. Maybe because I know I'll never be going back to that two-story house in the suburbs that I once called home.

"You look like you've never seen corn before," a voice says. Startled out of my daze, I look up to see Tyler looking at me in amusement from the top of the stairs.

"She's basically been in a cage for two years. Give her a break." Rebecca gives me a knowing smile as she walks past Tyler and into the house. I go up the stairs with Alfie, and Tyler holds the door for us, still looking at me like I'm a little kid who got way too excited over nothing of importance.

"I harvested crops in the Reserve, I know what corn looks like," I tell him, but he acts as if I haven't spoken. Without even a glance, he walks right by me.

"Welcome to our humble abode," Alfie says grandly, throwing out his arms for emphasis as he grins at me. We're in a living room, I assume. There's a cream-colored couch that's sagging with age, and a TV gathering dust from not being used for a long time. Bookshelves line the walls. Thin, white curtains hang from the windows. The entire room is lit by the natural sunlight, but I can spot dozens of candles that must give the place light at night.

"What do you think of the place?" Rebecca asks me as she lazily tosses her backpack onto the couch. "Nice, isn't it?" I nod.

"Is it just you four here?" I ask, taking in the large kitchen. A long wooden table takes up the attached dining room. This house is bigger than any house I've ever been in, and I think it could easily fit about 30 people if they didn't mind sharing space. Maybe the guy out there with the gun lives here, too.

"Hell no," Alfie scoffs, striding past me. "We're barely a quarter of the number of people here." With that, he bounds up the flight of stairs separating the living room from the dining room, screaming "RISE AND SHINE" at the top of his lungs.

Within minutes, about a dozen people sleepily make their way down the stairs. Most of them appear to be in their 20s and 30s, but there is one man with graying hair and wrinkled skin, and one boy who seems to be around Annie's age. The little boy stares up at me as he walks by. Just seeing him makes my heart ache for home, but I push it aside. I just have to stay away long enough to find my father.

Each person looks at me with a slight bit of interest before moving on to their morning routines. Everyone goes off in different directions with a purpose while I just stand here, unsure of where to go and what to do. I feel useless, and I can't stand it. Turning around, my eyes search the home until they find Tyler, who's taking canned food out of his pack and putting it away in the cabinets in the kitchen. I make my way toward him.

"Need any help?" I ask him quietly, feeling uncomfortable with all the people looking at me curiously as they walk through the kitchen.

"New plaything, Tyler?" says a tall guy with wavy brown hair as he walks toward us. His light blue eyes stare at me confidently, daring me to look away. I refuse, causing him to smirk.

"No," Tyler mutters under his breath, and I'm not sure whose question he's answering as he continues unpacking without looking at either of us.

"I'm Damien," the guy announces to me as if I'd been dying to know.

"Rachel," I say evenly.

"I like her," Damien comments, finally looking away from me to open a drawer and take out a plastic water bottle. "I mean, she's not as pretty as the last one, but she's got a decent body." I feel my cheeks heat up at his words, and I try to think of anywhere I could go that isn't here.

Tyler slams the cabinet door closed, causing me to flinch in surprise and look back down at him again. He throws his bag over his shoulder and stands up, storming past me without a word. His face hardens with anger.

"Hey," the wavy-haired boy continues. "Maybe you won't let this one die."

SIX

EVERYTHING AFTER THOSE WORDS HAPPENS IN A FLASH. TYLER'S fist connects with Damien's nose. Before Damien can react, Tyler slams him against the kitchen wall, his hands around Damien's neck, squeezing so tight that his fingers are turning white while Damien's face is turning red. Blood is dripping out of Damien's nose and onto his gray shirt. I feel like I should do something, but my body remains frozen in place, and all I manage to do is shout, "Stop!"

Either Tyler ignores me or he doesn't hear me because he doesn't even blink. I don't know why I expected to be any help in ending this. He has no intention of stopping, and the words of some girl he doesn't know won't change anything.

Damien lets out a choked laugh, dropping his water bottle. With little difficulty, he wraps his hands around Tyler's wrists. I can tell that Tyler is strong, but he's not strong enough to inflict the amount of pain that he wants. Damien pries Tyler's hands away and shoves him back forcefully enough that he loses his balance and ends up sprawled by my feet.

"Enough!" An authoritative voice yells the second Tyler scrambles to his feet and Damien surges forward. Both boys freeze in place as a woman steps in between them. "How many times are you two going to go at it?" She demands, her dark eyes narrowing at each one of them. Neither boy answers her nor meets her eyes, although Damien is smirking again.

"Won't happen again, Angie," Damien promises.

"Yeah," she huffs. "You keep saying that. Maybe one day it'll be true." She waves them away, grabbing a box of cigarettes from her pocket with a heavy sigh. Lighting one, she seems lost in her own world for a moment as she takes a long drag. With her free hand, she rubs her eyes tiredly until they come across me still standing around like a useless rag doll. "Oh, hello," She smiles warmly at me, emphasizing the faint wrinkles on her face.

"Hi," I reply in a voice barely above a murmur, clearing my throat awkwardly.

"Are you staying with us?" She asks, taking in my Reserve outfit as she exhales smoke again.

"Just until I find my father, David Collins." I nod.

"Oh, okay," she nods as well. "He should be back tonight, but you're welcome to stay as long as you want. I know he'll be happy that you're here. He's talked about you quite a bit to me."

"Thank you."

"No problem. I'm Angie, by the way," She holds out her hand and I shake it firmly.

"I'm Rachel," I say for what feels like the 20th time in the last few hours.

"Well, Rachel, let's find you a place to rest. You must be exhausted." Angie leads me out of the kitchen, tucking a strand of dark red hair behind her ear.

"Mama," A girl with hair like Angie's calls as she walks by, giving me an annoyed look. "No more strays in my room."

"Don't mind her," Angie chuckles. "I can never get that girl to behave."

"There's an extra bed in Tyler's room. You know, since his little girlfriend's gone." Damien suggests as he walks past us, holding a rag on his nose and going out the front door without waiting for anyone's reaction. Angie sighs again, shaking her head.

"He's right, though. Tyler, would you be okay with Rachel taking the extra bed?" She says to him as he starts to walk up the stairs.

"Whatever," is his reply.

"Are you okay with rooming with him? You can take this couch if you would prefer not to share a room with a guy, but I wouldn't advise the couch if you want any sleep. Some people stay up late and hang out on this floor." She looks at me with concern.

"It's fine," I say, even though it isn't. I've lived with 2 sisters my whole life and never once shared a room with a guy. I'm uncomfortable, but it doesnt sound like I have much of a choice.

"He'll show you around. If you need anything, just let me know." Angie says with another smile before patting me on the shoulder and walking back into the kitchen.

I follow Tyler up the stairs and down a long hallway, entering the last door on the right. It's a simple bedroom with white walls and dusty wooden furniture. One twin-sized bed is on each side of the room.

Tyler tosses his backpack on the bed to my left, so I make my way to the bed on the right and take off the messenger bag that I had nearly forgotten about. My body feels heavy, void of any energy from all the running and excitement of the past few hours.

I sit on the edge of the bed as Tyler turns to face me. I know he's not going to explain what's going on with him and Damien, and even though I'm curious, I wouldn't dare pester it out of him. Here in this room, with the early rays of morning sunlight shining through the window and casting a warm glow on his face, I can finally see all of his features. His cheeks are slightly sunken in, and there are dark circles under his eyes. I can see that his eyes are not brown like I originally thought. They are a dark blue with a hint of gray, like the color I think of whenever I think about the ocean.

But that's not even what sticks out to me. What takes me back is the look in his eyes. I'd always heard of the "thousand-yard stare" but never seen it in person until now. Just by his eyes alone, I can tell he is someone who has experienced more pain than anyone should ever face. He has seen things that I cannot begin to imagine, and he has probably lost more people close to him than I can ever dream of losing.

Will my father have that look? I'm anxious to see him after being away from him for a year. Just the idea of seeing him soon because I managed to find the rebels is still surreal to me.

"My clothes are in that dresser over there, but there's plenty of room for your clothes in the closet," Tyler says to me, bringing me back to reality. "Angie will get together some clothes for you later. I'll be up in five hours, but you can sleep longer than that if you want." I yawn without meaning to as I nod in response, feeling so exhausted that I doubt I'll remember his words when I wake up. Slipping off my mud-stained sneakers, I lie back on the bed and shut my eyes.

As I begin to drift off, I can hear Tyler already snoring softly, along with the muffled sounds of people laughing downstairs. For the first time since I climbed over the Reserve wall, I somehow get the feeling that I don't need to be afraid anymore. Maybe, by some miracle, everything will be okay for a little while.

I'm finally able to rest and be at peace. . .until the loud ringing of a bell outside forces my eyes open again. I grumble in complaint as I reach for the pillow on the bed so that I can hold it over my ears, but as I do that, I see Tyler shoot out of bed with more speed than I could ever hope to have the second I wake up. He shoves his feet into his hiking boots, and I give him a curious look as I sit up.

"What's going on?" I ask, wondering if I should be doing something.

"Outsiders," He answers quickly, grabbing his gun off of his dresser.

"What?" That's my intelligent reply. As he strides out of the bedroom, I grab the knife on the dresser and follow him out.

"Remember how I said that the Émigrés aren't the only enemy you have to worry about?"

"Yes," I do my best to keep up with him as he nearly sprints down the stairs and out the open front door.

"Outsiders are just one of the potential dangers that we have to deal with out here. Every so often, a group of them tries to come into our camp and steal anything that could be of use to them. When that bell is rung, it means some of them have gotten past the people guarding the camp, and we need to finish the job." He explains, stopping so suddenly that I nearly run into him. He turns to face me, an annoyed look in his dark eyes. "Which is why you need to stay here."

"What? No!" I sputter in protest. "I hate being useless. I had a job in the Reserve. A. . .a purpose. Now I have nothing all day. I'm going to help."

"Sometimes, the most helpful thing to do is stay out of the way," Tyler growls, grabbing me by the shoulders and pushing me back into the house. I try to pull his hands away and hold my ground, but it's no use. He won't let go, even when I'm back inside the house and he stops pushing.

"I want to help," I say firmly.

"A little knife won't do you much good. You wouldn't be able to handle even one of them."

"Just let me try." I hate to sound like I'm pleading, but I'm running out of options. He gives me an exasperated look.

"Look, kid-"

"Don't call me kid." The words slip harshly out of my mouth before I can stop them. Tyler stares at me as if I've gone insane.

"You ever kill anyone?" He demands. I shake my head no. "You ever seen a dead body?"

"Yes," I answer, my voice cracking with emotion as the memories come back. While my family was on the run from the Émigrés, it wasn't uncommon to come across a dead body, or even several all in one place. Émigrés were killing those who didn't surrender, and people were killing each other for things like food and clean water. We'd come across a body every now and then, and my parents would always cover Annie's eyes and tell us to look away, but sometimes my curiosity would get the best of me. I still don't understand why I ever looked. The images I have of the dead still haunt me. Eyes that stare without seeing, blood staining their clothes and the ground around them. . .men, women, children. . .the smell. . .the sound of the flies buzzing around them. . .it never got easier to experience, but it was something we all had to learn to deal with. "I can handle it."

"Regardless of what you think you can handle, it's not safe. And I highly doubt you'd like what you saw if you came with us. Just stay here. You won't be alone." With that, he finally let go of my shoulders and quickly made his way out the front door and into the surrounding forest.

SEVEN

I watch Tyler until he disappears. The area around the doorway gets eerily quiet, everyone else already going into the forest or staying put inside the house. For whatever reason, staying put is ripping me up inside. Can I really just hunker down and wait anxiously? He has a point, I'm not trained to fight.

"Are you new here, ma'am?" A new voice startles me. Deep, articulate, and slightly raspy. I look up to see the man with dark skin who appeared to be older than everyone else here. He smiles at me, reaching out a hand to shake mine. "You must be Rachel. I'm Abraham, but you can call me Abe." He says as I shake his hand.

"Nice to meet you," I say.

"Nice to meet you, too," He says, hobbling away with his cane.

"What are you doing?" I ask. "Can I help?"

"I'm checking to make sure everyone that stays inside during a lockdown is here," He explains, opening another room and checking inside. I look over his shoulder to see that it's an empty bedroom. "I'm nearly done, but. . .I can't find Jacob." His brow creases with worry.

"What's he look like?" I ask, happy to help.

"He's just a little boy. About this tall," He puts a hand up to his chest. "Youngest one here. Brown eyes and hair like you. But he's deaf. He wouldn't have heard the alarm and he won't hear me calling for him." My heart sinks.

"If he's not in the house, where would he be?"

"Either playing in the barn or in the woods," Abe's grip on his cane tightens. "I didn't see him out front or out back."

"You stay here, I'll look for him," I say, throwing caution into the wind. I've never met this child, but I can't help thinking of my sister Annie.

Before Abe can convince me otherwise, my legs seem to move on their own and I'm in the barn searching every corner. When I come up empty, I make my way back outside. I check the porch and back deck once again. Nothing. I jog out to the chicken coop, searching high and low. Nothing. Circling back to the house, I feel dread rising up in me.

"Did you find him?" I hear Abe call from the doorway.

"No," I reply. "Where does he like to play in the woods?"

"The river. It's that way. It's not far. He never goes far," He points east.

"Thank you, I'll get him," I promise as I take off. Clutching my knife firmly, I enter the trees and begin to search. Am I scared? Yes. I'm beyond terrified, but I can't just stand there and do nothing. If I can't help a child, who can I help? If I couldn't handle an outsider, I'd never be able to handle an Émigré, and if I couldn't handle an Émigré, I might as well welcome death with open arms. My father would never do that, so neither will I.

As I go deeper into the woods I walk to make less noise, trying my best not to make a sound. The forest is eerily quiet; the only sound I can hear is a faint breeze rustling the leaves on the trees. I don't know how much use I'll be, since I don't know all of the rebels yet and therefore won't know if a stranger is a rebel or an outsider, but I can at least find comfort in the thought that I can try to aid Jacob if he needs it.

Suddenly, I'm yanked roughly from behind, and before I can face my attacker, I'm turned and slammed against the trunk of a tree. A red-headed girl now stands in front of me, one of her hands holding me firmly against the tree while the other quickly presses the cold blade of a knife to my throat. Angie's daughter.

"Drop the knife," she demands quietly, pressing the blade harder against my skin. I reluctantly do as she says, swallowing hard as my mind feverishly tries to search for a way out of this. Was she a rebel?

"I'm a rebel," I try to say in a confident voice, trying my hardest not to avert my gaze from her calculating cobalt eyes.

"Like hell you are," She lets out a single chuckle, looking at my stained, white Reserve clothes in disgust. "You're not one of us."

"Unfortunately, she actually is." A familiar voice says lazily. "She's new." Damien walks by without looking at me, his eyes on the lookout for outsiders as he holds his rifle at the ready.

"Oh, okay then," The girl looks back at me with an awkward smile, pulling her hands away. "My mistake."

"It's fine," I breathe deeply in relief, attempting to slow down my racing heart.

"What are you doing out here if you're new?" She frowns, and I can tell her guard is still up with me.

"Looking for Jacob. Abe thinks he's in here." I answer.

"Shit, the little kid? Swear that old man is useless." She hisses.

"We'll look for him, too," Damien promises.

Grabbing my knife again, I look around for Tyler. Damien and the red-headed girl continue walking to my left, and I can hear him muttering to her as she looks back at me warily. Her eyes seem to warn me that one wrong move and she'd attack me again. I make my way forward instead, hoping that Jacob hasn't changed course. It might be safer to go with Damien and the girl, but after what had just happened, I really didn't feel comfortable enough around either of them.

I'm starting to realize how different life is here compared to the Reserve. In the Reserve, we all work together because we have to. We go through our daily routines the same way every day without fail.

We'd wake up, maintain the crops, work to construct more houses, and go to bed. Here, you definitely have the freedom to do as you please, but it comes at a cost. You constantly had to make the right decisions, even at a split-second's notice, if you wanted to survive. Anyone you came across could be your enemy, even if they were human.

Picking up my pace a little bit, I come across a hill tall enough that I can't see over it. I'm hoping that once I get to the top, I can easily see where Jacob is and if there is anyone else nearby that could be an outsider. But as soon as I make my way up, a man appears at the top. His clothes are torn in multiple places, and he's covered in dirt, scratches, and bruises. I've barely been with the rebels, but I've already noticed that they are better kept than this man.

Going with the assumption that he's an outsider, I get my knife ready to do who knows what. As if to confirm my suspicions, he gives me a toothy smile, holding up a gun.

"Hello, there, pretty lady," He drawls, aiming the gun at my head.

EIGHT

As I try to think of a way to talk him out of shooting me, I see Tyler coming up behind the man, and my eyes instinctively look at him. But, by doing that, I make the man curious, and he starts to turn his head around.

"Hey," I say loudly, desperately trying to get the man's attention away from Tyler. He focuses back on me, and I do everything in my power to look at his brown eyes rather than at Tyler. "Are you. . .going to kill me?" I ask, my voice shaking. I just have to distract him long enough for Tyler to get close, and Tyler's almost close enough. The man smiles at me, sending a shiver down my spine.

"That's the plan," He tells me, getting ready to pull the trigger.

Tyler spots the gun and immediately surges forward, his hands trying to yank the gun away from the man. The man still tries to shoot me but fails, his bullet going too far to my left thanks to Tyler's efforts.

I move forward to help Tyler get the man's gun, but in that split second, Tyler manages to pull the man's arm far enough to cause him to be in enough pain to drop the gun with a strangled grunt. The man retaliates by facing Tyler and punching him in the stomach with his other hand. Tyler doubles over, and I lunge forward to grab the gun while the man is distracted.

With the gun now in my possession, I let the knife drop to the ground and put my foot over it so that the man won't get a hold of it. Tyler has now tackled the man to the ground and is trying to pin him down while the man struggles to get free. I can see that Tyler is trying to get his gun out of his boot, but he's having too much trouble trying to keep the man's arms down.

"Shoot!" Tyler screams at me, the man finally getting an arm free and punching him in the face. I hastily hold the gun up with shaking hands, but I have no idea what I'm doing. What if I hit Tyler?

I aim for the man's head as Tyler struggles to pin him back down. Hoping like hell that I won't miss, I fire. My eyes shut and my body jerks due to the gun recoiling back at me, causing adrenaline to course through my veins and my heartbeat to skyrocket. I hear the man cry out in pain and open my eyes to see a bullet wound in his shoulder.

"Sorry!" I blurt out automatically. Sorry? Did I really just say that? He was going to shoot me. There was nothing wrong with fighting back. I had to shoot him.

It suddenly feels as if I can't get enough air in my lungs. My body starts to go numb as I back away. I just shot someone, and I can't seem to wrap my mind around it. The man's blood stains my vision and his screams ring in my ears.

Movement in front of me forces me back to reality. Tyler has taken this opportunity to shove the injured man away, scrambling to his feet and pulling out his gun. He takes aim and fires, his bullet hitting the man right between the eyes.

I gasp at the sight, my free hand flying to my mouth as I squeeze my eyes shut. The image still burns in my mind, and I feel bile begin to rise up in my throat. The numbness returns to my hands and legs, and it's like my entire body is shutting down. I'm now realizing the obvious; seeing a dead body and seeing someone die are two very different things.

"I told you not to follow me," Tyler says in a low voice. My eyes slowly open, and I try to keep them focused on him and not on the dead outsider. The image of Tyler firing the gun and the bullet killing the man continues to reply in my mind. I take a shaky, deep breath as I take my hand away from my mouth.

"I'm fine," I say forcefully, more to convince myself than to convince him.

"Sure you are," Tyler mutters sarcastically. "You're not pale as a ghost or anything."

"I'm fine," I say again, louder this time. The image of the dead man is still in my mind, already haunting me. "I was looking for Jacob. He wasn't in the house."

"He wasn't?" Tyler's anger falls and is replaced with concern. I feel my eyes welling with tears. "Right, come on." He takes the gun away from me and picks up my discarded knife as well, putting it in the pocket of his pants. Placing a hand on my back, he forcefully begins to guide me out of the forest. I follow him in a daze, only somewhat aware of how close he is to me.

"You're just. . ." I swallow heavily, picturing the bullet wound as I blink. "You're just going to leave him there?"

"No, we'll take care of it," Tyler answers vaguely. I realize that he's glaring at me. "This is why I told you not to come. I was going to sneak up to that outsider and stab him in the neck, quick and easy." He growls, letting go of me momentarily to pull out a pocketknife and show it to me to prove his point.

"Sorry," I say distantly, unable to focus on anything other than the fact that I had just seen someone die. It was kind of incredible how I hadn't seen anyone die before. I'd seen a lot of dead bodies but never watched someone lose their life.

"I don't like wasting ammo. My gun is a last resort, and I wouldn't have needed to use it if it wasn't for you." He rattles on, oblivious to the fact that what he's saying isn't registering to me.

Up ahead, I can see Alfie and Rebecca running towards us, along with a man that I haven't seen before. I'm so distraught I barely take in the stranger or bother to ask his name.

"Are you both okay? We heard gunshots and came as fast as we could." Alfie pants, eyeing us with concern.

"I'm okay," Tyler responds. "She's okay too, for the most part. Just a little shaken up."

"I told you," I hiss, glaring at him. "I'm fi-"

"Bec," He interrupts me. "Would you mind walking her back?"

"No problem." Rebecca smiles at me, wrapping an arm around my shoulders as soon as Tyler lets me go.

"Alfie, I'll need you to look for Jacob. He's probably by the river." Tyler says and the boys start walking toward the dead man, while Rebecca leads me back to the house.

"What are they going to do with the body?" I ask her, finally starting to breathe normally.

"Burn it," she replies.

"But won't that attract attention?" I wonder, thinking about all the smoke that would cause.

"Not any attention that we can't handle." She says confidently, looking at me again. "Hey, don't worry if this stuff freaks you out. That's normal."

"I've just never seen someone die before," I admit, the image of Tyler shooting the man flashing through my mind once more.

"It doesn't get easier to see. At least, for me, it hasn't. I'd like to think I'm tough enough to handle it, but I guess some part of me will always hold on to the fact that we're all human. I can't be a heartless killing machine, even if I want to be." She tells me, removing her arm from around me as we approach the red brick house.

"Have you ever killed anyone?" I ask her out of curiosity. A distant look clouds her green eyes as she nods.

"Two outsiders. I killed one with a gun and the other with a knife. I don't think I'll ever get over either of them." She stops once we're inside the house, giving me a sad smile. "You really should get some sleep. I'll see you later."

"Yeah." I nod as she walks off. I know I probably won't be getting any sleep anytime soon, but I go to Tyler's room anyway. Lying on my bed, my sweaty clothes sticking to me, I try to think about anything other than the outsider with a bullet between his eyes. I try not to think about how effortlessly Tyler killed him, and how it didn't seem to affect him in the slightest. But by trying to think about something else, I only manage to think about Damien's words. If I was correctly piecing together what he had said to Tyler, I'm in a bed that once belonged to a girl who is now dead.

I almost want to laugh. . . or cry. . . because all of this combined would make it impossible for me to sleep when sleep is all I need right now. I hadn't slept all night, and as tired as my body is now, if I do manage to sleep, I know I'll only have nightmares.

Closing my eyes, I hope for the best and prepare for the worst.

NINE

WHEN I WAKE UP, MY BODY IS STIFF, AS IF I'VE BEEN ASLEEP FOR
an incredibly long time. This surprises me, considering how my mind
had been going crazy before I went to sleep. I did have nightmares as
I slept, just as I had predicted, but the fact that I had managed to
sleep through them was a miracle.

The nightmares were strange. . . stranger than any other nightmares I could remember having. In these, I remember seeing the
image of Tyler shooting the outsider again, but then everything
shifted, and I was the one pulling the trigger that killed that man.
And then everything shifted once more, and Tyler was the one
pointing the gun at me, right between my eyes. I had woken up when
he had pulled the trigger.

The look in his eyes, so cold and free of emotion, terrifies me to
the point where I'm relieved that he's not in the room at the moment.
I understand that people have to kill in order to survive out here, but
for someone to be able to do it so easily disturbs me. I probably should
have expected it, but somehow, a part of me wanted to believe that
the invasion hadn't brought out the worst in all of us.

Rebecca said it wasn't easy for her, but was it easy for Alfie?

For Damien? For the red-headed girl? Would it become easy for me? I really hope it won't. The thought of losing my humanity reminds me too much of the Émigrés. I don't want to be anything like them.

"Oh, good. You're awake." Tyler's voice startles me as he enters the room. His navy eyes send a slight shiver of fear down my spine as they meet mine and remind me of my nightmares. A black eye is starting to form on his left eye, and I'm reminded once more of our confrontation with the outsider. I look away from him. "I was just coming to tell you that we're eating dinner if you'd like to join us."

"Dinner?" I gaze out the window in confusion. "I was asleep for that long?"

"It's understandable," is all Tyler says.

"Did they find Jacob?"

"Yeah, Alfie did. He's fine."

"I'll just eat here. I have some food." I tell him, hauling my messenger bag onto the bed. "You can take the canned food I brought." I take out some of the canned beans and vegetables that I had saved while in the Reserve. He stares at me quietly, seeming to ponder something.

"Come eat with us. You need the food, and you're going to want to meet everyone." He insists, taking the cans and leaving the room. My stomach growls loudly, as if to agree with him, and with a sigh, I reluctantly make my way downstairs.

People are crowded around the kitchen counter, filling their plates with the food provided. The heat from everyone cramped in one place and the summer air makes the air feel thick. It's almost making me claustrophobic. I hesitantly make my way over, careful not to get in anyone's way. Angie is standing by the counter, handing me a plate with a friendly smile.

"Take as much as you want," she tells me.

There's a pot of beans, a small bowl of cooked fish, a plate full of some kind of cooked meat, and a bowl of canned pineapple. I take some beans, meat, and pineapple, careful to not take too much even though I'm starving. There are a lot of people to feed here, so there is no need for me to be greedy.

I spot a small pile of candy bars that someone must have scavenged from a supply run somehow. There's one chocolate protein bar, three mini Snickers bars, and several Hershey mini bars. I go to grab the lone protein bar, only to see another hand snatch it away. I turn to see the greedy thief who deprived me of chocolaty goodness.

"You snooze, you lose," Damien gives me one of his trademark smirks, opening the wrapper and taking a huge bite of the bar before starting to fill his plate. My confusion, surprise, and anger all go unnoticed by him, but I won't give him the satisfaction of an outburst. Instead, I make my way to the dining room table.

There is one seat open between the red-headed girl and the boy that was with Alfie and Rebecca earlier. I take it as quietly as possible, hoping not to disturb the many conversations going on around me.

"Hey, that's my seat, newbie," Damien's voice snarls from behind me. I turn to face him, giving him a look that I hope conveys that he doesn't intimidate me.

"You snooze, you lose," I say with a shrug, turning back to my food and taking a bite of the beans. He laughs bitterly behind me, but thankfully, I can hear his footsteps leaving. I breathe a sigh of relief.

"Would you look at that?" The red-head gives me an impressed look. "The little Reserve girl's got some backbone. What's your name?"

"Rachel," I tell her.

"I'm Molly." She grins at me. Looking me up and down, she notices the sweat on my face and my flushed cheeks. "Aw, sucks without air conditioning, doesn't it, Princess?" She gives me a mocking point before turning back to the kitchen and heaving a sigh of her own. "Well, it was nice meeting you, but I better go over there before Damien and Tyler kill each other." I follow her gaze to see that Tyler is sitting on one of the stools by the countertop as he eats and that Damien had joined him since I had taken his seat. Molly grabs her plate and walks over, taking a seat on the open stool between the two boys.

"Nice to meet another Reserve escapee," the boy next to me says, offering me a shy smile as I face him. "I'm Elliot." He extends his hand, and I shake it while returning a shy smile of my own. He seems to be around my age, but his baby blue eyes and curly brown hair make him look like he could be younger.

"You're from the Reserve as well?" I look at him in surprise. I never realized how many people had left, just like I had. He nodded.

"I left about seven months ago. Don't worry about the people here that give you a hard time about being from the Reserve. They'll stop eventually."

"I don't get why they'd give people a hard time about being from there anyway," I say, poking the mystery meat on my plate with my fork.

"They see people from the Reserve as being weaker than they are. Obviously, this isn't always the case, but some of them still see us as cowards who can't think for ourselves."

"That's stupid," I snort, although, in the back of my mind, I wonder if Tyler sees me that way. Maybe not, since he seems to respect my father. Then again, why the hell do I care? "It takes courage to escape. And it's not easy."

"You're telling me," Elliot laughs. "Once they see that we're willing to fight, though, they usually stop teasing us about being from the Reserve."

"They just got lucky that they escaped the invasion," I mutter, finishing off my beans. "I don't see how that makes them any better than us." In all fairness, I got lucky, too.

"Hey, I'm just telling it like it is." He smiles. "We Reserve folk do have an advantage, though."

"You think so?" I shoot Elliot a curious glance. I'd never thought about humans from the Reserve having an advantage.

"Yeah. We got to see one portion of what the Émigrés were up to. We've been closer to them than most of the rebels ever have."

"But none of us know what it is that they're up to. . ." I point out, shifting my meat around my plate with my fork again.

"Doesn't mean we can't theorize." His eyes sparkle in excitement before looking back down at my plate. "Hey, you can eat that, you know. It's just squirrel meat. It's edible."

"What's it taste like?" I glance at the meat with some curiosity.

"It has the texture of chicken, and tastes kind of like it too. . .but not really."

"I'll take your word for it," I eat a small bite, chewing it thoughtfully. He's right. The only way to describe it is somewhat like chicken, but a lot tougher and drier.

"Not bad, right?" He looks hopefully at me. I shake my head in agreement.

"Anyway, what do you theorize, then? I've never been able to think of a logical explanation for what they're doing." I shift the conversation back to our earlier topic.

"Well," He turns to face me completely, abandoning his plate of food. "Remember how their huge ship landed in France?" I nod, and he continues. "Nobody in the world knew what was going on, and for a little while, that ship was just. . .there. Not doing anything. Then, they nuke the hell out of France and start nuking around the globe. Everybody panics, there's no more news on TV, nobody understands what's going on, and then they start putting us in the Reserve. When I think about all of this, I really don't think they came here with the intent of wiping out humankind. They had some other motive."

"But what motive? Maybe they want to study us. However, they told us that they were a dying race, and that's why they came here. Was it really nuclear warfare that was causing them to die out? Who exactly were they fighting? And why did they stop their nuclear attacks?" Elliot pauses as if waiting for me to respond.

"Um. . . maybe they ran out?" I offer weakly.

"That's the thing." His eyes spark to life again. "Do you really think a species that has the technology to come here would just conveniently run out of nuclear weapons? And there are many places where they didn't use nuclear weapons at all. Take the Divide, for example. Despite being damaged, those cities still had resources to be scavenged. After the attacks, none of us were dealing with the after-effects of a nuclear bomb. No fallout, no contaminated food or water. . .nothing. They must have used lasers, like the lasers that are fired from their ships and guns. So why did they stop? They want survivors, and I think they want to use us for something."

TEN

MY THOUGHTS SHIFT BACK TO WHEN I HAD FIRST MET TYLER IN the Divide, and he had told me that the Émigrés were using us. I think about the tracker bracelets, the controlled lives we had to live, and I begin to feel sick.

"What do you think they're using us for?" My voice is barely a whisper. Elliot seems to notice my fear, and his excitement vanishes. He places a comforting hand on my shoulder before continuing.

"I have multiple theories for that question. They might want us to help them build a weapon, they might want to go all Nazi on us and perform experiments, they might want us to help fight their war back on their own planet, or they might just want us to help them with life on Earth as much as possible. Then, once they don't need us, they'll. . ." He trails off, looking at me with concern.

"They'll kill us." I finish for him, looking up at him to see that there is a trace of fear in his eyes as well. As much as it excites him to try to find all the answers, he still fears death. "Hey, let's change the subject," I suggest quickly. The more I see him afraid, the more I remember why I should be afraid.

"Sure. Anything else you want to know since you're new here?" He offers, going back to eating his food.

"Um, there is one thing. . ." I mull over whether or not I should ask about the tension between Tyler and Damien. It's not really my business, but maybe a little gossip would take my mind off of the Émigrés for a little bit. "Why does it seem like Tyler and Damien hate each other?"

"I figured you'd want to know about that," Elliot gives me a knowing smile. "The way they act towards each other always makes new rebels curious. Long story short, they've both been through a lot, and they both have their own way of dealing with what they've been through. Tyler keeps to himself, and Damien lashes out. They argue with each other a lot because even though we have no distinct leader here, Damien likes to think that he's our leader anyway, and sometimes he feels like Tyler is stealing his spotlight."

"But what about the girl?" I press, wanting to know more. "From what I've gathered, Tyler lost someone close to him, and Damien gives him a hard time about it."

"Oh, yeah, that's Leisel. Leisel Rhodes. She was an original rebel, like Tyler and Damien. When the rebels first got together, they had everyone partner up so that each person always had someone watching their back. They still enforce that now, so my partner is Molly, Alfie's is Rebecca, Damien's is Grace, and Tyler's was Leisel.

"Others have told me that when Damien first got here, he didn't want a partner. He would always do everything solo. It seemed like that's what Tyler wanted, too, but eventually, he liked having Leisel as a partner. They were a good team, and they became pretty good friends from what I saw.

"The problem was that Damien developed an infatuation with Leisel, and when she wouldn't give him the time of day, he assumed that she was hooking up with Tyler-"

"Was she?" I interrupted, suddenly finding myself more curious.

"Not that I know of. If they were together, they did a good job hiding it from all of us. Anyway, so then Grace came along, and it was like Damien latched onto her to forget about Leisel. It seemed to work, too. She became his first partner, and-" Elliot stops suddenly, his eyes flickering to something behind me. I turn around just in time to see Tyler take Molly's old seat, loudly setting his plate on the table. My cheeks flush immediately. Had he heard us talking about him?

"Don't stop talking just because I'm here," Tyler says, looking at Elliot and me with some kind of emotion I can't place as he takes a bite of what looks like fish. He doesn't look angry, so maybe he hadn't heard us.

"Um, I was just. . .leaving. . ." I stammer, quickly getting up and taking my plate over to the sink. The memory of Tyler shooting the man still plagues me. It's all I see when I look at him, and I still can't bring myself to be around him. "Bye, guys," I say awkwardly as I pass the table on my way to the stairs. Elliot smiles at me and waves good-bye, while Tyler just looks at me briefly and nods.

As I walk up the staircase, I find Angie as she comes down. Pushing aside all thoughts of the Émigrés, the Reserve, the outsider, Damien, and Tyler, I put all my focus on what I came here for in the first place: to see my father.

"Hey, Angie, you said my father would be back tonight, right?" I ask her, causing her to stop in her tracks.

"Yes. If everything goes according to plan and they move quickly, they should be back tonight. I'll send him up to your room as soon as he gets here." She tells me before heading back down the stairs.

I go up to the room I share with Tyler and sit on my new bed. My body is begging for sleep once more, and every muscle seems to ache, but the excitement of seeing my father again makes me forget about that and everything else. Tiredly leaning against the wall that my bed is pressed against, I gaze out the window and wait.

I WAKE UP WITHOUT REMEMBERING THAT I HAD EVER FALLEN asleep. The morning sun peeks through the window and judging by that, I know I at least got another six hours of sleep. Sitting up in bed and stretching myself awake, I look over to see Tyler sitting on his bed, his eyes focused intently on a Rubik's cube as he tries to solve it.

"Morning," He greets me without looking away from his task.

"Good morning," I say back, sighing as I start to remember everything from the night before. I had waited for what felt like forever, just hoping that I'd see my dad walk up the steps to the front porch, but I never saw it happen. "They didn't come back, did they?" My voice sounds more like a statement than a question, and I hope he knows what I'm talking about. He shakes his head, and I feel my heart fall.

"Don't worry too much," He tells me, pausing a little to plan his next move in solving the cube. "Nobody ever gets back when they say they'll be back. Like that day I found you. We got back a lot earlier than we planned because Alfie and Rebecca found those hovers." So, that's what they call those motorcycle things. I nod, taking a deep breath. Tyler finishes solving the Rubik's cube, and I feel myself smiling at him.

"That's impressive," I say. "I could never figure out how to solve one of those."

"It's not that impressive." He chuckles softly. "I'm not one of those geniuses that can solve it in under a minute or anything. I just looked up how to do it and practiced."

"It's still impressive to me," I admit, leaning my back against the wall as I face him.

"Thanks, I guess." He offers me a small smile, setting the Rubik's cube down on the nightstand in between our two beds before laying back down on his bed and looking up at the ceiling. "You know, the first time I ever solved it was exactly one week before the invasion. I still remember that." He gazes straight ahead and his eyes cloud over, his mind most likely taking him back to simpler times.

"One week before the invasion. . ." I try to think back to that time. "The last thing I remember before the invasion was arguing with my older sister, Mary. I had just gotten done with dance practice, and she was supposed to pick me up. She forgot, and I was already having a bad day since I'd failed my biology exam that morning, so I called her and was yelling at her. When she finally picked me up, I didn't even listen to her apologize, and we spent the whole ride arguing." I laugh quietly. "It's weird that I remember that fondly. I thought that was one of the worst nights of my life back then. Everything was so much simpler." I realize how much I've been talking and shut my mouth, looking at him in embarrassment, but he doesn't seem to mind.

"Tell me about it," Tyler agrees. "I'd rather fail a biology exam every day than deal with aliens."

"Definitely," I laugh again, louder and more naturally this time.

"So, you were a dancer?" Tyler's eyes focus on me, and my eyes automatically shift to the floor.

"Yeah," I nod.

"What kind of dance did you do?"

"Ballet and contemporary," I answer. "What about you? What did you do?"

"I played soccer, basketball, and ran track." He told me, picking up the Rubik's cube and starting over.

"How old are you?" I ask him, now curious to know.

"20," He replies. "I had just graduated high school when the invasion happened."

"Were you going to go to college?" The questions were just flying out my mouth now, and I couldn't stop them. I expected him to tell me off, but to my surprise, he didn't.

"I got a track scholarship to Northwestern." He answers with a nod. I feel my mouth drop open.

"Really? Wow, that's amazing!" I congratulate him, feeling more impressed and less scared as he talks. Right now, he's just a normal boy who loved to play sports, not someone who can kill another person without hesitation or a hint of remorse.

"Not that it means anything anymore. . ." He sighs, forcing as much of a smile as it seems like he can probably manage. Sadly, he's right. If colleges were used at all now, it would be because survivors were taking refuge in their abandoned buildings.

"Maybe when this is all over, they'll reopen and you can go back." I try to tell him cheerfully, attempting to think positively.

"Yeah," He snorts. "Maybe. If I'm not dead or 85 years old by then." Tossing the unfinished Rubik's cube aside, he opens the night-stand drawer and pulls out a tiny, red bag of candy that I recognize immediately.

"You have Skittles?" My voice is almost accusatory as if he should have disclosed this information to me as soon as I arrived here. I hadn't seen Skittles since the beginning of the invasion when my family and I were rummaging through an abandoned convenience store for food.

"Yes. They're my favorite. And with all this talk about the past, I think I deserve a pack." He smirks at me, and I find myself smiling back for some reason. He opens the pack, and I watch as he starts rearranging the candies by color on his bed sheets.

"What are you doing that for?" I wonder aloud.

"I don't like the orange ones." He says simply, scooping them up and then holding them out in my direction. His eyes meet mine again, and I realize he's expecting me to take them.

"Oh," I murmur as I hesitantly lean forward and hold out my hands. He drops the little orange candies into my hands before taking some of the green ones and tossing them into his mouth.

"Want any other ones?" He asks, his slightly bored tone implying that he's only trying to be polite. Shaking my head no, I eat the five orange Skittles he's given me one at a time, savoring the sickeningly sweet taste that's now foreign to me. The Reserve only gave us a portion of the fruits and vegetables that we grew, along with a few canned goods that we could obtain from them if we gave them more of our share of the crops. I hadn't had anything this artificially sweet in ages.

"I dread the day I run out of these," Tyler sighs. "I remember how happy I was to find some for the first time. It felt like home. But I knew I didn't want to waste them. When things got bad and food was scarce, before I came here, I would grab a bunch of sugar packets from restaurants. It would hold me over and give me energy until I found real food."

I gape at him, imagining a world so desolate that tiny sugar packets are all you have to keep you going. The Reserve suddenly feels wasteful in comparison. Every day at the market were hundreds of fresh baked goods. The cookies and bread were always still warm when we bought them. Looking back they probably threw away whatever didn't sell and no one else ate. Those thoughts combined with the sugar suddenly make me feel sick to my stomach.

Tyler finishes all of his Skittles just as someone knocks on the door. He tells them to come in, and Angie walks into the room. My heart leaps in my chest as I wonder if this means what I hope it means. Is my father back?

"I just came to talk to Rachel. Sorry if I interrupted anything." She apologizes.

"You didn't," Tyler says before I can even open my mouth as he walks out of the room.

"I wanted to let you know that I found some clothes that I think might fit you, and I put them in the closet. Here's some soap and shampoo if you want to take a bath." Angie hands me an unused bar of soap and a clear bottle of shampoo that's halfway full. My heart falls and I try not to frown. My father still isn't back.

"Thank you," I say quietly, suddenly realizing how dirty and disgusting I am at the moment. I'm literally covered in dried sweat and dirt. I look at her gratefully.

"To take a bath, there's a well out there with buckets next to it. You might need to take a lot of trips to get the right amount of water in the tub, but believe me, it's worth it. The bathroom is the door right across from this one. Here's a toothbrush for you."

"Is there anywhere for me to wash my sheets and clothes, too?" I ask her, taking the packaged toothbrush.

"I'll wash them," she promises. "Just leave the clothes on your bed." Walking over to the closet, she pulls out two blue towels and hands them to me before telling me that she tried to find clothes that she thought would fit me, but I would have to try them on for myself and let her know if they didn't fit.

Luckily, I ran into Rebecca on my way out to the well. She shows me where it was and grabs another bucket to help me fill the tub. With her help, it only takes us three trips to the well to fill the tub completely. Closing the bedroom door and locking it, I quickly stripped out of my clothes and left them on the bed. Hoping that Tyler wouldn't try to barge in anytime soon, I hastily wrapped myself in one of the blue towels and took the soap, shampoo, and extra towel with me on my way to the bathroom.

ELEVEN

I bathe quickly, knowing by the muffled sound of doors opening and closing that everyone here was getting started on their day and I would get left behind in a heartbeat if I didn't hurry. As fast as I can, I dry off, wrap the towel around me once more, and pad my way back to my room. Finger-combing my hair and attempting to put it back up in a bun with my only hair elastic, I look through the closet of clothes for something to wear. Grabbing the first pair of pants and shirt that I can find, I get dressed and nearly stumble down the stairs as I try to slip on my shoes at the same time. I regain my balance just long enough to run into Alfie as I head toward the kitchen.

"Ah, there she is!" He exclaims as if he's been looking for me all his life, barely flustered by the fact that I've just rammed into his chest.

"Sor-" I begin to apologize for running into him, but he interrupts me.

"Have some eggs." The next thing I know, he's nearly shoving his plate full of fluffy scrambled eggs into my hands. I'm so caught off guard that the plate begins to tip sideways, and the fork balanced on the edge of it begins to fall. Alfie catches it easily with his left hand while his right hand steadies the plate in my hands. Handing the fork to me, he gives me a friendly grin before turning away.

"Uh, thanks," I managed to say to him as he goes back into the kitchen. I turn toward the dining room, which is already full of people. The only seats that are open are the ones that belong to Alfie and Damien if I remember correctly.

"Don't even think about it." A rough voice whispers harshly in my ear, causing me to nearly drop my plate in surprise. Damien walks past me, shooting me a look that could cut through steel.

"Wasn't planning on it." my voice stutters, and I clear my throat and stand up straighter in order to appear more confident than I sound.

"Sure you weren't," He rolls his eyes as he continues walking. "You better watch your back, little girl. I'm warning you."

I respond with an eye roll of my own that he doesn't catch as I go to sit on the cream-colored couch in the living room. I find the little boy from the forest already sitting there, slowly eating his plateful of scrambled eggs. He looks up at me with auburn eyes that contain the warmth and happiness that seems so rare these days, and I can't help but smile at him.

"Hi, again," I murmur automatically, waving at him.

Jacob waves back to me, his cheeks flushing a shade of pink that immediately reminds me of Annie. I feel my heart clench and force my gaze back to his eyes so that I can forget the pain of missing her.

"Would it be okay if I sat with you?" I ask softly, motioning to the couch in case he can't understand me. A part of me wishes I had bothered to learn sign language while in the Reserve. I know Tina did. He nods, giving me a shy smile and seeming to understand my lips. I beam back at him as I take a seat on the couch. I peek at him from the corner of my eye as I begin to eat my eggs.

"I'm Rachel," I add quickly, realizing I hadn't introduced myself. Then I take a moment to slow down my words so he can understand easier. "Do you always sit here by yourself?" I hope he doesn't feel like

I'm pestering him. I'm just curious, plus talking helps me feel less awkward. He responds with a shake of his head.

"He likes to sit with me," Abe replies as he sits across from us and starts to eat his breakfast as well.

"I assume you know sign language," I say, and Abe nods. "Could you tell him my name is Rachel?" Abe nods again, taking a drink of water before signing to Jacob. I watch carefully, trying to remember the motions he uses. Jacob smiles at Abe and then at me.

I watch as Jacob digs into his meal, his arms clutching his plate and his hands shoveling food as if he hasn't eaten in days and knows he won't eat again. He leans over his plate protectively, as if someone is going to snatch his food at any moment. I try not to stare.

"Is he...from the Reserve?" I look at Abe.

"No. He has always been on the run until Tyler found him. He told us his parents got captured and taken to the Reserve while they were protecting him." He answers.

"Wow," I look at Jacob again, feeling my heart ache. "This place must be such a welcome change for him."

"What do you think of the place?" Abe asks.

"It's. . .it's nice." I stumble over my words as I try to find the right way to answer him, sounding like I'm talking about something as normal as a new college dorm room instead of a house of survivors of an alien invasion. "There's just a lot of people here. I'm having trouble remembering names already."

"It'll get easier," He promises.

"And you guys have it a lot better than I expected. The Reserve made it sound like you guys were living in caves with little to no food or water." I admit.

"We're doing the best we can. I know it used to nearly be that bad at the start of the invasion, with everyone panicking and frantically trying to do what they could to survive, but once we started forming the group that we did and established a system, things worked out." He explained, but unfortunately for him, curiosity is starting to bubble within me, and I start blurting out questions.

"How bad were things back then? And how did you guys establish this place and the rebels?"

"Well," Abe begins, and I'm relieved that he doesn't sound annoyed. "After the Émigrés swept through the area, survivors started gathering in the basements of buildings in the Divide. It seemed to be the safest place at the time, but everyone was restless and scared and hungry. People argued all the time and some even killed each other for food. It was probably a good thing that the Émigrés found them there and scattered them out."

"You make it sound like you weren't there," I state, watching him carefully as his eyes cloud over, taking him back to the past.

"I wasn't. After I escaped the Émigrés, I found Angie. I had been a friend of the family before the invasion, and this was their home. I came here and found that they had all survived, and we've been taking in survivors ever since."

"How did you escape them?" My voice sounds demanding, and I try to soften it. It's not his fault that he managed to escape and my family didn't. He pauses for a moment before beginning to explain.

"My home is in a field, so I could see them coming long before they were at my doorstep. I could just tell they weren't there to rescue me or anything like that. I live alone, and there's a pull-down ladder in my closet that leads to the attic. I went into the attic, pulled up the ladder, and closed the door. I could hear them knock before they kicked down the door. They were saying things like, 'If you can hear us, stay calm and stay where you are. Surrender and we will take you to safety. Resist and we will be forced to shoot.' Something like that."

His words remind me of my own capture. Chills run down my spine as I remember their white clothes, white helmets with thick black visors covering their eyes, and their strange silver guns pointed right at us. Nowhere to run. Nowhere to hide. We were outnumbered and surrounded. It was either surrender or die. Some would say we made the cowardly decision.

TWELVE

"ALL I COULD DO WAS PRAY THAT THEY WOULDN'T SEE THE WAY to the attic." Abe continues, the wrinkles on his dark skin becoming more prominent as he grips his fork tightly. "That was my only hope. And thankfully, they didn't. I waited for hours until I was sure they were gone before I came back down and started to plan what the hell I was going to do."

Jacob sneezes, and for a moment, Abe and I are brought back into reality, looking down at him as if noticing him for the first time.

"Bless you," I find myself saying to him. Jacob signs back, which Abe translates as 'thank you'.

Suddenly I wonder where Jacob's parents are. Is he related to Angie? His brown hair and tanned skin suggest otherwise, and he doesn't look like anyone else I've seen here. My heart sinks at the idea that his parents might be dead. For the past two years, I think the majority of us survivors have tried to cling to the hope that anyone from our past that we haven't seen is still alive, but the reality is much grimmer than that.

My best friend was a girl named Callie Michelson. I had known her my whole life. She was my age, went to school with me, and lived right across the street. When we were little, we would pretend to be chefs and make soup out of grass, mulch, leaves, flowers, and water from the hose. We'd never eat it, but we always pretended like it was the best thing ever created. We would play Harry Potter and pretend that we were witches as brave as Hermione, waving chopsticks around like they were our wands.

The last time I saw her was when we had gotten ice cream at the local ice cream shop after school. I had gotten my favorite chocolate sundae with whipped cream and sprinkles, but it sat melting in front of me as my eyes fixed on the TV. For over a week, there had been continuous news coverage of the strange ship hovering over France.

"It's gotta be aliens. It's gotta be." Callie was telling me, absent-mindedly braiding and unbraiding her honey blonde hair as she stared at the TV, her strawberry ice cream untouched as well. "Wouldn't that be so cool?" Her green eyes looked at me, and I remember them sparkling in excitement. "I mean, think about it! When we're old and have grandkids of our own, we can tell them we were alive when aliens first came to Earth."

She didn't think they were going to hurt us. A week's worth of inactivity from the ship and no new information had put plenty of people at ease. We all thought our governments had everything under control. But we were so wrong.

I haven't seen her since. She's not in the Reserve, and she's not here. Her older brother, Ross, with his gorgeous green eyes and tousled brown hair, who I had a crush on since I was in first grade, was nowhere to be seen either. I remember the last time I saw him as well. In that same ice cream shop on the same day I last saw Callie, he was two tables down from us with his friends. They were all watching the TV just as intently as we were.

"This could be it for us, you know," He was saying, his expression serious. "They could attack, and we could all die today."

"They won't attack." One of his friends scoffed.

"You don't know that!" Ross had growled, turning to face his friends with an expression that made even me afraid two tables over.

"We don't even know if they're aliens." Another friend pointed out, unfazed by his friend's sudden outburst.

"What the fuck else would they be? What kind of ship in this world has ever moved like that? Stayed up in the same spot for that long?" Ross threw his hands up in the air. "Like I said, these could be our last moments, and we're sitting in a fucking ice cream shop, watching life go on around us without actually living it."

His friends started making fun of him, mockingly telling him to carpe diem and get laid. Maybe some of them didn't want to be afraid and were in denial. Maybe some of them honestly didn't think aliens were a bad thing, like Callie. But Ross had been right. We should have spent the last few moments of our normal lives doing everything we'd ever been too afraid to do, taken every opportunity, crossed off things from our bucket list. . .

I had known that things were going to change, and I dreaded the idea of them getting worse, but my parents had constantly assured me that everything was going to be fine. However, Ross' words had sparked something in me, and for a moment, I wanted to throw nerves aside and tell him I'd had a crush on him for years, and maybe even kiss him. But even then, I had been too afraid. Before the invasion, I always let fear consume me. It thrived within me, rendering me silent and immobile until the invasion set me free, and I had no choice but to do things despite how afraid I was.

I left the ice cream shop moments later. I had dance practice, and then Mary picked me up late and took me home. We argued, and even though that had seemed like such a bad day, everything had seemed normal. Then the invasion began. And now Ross was gone, just like Callie. All of my past friends, the boys I've had a crush on, the girls that teased me, the boys I'd dated, my relatives. . .they could all be dead. I feel sick to my stomach, and set down my plate.

"Are you okay?" Jacob's voice brings me out of my nostalgic trance and I feel him tap my arm. He looks up at me with concern, and I notice he spoke up to get my attention.

"Yeah. I'm fine." I assure him, smiling as if to prove it. He signs back with a frown. Abe translates that I look sad, and I quickly backtrack.

"Oh, no. No. I'm fine." I promise, smiling so wide my face hurts.

"Newbie," Damien's voice interrupts us, and I'm somehow relieved. I turn around to see him standing next to a girl I haven't seen before. She's completely opposite of him, physically. While his hair is dark brown and wavy, hers is light brown and straight. While his eyes are blue and cold, hers are brown and warm. He leers at me, while she gives me a friendly smile. He stands tall, tan, and muscular with his rifle strapped to him, while she is nearly a foot shorter, thin, and pale. It's almost comical to see them together. "Stop being useless and help Grace out." He commands, giving her a quick kiss on the cheek before walking out the door. I feel my mouth drop open and quickly work to close it. So, this was Grace. She looked a lot different than I expected.

Jacob grabs my plate, taking it off the table.

"Oh, you don't ha-" I start, but he continues on past me. With that, he and Abe go into the kitchen. I walk toward Grace, trying to keep my expression neutral despite the fact that I'm still in shock that she's the one with Damien.

"So, you're the one who tamed the beast," the words fly out of my mouth before I can stop them. Great job, Rachel, call the girl's boyfriend a beast. Amazing social skills.

She gives me a confused look, but before I can apologize, understanding flashes across her face, and suddenly she's laughing, her laugh as pleasing to hear as the sound of wind chimes tinkling together during a faint summer breeze.

"I guess you'll just have to call me Belle," she jokes before leading me out the front door.

"How'd you do it?" My mind somehow seems to think that it's suddenly okay for me to say whatever I think. "Sorry," I add.

"It's alright," Grace smiles gently. "I don't really understand how it all worked out either. I used to be really afraid of him, and we wanted nothing to do with one another, but. . .then something changed. I was in this chicken coop here," she points at the wooden structure as we enter it.

"And I was feeding them like I do every day. But then, the bell rang, two at a time, which meant multiple outsiders had gotten through. I didn't think I had enough time to make it back to the house, so I just hid here. But an outsider must have thought this coop would be a good place to hide too. Because he came in and I was suddenly in front of a man holding a bloodied axe. He came toward me and I knew he was going to kill me, so I just started pleading and praying and trying to accept the fact that I was going to die, when all of a sudden, I hear a gunshot and the man is lying on the ground in front of me. Damien had shot him. He knew I was in here and wanted to check to make sure I was okay. Everything just kind of escalated from there."

"Wow. . ." is all I can think to say as I follow her lead and help her feed the chickens.

"I knew from then on that he wasn't as bad as I made him out to be, and I wanted to get to know him better. We talked a lot, and we got to know each other over time, and we ended up becoming close friends. That's when he became okay with the idea of me being his partner. Since then, we've just gotten even closer. I guess you could say he's my boyfriend now, but that just sounds weird during this time. We don't live in a world where we can go on dates and buy each other things, but that's okay. He's my partner and my best friend, and he helps keep me together no matter what happens. He saved my life, and I don't think I can ever repay him for that."

A silence falls between us as I try to imagine a kind, loving Damien. It's difficult. I haven't been here long, but my image of him has already been tainted. The way he treats me and the way he treats Tyler does little in his favor. I can't picture him the same way that Grace can, and I doubt I ever will. He's a different person with her.

"I've never had anything like that," I tell her, and I'm not sure if I'm saying this to fill the silence or if I just feel the need to open up to her after she had opened up to me. "I mean, I've had a few boyfriends before, and there were some that I was very close to and liked very much, but it never. . . nothing ever felt like what you just described."

"Well," she ponders as we finish feeding, leading me back out the door. The wind has picked up and the clouds have built up and darkened, hinting at a storm. "It's not as if those relationships are a waste. You're always learning with each relationship, and I think it'll be like that until you find the right person. I don't even know if Damien's the 'right' person for me, but being together feels right, and that's enough for me right now."

"That makes sense." I nod. Truthfully, relationships are the last thing I should be worried about. But having a crush and having a boyfriend would definitely bring back some normalcy in my life. I can't imagine attempting a relationship in a world like this, but I guess anything's possible. Every past relationship I've had was started because the boy was brave enough to try to make things go past friendship. I can't be held back by fear anymore. I don't have that luxury.

I've already escaped the Reserve; something I never thought I would be capable of doing, as much as I wanted to do it. I've shot someone. I've hitched a ride with a strange boy that I don't know anything about. Why should I let anything else stop me? If I want to be friends with someone, I'll have to push forward. If I want a relationship, I'll have to step out of my comfort zone and try my best to make it happen. If I want to live, I'll have to do things I'm afraid of. I can't afford anything else.

Up ahead of us, I can see Tyler off in the distance, running around and lifting things in the space of grass beside the house. He doesn't seem to be doing chores, and I can't quite make out what he's actually trying to accomplish.

"What the hell's he doing?" I ask Grace, my voice nearly lost in the wind as it whips harshly around us.

"Training," she raises her voice so that I can hear her. "Pretty much everyone here trains once a day at some point." Something in my brain clicks. Of course, they're training. They want to one day take back the Earth from the Émigrés. And that's another step in the right direction for me to push past my fears and start living. I should be too terrified of the idea of confronting the Émigrés, but I won't let that happen. Seeing Tyler should make me afraid again, but I won't let it. I begin running toward him.

"Wait!" Grace calls out, grabbing my wrist. "What are you doing?"

"I'm going to join him," I say simply, but she doesn't let me go.

"He prefers to be left alone when he's training." She explains, shooting me a warning glance. I shrug, easing out of her grip.

"He'll have to get over it." I grin at her, running toward him once more.

THIRTEEN

As soon as I make it to where Tyler is, tiny, scattered raindrops have begun to fall, cooling my skin from the late summer air. Tyler is doing push-ups, the muscles in his arms rippling with each one. I clear my throat to let him know I'm there, but his eyes remain focused on the ground. Frowning at him, I try a different approach.

"Mind if I join you?" I, unfortunately, have to nearly shout over the wind so that he can hear me.

"Can you even do a push-up?" He huffs out as he rolls over on his back and gives himself a short break before starting crunches.

"Does it matter?" I retort back, crossing my arms over my chest. "I want to train."

"Train on your own time then." He snarls between crunches, finally looking at me only to glare, his eyes an intense swirl of sapphire and gray, like the ocean as a storm starts to take over.

"You know I don't know what I'm doing. I want to train with you."

"Yeah, well, I want a lot of things, but we all have to suck it up and realize that the world doesn't revolve around us." He stands up, his breathing heavy as he goes toward a row of makeshift wooden targets. "And you're not my problem."

"Make me your problem," I demand, feeling the rain starting to fall harder. "You need a new partner, don't you?"

"I need food and I need water. I don't need anything else." He insists, pulling the familiar knife from the pocket of his pants and running his finger gently along the blade.

"You know that's not true." I feel my anger rising as I take a step toward him. "You need-"

"I also don't need you to be smart with me, kid. You get my goddamn point." He bites back just as angry.

"Will you stop calling me 'kid'?" I throw my hands up in the air exasperatedly.

"Will you stop bothering me?" He throws his hands up as well, mocking me.

"You're full of shit!" I yell at him, getting more frustrated by the minute. I shouldn't let him get to me, but I can't help it. I've been too on edge, too worried about my father, too worried about almost dying, and too worried about the rest of my family to be able to control my emotions and let things go. "Why can't you just treat me like a normal human being? Why can't you help me, just once? Why can't you act like you care about someone other than yourself?"

"Are you fucking kidding me?" His voice rises as he looks at me once more, rainwater matting his hair and running down his reddening face. "I saved your life! Or did you just conveniently forget that?"

I don't say anything back, just stare at him as the rain drenches me. He's right.

"I could have left you for dead, but I didn't. I probably should have, knowing how much you would slow me down and put me more at risk, but I didn't. I'm not that heartless. I don't leave people behind in the Divide. Day to day, I'm preparing to risk my life to save the human race as a whole. I gave up my life a long time ago to protect this planet, so what kind of person do you think I am?" He's still yelling, his face just inches from mine, but I don't cower away.

"You're right. . ..I'm. . .I'm sorry." I say quietly, so quietly that I'm not even sure if he can hear me over the wind and the rain. He lets out a frustrated exhale, his fists tightly clenched, even the one holding the knife.

"I'm not trying to make things more difficult for you," He begins in a calmer voice, taking two steps back. "You have to understand that out here, if you want something, you have to do it yourself."

Looking back at the targets, he stands in front of the one on the far left, readying his knife. Despite the rain, he takes aim, and in one swift motion, throws the knife at the target. The knife slices through the air and hits the target dead center. I try not to gape at him.

"You see that?" He turns back to me, pointing at the target as if I've recently turned into a completely oblivious moron within the last five minutes and wouldn't notice someone throwing a knife right in front of me. "No one taught me how to do that. I practiced on my own. I'm out here everyday training alone, and it's been that way for two years. And with two years of hard work, that's just one of the things I've been able to do. No one helped me. I did it on my own. And I'm not the only one here who can do that."

"Okay, I get it," I tell him defeatedly, turning back toward the house. "Sorry for bothering you." I start to walk back to the house, feeling like the biggest idiot on the planet. I should have listened to Grace.

"Rachel, wait," Tyler calls out over the rain, and I freeze. That's the first time he's used my name since he met me, and although it hasn't been that long, it still catches me off guard.

"What?" I turn to face him, trying to look pissed off again but probably failing miserably.

"I'm. . .." He looks confused, and I wait for him to figure out how to say what he's trying to say. "I'm sorry too, okay?"

"Okay. . ." I mumble awkwardly, getting ready to go back into the house, but he grabs my shoulder and turns me back toward him, the heat of his hand contrasting sharply with the chill of the rain and sending goose bumps down my arm.

"I get why you want help. I get why you want to become a part of this. But. . .I'm not. . .I'm not a coach, teacher, instructor, trainer, whatever the hell you want to call it. I don't have the patience."

"I understand," I tell him, ready to go back into the house once more, but his troubled sigh keeps me still as I realize he's not finished talking. He runs a hand over his soaked, chestnut-colored hair as he looks away from me, mulling over his next words.

"But. . ." He begins, focusing his eyes back on me hesitantly. "I should at least try. You did come to me for help, and if you're going to keep tagging along with me after I tell you not to, you better know what you're doing."

He walks back to the target, and I try my best to erase the goofy, triumphant grin from my face.

"Thanks!" I call out as I break into a light jog to catch up to him. He yanks the knife out of the target, turning back to me and pointing it in my direction.

"Five push-ups. Let's go." He commands, now pointing the knife at the ground. I nod, dropping down on the mud-soaked grass, and begin.

———

Tyler has me do five push-ups, five crunches, and one lap around the open area surrounding the house. Then I repeat all of it. Again and again, five times total. Even though I haven't worked out like this since before the invasion, the workout isn't difficult, but Tyler insists on starting out slow and easy and then building up the intensity. Plus, my push-ups and crunches are absolutely horrible, which Tyler doesn't fail to point out or try to fix.

We then move on to throwing the knife at the target, and as expected, I'm terrible at it. By the time I finally manage to actually get my knife on the target at all thanks to Tyler's multitude of advice, the rain has intensified, and a loud rumble of thunder causes me to flinch on my next throw. I miss the makeshift target completely.

"Scared of a little thunder?" Tyler calls out as he retrieves the knife.

"No," I reply loudly and firmly. I'm not supposed to be scared of anything. Tyler jogs over to me, handing me the knife as he gives me a look that I can't place.

"It's okay to be afraid, you know," He tells me as if he's reading my mind, looking out at the clouds as lightning flashes across the darkest ones in the distance. "There's nothing wrong with it." He pauses, looking like he wants to say more but he's not sure if I'll really listen. I stay silent, letting him know that he can continue. "I'm afraid constantly. So is everyone here, as much as they don't want to admit it."

I lift up my arm to throw again, but he faces me, holding up a hand as if to say, 'Stop'.

"Being scared doesn't mean you're not brave." He continues after another rumble of thunder has passed, looking me in the eye. "Being brave just means you're scared but you do it anyway. Fear is what makes us human. Fear is what keeps us alive out here."

It's almost as if he's not really talking to me, just reciting something he's been telling himself for a long time. I wonder if he's tried to internally tell himself not to be afraid as much as I have tried to tell myself that, only to realize that fear is a natural response.

"That's enough for today," Tyler says quietly as the worst of the storm comes closer. It's only then that I realize I'm shaking and my teeth are chattering. I nod, following him into the house. The rain has turned the grass and leaves a bright, refreshed green, and there are people placing buckets all around the house to collect the rainwater.

"Free shower!" Alfie exclaims as he runs out the front door. Rebecca follows him at a more normal pace, holding the door for us as we shuffle inside. I almost laugh as I see him start to dance in the rain out of the corner of my eye.

Tyler and I make our way inside and trudge up the stairs, practically leaving puddles in our wake. The minute we're in our room, I start to tug off my soaked clothes. I don't even care that Tyler's in here, I just need to get these clothes off me and I need to get warm again. He seems to have the same mindset as we change out from our wet clothes and into some dry clothes, our backs to each other the entire time. I'm too cold and exhausted to feel nervous or self-conscious.

Tyler finishes getting dressed before me and leaves the room, and I take a moment to gather my discarded clothes and throw them in the basket for dirty laundry. After that, I head downstairs as well, finding that Angie was giving out what appeared to be bowls of soup for lunch. Eagerly grabbing a bowl, I went toward the cream-colored couch only to find Tyler already there.

Just because it's supposedly okay to be afraid doesn't mean you have to be afraid of him, a voice in the back of my head tells me, and I hesitantly sit on the other end of the couch. Someone has started a fire in the fireplace, and there are blankets on the cream-colored armchair to my right. I grab one and curl up on the couch, eating my soup like it's the first meal I've had in years. It's simple, a clear broth with some vegetables, meat, and spices, but it's warm and just what I need.

A silence falls between us, but for some reason, it doesn't feel uncomfortable. Sure, we don't have a TV to drown out silences while we eat, and neither of us has the opportunity to pretend to watch baseball in order to avoid conversation, but that doesn't seem to matter. I think we're finally getting to a point where we can be in the same room and not feel awkward or feel the need to pretend like the other person doesn't exist.

"Hi," Jacob plops down in the space between us, a bowl of soup in hand.

"Hey, Jacob," Tyler and I say in unison. Tyler ruffles Jacob's hair playfully, and at that moment, I see the depths of his oceanic eyes spark to life. A genuine smile, unlike any smile I've ever seen him give, graces his features as he and Jacob playfully shove each other back and forth. Jacob cries out in protest, working to steady his bowl. I set mine down and reach out to help him, and he smiles up at me gratefully.

"You started it!" Tyler points at him, then signs. Jacob vehemently shakes his head.

"Did too!" Tyler argues, sticking out his tongue.

"Boys, boys, boys," Abe's calm voice quiets them immediately. "Some people are trying to sleep." He reminds them of the fact that everyone here sleeps at different times, and some are sleeping now even though it's not night. Tyler chuckles softly and shoots Jacob a knowing look. Jacob crosses his arms over his chest, looking like he's trying to refrain from rolling his eyes. A loud bang of thunder brings us all back to reality, and everyone goes back to eating their soup.

As soon as I finish off my soup, I head back upstairs for a nap. I like having the freedom to nap and to work out, but I do miss my family in the Reserve. The more I think about it, the more I'm not really sure if I want to go back after my dad comes back. I really like it here, and I think they'd like it too. My mind runs through several different plans to help them escape the Reserve as I drift off.

FOURTEEN

WHEN I WAKE UP, THE STORM IS GONE, AND MY HAIR IS ALMOST completely dry. Once again, it seems as if I've slept longer than I intended. The only reason I woke up was because Tyler came to tell me that dinner was ready.

It's a meat and beans kind of night again, but I'm so hungry already that I'm nearly overjoyed despite the repetition. I fill my plate and sit next to Jacob on the couch, and Abe joins us as well. We make small talk as we eat, and in no time at all, the sun is setting and the candles are being lit.

But just as everything begins to quiet down, an enthusiastic cheer from outside sends everyone back into excitement. My heart soars, thinking that the only explanation is that my father is back. Everyone I recognize is currently inside this house. It has to be him, back from his supply run. I rush to the window to see who it is, Elliot and Molly joining me seconds later. By the time I can see the outline of two people in the distance, nearly every rebel is surrounding me, craning to see who's outside.

It looks like a man and a woman, but I quickly realize that the man is not my father. He's much younger, probably in his late twenties. Heat floods my face as tears begin to sting in my eyes. I know I'm supposed to be patient. I know that almost no one gets back when they say they will be out here. But that doesn't mean that waiting is easy for me. And right now my mind is thinking the worst.

I feel a hand on my shoulder and turn to find Angie giving me a comforting smile.

"He'll be here soon," She promises, giving my shoulder a squeeze. I can only nod.

"Hey, come on! That's Garret and Brianna, you have to meet them," Elliot insists to me, unaware of the unshed tears in my eyes as he practically drags me outside. The air is thick with humidity, and the drenched grass causes water to seep into my shoes. The man who I assume is Garret comes forward, smiling at the crowd of rebels coming to greet him.

"We didn't find much, but we found these," He says grandly, pulling out two bottles of whiskey from his backpack. A few cheers run through the crowd.

"Bonfire tonight!" A voice that I swear belongs to Damien yells. More cheers.

"Yeah, just what we need, drunk men," Brianna mutters sarcastically with a roll of her brown eyes, an amused smirk on her lips.

"Lighten up, babe," Garret insists, throwing his arm around her as we all head toward the backyard of the house. Damien starts up a fire in what looks like a fire pit, and everyone who's outside begins to spread towels around it, sitting on the towels to avoid getting wet from the grass. I sit next to Elliot in a daze, trying to think about anything other than my father.

Moments later, a decent-sized fire is burning, and Grace and Tyler have joined us, Tyler holding a guitar. The first bottle of whiskey is passed around as the sun continues to set, casting everyone's face in an orange glow. It'll only be a few minutes before it's dark out.

"You know what I miss?" Garret nearly bellows to the group, running a hand thoughtfully over his dark stubble. Elliot takes a swig of whiskey and hands it to me, and I pass it to Molly without taking a sip. Even though laws mean nothing anymore, alcohol was never something I drank before the invasion, and it's not something I want to drink now. "I miss Chinese takeout. There was a local place by my apartment, and they had the best goddamn General Tso's chicken in the world." Garret finishes, earning some laughs and some sounds of agreement.

"I miss sushi." Brianna follows up. Garret snorts, causing her to glare at him. But even from across the fire, I can see him mouth "sorry" with a playful grin and give her a peck on the forehead. I wonder if they're a couple too.

"I miss pizza!" Alfie hollers, getting some louder noises of agreement.

"Coffee!" someone else yells.

"Tea!" Elliot yells back.

"Diet Coke!" Rebecca follows up.

"Beer!" Damien exclaims.

"Cheesecake!" Molly shouts.

Food after food is named until people start slurring their words from the whiskey and the chatter dies down. Tyler begins strumming his guitar quietly and casually.

"You two," Garret points at Grace and Tyler. "Sing us a song. Like last time." Grace laughs softly as Tyler sighs.

"That was so long ago," Tyler complains, taking another sip of whiskey as the bottle comes around. "What song did we even sing?" Grace shrugs, but Garret is quick to answer.

"Freefalling by Tom Petty."

"Please don't do that one again," Damien groans, and I'm expecting Tyler to snap at him, but he doesn't. He and Grace just start whispering to each other, trying to come up with what song to sing, I assume. After a few moments of debate, they both nod, and Tyler starts strumming on the guitar as they both begin to sing in harmony.

"Sometimes I feel like I don't have a partner,

Sometimes I feel like my only friend,
Is the city I live in,
The city of angels,
Long as I am,
Together we cry."

I recognize Under the Bridge by Red Hot Chili Peppers immediately. It instantly reminds me of summer vacations to the beach, of my father handing out sparklers, of burgers and chicken fresh off the grill. I close my eyes and let their voices take me back to when things were simple, and it seems as if everyone else is doing the same as a hush falls over the campfire as Tyler and Grace continue to sing.

Tyler sings well, which is surprising enough for me since his voice is normally so cold and rough unless he is with Jacob, but it's Grace's voice that blows me away. Her voice is so melodic, hitting every note with perfection that I swear I could die happy listening to her sing for the rest of my life.

Garret immediately joins in at the top of his lungs, startling us all into laughter. Alfie joins in just as loud, and soon, the majority of us are singing along. We sing the rest of the song together, each of our voices becoming stronger and happier as the lyrics remind us of the pre-invasion days, where home meant something entirely different than it does now. When the song is over, we clap and cheer for Tyler and Grace, and everyone is smiling.

Moments later, everyone dissolves back into their mindless chatter, and Tyler sets the guitar aside. The next bottle of whiskey starts to go around, but Damien snatches it away and takes off without a word. He raises his middle finger to everyone's protests and gives us all a wink and a smirk, and I watch as Grace frowns and goes after him.

Elliot starts telling me all about the Red Hot Chili Peppers and how he always wanted to see them in concert but never got the chance to, his words slightly slurred and his excitement intensified. I'm sort of listening, but I can feel my eyes starting to close and my mind starting to drift off, and the darkened sky isn't helping. I need to sleep again. Saying goodnight to him, I go over to Tyler.

"I'm going to bed," I tell him, unconsciously yawning. "Try not to wake me up when you come back in."

"No problem," He slowly gets to his feet, grabbing the guitar. "I should get to bed, too. I'll come with you." With some whiskey in his stomach, he seems a lot like the Tyler that Jacob gets to see. A smile tugs at the corner of his lips, his cheeks are slightly flushed, and his eyes are bright again. I wonder if he always used to be like this before the invasion. . .happy as if there was no reason not to be. Not like now, where a smile is foreign and his face and voice rarely show any emotion other than anger.

As we walk toward the house, the sound of someone yelling to our right stops us short. Tyler and I look at each other in confusion, and I watch his expression to see if he becomes alarmed. He places his guitar against the side of the house and goes toward the noise, and I reluctantly follow. Moments later, we come across Damien in the distance, towering over Grace. One of his hands grips Grace's wrist, while the other holds the whiskey bottle. Even in the dark, I can tell from Grace's expression that she is crying. I pick up my pace and go past Tyler.

"How many fucking times do I have to tell you to leave me alone when I'm here? You stupid bitch!" His words are laced with venom, fueled by alcohol.

Here? Where is here? As I come closer, I can see what looks like wooden crosses sticking out of the ground. Is this a graveyard? I can't make out what the crosses say, but I can't imagine what else they'd be for and why Damien would be here.

"I just wanted to make sure you're alright," Grace's voice is trembling, and she's too focused on him to see me.

"I don't need your help," Damien snarls, gripping her wrist tighter until she cries out in pain. I'm sprinting toward them now.

"Damien, put the bottle down, please," she begs.

"You don't get to tell me what to do!" He roars, and even as I run I can see his hand let go of her wrist and slap her hard across the face. The slap rings in my ears and I feel anger rise within me.

"Hey!" I feel myself shout, and Damien and Grace immediately look toward me. I'm ready to yell at Damien, regardless if it won't do any good, but Tyler springs into action before I can open my mouth. He slams Damien against the trunk of a tree, pressing his gun into Damien's forehead. I rush toward Grace to comfort her, but my eyes are focused on Tyler's gun, panic rising in my gut.

"Go ahead," Damien smirks, his words slurred and his eyes glazed. "We all know you want to." Tyler clicks the bullet into place, and I hear Grace let out another sob.

"Tyler, please! Don't!" She yells, falling to her knees. She still loves Damien, even at his worst.

"Tyler," I go toward him.

"If you ever hit her again," Tyler begins, his voice loud and enraged. "If you even look at her wrong, I swear I won't hesitate to send a bullet through your fucking skull," With a final shove, he lets go of Damien and lowers the gun, walking away.

"Is that a promise?" Damien laughs.

"It's a guarantee. " Tyler says in a final tone, picking up the whiskey bottle and going back toward the house. I help Grace up and put my arm around her, following Tyler. We run into Garret and Brianna on the way back, and with a quick explanation from me, Garret goes back to take care of Damien and Brianna takes Grace up to her room.

As Tyler and I go to our room, the Tyler I know is back. His mouth is a thin, hard line, his eyes zapped of any spark of life. He drinks out of the bottle regardless of the fact that Damien was drinking from it just moments ago. With a heavy sigh, he collapses onto his bed as I take off my shoes and turn off the solar-powered lantern lighting this room, plunging us into darkness.

With my eyes unadjusted, I reach out my hands to feel my way toward my bed. As soon as I feel my legs hit the mattress, I sink down and pull the covers over me, ready to give my body rest and bring me one day closer to my father's return. My mind is still reeling from what just happened, and I want sleep to take my mind away from the thoughts of Damien treating Grace like that and wondering how many times he's done that before and if she just quietly put up with it.

"You know what's strange?" Tyler's voice snaps my tired eyes open, and he continues without waiting for a response. "As soon as the bombs hit. . .as soon as we started running for our lives. . .we became different people. We wanted food? We took it. We wanted guns? We took them. Everything became about survival, and suddenly. . ." he pauses, and I can hear him take a swig of whiskey as the liquid sloshes around the bottle. "I'm a man without a name."

As he pauses again I find myself more awake, trying to figure out his words and what he could be trying to say. Why does he think he's a man without a name? My mind keeps spinning as I wait for him to tell me.

"With everything the way it is now, my name means nothing. I could tell you it was Mark Smith and you wouldn't know the goddamn difference because that's the kind of world we live in now. And even if I tell everyone I meet what my real name is or if I give them a new name, it doesn't matter. To the Émigrés, I am just a target for them to shoot. To the rest of humanity, I am another soldier whose purpose is to fight for them." The anger seeps back into his voice, but he doesn't let the emotion overpower it, even in his mildly drunken state.

"They don't know that my favorite candy is Skittles. They don't know that I taught myself how to play the guitar and solve a Rubik's cube. They don't know that I like to run for miles just to clear my head and that sometimes I'll wake up at the ass crack of dawn just to watch the sun come up. They don't know anything about me and they don't care. I don't have a name. On the day of the invasion, I became a soldier of the Earth. I am nothing but a soldier."

I know he doesn't want me to respond, and there's really nothing for me to say. So I stay quiet as I stare up into the darkness at the ceiling, his words running through my brain. I already know that the Émigrés don't see us as anything but an enemy. But to imagine the rest of the people left in this world not seeing the rebels as actual people but just as soldiers throws me off. I never thought of it that way; when people think of us, they do not think about who we are, only what we do.

The more I stay here, the more I don't want to go back to the Reserve when my father gets back. I am a rebel now. I'm not the girl who does ballet, who paints each of her nails a different color, who loves red velvet cake, and who stays up all night just to finish a book. I'm not the girl who's too afraid to talk to Ross Michaels, who finds peace being near the ocean, and whose favorite color is blue.

I am nothing but a soldier of the Earth.

FIFTEEN

When I awake the next morning, I find Tyler still asleep. I can tell by the morning sunlight streaming through the windows that under any other normal circumstances, Tyler would have been up already, but last night's drinking took a bit of a toll. Even though I'm no drinker myself, I'm sure that the slightly malnourished and probably dehydrated state of everyone's bodies here would cause a little bit of alcohol to go a long way.

So, I let him sleep and sneak quietly downstairs. It's possible that he might wake up later and be a little angry that no one woke him earlier, and maybe he'll be especially mad at me, but I could really care less. As much as I find myself starting to like Tyler as a person, getting him to like me is the least of my worries. Roommates don't have to be friends; they just have to tolerate each other.

I fill a cup up with some of the water from a large plastic container on the kitchen counter, knowing by now that all water that's been purified goes in that container. Shuffling past some other rebels, I head back up the stairs and tiptoe back into the room I share with Tyler. Placing the water on the nightstand, I quickly leave without a sound.

That's what people need when they're hungover, right? Water? And. . .Advil? But I have absolutely no idea where any Advil would be. . .if there even is any here. He'll have to get some on his own if he wants some.

Grabbing a package of peanuts from the counter and eating them on the go for breakfast, I make my way out to the barn to feed the chickens. I don't know where Grace is or if she's already fed them, but I might as well check. And to my surprise, the chickens are fed, and I can only assume Grace fed them and it's later than I thought, and she's at least doing somewhat okay after last night.

As I go back inside the house, everyone seems to be either still asleep, awake and hungover, or just taking it easy. It seems as if today is an established easy day, and I can't help but think that if the Émigrés knew where we were, now would be the perfect time to attack us. The thought sends a slight shiver of fear down my spine, and pretty soon I find myself back in my room, changing into clean clothes before taking off outside for a run to keep my body and my mind occupied.

I take a lap around the open area surrounding the house, stretch, and then start off into the woods. I have no idea where the hell I'm going, but the urge to train is even stronger than it was yesterday.

If you want something, you have to do it yourself, Tyler's words ring in my ears, and I pick up my pace. I will not be weak. I'll show him, and everyone else who doubts me that I am capable of taking care of myself as well as fighting for humanity. Dance taught me the importance of hard work and determination, and my father taught me to be strong, and that when things go to hell, there is always someone worth dying for. You do what you have to do to protect the ones you love.

I think of Annie's laughter as I run, trying to distract myself from the memories of the outsider that come creeping back as I make my way through the familiar-looking area. When the image of Tyler's bullet hitting the outsider right between the eyes starts to edge into my mind, I think of how Annie used to call me "Chel" when she was younger and still learning how to speak. Even as she began to learn, pronouncing my name was still difficult, and she ended up calling me "Ay Chel" for a while.

I picture how Mary looked calm, cool, and collected walking through the halls of high school on her first day of senior year, whereas I was a shaking, blushing mess of a freshman who couldn't speak without squeaking. She was always so effortlessly beautiful, and I envied her and looked up to her more than anyone. Kind, confident, fearless Mary Collins; the type of girl that I could imagine saving the world. . ..the type of girl that would risk everything to let her sister escape instead of escaping herself because she knew how much it meant for her sister.

Running back to the house, I stumble across the graveyard I had discovered the night before, and to my surprise, I find Grace there. She's kneeling in front of one of the wooden crosses and doesn't even look up as I jog toward her, breathing heavily from my run.

"Sorry to intrude on you," I say what I feel should be said, instead of just running by her and pretending she's not there. "I didn't realize-"

"It's okay," she interrupts me, finally looking up at me with a distant expression. I glance at the cross she's in front of, seeing the name "Patricia Simmonds" carved into it. Each cross, I realize, has a name carved into it. Thomas O'Brien. Jason McCann. Sara Enders. Richard Mallory. Liesel Rhodes. The crosses fill this small, open space, each representing a human life lost in this war. I never knew any of these people, but my heart still aches for them. Being buried here means they died fighting for the remaining human race, whether going on supply runs, guarding the rebel hideout, keeping a house full of people running smoothly, or just offering a chance for everyone to smile and forget about the war for a little while. They could have died by Émigré lasers, by outsider bullets or stab wounds, or by illness, or by. . .suicide. . .but regardless, they died much too soon.

"Damien's not a terrible person," Grace insists, tearing my eyes away from the crosses. "He'd never hit me before that night. Not once. And he apologized so much this morning, too. He just isn't the same with alcohol. . .but, hey, why am I making excuses for him, right?" She lets out a laugh that's far from genuine, looking at the cross of Patricia Simmonds again.

"Why did you go after him?" I ask her. She gives a sad smile that doesn't reach her eyes.

"Because I knew he was going to go here. And I knew that alcohol just fuels his anger and sadness. His mom, Patricia, was killed by Émigrés on a supply run. She was all he had left, and she died right in front of him." Just like that, tears fill her eyes and she looks ahead, deeper into the woods. "Just beyond there is a cliff. We all know it's there, and it's high enough that if you hurl yourself off the edge, you'll die the second you hit the ground. And I'm afraid that one day, I won't be enough for him, and he'll go to the edge and jump off, just like Sara did." Her eyes glance quickly at the cross of Sara Enders.

"But he wouldn't do that. He wouldn't leave you." The words fly out of my mouth regardless of the fact that I barely know Damien. The urge to comfort Grace numbs all logical thinking.

"I hope with all my heart that that's true." She offers me another attempt at a smile. "We should get back to the house. . .before anyone has a chance to wonder where we are." As much as she tries to hide it, I still catch the desperation in her tone. She's spent all the time she can take here, and she wants to leave before she starts to break down.

We walk back to the house in silence, and the moment we step inside, a groggy-looking Damien takes Grace into his arms. As I step aside to give them space, I see Tyler trudging his way down the stairs, drinking the water I had given him this morning. As soon as he sees me, he gives me a nod and comes toward me.

"You train already?" He gestures toward my sweaty appearance.

"Not really. All I did was run. How are you feeling?" I notice that his eyes are slightly bloodshot. He shrugs.

"I'm okay. I've been better, but I've also been a lot worse. Thanks for the water, by the way."

"No problem. So, are we just going to train later today, then? Or. . ." I trail off in case he wants to decline, although I'm hoping he'll say yes.

"Sounds good." He shakes his head in agreement before heading off into the kitchen. Trying to refrain from looking too happy at the thought of training, I start stretching as I realize I have absolutely no idea what else to do for the rest of the time being.

I can see Alfie and Rebecca through the dining room window, training at the makeshift targets. Although I know they wouldn't mind if I joined them, the fact that I already went through some trouble to get Tyler to train me is enough to make me wait to train. Glancing around the house, I try to find something to do. Maybe I can clean the kitchen?

"Rachel!" a voice calls from the top of the stairs. I look up to see Elliot smiling down at me. "Come up here. I want to show you something." Confusion and curiosity make me follow him quickly, and he leads me into what I assume is his room. Bookshelves line the walls, every shelf full of books. It's an impressive collection, especially during this time. He gestures grandly at the books which earns a grin out of me.

"These are all yours?" I count six bookshelves in all, and I can't imagine how many books are here in total.

"Yup," He replies proudly. "While everyone else searched houses and stores for food and soap and things like that, I searched for books. I couldn't help it." He shoots me a sheepish grin. "I still like to read more than anything."

I run my finger along the spines of the books closest to me. All Quiet on the Western Front, Hamlet, To Kill a Mockingbird, The Odyssey, Harry Potter. And the next shelf contained dozens of books about things like first aid, CPR, and camping. I know Elliot's just showing me this because he could tell I felt out of place, but I'm beyond grateful. The amount of books in front of me is incredible.

"This is amazing," I say in true awe. I haven't seen this many books in over two years. "Are the books downstairs yours too?"

"You bet." Elliot nods, beaming at me. My eyes fall on an aged copy of The Sun Also Rises by Ernest Hemingway, and I look at Elliot hopefully as I grab the book off the shelf.

"Would it be okay if I borrowed this one?"

"Oh, of course!" He gestures at the bookshelf. "Feel free to borrow any book you want any ti-"

The sound of the bell interrupts us, and I feel the panic rising in my gut as my eyes immediately look out the window. It rings one at a time, unlike the two-at-a-time rings that signaled the coming of outsiders.

"What's that mean?" My voice is a choked whisper. "Émigrés?"

"No," Elliot shakes his head, suddenly looking like a soldier snapped to attention. He begins to quickly look through his room before pulling out a first aid kit. "It means someone just got back from a supply run, and they're hurt."

My father.

SIXTEEN

The book drops from my hands as I run from the room and down the stairs. I nearly collide with Tyler as I run out the door, and I can hear him running after me.

"Rachel, wait!" His tone is urgent. He doesn't want me to go. There's something he doesn't want me to see. He knows this has something to do with my father. I pick up my pace instead of stopping, running towards the sound of the ringing bell. Tyler passes me but doesn't stop me, probably assuming it's no use to try to keep me away. I follow him as quickly as I can, trying not to trip over the roots of the trees in the forest.

In a few agonizing moments, we reach the small building I saw when I first arrived here, and I see the same guard from before. Beside him is an extremely tall, muscular man with dark skin shiny with blood. He is standing alone next to a hover, and my father is nowhere to be seen.

"What happened?" Tyler demands as Elliot rushes forward to attend to the man's wounds. Within seconds, Damien, Molly, Alfie, Rebecca, Angie, and Garret are beside me, but it doesn't take long for tears to cloud my vision. If my hectic train of thought is correct and this man was on a supply run with my father, my father is dead.

I can feel my heart breaking even as someone slides a comforting arm around my shoulders. I look up and blink through my tears, seeing Rebecca next to me. Her expression isn't hopeful. It's distressed, and yet she decided to comfort me.

"We found the mothership." The man explains through a gasp of pain.

"You mean the ship those freaks came here on?" Damien's voice is enraged. The man nods.

"We were scoping it out in the trees far away from the actual ship. Trying to see what they were up to. Trying to see if there were any ways to get in. . .if they had any weaknesses. But they must have seen us. Next thing we know, we're surrounded by them. And what's weird. . .what's weird as hell is that they weren't shooting us with lasers. They had these. . .these darts. Anyone that got hit seemed to slowly go unconscious, and they would drag them away. The only reason I escaped was because I got to a hover in time."

"So, the rest of your group isn't dead. . .they were kidnapped?" Angie asks in disbelief. The man nods. I suddenly feel like I'm going to throw up. Those disgusting, emotionless, vile creatures took my dad. And for what? To study? To experiment on? I slip out of Rebecca's grasp and find myself taking off back toward the house.

"How'd you get hurt?" Garret's voice is the last thing I hear.

Once I'm out of the forest and inside the house that no longer feels like home, I go up to my room that no longer feels like mine. I grab my messenger bag from the Reserve and start angrily shoving some things inside. A jacket. The knife I sort of borrowed from Tyler. And. . .the gun I took from the outsider. Where is that gun?

I have to leave. I have to get out. I need that gun.

Displaying emotions similar to a toddler throwing a temper tantrum, I furiously toss aside any useless crap and look under both beds, ignoring the tears that stream down my face. Not finding it, I search through every dresser drawer before opening the drawer on the nightstand. I find the stupid Rubik's cube and the selfish stash of Skittles, but of all things, it's a pile of photographs that makes me freeze.

I see Tyler and Alfie looking up at me through a Polaroid photograph, smiling so wide they look like children as if a war wasn't going on despite the dirt and blood on their faces. The photograph is dated in marker on the bottom, indicating that this photo was taken about a year after the invasion. Below the date are the names Alfie Mallon and Tyler Forester, scrawled in sloppy penmanship.

The next photo was of Tyler and a blonde girl, dated three months after the invasion with the names Tyler Forester and Liesel Rhodes on the bottom. Tyler's arm is casually around her shoulders, and even though he's smiling away from the camera like he wasn't ready for the picture to be taken and was talking to someone else, Liesel is looking directly at the camera and smiling as if she knows all of your secrets.

"What the hell are you doing?" Tyler's voice startles me, and I whirl around to find him standing in the doorway, looking at me with a mixture of irritation and confusion.

"Looking for my gun," I reply to him, feeling my emotions starting to return as I resume my search.

"Your gun?"

"The gun from the outsider that you killed."

"Why?"

"Because I'm leaving." I huff as if it were the most obvious thing in the world.

"You don't even know how to shoot well." He points out with a sigh of annoyance.

"Does it look like I care?" I snarl as I look at him again, only to see that he's holding my gun. "Give it," I demand, turning back into a five-year-old child as I stomp toward him and hold out my hand. He doesn't hand it to me, only puts it in his backpack without a word. He closes the door with his foot as if a closed door would keep me here. "Give it!" My anger starts to simmer to the surface as I reach for his backpack, but the second I raise my hand, his hand flies forward with impeccable speed, wrapping tightly around my wrist and easily lowering my arm back down. His other hand grabs my other wrist, holding me still.

"Let me go!" If I had been held by anyone else, the venom in my voice might have been enough to get them to let me go. But Tyler doesn't move. In fact, he acts as if I haven't spoken.

"Not only are you not trained enough, you're hardly in the right mindset to handle any type of weapon." His voice sounds harsh like he's trying not to yell at me. And for whatever reason, that just makes me angrier.

"I'll go without a gun, then!" I cry out, attempting to shove him aside with no luck. He rolls his eyes.

"Don't be stupid, ki-"

"I swear to God, if you call me kid, I'll rip your eyes out." I hiss, my frustration going past its boiling point as my threat only manages to cause his lips to twitch upward as a chuckle slips past them. My life is falling apart all around me, and he has the audacity to laugh at me!

"Just-" He begins.

"Let go of me!" I shove him away again, and this time he lets go by choice, but he still blocks my path to the door. "What the hell is your problem?"

"What the hell is my problem?" He looks at me like I've gone insane, which at this point, I may have. "What the hell is your problem? What good do you think leaving is going to do?"

"Well, I'm not going to sit on my ass for the rest of my life like you guys are. I'm not going to waste precious minutes 'training' for nothing while people continue to die. I'm not gonna sit around campfires drinking myself stupid and making myself the easiest target on the face of this Earth. You guys act like you're doing something great, but it's been two years and you've done absolutely nothing!" I'm so upset that I'm shaking, and my throat burns from yelling.

"Do you really think a war gets won by just waltzing into enemy territory? Do you think training and planning don't accomplish anything? Do you think an army gets built overnight? We don't have things like airplanes and computers and phones and tanks anymore, so I sincerely apologize on behalf of all rebels for taking longer than your liking to find a way to win, and for trying to find ways to enjoy ourselves while we still can with the numbered days we have left." Tyler growls, his tone dripping with sarcasm. "But now that we've found the mothership, we can finally get this war started and become nothing but soldiers just for you. Happy now?" A silence falls between us, thickening the air with tension as each second passes.

"I'm sorry," I answer, taking a deep breath. I've acted on impulse and lashed out all because I'm scared of losing my dad. "I'm just. . .so frustrated. Because no matter what you or anyone hear says, they still have my dad. And even if he's alive right now, who knows how much longer he's got?" Just saying those words brings the tears back to my eyes, and I clench my fists as if that will help keep them from spilling over. I can't keep crying like this. It doesn't help anything.

"Rachel," Tyler exhales tiredly, saying my name as if he's scolding a pet for behaving badly. "They've got four other rebels including your dad, and they probably have dozens more humans in that ship for all we know. Everyone here is just as worried as you are and wants to rescue your dad just as much as you do. We know we don't have a lot of time. But you running off would just add another body to the count, and I don't want to be the one to tell your dad that you're dead when we rescue him."

When. Not 'if'. When. Somehow, even his confidence in the rebels doesn't comfort me. My dad has always been the strongest person in the world in my eyes, and if he's dead, in my mind it's only a matter of time before everyone else is too. But as wonderful as the idea of leaving seemed during my frustration, now that I've calmed down a bit, I know it's a stupid idea. I don't even know where the mothership is. Only that man does. To add to that, it took them nearly two years to find it, and only one person made it back.

"Fine. I'm not leaving." I reluctantly say as I sit down on my bed, wiping my eyes dry.

"Good," Tyler replies.

"Can I have my gun back now?" I hold my hand out toward him again, but he only shakes his head.

"Of course not," He scoffs, nodding out toward the hallway. "At the very least. . .not until you can use it well."

"You really piss me off," I say as I get up and follow him out the door, dreading the idea of training with someone that I was justifiably annoyed with me.

"Don't think I enjoy your company either, kid," He bites back, actually letting out a laugh as I hit him as hard as I can on the shoulder for calling me 'kid' again.

"You obviously don't value your eyes very much." I remind him of my earlier threat as we walk down the stairs.

"You wouldn't hurt a fly." He shrugs. "In all seriousness, you should also learn to keep your emotions in check. You'll need that skill out here if you want to survive."

SEVENTEEN

As we reach the bottom of the stairs, I realize why no one else in the house seemed to have noticed our shouting match. Elliot and Angie are still tending to the man's wounds as he lies on the couch, pointing at what looks like a map on the coffee table as nearly every rebel stands around him, listening intently and adding in some ideas every now and then. The place is bustling with noise, and our argument was nearly some sound in the background.

Tyler and I slip out the front door without anyone noticing. I follow him out to the makeshift targets as he pulls my gun out of his backpack. Opening a small wooden box by one of the targets, he takes out some bullets and loads them inside.

"Are you sure you're not wasting ammo teaching me how to shoot?" I look down at the little box in dismay.

"Don't worry, we have plenty," He assures me, walking away from the targets and gesturing for me to follow.

"Where?" I wonder aloud, but he doesn't answer me. Instead, he immediately starts informing me about what kind of gun I have and how to use it. He tells me about how everything works, making sure he has my full attention and that I've completely calmed down from my earlier breakdown before handing me the empty gun and instructing me on how to hold it. Then how to load it. Finally, he shows me how to shoot it.

He monitors my every move, standing just inches away from me. Every bullet that misses the target is another mistake that he knows exactly how to correct, and even shots that make it onto the target get critiqued fully by him. He critiques my stance, where I'm looking, my aim, and how I'm holding the gun. It gets to the point where I'm sure he would criticize me if I moved just a centimeter in the wrong direction.

When my shots were finally nearing the center of the target every time, Tyler decided that was enough for today, and I agreed. He then suggested that I help him take some buckets of water from the well to the house since the buckets were heavy enough to help build some arm strength and we would both need the water for baths later.

"I know I'm a bit hard to deal with," I begin as we walk from the well to the house with our buckets in hand for the second trip. Tyler snorts, and even though he's walking in front of me, I'm sure he's rolling his eyes. "But I really do appreciate you putting up with me and helping me out. Thank you."

"Mhmm," Tyler grunts in reply.

"I don't know why you do it," I admit, my breathing getting heavier as I work to heave the large bucket of water along. I glance at Tyler jealously as he easily holds one bucket in each hand, walking at a steady pace.

"I don't know why I do it either," He agrees.

Before I can continue talking to help take my mind off of how heavy the bucket is, movement to my right catches my eye. In the woods where we walk is a guy who looks probably a bit older than Tyler, and I can only assume he's a guard by the rifle he holds and the fact that he waves at us and that Tyler nods back. The boy is walking away from the house instead of towards it, so he must be going back on duty after getting lunch or something.

But it's not the fact that I've never seen him here before that I find myself staring. His skin is perfect, free of any blemishes, bruises, scars, freckles, or scratches. His shiny brown hair looks like it belongs in a shampoo commercial, and his beaming white smile is advertisement worthy. He's like the Ross Michaels of the Ruins.

Even as he continues walking, I crane my neck to get a good look at him. Seriously, how can someone look that good out here? Is he hoarding all the hygiene products? Was he a celebrity before the invasion? Have I seen him on TV or in a movie before?

The vibrating, loud clang of my metal bucket against a hard object brings me back to reality, and by the time I look forward, I've run directly into the trunk of a tree. Stumbling backward, I find myself on my back and drenched in water before I can regain my balance. And to make the situation even better, I can hear Tyler burst into laughter in front of me.

"Yeah, you're a ballerina alright," He manages to say as his laughter dies down and he sets his buckets aside. He walks toward me, smiling that genuine smile so rare that I almost forget to look pissed at him for laughing at me. "I can tell by how graceful you are."

"Ha ha, you're hilarious," I drone sarcastically, trying to wring out my soaking wet clothes but failing miserably.

"Mademoiselle," He says in a dramatic voice, extending a hand to help me up as he tries not to smile.

"Screw you," I glare up at him, still wringing out my clothes, and yet for some reason, I'm also fighting off a smile.

"Oh, come on, you're not gonna sit in the dirt all day, are you?" He raises an eyebrow.

"I can get up on my own, thanks," I tell him, finally getting to my feet.

"Suit yourself," He shrugs, handing me one of his buckets.

"Such a gentleman!" I exclaim in my own dramatic tone.

"You bet I am. I'm always here to help girls that get distracted by Cole and run into trees."

I feel my cheeks flush. Even while walking in front of me, he still put two and two together to realize why I'd fallen. I clear my throat.

"I just thought I recognized him from somewhere," I say nonchalantly, trying not to even think about the guy who's supposedly named Cole.

"Yeah, sure, that's what they all say." He gives me a knowing look.

As we walk back to the house, I'm amazed that we can go from screaming at each other to joking around so quickly. And even though Tyler seems to be mostly stiff and full of angst, I think in moments like this, I'm finally getting to see what he's really like. . .who he was before the war. It makes me wonder how different everyone else here could have been. Maybe Damien was a lot nicer, Alfie was even happier, and Grace wasn't as quiet. I know for me, I've become a lot bolder with the things I choose to say and do, but maybe I'm a lot more noticeably different to people that knew me before the war.

When we enter the house after setting aside our buckets, we're immediately greeted by the smell of cooked meat and vegetables. The injured man is no longer on the couch, and Angie and Elliot are both eating at the dining table, along with Molly and Garret. And although Angie tries to hide it, I can tell she's relieved that I don't look as upset as I did this morning. Everyone looks a bit sadder and a bit more stressed, sure, but it's easy to see that they've been dealing with situations like this for a long time, and there's relief in knowing that those rebels on the mothership could very well be alive.

I grab a plate of food and take a seat on the couch next to Tyler, feeling an overwhelming sense of urgency once more. Every second of my life that isn't working toward getting on that ship and getting back my father feels like a second wasted. As the gears in my mind spin to formulate some type of plan, I turn toward Tyler.

"Hey," I interrupt him from eating, and he looks up from his food with a hint of annoyance. "I need to get back to the Reserve to tell the rest of my family what's happened. Do you think it's possible to go back?"

"It's possible," He's gone back to looking at me like I've gone mad.

"But are you really willing to risk your life just to tell them a message?"

"They're my family," I tell him with a roll of my eyes. "I'd like to visit them, too. Make sure they're okay and all."

"And how exactly do you plan on getting there and getting in?"

"You'd help a poor, little, mademoiselle out, right? Being the gentleman that you are," I bat my eyelashes excessively, smirking when I see him try not to smile.

"I don't have any reason to go to the Reserve. I don't have family there." He says simply, going back to eating his food. But before I can argue, Elliot comes out of nowhere and plops down on the couch in the space between Tyler and me.

"Well, we've been talking about going to the Reserve for a while now, haven't we? To get a good idea of the area to help plan how we're going to set them all free at once and destroy the place, to update the people on our efforts, and to visit our families and friends if we have any there," Elliot informs matter-of-factly, earning a grumble from Tyler and a beaming smile from me.

"Great! When's the soonest we could leave?" I ask Elliot.

"Well, theoretically-" Elliot begins before Tyler cuts him off.

"You're not ready." He states, looking directly at me. I gape at him.

"What the hell do you mean? It's an in-and-out type of mission, right? Plus, you're my partner and-" This time, he interrupts me.

"We're not partners." He says it so strongly that I'm taken aback. How is it that once things finally start to seem okay between us, it all ends up going to hell in a matter of seconds? It's like he wants to push people away.

"Well, what does it take for me to be your partner? Hate to break it to you, but we don't exactly have the next two years to bring me up to your expectations." I argue.

"That's why you won't go," Tyler says as if it's the most obvious solution in the world.

"Tyler, come on," Elliot shoots him a warning look, and Tyler raises his hands as if everyone's conspiring against him.

"Look, I'll go to the Reserve in your place. I'll tell your family whatever you want and let you know exactly what they say in response, word for word." He promises.

"You don't even know what they look like!" I let out a bitter laugh.

"You just have to tell me-"

"And what if you still end up talking to the wrong family? How are you going to find the right family before the Émigrés find you and discover that you're a rebel?" I point out, watching his mouth set into a hard line. "What does it take for me to be your partner?" I repeat, louder this time.

"You're not going to be my partner-"

"Just tell her what it takes." Elliot insists, and for a second, I think Tyler's going to punch him in the face.

"Fine. Whatever. You have to be able to defend yourself and not rely on me to protect you. The whole point of a partnership is that it's balanced. You help each other out while doing what you need to do. I can't spend all of my time, focus, and energy trying to keep you from getting shot to death." He says, his tone implying that I'm nowhere near good enough.

"So, when will I be good enough to-" I start.

"I don't think you understand," He interrupts once more, standing up and glaring down at me. "I'm not going to be responsible for any more deaths, okay? No one else is going to die because of me. You got that? No one." Although he's not shouting, his voice is harsh enough to convey his frustration. With that he stomps off, leaving Elliot and me sitting uncomfortably on the couch. My mind jumps back to the crosses out in the woods, and the photograph of the blonde girl who smiles like she has you all figured out.

"Was that. . ." I look at Elliot hesitantly. "Was he talking about Liesel?"

"Yeah," Elliot nods, suddenly looking a lot older as he lets stress and exhaustion take over his features.

"Why does he think he's responsible?"

Elliot looks at me sadly, causing my stomach to clench in anticipation. Leaning toward me, he speaks in a low murmur so as not to draw any attention to us.

"He thinks he's responsible because the bullet he fired was the bullet that killed her."

"You mean. . .he. . ." I struggle to form a coherent sentence as my mind tries to wrap around Elliot's words. "He shot her?"

"It was an accident," Elliot nods. "It was dark, and an outsider had gotten in. When Liesel and Tyler went out to help everyone find him, they split up to cover more ground. The outsider found Liesel and must have snuck up behind her and grabbed her before she could react. He held a gun to her head and walked toward the house, demanding food, weapons, and supplies before he would let her go alive. Tyler approached them from behind at an angle, preparing to fire at the man, but everything just went wrong. The man must have heard Tyler because he whirled around and held Liesel up, and by that time, Tyler had fired, and the bullet struck Liesel in the head."

EIGHTEEN

I TAKE A MOMENT TO LET HIS WORDS SINK IN AS MY MIND begins to visualize the events that led to Liesel's death. The amount of guilt Tyler must have felt would be unbelievable. Going through that forest alone at night to search for one enemy would be enough to put anyone on edge, and seeing the enemy holding your friend at gunpoint would prompt anyone's mind to think of the quickest solution. He was only doing what he thought would be the quickest end to the situation and the easiest way to prevent anyone else from getting hurt. I can only imagine how horrible it would be to accidentally kill your friend when you were only trying to save her.

"What happened after that?" I ask, my voice sounding unbelievably quiet as I grip the edge of the couch.

"Well, as you can imagine, Tyler was pretty much a wreck the second he realized what he had done. He starts losing it. . .screaming, running toward her. . .and in the meantime, the outsider is aiming his gun at him. Thankfully, before he can get a shot and I can even get my gun out, Rebecca nails him with her gun. Alfie also fired. And that was that. Damien blamed Tyler and hated him for it, and Tyler blamed himself and hated himself for it, too. That's why they are the way they are now."

"It's not his fault," the words tumble out of my mouth forcefully. It was just an accident. A rare collision of decisions that led to a horrible coincidence. Elliot nods.

"I know, but convincing either of them that is nearly impossible right now."

"I'm going to go talk to him." I stand up, setting my plate of food on the table.

"Wait, you're not going to talk to him about what I just told you, right?" Elliot immediately stands up as well, panic washing over his face.

"Of course not," I shake my head.

"Good. Because he would kill me if he found out that I told you." He laughs nervously.

"Well, doesn't pretty much everyone here already know the story anyway?" I raise a brow.

"Yes, but no one talks to him about it. I think he'd like everyone to pretend that it never happened, so no one brings it up."

"Gotcha. Well, I'll see you later. I need to change out of these wet clothes, too." I tell him, just now remembering that I'd spilled water all over them.

"I was going to ask you about that." Elliot loses his grim expression and smiles at me. "Did you fall into a puddle or something?"

"No," I shrug with a grin of my own. "Just ran into a tree while holding a bucket. You know, things people normally do when they're trying to transport water from one place to another."

"Nice," Elliot laughs. "Well, see you. And hey, I know this isn't the best plan, but if no one agrees to go to the Reserve before we go to the mothership, I'll go with you."

"Thanks, Elliot," I'm smiling from ear to ear now, but he's up the stairs before I can even think to hug him. As I follow him up the stairs, a girl I haven't seen here before comes stomping down, forcing us to the right side of the staircase. Her cold eyes look me over as she passes me.

"Who is this?" She turns back to Elliot, halting momentarily just one step below me. Her intense gaze and solemn expression don't match her light tone, and it sends a chill down my spine. Although her features are dainty and sweet (big blue eyes with long, dark eyelashes, long brown hair, full pink lips), her body language and expressions convey a different image. There's something off about her. . .like the war knocked her a bit off her rocker and she never recovered.

"This is Rachel. She's new." Elliot explains.

"Hey," I wave at her, offering her a smile. She just gazes at me some more in silence, successfully erasing my smile in an instant.

"Hmph," she gives a half shrug, and with that, she continues down the stairs and into the kitchen. I look back up at Elliot in confusion.

"Uh, who the hell was that, and what the hell is up with her?"

"That's just Kira. Don't worry about her, she's just weird." He shrugs, walking back up the stairs.

"Yeah?" I chuckle.

"She just stays in her room all the time. She's got the room right next to you and Tyler, actually."

"She doesn't train? Go on supply runs? Help out?"

"Nope," Elliot responds. I'm a bit taken aback. I thought everyone played a part here. That's how things seemed to work out. You play your part, and in return, you get to live here, get food, and get protection. How anyone could just live here and not try to help is beyond me.

"Who's her partner?" I ask.

"Her brother, Cole. He's a guard, so she doesn't actually need to fight if she doesn't want to."

"Oh," I murmur. So Cole is her brother. That makes sense. Her eye color, hair color, and skin tone match his perfectly from what I remember. I shake my head as I realize I'm getting distracted from what I need to do. I can't waste any more time. "See you," I say to Elliot again as I go toward my room. Walking in, I find Tyler on his bed, fiddling with the Rubik's cube once again. I clear my throat to let him know I'm there, and he looks up at me with an expression that seems more emotionless than anything.

"What?" His voice is cold.

"I get where you're coming from-" I begin.

"Do you?" His tone becomes slightly mocking.

"Just let me talk, alright?" I raise my voice in the hopes that he won't speak up again, and thankfully, he just lies flat on his bed and stares up at the ceiling. "This is my family we're talking about. They're the reason why I do everything that I do, and right now, I need to go to the Reserve. I need to make my escape from there worth it. I have to give purpose to all of my efforts so far. I can't just sit back when my family's on the line. Surely you understand that. . ."

His expression doesn't change, but I think of something that I've never bothered to think about before: that I've never seen his family. There is no one here that seems to be his family, and he said so himself that they aren't in the Reserve. Is he the last one left? My heart falls as I try to force out the rest of what I need to say.

"So, I've come up with a bit of a plan. When's your next supply run?"

"Not for a while," He sits up, glaring at me now. "But there's no way in hell you're going."

"I'm going to the Divide tonight," I tell him with as firm of a voice as I can muster.

"No, you're not," Tyler raises his voice.

"I am. I get that I have to have a partner before I can go anywhere. It's the rebel system of making sure everyone has someone to keep them accounted for and provide backup. So, I'm going to prove to you and everyone else that I'm ready. You can come with me or stay here. . .I'll find some other way to go. But I'm doing this to show that I can handle myself out here and that I can be your partner or anyone else's partner if you won't take me, so if you don't come and I don't make it back, you can tell my father I'm dead." I can't imagine how angry he is with me right now, and at this point, he's probably wishing he'd left me for dead in the Divide, but I'm running out of options. I'm scrambling for a way to keep my family together and keep us alive.

"This isn't some kind of game," He's on his feet and in front of me in seconds, his fists clenched so tight that his knuckles are white. "You want to go out there and die? Fine, be my guest. I'll gladly come and watch." He walks past me and out the door.

"I'm leaving as soon as the sun goes down," I say to him, sighing as he doesn't respond. I close the door and change from my wet clothes to some dry clothes. I make sure that everything I'm wearing is dark and easy to move around in so that I'm ready for the Divide when nightfall hits. Leaving out a jacket and packing a small, shoestring bag with a flashlight, I head out to the training area. I have no idea where Tyler is, but I don't need him to help me practice what he's already taught me.

"Got any extra knives?" I say to Molly as she practices throwing knives at one of the targets. After hitting the target almost perfectly in the center, she nods.

"Yeah, I'm actually done with these, so you can use them." She hands me three knives that are about equal in size.

"Thanks!" I call out to her as she goes back toward the house.

"Keep practicing." She calls back at me. "Then one day, you'll be a force to reckon with."

Her words earn a smile from me, and I begin practicing with some enthusiasm. I only stop when my right arm begins to get tired, and then I move on to push-ups, crunches, and laps around the house. My father would have been proud of my work, no matter how easy it seemed to him, but I'm not done yet. I need to practice shooting more.

Unfortunately, Tyler still has my gun, and I'm sure he either has it with him or put it somewhere where he knows I most likely won't be able to ever find it. It would be a waste of time to look for it, so I'll need someone else's help.

I look around the area as I stretch, hoping to find someone who not only has the ability to help me but will also actually be willing. Spotting Elliot reading a book on the porch, I call out to him to come over.

"Who's the best shooter here?" I ask as soon as he reaches me. "And don't say Tyler. . ."

"Okay, um. . .best shooter here right now. . .um. . .Marcus, but he's busy-"

"Marcus?" I look up at him in confusion as I stop stretching.

"He's the guy who came back hurt from the mothership."

"Oh," is all I say in response, the image of him covered in blood returning to my memory.

"Well, there's Garret, but he and Brianna are hunting right now. Then Damien. . .."

"Anybody but him." I groan, causing Elliot to smile.

"And then Cole. . ."

"Cole?" I heard his answer, but I'm a bit surprised for some reason. It would make sense for him to be a good shooter, though. He is a guard after all. I guess I'm just surprised I hadn't thought of him myself. Springing to my feet, I glance off toward the woods as Elliot nods. "Got it. Thanks." I start to take off.

"Be careful, Rachel," Elliot says, his warning tone bringing me to a halt. I look back at him. "I understand why you're so driven to be a part of this war, but remember, Tyler has good reasons for wanting to keep you out of it." He offers me a small smile as if to show me that he's not going to hold me back, but he does want me to understand what I'm getting myself into.

I nod back at him. I do understand. Yes, sometimes the urge to do everything I can to save my family clouds over my other thoughts and I don't think about my own safety, but deep down, I know the risks. I know that death is something that no longer lurks in the shadows waiting for its chance to strike, but rather waits patiently behind the nearest corner for the moment I walk mistakenly in its path. I'd be a fool to assume that I'll make it out of this war alive.

"I'll be careful," I murmur. He smiles wider before heading back into the house, and I take off toward the woods once more.

I find Cole patrolling along a chain link fence, rifle at the ready. When he spots me, I wave, and a hint of recognition washes over his features.

"Is something wrong?" His voice is barely above a whisper, and yet it's so melodic that I have to refrain from rolling my eyes. He's not even like Ross Michaels. . .he's worse. He's that guy in high school that's too good-looking to be real and seems to have a brain the size of a fruit fly, but yet somehow manages to manipulate everyone into getting exactly what he wants. I put my guard up immediately. It may be wrong to judge, but in this world, better safe than sorry.

"No, nothing's wrong. I just heard that you were a good shooter, and I need some tips." I answer, keeping my voice low as well.

"Oh," He looks down at his gun and then back at me, offering me a charming smile. I try my best to smile back and appear friendly, keeping my suspicious feelings below the surface. "I'm not really the expert here. You should talk to Garret. . . or Marcus-"

"Well, I'm talking to you," I say in the sweetest tone I can muster.

"Okay then, don't be too disappointed if you don't find my tips very helpful." He chuckles softly.

"At this point, I'll take any help I can get."

"Alright, if you insist." He shrugs, walking in the direction of the house. "Let's go somewhere where we can talk." I follow his lead as he goes out of the woods and towards the backyard of the house where the targets are. Alfie and Rebecca are sitting on a low, old-looking wooden table, and Cole makes his way toward them.

"Alfie, would you cover for me?" Cole asks, handing over his gun, helmet, and bulletproof vest.

"Yeah, sure. No problem, man." Alfie takes everything with a nod, quickly shooting me a wink and a knowing look as he heads off into the woods. I can't help but smile as a quiet laugh slips under my breath, shaking my head as if to say he's got it all wrong. He just smirks, making quiet kissing noises behind Cole's back before turning back around and walking toward the woods.

Rebecca gets up as well, smiling at me as she makes her way toward Alfie. She gives him a quick kiss on the lips before going into the house, and I find myself gaping at them.

"They're a couple, too?" I turn to Cole in disbelief. He gives me an amused look.

"Yes. You didn't know?" He sits on the table. I shake my head, sitting next to him but making sure that I'm not too close.

"Is everyone here in a relationship with their partner?" I ask with some sarcasm, causing Cole to laugh.

"No, of course not. Alfie and Rebecca were a couple before the invasion even started. So were Brianna and Garret. The only couple here that's formed since the invasion is Damien and Grace."

"Good to know. Let's get to the point." I urge, giving him my full attention.

"Okay, well. . ." he pauses, seeming to plan out his words. "The first bit of advice that I can think of is leading. When you're trying to shoot a moving target that's ahead of you, the best thing to do is lead, which means fire so that the bullet will go ahead of them. So when they're running from your left to your right, shoot ahead of them at your right. This way, by the time the bullet reaches them, they'll run into it."

"Alright, got it. What else?" I nod, trying to memorize his every word while visualizing what he's suggesting.

"Um. . .you should hold the gun properly. Like-."

"Tyler showed me that," I interrupt. "What else?"

"Uh, don't panic?" He tries to add, smiling at me sheepishly.

"That's it?" I frown at him.

"That's all I've got. I told you I'm not the expert here." He reminds me.

"Right," I sigh, getting off the table. "Well, I should let you get back to guarding this place. Thanks for the advice. I really do appreciate it." Smiling at him naturally this time, I start to walk back toward the house.

"Wait," Cole calls after me, causing me to turn around. "I never got your name. . ." His charming grin is back, and I'm immediately on my guard once again.

"It's not important," I assure him, walking backward.

"I'd still like to know." He insists, walking toward me. "I'm-"

"Cole." I finish for him, and I find myself smirking a bit as he stops walking and looks at me in surprise, wondering how I knew his name. "I know who you are. Tyler told me."

"So, what's your name, then? Because if you don't tell me, I'm just going to refer to you as 'the girl who ran into a tree'." Now he's the one smirking at me, and I feel my cheeks flush scarlet. I didn't think he saw that, but he must have heard the sound of the bucket hitting the tree and turned around.

"Rachel," I answer him, walking back to the house without waiting for a response.

"Rachel," I hear him repeat. "You know, Rachel," He calls out, louder this time as I'm further away. I don't turn around, but he continues. "If there's any other bit of advice I can give you, it's that you shouldn't be so distant. If there's anything I've learned in this war, it's that friends make things easier." That last bit makes me stop, and I turn to face him. He's still smiling, but he doesn't look like he's teasing me, which is what I expected. He looks like he means what he's saying, truly, and he's trying to help me out again. And yet, I still feel just as defensive as before.

"And if there's any advice I could give you, Cole, it's that you shouldn't be so trusting. If I've learned anything in this war, it's that you can't trust anyone. Not even your friends."

NINETEEN

I leave him standing there and finally go into the house, plopping onto the couch with a heavy sigh.

Where the hell did that come from? When did I start preaching that you can't trust your friends anymore? I feel like I'm turning into Tyler. I'm pushing people away the second for the smallest of reasons, just to make sure I won't get hurt. What is wrong with me? Why am I getting so edgy over someone just because they look manipulative and seem like the kind of person who is used to getting their way? I trust Elliot. I trust most of the rebels here. I'm even learning to trust Tyler. And maybe I shouldn't trust them so quickly, but if I can, why can't I trust Cole? For heaven's sake, he gave me advice on how to kill someone! And now the same person that came to him for advice is telling him that they don't trust him. Brilliant.

"Why the glum face?" Elliot takes a seat on the couch beside me, looking at me curiously while offering a comforting smile.

"I'm an idiot," I say simply.

"Why do you say that?" His brows knit in confusion.

"I basically implied to Cole that I don't trust him." I sigh, looking up at the ceiling to avoid his gaze.

"You don't? Okay. . .why is that?"

"I just. . .I don't know. He gave me a weird vibe. . .seems manipulative. . ."

"Well, if it helps, he's not manipulative," Elliot assures me. "But he did have very rich parents, so I've been told. I always assumed that's why he and Kira are so proper. And sometimes snobby." He chuckles.

"With all the outsiders lurking in the woods, it's just made me wonder if anyone here isn't looking to help humanity, only to help themselves, no matter who gets hurt in the process," I admit.

"It's possible that there could be someone like that here, but Cole's been here almost as long as I have, and he's been a great guy so far."

"That's why I said I'm an idiot." I smile sheepishly at him.

"You're not an idiot. You picked up on something you didn't like about him, and it made you wary. I think it's perfectly acceptable to be on your guard in an alien invasion, no matter who you're dealing with." He gives me another comforting grin, and I feel my mood starting to lighten.

"When you put it that way, I don't feel too bad," I say.

"Good. Glad to help."

"So, what have you been up to all day?" I switch topics, leaning back into the couch and beginning to relax.

"Training and reading. Same old, same old." He replies, holding up a copy of War & Peace.

"Sounds fun. I bet reading's a nice escape." The more I think about it, the more I'm surprised that I've only seen Elliot reading here.

"Definitely. Reading and sleeping are the best ways to escape." But just like that, the spark in his eyes is gone, and a distant tone takes over his voice. "As long as you don't have nightmares. . ."

I feel my stomach clench. He's right. Sleeping is one of the few ways we can escape the harsh reality of our world now. It's the only time when the stress of the day melts away and we can erase the sight of the dead and the suffering and the enemy that we face, and truly begin to imagine we are somewhere better. . .somewhere safe, like home.

But sometimes we aren't greeted with those happy images when we drift off. Sometimes the things we wish we could forget replay in our minds over and over. They can prevent us from falling asleep or wake us up in a cold sweat, shaking in fear with tears in our eyes, a silent scream on our lips.

The sight of cities being blown up, of bodies littering the Earth, and of cold, hateful violet eyes haunted me in the Reserve. And now the images of a man with a bullet hole between his eyes are burned into my brain, along with the image of Marcus covered in blood, and the thought of my father being subjected to every torture imaginable.

I can only begin to imagine what images haunt the others here when all they want is to get some sleep. Tyler could see Liesel, shot by his bullet and dead before he can reach her. Rebecca could see the two outsiders she killed, trying her best not to let the guilt of killing two people consume her. Damien could see his mother taking her last breath right in front of him. I don't know what things Elliot has seen in this war that he tries so hard to forget. All I know is that it has scarred us and we're doing whatever we can to move on.

"Fresh squirrels! Get 'em while they're hot!" Garret bellows, startling me out of my thoughts. I see him walking toward the kitchen with his hands full of skinned, fire-cooked squirrels, grinning triumphantly. Brianna walks behind him, holding a rabbit and a crossbow.

"You should probably eat before you leave," Elliot suggests, and with a nervous pang in my stomach, I realize the sun is starting to set.

I eat quickly and quietly with Elliot, thinking about how I'm going to survive in a place that nearly killed me the second I stepped foot in it. My nervousness makes it difficult for me to want to eat, but I eat anyway, knowing my body needs it and how lucky I am to have food to eat and a safe place to stay for now.

By the time the sun has set, the realization that this could be my last few moments alive hits me full force. I have to try to keep my breathing even as I put my shoes on, and I'm already sweating despite the chilly night air already cooling the house. Trying to keep a smile on my face, I say goodbye to everyone else, hoping it's not goodbye forever.

"You look better in black," Molly says to me, taking in the black pants, black shirt, and black boots I'm wearing. I didn't intend to be dressed in all black, but most of the clothes here are black or dark gray. They avoid clothes that are colors that would make us easy to spot, and they avoid white, especially because it's associated with the Reserve and the Émigrés. "You look like one of us." It's strange to me how a color that once stood for darkness now stands for the good, and the color that stood for the right, the just, and the pure now stands for the evil.

"Thanks," I tell her, and momentarily, I don't have to try that hard to smile.

"You coming?" Tyler mutters as he walks past me, striding out the door. I reluctantly follow, seeing Alfie and Rebecca on two hovers in the open area in front of the house. Alfie smiles at me and hops off, making his way toward me.

"Hey, want me to teach you how to ride one of these?" He asks.

"Don't be an idiot. She's not going to learn in five minutes." Tyler rolls his eyes, fighting off an amused grin.

"Another time, then?" Alfie looks at me expectantly.

"Another time." I nod, feeling like maybe everything will be okay and I can come back safely. I'll be Tyler's partner, and Alfie can teach me how to ride a hover.

"Okay, Rebecca and I will be your backup tonight. You got this." He gives me a firm pat on the shoulder, and he and Rebecca take off together on one of the hovers before I can formulate a protest.

"Did you know they would tag along?" I demand at Tyler. He just shrugs, which causes some anger to wash away my nerves. "I didn't want anyone else coming. No one needs to risk their lives for this."

"Oh, but it's fine if I go with you?" Tyler scoffs, getting on the hover with a shake of his head.

"I said you could stay here." I remind him.

"And what would that prove? You can't even ride a hover, so it would take you at least a day to walk there. How would I know you wouldn't just wait in the woods and come back, claiming that you'd survived a supply run, when really, you're just showing me some more cans you brought from the Reserve?"

"I'd never cheat." I hiss through gritted teeth.

"I don't know that." He replies.

"Ugh, is there ANYONE else I could partner with? I'd take any other human on this planet other than you right now." I huff, my frustration with him only getting amplified by my anxiety.

"Nope. No one else." He smirks. "And if there was, they'd want you to prove yourself too before they ever considered you to be their partner."

"So, what did everyone else here do to prove themselves, then?"

"What you failed to do, or what you're about to do. They either killed an outsider or went on a successful supply run. Except they actually waited until we had a run planned before they decided to go out to the Divide. And in the meantime, they learned how to fight and shoot well." He's trying to tempt me to turn around. . .to walk back into the house, call things off, and forget about being his partner. But I won't.

"Well, like I said, we don't have all the time in the world, so let's get moving." I finally make my way toward him when another voice stops me.

"You guys aren't going without saying goodbye to me, are you?" Elliot says as he approaches us, giving us his friendly grin that's impossible not to smile back at.

"Bye, Elliot," Tyler calls out mockingly, pretending to turn on the hover. When they both laugh, Tyler hops off the hover to hug Elliot goodbye, and I watch as Elliot whispers something to Tyler, and Tyler's smile vanishes. I'm not close enough to have any idea what

Elliot said, but Tyler just nods and gets back on the hover.

"Have fun out there," Elliot says to me as he comes toward me. His sad smile makes me realize once again that this could be my last few moments if something goes wrong. I try my hardest not to cry as I wrap my arms around him, trying to relax as he hugs me back. Neither of us let go for a long time, and knowing Elliot's way of always figuring things out, he probably understands exactly what I'm thinking and what I need. He was basically my first start of friendship here. . .my first taste of what life used to be like before the war. I don't want to leave him and let go of that small comfort, but I'm going to have to face my fears despite the risks.

"I survived once. I can survive again," I tell him as we let go. He smiles at me like he's proud of me, and I feel my heart clench. I want to hug him again and never let go this time. I want to stay here and pretend everything is fine, even though it isn't.

"That's what I like to hear." He gives me a pat on the back, nodding at me as if to say 'everything's going to be okay', before walking back into the house. Taking a deep breath, I turn back to Tyler, ready as I'll ever be to take on hell.

"You two lovers now or something?" Tyler comments as I climb onto the back of the hover he's on. He hands me a helmet with an irritated look, and I make sure I look just as annoyed with him as his eyes meet mine.

"Jealous?" I raise a brow as I slip on the helmet.

"Hardly." He replies, facing forward and turning on the hover, taking off before I can say anything else.

A long trip to the Divide would have given me some time to calm my nerves, but it seems like we get there in seconds. I've barely started to give myself a mental pep talk by the time Tyler parks the hover next to the last tree before the damaged buildings of the Divide start. As we get off, I attempt to stay relaxed and not let the silver Emigre ships patrolling up ahead intimidate me. I realize we're not at the same spot where Tyler found me. You can't even see the wall of the Reserve from this section of the Divide.

"Here," Tyler clears his throat, and I look toward him to see he's been trying to hand me a gun. . .my gun, the gun I had claimed was my own that once belonged to an outsider. I look at him in confusion, wondering what made him decide to give it back. "You're going to need more than just a knife." He says simply, walking toward the buildings.

"So, what's your plan?" I lower my voice as we get further from the trees and closer to the buildings. Rebecca and Alfie are nowhere in sight, but judging by the fact that I can only hear the faint hum of the ships' engines and not the sound of lasers, they should be fine.

"I thought you had a plan. You're the one trying to prove something." He shrugs.

"I do have one. It involves you searching the buildings over there." I point at the buildings on my left. "And me searching the ones over here." I point to my right. "We work our way in and meet in the middle."

"And what makes you think I'll follow your plan?" He looks back at me to give me a signature glare.

"You can just sit here if you want." I offer with fake kindness, an exaggerated smile on my face. Tyler stops short and faces me, forcing me to stop as well.

"You're not going in there alone." He growls.

"Yes, I am. I need to prove that I can handle this myself, remember?" I point out.

"I don't care. You won't last five minutes in there."

"I thought you came here to watch me die." I offer him a scowl, walking past him. He grabs my arm, forcefully turning me toward him.

"Don't-" He begins, but my outburst interrupts him.

"I'm not Liesel, Tyler!" The words fly out my mouth loudly enough to attract attention if Emigres patrolled on foot. Tyler's eyes widen in surprise, and even I'm a bit shocked at what I just said, but I don't take it back, even as I feel a blush creep into my cheeks. His expression darkens as he lets go of me.

"No, you're definitely not." He mutters harshly, turning and walking toward the buildings I pointed out. I should feel happy that he's doing what I want and giving me a chance, but I feel like I've been punched in the stomach. I know he thinks of Liesel every time I take a risk, so he feels the need to hold me back and make sure there's never another innocent death on his hands. But I'm not her. I'm a completely different person who has her own goals and motivations. Still, the way he spoke to me just now made it sound like I could never compare to her. . .that he thinks I'm worthless because I'm not the one person who was good enough to change his mind about having a partner. That's what stings.

"More motivation to prove you wrong, then," I murmur under my breath as I watch him disappear into an alleyway.

I place the gun in my bag and make my way toward the buildings to my right, choosing to slip inside the one that looks the most intact. An Emigre ship is approaching from my left, a spotlight lighting up the ground underneath it as it patrols at a slow, steady pace. The pilot doesn't see me yet, but if I don't hurry, it will.

I take off running towards an almost completely intact white brick building, sprinting inside the busted-in back door. It's completely dark inside and I can barely see, but I keep running so that the light of the ship won't catch me as it passes.

All of a sudden, my right foot catches on something and I fall to the ground hard. My knees hit first, and then the palms of my hands slam against the ground as I try to prepare myself for the impact. The pain comes immediately, but I don't dare make a sound. I bite my lip so hard to keep from crying out that I can taste blood.

The humming of the ship gets louder, and soon, I can see its light shining through the back doorway. The light doesn't reach me, but for a moment, it illuminates what I tripped over.

Right in front of me is the body of a man, completely dressed in white, his neck twisted at a completely unnatural angle and his green eyes staring straight at me without blinking.

TWENTY

Panic shoots through my body, freezing me in a state of shock. I feel a scream bubbling up in my throat, but the light of the ship still illuminates the body, and I know I have to do everything I can not to make a sound. Shutting my eyes, I pretend I'm somewhere else.

I imagine my bedroom back home, in my actual home. Pale pink walls, ballet slippers on the doorknob, a bookshelf full of books arranged by color, pictures of me and my friends posted on a corkboard above my desk. I am there, not here. Everything is fine. I'm okay, and everything is fine.

I take several deep breaths, doing everything I can to keep myself calm and stop my body from shaking. I bask in the sense of false safety and comfort, letting it relax my nerves and slow my thoughts. The humming of the ship's engine has passed, but it takes a few moments until I'm ready to open my eyes.

Sliding backward a bit, I fish through my bag until I find my flashlight. I know there's a dead man in front of me, but that doesn't change the fact that I can still hardly see anything in this darkness. I need to figure out my surroundings and realize what kind of danger I'm in.

Now that my adrenaline rush is starting to fade, I can feel the stinging pain in the palms of my hands and on my knees from my fall. Ignoring it, I turn on the flashlight and take a look around, as much as I don't want to.

It looks like this was a shop for sale before the invasion. There is absolutely nothing in here. No shelves, no newspapers, and no empty cans littering the floor. . .just tiny pieces of glass scattered by the broken windows.

So why is there a dead man in here with a broken neck? This couldn't have been some kind of accident. Someone else killed him, but who? And why? And where were they now?

I take a look at the dead man again, holding my breath for a moment as the beam of my flashlight illuminates his unblinking eyes. Green eyes, not violet. Dressed all in white.ro Probably from the Reserve. Not a single drop of blood anywhere, his neck at an unnatural angle. He couldn't have been killed by an Emigre. No Emigre would go through here on foot, and if they did, they wouldn't try to kill someone by snapping their neck.

I notice his pack for the first time: a simple, white threaded messenger bag just like my old one. I step forward slowly, as if trying not to disturb the man. Hesitantly, I reach forward and lift up the flap. The bag is completely empty.

Running all my observations through my mind again, the only plausible explanation I can think of is that this young man tried to escape the Reserve just like I did, his bag full of food. But an outsider must have been roaming through the Divide and killed him in order to take his stuff. I would need to not only be on my guard for the Emigre ships but also for outsiders as well.

I can hear the low hum of a ship's engine again, this time out of the front of the building. As I slowly make my way to the window to get an idea of where the ships are, the sound of lasers being fired and a male scream of pain pierces the air.

"Tyler?" I breathe, my mind automatically thinking the worst and going into panic mode. I gaze out the window, my heartbeat thudding in my ears as fear pulses through my veins again. Someone is on the ground about 15 feet away, still screaming in pain. The ship has already flown past, apparently leaving him to die. Throwing all caution into the wind, I dash out the front door.

I reach him in seconds, and to my relief, it's not Tyler but another Reserve man dressed in all white. His abdominal area is completely stained dark red with blood, and he's not getting up, just screaming.

"Okay, okay, shh, everything's going to be okay!" I tell him, waving my hands around stupidly as I look at his wound again to try to figure out what the hell I should do. Bad idea. Too much blood. And he can't seem to move, so the laser must have hit his spine, too. His eyes focus on me for the slightest second and I notice his eyes are the same color as the man with the snapped neck. Maybe they were brothers.

"Is there someone else out here? Not an alien, but a human. Do you know where they went?" The questions fly out of my mouth, but he just keeps screaming, and I realize he's screaming for his mother. My heart breaks as his green eyes look up at the sky, his face contorted in pain. I'm watching a twenty-something-year-old scream for his mother, who may not even be alive anymore because he's in so much pain and probably scared out of his mind and thinking he's going to die. And judging by the amount of blood he's lost, he probably is.

"It's okay." I try to make my voice soothing, taking his hand. His gaze focuses on me once more and he looks at me in confusion.

Suddenly, the humming sound returns, and I look up to my left to see that a ship is heading straight toward us. The man's screaming has resumed as I frantically look for a way out. There's another building with an open door about 20 feet ahead. I could make it if I run now, but would I be able to take him?

"Come on, let's go." I try to keep my voice light and positive, letting his hand go and attempting to lift him up. But it's no use. I'm not strong enough. "Come on, help me out here," I say, but he just screams in pain, and I'm sure I'm not helping his injury by trying to move him. I can hear the ship getting closer, and soon, its light will find us. Even if I miraculously manage to get this man to safety, without any medical care, he wouldn't last much longer.

"I'm sorry, I'm so sorry," I whisper as I blink away the tears in my eyes, already hating myself when he looks at me again. I gently place him back down to rest and take off toward the building. By the time I get inside, I can hear the lasers again, and the screaming stops. When the hum of the engine fades away, the silence is deafening.

I'm shaking again, trying to breathe normally as the tears fall freely down my cheeks. Maybe I'm not cut out for this. I don't even know those two guys, but I'm already a mess now that they're both dead. There's someone out there killing innocent people, and it's only a matter of time before they find me or one of the other rebels. If that person finds the others, they'd be able to defend themselves and make it out okay. I'm almost positive. Me, on the other hand, well. . . I don't even think I'm in the right state of mind to take on a punching bag.

Should I try to find Tyler and get him to take me back? I'd be letting him win and proving him right, something I definitely don't want to do, but I'd rather be alive than dead. But. . .no. . .I came all the way out here to do what I needed to do to make sure I'm there when they find my dad. I'm the one that has a chance to bring my family together, and multiple people have made sacrifices, no matter how small, to get me here. I need to get myself together and get some supplies.

With a deep breath, I wipe my eyes and stand up, finally taking in my surroundings. I realize with some relief that I'm finally in a convenience store. Although it's small and there's barely anything on the shelves, I turn on my flashlight and have a look around.

As I move toward a shelf that seems to be covered in empty boxes of candy bars, I feel something other than the tile floor underneath my feet. Looking down, I shine my light on it to discover some medical tape and a small flashlight. It's like they were dropped here.

These must have belonged to the man who I had just saw. Something must have made him drop everything and run.

The second my mind starts to hypothesize what could have happened, I hear the sound of footsteps. Whoever they belong to is trying to be quiet, practically tiptoeing, but I'm on high alert and still full of adrenaline. I cower behind the shelf I'm standing in front of, peaking around the corner just enough to try to see who's coming.

Whoever it is, they're coming from the back of the store, almost as if they're coming from a side door or back entrance. As I crouch behind a shelf full of empty boxes, the footsteps become slightly louder, and I can hear that there are two voices.

"You shoulda seen it, Carol," a deep male voice whispers. "I snapped his neck like his bones were made of twigs." He lets out a small laugh that could almost pass for a quiet exhale, and I immediately think of the man that I tripped over. These are the killers, and they're only a few feet away from me. I don't dare move, and I struggle to keep my breathing as quiet as possible.

"I almost got that other guy," the female voice, Carol, whispers back. "But he ran right into the line of fire. Those goddamn aliens actually did my job for me."

"You still got all the stuff from his bag, right?" The man asks.

"Yeah." Her voice gets a little louder when she thinks they're alone, sounding so close it's like they're standing right next to me. "That little shit was crying for his mommy. Fucking hilarious." They both laugh under their breath, and in an instant, I can feel anger washing away my fear.

They killed those two men. Two innocent men, just trying to be free. All those men wanted was to escape like I did, but it wasn't even aliens that put an end to it. It was fellow humans. Do we all have to be allies with one another? No. But we still want the same thing: to have our planet back and make it the way it was before. We shouldn't be killing one another.

I can hear their voices coming closer. Their heavy footsteps send tiny vibrations through the floor. As much as I try to stay calm, I can feel the panic spreading through my body. It seizes my stomach tightly, making my hands shake and my breathing sound unnaturally loud and disjointed. They're coming in my direction. In a few seconds, they'll see me. Crouched in the aisle with nowhere to hide. As quietly as I can, I pull out my gun from my backpack. Ignoring the fear still stirring in the pit of my stomach, I stand up and make myself known when they walk to my aisle.

They are about five feet away from where I stand. The man is tall and extremely muscular with a thick, dark beard. The woman seems thin and pale, but her arms ripple with strength as she clutches a knife stained with dried blood. The minute their wild eyes lock onto mine, they both freeze.

TWENTY-ONE

"Shit," the woman flinches in surprise before recovering in almost an instant. With a smirk, she raises her knife in my direction.

"Don't move, or I'll shoot!" I threaten, hoping to latch on to the comfort of knowing that I have a gun and they don't seem to.

"Do you even know how to use that thing, honey?" the woman coos, and for the first time, I notice she's wearing a cross around her neck. This surprises me, but I try not to let it ruin my concentration. If she was religious before, she's probably lost all of her faith by now.

"I could snap your skinny little arm in half before you even fired a shot." The man grins, cracking his knuckles for emphasis as he begins to walk toward me.

"I said don't move!" I yell at the top of my lungs, trying to sound more menacing than I appear. The man stands still with a smirk of his own.

"Alright, darlin'," He laughs. "Tell you what, how about you just let us go and we'll let you go? No one gets hurt. Sound good?"

"That's not happening," I say firmly. Sweat is dripping down the back of my neck, and my knees are shaking, but I'm the one with the gun. I can do this.

"And why's that?" The woman is still smiling at me in a way that sends a chill down my spine. She playfully runs her finger lightly up and down the blade of her knife.

"You killed those two people from the Reserve," I tell them.

"Oh, I'm sorry dear, were they your friends?" She pouts comically at me before grinning again.

"Doesn't matter. They were innocent. They weren't the enemy. You had no right-" I begin, but the man interrupts me with a loud burst of laughter.

"It's the end of the world, babycakes! We've got every right to do whatever the hell we want!"

I glare at them as they laugh at me, obviously not taking me seriously as a threat and just talking to me purely for amusement. But if they're going to talk, I might as well keep them talking.

"If you want to kill, why not just join the rebels, then? You wouldn't have to kill any innocent humans just to get food and supplies."

"Because the rebels are full of shit." The woman replies with exaggerated emphasis, as if I'm a slow child and this was common sense.

"Yeah," the man agrees. "They actually think they can take on a bunch of aliens that have already managed to wipe out most of the planet. They don't stand a chance. As soon as they fight, they'll all be slaughtered. We've all managed to not get captured. It's every man for himself now."

So that's why outsiders exist. They're not only made up of insane people who love to kill for the sake of killing, but they've also got people who think it's impossible for humanity to survive at this point and have decided to just fend for themselves, no matter who else gets hurt in the process.

"You're wrong," I tell them. "Humans will find a way to win this.

Maybe not in your lifetime, but they will. They always find a way to make it-"

"Alright, enough bullshit." The man comes forward again, and I snap into action.

"I said don't move!" I yell as I fire the gun with shaking hands, momentarily relieved that I managed to shoot him in the chest.

He goes down, and as my heartbeat pounds in my head, I take several steps back as I aim at the woman. She's now shouting every insult in the book at me, her face scarlet with rage. She throws her knife, and I barely manage to jerk my head out of the way, hearing the blade whoosh past my right ear. When she pulls out another knife and springs towards me, I fire again.

Because she's so close to me, the bullet nails her right where I want it to: in the heart. Her dark eyes glaze over and she falls forward, but no matter how quickly I move back, she still ends up falling on top of me and knocking me to the ground. I can feel her blood seeping through my shirt even as I frantically try to push her body off me and spring to my feet.

My ears are ringing as I stand up, looking down at the body of a woman named Carol who was alive just moments ago. Her blood, almost black in the dark of night, slowly seeps across the tile floor toward the tips of my shoes. Swallowing hard, I step over her body toward the front door of the store. As I walk like a drunk in my panicked haze, I nearly stumble over the man and realize he's still alive. His ragged breathing drowns out the sound of my heartbeat for a moment, and his eyes, the color of coal, look up at me.

His gaze isn't pleading. His expression isn't sad. He just looks at me weakly with an ounce of hatred, but also understanding. It's as if he's saying "You do what you've gotta do. I've put up one hell of a fight, as much as I don't want to die by the likes of you".

"I'm sorry." I find myself choking out as I raise my gun again at his head. I close my eyes as I fire, letting the tears spill out as the sound of his breathing disappears.

A few moments pass by before the familiar hum of an Émigré

ship brings me back to reality. I can't stay here and waste any more time freaking out. I need to leave if I want to live, so I take a deep breath to get myself together as I wait for the ship to pass. Once the sound of the engine is a good distance away, I make my way toward the door to see if there's any more. But the second I reach the doorway, someone else is already there.

Startled, I almost drop my gun as I run into them. Fumbling to get a grip on the gun, I look up just in time to meet a pair of eyes that I can recognize even at night.

"Are you okay?" Tyler demands, probably a little louder than he should. He doesn't give me any time to answer as he shines his flashlight directly in my face, temporarily blinding me. "We heard gunshots and came as fast as we could." Using his free hand to pull the gun out of my hands, he inspects every inch of me from top to bottom, his gaze freezing at my stomach.

"You're bleeding! What happened?" He's practically shouting, and I look down to see what the hell he's talking about. Even in my slight daze, I notice the bloodstain on my gray shirt, and the memory of shooting the woman burns in my mind as if it's happening again.

"That's not my blood," I tell him simply, pushing my way past him. I can see his face just long enough to watch his mouth drop open and then morph into a shocked smile, all in a split second. But I continue walking, only thinking about the man and woman I just killed. The look in their eyes after I'd killed them, the sound of the man struggling to breathe, the recoil of the gun after I fired each time, the deafening sound of the gun firing, the sight, and smell of the blood. . .

"You did that?" Tyler sounds elated, and he must have looked inside the store. "You killed both of them?" He already makes it sound like I had every reason to kill them. . .like I wouldn't have fired the gun unless I needed to, because he already knows me that well. It's like he's not even bothered that two people are dead because of me. How does he know I didn't just panic and kill two innocent people?

Alfie and Rebecca are coming toward me, looking at me with concern.

"Rachel," Rebecca says, as if trying to wake me from a nightmare. "Rachel, are you alright?"

"Yeah, fine." I nod, but I don't look at either of them, and my voice sounds foreign. Too high. Too sluggish.

"Rachel, are you sure you're okay?" It's Alfie speaking this time, but his voice sounds muffled and far away. All I know is that I need to keep walking, as difficult as that is to do.

"Yeah," I say again. "Let's go. Come on." I try to wave my arm to convey my sense of urgency, but it's like my arm is no longer attached to my body. It barely lifts up.

"Rachel," Tyler's voice again, and I can see him make his way in front of me, his brows knitting together as he frowns at me. "What's wrong? Are you-"

"Yes, I'm fine. Now, will everyone stop asking me?" I attempt to shout to get them to back off and to help me snap out of this funk, but my voice only gets a little louder, and I realize I'm beginning to hyperventilate. Out of the corner of my eye, I can see a body on the road, and I know it's the man with the green eyes who I couldn't save. And in the building right across from him is the man with the matching green eyes and a broken neck.

I can hear the man screaming for his mother as my vision starts to get spotty. Bile rises in my throat. My legs start to wobble, and the ringing in my ears gets even louder. I can feel someone trying to hold me up, but it's too late. Everything goes black.

When I come to, I find myself lying flat on the ground and looking at the ceiling of a building, and then staring up into Tyler's familiar ocean blue eyes, his face illuminated by a flashlight.

"How are you feeling?" He says calmly, nodding at Rebecca, who comes forward and holds a water bottle up to my lips. I take several sips, looking at her with an expression that I hope conveys gratitude.

"Okay," I manage to say, realizing that my head is elevated on his lap. "How long was I out?"

"Not very long," Rebecca says. "We brought you in here and laid you down only moments ago."

I take a look around, realizing gratefully that we're not in the same building I was just in. This looks like it was once an electronics store. There are broken TVs and speakers everywhere. I try to sit up, but Tyler gently pushes me right back down.

"Whoa, whoa, whoa, easy there," He cautions me. I don't argue, feeling slightly dizzy once again. He holds up my head and slides away before slowly placing my head down so that I'm lying flat on the floor again.

"Why did I pass out?" I'm asking myself this more than I'm asking them, but they still answer.

"Extreme fear, I think. Elliot said it's called vasovagal syncope." Rebecca explains. "Something freaks you out so much that it triggers you to lose consciousness. It happened to Sara whenever she saw blood, so we learned how to deal with it."

"Yeah, we have to make sure you lie flat so that blood flow to your brain can be restored immediately. Otherwise, you could have a seizure. But we decided to elevate you a bit once you woke up so that we could give you some water. Dehydration could play a part in this, too." Alfie informs me, seeming proud to have remembered all of this.

It only takes a few moments for the memories of everything that happened here to start to come back. As much as I try to stop thinking about the faces of the dead, I can still see them as clearly as if I was standing right in front of them right now.

"I'm sorry," I say to all of them, closing my eyes as the tears come back.

"Sorry for what?" Tyler says in confusion.

"Screwing everything up. Thinking I could do this." I feel someone take my hand and open my eyes again to see Rebecca trying to give me a comforting smile, although I can see the sadness and confusion in her eyes.

"But you didn't screw up. You were able to do this. You did exactly what we all hoped you were capable of doing. I didn't think you had it in you, but you proved me wrong." Tyler tells me. I crane my neck to look up at him. He looks like he's proud of me, and it makes me sick.

"I killed two people, Tyler! How the hell am I supposed to be happy about that?"

"But. . .they were outsiders, right?" Tyler frowns. "You killed in self-defense-"

"What's it matter if they were outsiders or not? They're still people, and now they're dead because of me." I choke out, trying to hold back a sob. "I confronted them because they killed two innocent people from the Reserve. I could have just let them go. Maybe they would have found me anyway, maybe not. But I couldn't let them go after seeing one man dead and watching the other die. As much as I debated whether to let them go and tried to stall them, I knew I was still going to pull the trigger. I'm no better than they are."

A silence falls over all of us, and I'm left staring up at the stupid ceiling again. In the back of my mind, I can still hear the man in the road screaming for his mother as he looks up at the sky. I wonder what he thought when he saw me. Did he think I was there to rescue him? Or did he think I was another killer? Maybe he was in too much pain to really notice me much at all, but either way, I left him for dead.

"You are better than they are," Alfie says quietly.

"I'm not-" I start.

"Yes, you are." Tyler snaps. "You're kind. . .you're smart. . .you actually give a shit about other people, even if you don't know them. . .you want to save the human race. . ."

I slowly sit up, letting go of Rebecca's hand as I wipe my eyes and turn toward Tyler, trying not to look at him in disbelief. His eyes lock on mine, determined and sincere.

"The first kill is hard for pretty much everyone," He continues. "This guilt you feel, you feel it because you're human. You haven't lost your humanity like they have. They killed those men. It's not your fault that they did. And who knows how many more they killed before that? But now that they're gone, they can't kill anyone else. You've saved more than just your own life, and I won't have my partner thinking otherwise."

Partner? My eyes widen at him, wondering if I heard him correctly. His mouth curves up into a grin, giving me all the confirmation I need. I find myself beaming back at him.

"Alright, now that our heroine is feeling a little better, what do you say we head out?" Rebecca gets to her feet, and with an unspoken agreement, she and Tyler are helping me up.

"What about supplies?" I bring up, suddenly remembering the reason why we came here in the first place.

"Don't worry, we got plenty," Alfie promises, pointing to his backpack as he walks toward the front door of the building. Before I can say anything else, I feel my body being lifted up in an instant. I let out a small yelp of surprise, and the next thing I know, I'm scooped up in Tyler's arms as if I were no heavier than a pillow.

"I'm sure I can walk," I tell him, laughing a bit as I wrap my arms around his neck to keep from flopping over.

"Yeah, you may be able to walk, but we're gonna need to run from Émigré ships, remember? Just trying to be on the safe side." He tells me as he walks toward the door. "Besides, you may want to close your eyes for a little while."

Just like that, my small moment of happiness is over as I remember the man on the road again. I close my eyes as instructed, and soon I can feel Tyler running forward. I can't hear the hum of an Émigré ship or the sound of their lasers. There's no sound of buildings being hit and parts of them being reduced to rubble. All I can hear is Tyler's steady breathing as his feet pound on the rubble-littered pavement and his heart beats strongly against his chest.

It's not long until Tyler goes from running to walking, and I assume it's safe to open my eyes. We're by the trees, and I can faintly make out Tyler's hover, hidden among the tree trunks. He sets me down on the hover seat first before getting on behind me. I look back at him in confusion.

"Shouldn't you be in front?" I ask.

"I don't want you falling off." He replies, putting the helmet on my head and turning on the hover. He presses a few buttons and readjusts some things until he can easily manage the hover, despite the fact that I'm sitting in front of him.

"I'm sure I'm fine now." I insist, attempting to slide off the hover before he accelerates it. But he doesn't move his arms, keeping me locked in.

"I'm not taking any chances." He says in a final tone.

"But-" I begin.

"Don't argue with me, ki. . .Rachel," He interrupts me, correcting himself before he calls me 'kid'. I shut my mouth, but I'm smiling underneath my helmet as our hover takes off into the woods.

TWENTY-TWO

The minute our hover reaches the rebel house, Elliot is on the lawn waiting to greet us. I can make out him talking to Rebecca and Alfie, but he keeps looking into the light of our hover as if trying to see if I'm okay. Tyler parks the hover and turns it off, sending the front lawn back into darkness. I take off my helmet as he gets off and turns toward me.

"Think you can walk okay?" He asks quietly. I nod. I'm still shaking like I've just gotten off the most intense roller coaster ride of my life, but I'm feeling a lot better than I was back at the Divide.

Tyler takes the helmet from my hands and starts to slide my backpack off my shoulders.

"Oh, you don't have to take that-" I start, but he's quick to interrupt.

"It's the least I can do." He walks toward the house as I get off the hover. Elliot's immediately in front of me.

"Hey," He smiles, looking relieved to see me in one piece. He must not be able to see the bloodstain on my shirt because it's so dark out. "Everything go well?"

"Yeah." I try to keep my voice firm, managing to smile back. I find myself not wanting to trouble him with what happened at the Divide. I don't want him worried about me. Or upset with me. I know I killed 'the bad guys,' so to speak. But, the fact is, I've killed two people. I feel like I've been branded as a killer already, that I'm a terrible person and deserve whatever bad things happen to me. "I'm his partner now."

"Really? I didn't think he'd change his mind so quickly. . ." Elliot trails off, observing me like I'm a lab rat in an experiment or a suspect in a murder case. I cross my arms over my chest, casually trying to hide the bloodstain. "Well, I'm glad he did," Elliot tells me, smiling again, but his voice is very controlled. He can tell something's up, that something happened and I don't want to talk about it. Not pressing me for any details, he walks back into the house and I follow.

I go straight to my room without speaking to anyone else, wanting nothing more than to go to sleep and pretend this all didn't happen. The room is dark when I come in, and I can hear Tyler already snoring softly. I try not to feel jealous of him as I make my way to my bed, collapsing on it without bothering to change my clothes. He didn't kill anyone tonight, so he's lucky enough to get some rest. Any bad thoughts plaguing him are gone for a few hours.

It's different for me. All of my terrible thoughts are still here, fresh in my mind and so vivid it's as if they only took place a few seconds ago. I can hear the screams, smell the blood, see the unblinking eyes of the dead. How did the rebels deal with this? How did they harden their hearts so that it wouldn't hurt so much? How did they control their thoughts so that they could only see what they wanted to see and forget the rest?

A sound outside the door causes me to sit up in bed, fully alert. My mind jumps to conclusions: it's the outsiders I thought I killed, it's more outsiders that followed us to avenge their deaths, or it's Émigrés. But really, it's the sound of a door closing and someone making their way down the stairs, yet I can't put my suspicions to rest or slow the pounding of my heart. Every hair on the back of my neck stands up as I look out the window to see what's going on.

A figure is walking out of the house and into the front yard. Even in the dark, I can tell who it is by the small, thin frame and long hair. It's Kira. She's walking toward the cornfield with a purpose. What could she be doing out there? Going to the bathroom? Meeting up with someone? I don't know, and I'm curious and unable to sleep, so I grab my flashlight and slip on my shoes.

Searching for my bag with the gun inside, I then remember Tyler had taken it. Not seeing it anywhere in the room or in any of the unlocked drawers that I carefully open, I can only guess that he stuffed it in the only dresser drawer that's locked. Mouthing every insult I can think of at his sleeping frame so that I can get out my frustration without waking him up, I sneak out with only a flashlight.

I can hear people talking softly at the end of the hallway, but I don't stop to see who they are or what they're saying. Going downstairs and out the front door as quietly as I can, I try to shut the door behind me without a sound. Striding out into the night, I make my way toward the cornfield.

I'm only a few steps away from the cornfield when I stop short. What am I doing? I can't sleep and my mind is restless, so I go after someone just because I think they're weird and don't know what they're doing. What kind of person does that? Who cares what Kira does in her spare time? I turn around to make my way back to the house, and only then do I see that Tyler is behind me. A string of curse words flies out of my mouth as I stop myself from walking into him.

"What are you doing?" He asks me, his eyes cold.

"What am I doing? What are you doing?" I fire back.

"You're not as quiet as you think you are. I wanted to see what you were up to. I can't imagine what that would be." There's some sarcasm in his voice as he looks out at the cornfield.

"Alright, alright, you got me. I wanted to see what Kira was doing out in the middle of the night."

"Why? You think she's working with outsiders or something?" He lets out a dry chuckle.

"Maybe. I don't know. I just. . .I don't know, okay?" I admit with an exasperated sigh.

"Let's go find out, then." He mutters with some false enthusiasm, marching off into the cornfield.

"Tyler-" I start, but he interrupts me.

"Don't make me drag you along. You're the one who wanted to follow her in the first place."

I follow him in silence, thinking better than to argue with him. The night air is cool and quiet, filled only with the sounds of our footsteps and our hands brushing the cornstalks we push aside. I try to navigate as quietly through the cornstalks as Tyler does, but it seems like every stray twig I snap under my feet and every stalk I bend aside is a gunshot slicing through the silent air.

Thankfully, we're out of the cornfield in a matter of moments and find ourselves in a decent-sized field. With Kira nowhere to be seen, Tyler heads into the woods on our left and I follow. The sound of crickets and other insects now fills my ears, making me think of the 'camping trips' my dad used to take us on when I was little. We only camped out in our backyard, but it was amazing to see how the woods seemed to come alive at night.

"There's your answer," Tyler whispers to me, stopping suddenly. I peer around him to see Kira up ahead, sitting on the bank of a stream lit up by the moonlight.

TWENTY-THREE

Kira has a flashlight on and her head is bent down, but I can't see why.

"What is she doing?" I ask out loud.

"Drawing, I think." He replies, and when I squint and try to look closer, I think he's right. She has a pad of paper in front of her, and she keeps looking up at the waxing moon and then back down at her paper, scribbling across the page. "Happy now?" Tyler looks back at me. I nod.

"Let's go back," I say, walking back the way we came.

"This way," Tyler murmurs, tapping my shoulder to make sure I heard him and follow his lead. "It's faster." When I'm sure we're far enough away from Kira, I speak up.

"So, you know where we are?"

He nods. "This is where I go on my morning runs. Actually, this way might not be faster than going through the corn, but it's easier."

A silence falls between us, but with it comes back the memories of everything that happened in the Divide, so I speak up again.

"I saw that you locked away my bag. You still don't think I'm capable of being your partner, do you?" I glance at him, my tone accusatory. "You just said anything you could think of to calm me down, even if you didn't mean it."

The surprise on Elliot's face when I had told him Tyler said I was his partner vividly replays in my mind, and I shudder as frustration starts to seep back in. His silence only fuels my emotions.

"What does it take for me to be good enough? What more can I do? I killed two people-"

"Shh," Tyler hushes when my voice gets too loud, and I realize we're nearing the house, where many people are still trying to sleep. I bite my lip as tears sting my eyes again. I refuse to let them fall. "Let's go for a walk," Tyler suggests, changing the route so that we're going deeper into the woods. I don't question him, just follow blindly, trying not to think about the evil I had done earlier tonight. "You are my partner, alright? So quit complaining." He mutters, slowing down his pace so that he's walking beside me instead of directly in front of me, although he's still a step ahead so that he remains in charge of where we go.

"Then why do you keep acting like I'm not?" My voice sounds whiny and I hate it.

"I'm not trying to make you feel inadequate. You did a good thing tonight, and you did it on your own. I meant what I said."

"Killing people isn't a good thing. They aren't the enemy."

"Some of them are." He argues. "Look, why don't you tell me what happened tonight? Help me understand why you did what you did."

"Okay," I sigh, picking up the pace as my emotions come back. I think about when Tyler and I first parted ways when we got to the Divide, and I ran into the nearest open building to escape a ship. "When I got into one of the buildings, I tripped over something. And when the ship went by, its light illuminated it, and I realized I had tripped over a body. He was wearing all white, but his eyes were green, so I knew he was from the Reserve. There was no blood and his neck was broken, so I knew he wasn't killed by an Émigré. The fact that his bag was empty proved it. Then I heard screaming. I thought it was you." I pause and without even thinking, I look over at him. His gaze remains fixed on the ground as we walk, his mouth set in a firm line.

"I ran out to see that it was another man, just like the one in the building. Dressed in all white, with green eyes instead of violet. He was hurt really badly. There was so much blood and I . . . he kept screaming for his mom . . . I didn't know what to do. I tried to move him, but I couldn't. The ship was making its way back again. I figured that even if I saved him, he wouldn't last much longer, anyway. It's not like we could get him to a hospital. So I . . . I left him there. I ran into the next building as the ship shot him down." The tears were falling freely right now, and every emotion I had felt in that moment was on the tip of my tongue, waiting to be blurted out. But Tyler didn't care about how much it hurt to leave the man behind. He didn't care how much more painful it was to hear silence instead of screaming. . .to hear the proof that someone was dead instead of the proof that they were alive. He just wanted to know why I killed two people.

"When I got in there, I could hear people talking about how they killed the man in the building and were about to kill the man I saw outside when the Émigré ship got to him first. I was angry and upset and whatnot so I . . . confronted them. I saw that they didn't have a gun like I did, so I knew I had the upper hand. They tried to reason with me to let them go, but I couldn't. Knowing that they were killing innocent people just to steal their belongings. When they got fed up with me and came at me, I shot them both down. That's it. That's what happened." I let out a long exhale as I wiped away the tears that had escaped, now barely walking. Surprisingly, it felt good to talk about it. I felt some relief. I'm not sure why because all I had really done was just prove that it had happened and it was real, but just getting all those emotions out suddenly made my body start to relax.

I realize that Tyler was now leading me up the steps of the porch in front of the house and we were no longer in the woods. Instead of going inside, he goes toward some outdoor furniture I'd never noticed before and takes a seat on the chair. He motions to the couch next to him, and I take a seat as well, glancing at him in confusion. But before I could ask him why we were sitting out here, he began to speak.

"My first kill was two years ago, right when I first came here. I remember everything about it. The sound of the wind moving the leaves on the trees, of the gun as I fired a shot, of the man screaming in pain, and how he sounded as he wheezed out his last breath. I remember seeing the clear blue sky with the sunlight peaking down through the trees and shining on his eyes as the life left him. I remember the blood staining his clothes. It was such a beautiful day . . . too beautiful for something so awful." He told me, his voice distant and his eyes glazed.

"He was an outsider who got past the fence. We called them 'invaders' back then . . . before we even really had a rebel group. But yeah, I get how you feel, to an extent. You're not alone. I remember how empty I felt and how much I thought about how wrong I was and about if he had family or friends that were looking for him. I thought about that a lot, even when I killed again. But it got to a point where I realized this was going to be something I would have to do if I wanted to stay alive and protect the people that mattered to me." He comes back to reality and looks at me with understanding, and I feel myself swallow nervously.

He's not like I imagined at all. He doesn't relish in the lives he took. Every life he takes still has a name and a face in his eyes. They are still a person, not just a piece in a game . . . an obstacle to get past. For the first time, I'm glad that I am his partner, and not anyone else's. Sure, things would have probably been easier with someone like Elliot, but I could have ended up with someone like Damien. Instead, I ended up running into Tyler right after I escaped the Reserve, and he was the only rebel currently without a partner. For some reason, it feels like this is how things were supposed to be, and I'm glad they worked out that way. Despite all of our differences, I think he and I could make this work. Because really, when I stop to think about it, we're not that different.

"Tell me something," Tyler says, noticing that I haven't spoken in a while and instead have just been staring at him. I blush and stare down at the charcoal-colored cushions on the couch. "Let's talk about something happier. What was one of the happiest moments in your lifetime?"

"Um," I glance at him curiously, wondering what this is about. Did he think I needed cheering up? Did I really look that gloomy? Or did he need cheering up? "Well, I was really happy about four Christmases ago. I was with my whole family making Christmas cookies on Christmas Day. It was snowing outside. We had a fire going in the fireplace, and everyone was smiling and laughing. I didn't have a care in the world. It was the last Christmas we had with my grandpa before he passed away, so it was really special to me." I thought about all my relatives and how I had no idea where they were, and the feeling of sadness started to creep in again, but I fought it off, trying my hardest to focus on only the good feelings associated with those happy memories.

"Mine's similar," Tyler said, causing my attention to shift back at him. "In the summer, we would always go up to visit my uncle in Michigan. He lived in the middle of nowhere, and there was a trail I could run on, a lake I could swim in, and a forest I could just walk around in for hours. The last time I was up there was 6 years ago, and that was the last summer before my parents divorced." I opened my mouth to offer my condolences, but he wasn't even looking at me, lost in his own world again. "I know the place didn't seem like much, but it was a paradise for me. The lake was always the perfect tempera-ture, and we could even catch some fish for dinner. The trail I ran on was just one big, long 4-mile loop, but it was all in the shade and I could even see the lake through the trees at some parts." He continued talking about that place in the middle of nowhere in Michigan, and I could feel my eyes slipping shut as I imagined it. He wasn't boring me, it was just that his descriptions were finally allowing my mind to have peace, and the sleep that I so desperately needed was starting to come.

When I opened my eyes, the sun was out, and I was back in my own bed. I look around in mild confusion to see Tyler stretching as he got up from his own bed.

"Morning," he mumbles, rubbing the sleep from his eyes. I was too out of it to respond. Last night wasn't a dream, was it? I looked down to see my flashlight at the foot of my bed. It wasn't a dream. My flashlight was always on the dresser. And I still had my shoes on. And I wasn't underneath my covers. I looked at Tyler as if I had just noticed him for the first time.

"You carried me up here?" I look at him in disbelief.

"Yeah," He shrugs. "I've carried you before. It's not like it's difficult."

"No, but. . .I mean. . .I didn't wake up?" Knowing how restless I'd been, surely I would have noticed someone picking me up and carrying me to my bed.

"Nope." Tyler shook his head. "You were dead asleep the whole time."

"Weird." I stretch my own muscles too, feeling them protest in pain from everything I'd been putting them through lately. Everything about last night slowly comes back to mind, and I glance at Tyler again. "Thank you. For all the help you gave me the other night." I say, hoping there's enough sincerity in my voice to convey how thankful I am. I now realize why he went through all the trouble he did.

I couldn't see it through my emotions and my tiredness, but he knew from experience how up and down my mind would be and how all I needed was to talk it out and then get my mind off it and rest. He knew exactly what he was doing and probably wasn't surprised at all by anything I said or did. The second he confronted me by the corn-field, he was already trying to help me. He knew exactly what I was going through and what would probably help, and gave up his night to do it. Sure, he didn't hug me or tell me 'everything's okay' and to just 'talk it out', but he tried to make things easier for me in his own way, and that's all I could ask for. He cared, and the small smile he gave me before nodding and heading downstairs was all the proof I needed.

TWENTY-FOUR

"So, I heard you killed two outsiders the other night," Grace says nonchalantly as we feed the chickens. I glance over at her in surprise. Word had already gotten around that fast? "We don't have to talk about it or anything. I just wanted to say I'm glad you're okay." She quickly adds, noticing my expression.

"Yeah," I say lamely, picturing the faces of the outsiders again. No matter what I did, I couldn't get the images of last night out of my head. And every time they came back to my mind, I'd have to fight back the bile in my throat and stop my body from shaking.

"Everyone was pretty worried about you." Grace went on, shooting me a comforting smile. "It's not every day that someone new here wants to go to the Divide at night. You were all anybody could talk about, and I think everyone's really happy that you made it back."

I momentarily stop feeding the chickens as her words sink in. Were they talking about how stupid I was for going there when I could barely hit a target any time I shot a gun? Were they wondering just how badly I would screw up and end up getting everyone else hurt or killed? And did hearing that I killed two outsiders change anyone's mind about me, or did they assume I got lucky? They wouldn't be wrong.

"I was very lucky that I wasn't alone," I mutter, imagining what could have happened if Tyler, Rebecca, and Alfie hadn't come with me. After killing the two outsiders, who knows if I would have ever made it back? And I hadn't even snagged any supplies.

Without waiting to hear Grace's reply, I headed back to the house, thankful that no one else had attempted to talk to me. I found Angie cleaning the kitchen from any remnants of this morning's breakfast, and I immediately joined her to keep my mind occupied.

Any time I started to think about what happened in the Divide, I focused on a smudge of food on the counter that I had missed, a dish that hadn't been put away, or a cabinet door that wasn't closed. I straightened books on the bookshelves, dusted off furniture, and swept the floors until Angie announced that the house was cleaner than it had ever been, thanks to me.

"Time for a meeting," Elliot told me as he walked by, bringing me back to the reality that I was trying to stay out of.

"Meeting?" I slowly followed him into the family room. "About what?"

"Going to the Reserve." He replied, sitting on the cream-colored couch where Alfie and Rebecca were already sitting. I took the last spot next to him as my stomach felt like it was suddenly filled with knots.

"You guys don't have to go to the Reserve just because I want to," I say, avoiding Tyler's eyes as he sits in the armchair next to the fireplace.

"Oh please," Damien snorts, and he glares at me as he hops into the other armchair. "We've been planning on going to the Reserve for ages. Newsflash: the world doesn't revolve around you."

"Anyway, let's get started," Rebecca announces loudly, taking the opportunity to give Damien an annoyed look, to which he responds with a scowl. "Alfie and I saw were in the Divide this morning. We saw that the flags in the Reserve are purple today. Someone died, which means we have a chance. Rachel is an important part of this meeting because she most recently escaped through the sewers, which seem to be the safest route for us to get in. She can help us find our way. So, at this point, who's all going?"

"I think it's me, Molly, Rebecca, Alfie, Tyler, and Rachel." Elliot answers. I shudder involuntarily, thinking about how I'll have to go through the Divide again to get to the Reserve. Clutching the edge of the couch, I think about my family and focus on their faces. "Anyone else thinking of going?"

"He would like to," Abe speaks up, gesturing to Jacob at his side. Every one of us looks over in surprise. None of us had realized that Jacob and Abe had walked into the room. Jacob gazes at us nervously, his small hands fiddling with the hem of his shirt.

"Absolutely not." Tyler refuses immediately. Jacob's face falls at Tyler's expression.

"He has family in the Reserve, too," Elliot argues, sitting up straight.

"Yeah? And who's going to keep him from outing all of us or getting himself killed?" Tyler glares at Elliot as if he's daring Elliot to challenge him.

"Oh shut up, Tyler," Rebecca groans, stunning all of us. "You need to stop acting like no one is capable of taking care of themselves. I'm tired of it." Her green eyes are bright and fierce, refusing to back down.

"He's 12 years old, Rebecca! He's just a kid!" Tyler protests, fixing his angry gaze on her.

"So were you at one point. And I'm sure if you were in his shoes, you'd be doing the same things he is and getting even more upset if no one let you go see your family." Rebecca snaps.

"It's not the same thing. I don't have a family to go to-" Tyler begins after a long pause, but Rebecca isn't having it.

"That's not his fault. Stop taking control of people's lives here. You're not helping anyone. Stop trying to save everyone. You can't." As soon as she hisses out those last words, Tyler's expression hardens and he stays silent, angrily looking down at the floor instead of meeting anyone else's eyes. "We all have our own sob stories. They don't give us the right to control other people or treat them like shit."

"I'm trying to protect him." Tyler insists, and it's obvious that all he wants is so desperately to keep everyone alive, even if it means trying to take control of their lives. But our lives aren't his to control.

"He didn't ask for your protection. Protecting everyone is not your job." Rebecca reminds him. A silence falls over the whole room. No one says a word or even moves a muscle for a few moments, and the air grows thick with tension.

"He does have a point, though," Alfie speaks up quietly, knowing he's the only one Rebecca would listen to at this point. He clears his throat as if to rid the air of the awkward tension. "Who's going to look out for him if he comes with us? As much as we'd like to all keep an eye on him, we've all got our own places to be and things to do and people to look out for."

"I'll take him." Garret's voice speaks up from beside me, startling me and causing me to look up. I hadn't even noticed he was there. "I don't have family in the Reserve. All of my focus would be on him."

"Alright," Rebecca says tiredly, squeezing her eyes shut as Alfie puts his arm around her and gently rubs her back.

"That's it then?" Molly stands up and forces a smile, looking beyond eager to get away from all the tension this short meeting brought up. "We all know how this is going to go. . . in-and-out mission, right?"

"Yup," Tyler mutters, standing up as well and leaving the room before anyone else.

"Tyler," Jacob tries to call out to him, but Tyler just walks right past him without a word, leaving Jacob standing by himself. I get up from my seat, ready to help erase the frown off Jacob's face, but Garret beats me to him.

"Don't worry about him, buddy," He assures him as he signs, leading him upstairs.

I watch as Damien gets up and gives Rebecca a pat on the back, as if someone standing up to Tyler was what he'd been waiting for since he got here. Everyone leaves the room, leaving just me and Elliot standing there. I think about the Divide again. The hum of the ships. The sound of their lasers. The screams of innocent people dying. I close my eyes and squeeze my hands so that my nails dig into my palms. I'll have to go through the Divide to get to the Reserve, even if it's only for a minute when I'm on the back of a hover. Just the thought of being there again makes me numb.

"I don't think I can go back there," I tell Elliot, my voice shaking. He gives me a look of understanding, and all of a sudden, I realize he must know about the fact that I killed two outsiders. Everyone knows at this point, I'm sure. I wonder if he thinks of me differently. "The beasts in the sewers . . . I mean, could we even fight them off if they found us?"

"You don't have to go back." He reminds me. "You don't have to go when we do. I can tell your family whatever you want me to tell them. I can take you back whenever you're ready."

I want to respond. I want to tell him thank you. But all that comes out of my mouth is a sob, and the next thing I know, all the emotions I've been keeping in are pouring out. Elliot's arms are around me instantly, and he guides me back to sitting on the couch. But all I can think of is everything I'm trying to forget. The fact that no one knows what's happening to my dad or if he's even alive is one thing. The fact that I've killed two people and seen an innocent man die is another. I'm falling apart and I don't know what to do.

When my crying eases up, I pull away from Elliot.

"H-how do you deal with all of this? How do you make the pain and fear go away?" I choke out.

"It doesn't go away. You never really deal with any of it." He replies, any traces of a comforting smile completely gone from his features. "It may seem like some of us have it together. . .that we know what we're doing. But we don't. We're all broken."

His words remind me of things that everyone used to say before the invasion when life was normal. . .things like, 'everyone you meet is fighting their own battle' and 'don't judge someone unless you've walked a mile in their shoes'. I know it's stupid of me to assume that everyone here is doing fine, but it's also easy to see how much happier everyone looks when your own world is falling apart. But Elliot's right. Of course he is. Practically everyone here has been where I am right now. I wipe my eyes and look at him.

"Your family is in the Reserve," I state. He nods. "I want you to know that when we liberate them someday in the future, I'll make sure they're safe. Even if . . . if you're . . . not . . . around anymore, I will make sure they're safe. I promise." I want him to know I have his back. As many times as he's been there for me while I've been here in this short amount of time, I want him to know there is someone who is there for him, too.

TWENTY-FIVE

No matter what happens, life goes on. As days go by and plans for going into the Reserve are formed, time doesn't stop for me as I struggle to shut out my tormenting thoughts. Whenever I try to go to sleep, I see their bodies the second I close my eyes. The outsider in the woods, the outsiders I killed, and the Reserve man they killed. And the man they left for dead. The man I also left for dead. When I try to practice shooting my gun or throwing knives, I see them again, but I step aside and calm myself down and get back to work. I cannot let these memories consume me.

I have people here that are helping me to keep it together. Elliot listens whenever I need to talk, and I feel comfortable talking to him. Rebecca is always making sure I have everything I need and looks after me the way my own mother would. Alfie looks for any possible opportunity to make me smile or laugh. Grace helps me get every chore done perfectly and shushes Damien whenever a cruel insult is aimed my way. Abe and Jacob teach me sign language so I can communicate with Jacob better.

And on nights when my thoughts turn into nightmares as I fall asleep and I wake up with a strangled cry, Tyler is up in an instant, knife in hand and ready to take on an intruder that's never there. He never gets mad at me for waking him up over something as simple as a nightmare, even with my excessive apologizing and uncontrollable crying. He just tells me not to worry and lets me talk about it if I want to or go back to sleep if I don't. Because he's seen it all before and felt it himself. When I wake up one night to the sound of him gasping for air and see him shaking and clutching the sides of his bed, I know it's true.

Some nights I can hear the muffled sound of someone crying in one of the other rooms. Other nights I'm woken up by a scream of someone else waking up from their own nightmare. Despite the smiles and the laughter of everyone during the day, it's now obvious to me that they're all going through exactly what I am, and some have it worse. We're all a little broken but still trying to manage to keep fighting.

I train as hard as I can during the day to keep my mind occupied and get my body ready. The soreness in my muscles is fading, and I can tell I'm getting stronger, even if it's only a slight improvement. Alfie teaches me how to ride a hover in a field far away from the fences enclosing the house, with Elliot and Rebecca as our protection. It takes me a while to get the hang of it, but he's patient.

Being the perfectionist I am, it didn't take long for my mood to turn sour. But he didn't get angry no matter how many times I messed up, he didn't yell at me when I got frustrated, and he didn't mind explaining things more than once. I wouldn't be surprised if he was the one who taught most people here how to ride a hover.

Time passes, days go by all too quickly, and pretty soon I find myself realizing that it's now the day before we leave for the Reserve. The sun is starting to set as reality sinks in. Everything seems normal, but underneath all the smiles and small talk, we know that tomorrow isn't to be taken lightly. Tyler gave me my gun back and I start to pack my things, but the second my fingers brush across the cool surface of the gun, all the memories of the Divide that I wish I could forget resurface full force. So I go outside and pretend like everything couldn't be better in order to keep calm.

I see Molly and Brianna talking by the makeshift targets, holding the knives I was just starting to get familiar with. It looks like Molly is giving Brianna throwing lessons, and judging by how well Brianna is doing, these lessons have been going on for a while. As I make my way to the backyard, I notice Tyler and Jacob sitting where we had that bonfire several nights ago. They've long since repaired the small strain in their friendship. Up ahead, Alfie and Rebecca are at the picnic table again, and I walk over to them.

Alfie is sitting on the table cross-legged, looking more childlike than anything, as he fiddles with what looks like long blades of grass. Rebecca is seated normally at one of the benches of the picnic table, watching him with amusement. But the love she has for him is so obvious in her eyes that I feel like I'm intruding, so I awkwardly come to a halt a few yards away, pretending to look at the sunset.

"Collins! Come over here!" Alfie calls out as he spots me. I think about politely refusing and letting them be, but with his playful grin, I have a feeling he won't let me go. Plus, he referred to me by my last name, which reminds me that at this point most people here know I am my father's daughter. I walk over and sit next to Rebecca. "Check this out," he tells me, holding up the grass that he's woven and knotted into a bracelet. "I made it for ol' Becky over here." He smirks at her, causing her to shake her head and grin at him.

"I'm honored," she proclaims dramatically, holding out her wrist. He slides it on and it hangs loosely on her thin wrist.

"Perfect!" He exclaims, looking at both of us expectantly until we both nod. "Want me to make you one?" He hops to his feet as he looks down at me, towering over both of us by standing on the table.

"Sure." I smile at him.

"Will do," He jumps off of the table, striding out further into the backyard in search of more tall grass, leaving Rebecca and me with just each other's company.

"He's an interesting one," I say, to fill the silence and keep my mind distracted.

"Tell me about it." She chuckles softly.

"How did you two meet?" I ask, hoping I'm not coming off as nosy already.

"High school," she replies with a smile. "We've been together for 5 years."

"Wow." I don't hide the fact that I'm impressed. "That's pretty amazing."

"It's not that big of a deal," she chuckles modestly, tucking a strand of her blonde hair behind her ear. "Are you ready for tomorrow?"

"No," I admit. "Are you?"

"Not at all." She lets out a sigh, twiddling with the grass bracelet. I shoot her a curious look.

"You've been back to the Reserve before, right? Since you left all those years ago." I assumed she would have visited her family at least once, but she shakes her head no.

"We had one mission a few months ago where we went back to the Reserve, but our goal was to only get one person back in. The rest of us were just supposed to stay out around the perimeter in case something went wrong. We had all agreed that Sara should be the one to attempt to visit her family. To put it lightly, she was the one who was losing it the most. She needed this more than the rest of us. She was able to get in and out without getting caught and with her help, we've been figuring out how to get more of us through undetected, but barely any of us have been able to visit our families yet."

I feel a pang in my heart as I think about my dad. All those days I spent thinking he would never risk coming back to the Reserve to visit us. He could have been just outside those walls, wishing he had the mindset to abandon the plan and the other rebels so that he could see us again.

"I think we'll be okay, though," Rebecca tells me, probably

assuming my silence was because I was worried. "We've got a great group of people going."

"Except for me," I can't help but mutter. Every horrible memory of these past few days parades through my mind like a slideshow of nightmares. I squeeze my eyes shut before opening them again, as if it would erase all those terrors from my brain. "I don't think I'm cut out for this."

"If it helps, I think you are," Rebecca insists. I shake my head but don't say anything, not wanting to argue. "I mean it. You escaped from the Reserve, made it through the Divide, and survived the Divide again after you intentionally chose to go back. I think you're definitely ready."

"But I did all those things with the help of other people," I mutter, still not feeling confident. Mary helped me escape, Tyler got me through the Divide and took me to the rebels, and he got me out of the Divide when I chose to go back again. All the things people think I'm brave for accomplishing, I never accomplished alone.

"So maybe you did have help, but you still did those things. You didn't just sit there in the Reserve and wonder what it would be like if you got past those walls, you actually went and did it. I know how hard and terrifying that alone can be, even if you have someone helping you. Same goes with the Divide."

Her words do little to comfort me. I'm still scared out of my mind for tomorrow, so much so that I know I won't be sleeping tonight. As much as everyone says this is a simple in-and-out mission and masks the danger with the excitement of seeing their families again, there is a strong possibility that this could go horribly wrong. If we get caught, maybe we'll just be captured and taken to the main ship or something. . .but they may just kill us. That's what I imagine they'd do, and that's what I'm afraid of. And maybe if things go wrong some of us could escape unharmed, but even if I manage to cheat death, one of these rebels here that I've gotten so familiar with could die, and I'm not ready for that.

I try to act like I agree with Rebecca and say a quick goodbye, going inside the house and grabbing a few survival books off of the shelf by the couch. Noting that it's getting dark, I also grab Tyler's solar-powered flashlight from upstairs. Making my way back out to the porch, I get comfortable on the bench with the charcoal-colored cushions and begin to read to take my mind off things.

I read about edible plants, how to start a fire, and basic first aid . . . simple things I wish I had learned long before the world turned into hell. By the time I finish what I've brought out, the sun has completely set, and it's dark out. Our journey to the Reserve is only a few hours away. Looking out across the yard, it's eerily quiet. No late summer breeze rustles the leaves on the trees tonight, and even the insects that fill the night air with noise are much quieter. I feel my gut clench nervously as I think to myself that this is the calm before the storm.

TWENTY-SIX

Everyone gets up early in the morning, which isn't a problem for me since I didn't sleep. I managed to get a few more survival books from Elliot and stayed up all night reading them so that I didn't have to think about anything else. I continued to use the flashlight instead of the lantern so that Tyler could get some sleep, but without his light snoring in the background as I read, I knew he couldn't sleep either.

As we each grab a Reserve outfit and change, I realize very quickly that this particular shirt and pants aren't the same ones I escaped the Reserve with. Someone must have grabbed mine by mistake. When we got to the Reserve, they gave us custom clothing that fit us perfectly. These pants, however, were too long, causing me to have to roll them up by the waist, and the legs of the pants were too wide, making me worry that they would get caught on something. The sleeves of the long-sleeved top went well past my fingertips.

"Um, these aren't mine," I say lamely to Tyler as he throws on a Reserve shirt that seems to fit him perfectly. Considering that he's not from the Reserve, I wonder why that is. He gives me a quick once-over.

"Well, the only other person that's going to the Reserve that could fit in your clothes would be Molly. Go talk to her." He advises. I go downstairs with Tyler at my heels. Seeing the familiar head of fiery red hair in the dining room, I go toward her.

"Hey, I think you grabbed my clothes by accident," I tell her, gesturing at my ill-fitting outfit. Molly glares at me, which takes me back.

"It wasn't an accident." She hisses. "I'm not going on a mission with clothes that don't fit me. I can't run around in something like that. Sorry." She doesn't sound sorry in the slightest.

"But-" I stammer.

"Not my problem, swan queen." She slams her feet into her shoes before plopping onto one of the dining chairs and lacing them up with a huff.

"Molly," Tyler speaks up, but she continues on in a louder voice.

"Look, I don't even want to go on this mission. I don't have a family in the Reserve. My family is here." Molly glances briefly in the kitchen and I look as well, seeing Angie putting our breakfast dishes in a pile. "But I'll be damned if Elliot can't see his family. I'm doing this for him. Nobody hurts him. . .I need to make sure of that. So figure something else out." With that, she gets up and storms past us, going out the front door before either of us can say anything.

"Don't take it personally. She's just . . . stressed." Tyler mumbles, gazing at the front door like he wants to go after her and talk to her.

"You can go talk to her if you want," I tell him as I roll up the sleeves of the shirt. He shakes his head.

"It wouldn't help. She just needs to be alone for a bit." He looks at my outfit again, and I can see him trying not to crack a smile. "I think someone's got some suspenders or something. I'll be right back."

I wish I could smile back, but I can't bring myself to. Molly made something very clear, which is that no matter how hard I've worked these last couple of days, I'm nowhere near their level. If anything, I'd just get in their way. So she's totally right. Why should she have to deal with clothes that don't fit when she's way more capable than I'll ever be?

"Here, use these." Tyler is back and handing me a pair of suspenders. I head upstairs to put them on in our room before packing up my messenger bag and going back to the dining room again. Tyler's putting his shoes on now, and I take the seat next to him and do the same.

"Those help?" He looks over at me. I nod. "Good." He leans back in his chair and closes his eyes, letting out a deep breath. I feel the urge to ask him if he's okay, but I already know the answer. His pained expression says it all. So I settle for another question.

"Need anything?"

His eyes open and his brows crease in confusion. "What?"

"Do you need anything?" I repeat, offering him a small smile. "You look a bit worried."

"I'm okay," He sighs tiredly, even though we both know he isn't. None of us are. I notice his hands are shaking. For a moment, I want to take them in mine and hold them for a bit . . . just to let him know that he isn't alone. If it were almost anyone else, that's what I would have done. But knowing him, the gesture seemed too intimate for him to appreciate. I give him a gentle pat on the shoulder instead, which is probably a bit too strange of a gesture itself, but what's done is done.

"We'll make it through this," I offer, trying to make it sound like I believe in that statement. As I start to lace up my shoes, I can see him nod before getting up and going out the front door. When my shoes are tied, I follow him out as well, seeing everybody pairing up and getting ready to go on their hovers. My nerves start up again, and I feel my stomach turn.

"Ready?" Tyler comes up to me, handing me the familiar black motorcycle helmet. I feel my breakfast coming back up and quickly offer an excuse to leave.

"Yeah, give me a minute. I just need to make sure I've got everything." I ignore the strange look he gives me and do everything I can to keep from bolting into the backyard. The all too familiar screams of the man I couldn't save and the outsiders I killed ring in my ears, the gory images that accompany them flashing in front of my eyes. Once I'm behind the house, I place a hand against the brick wall and prepare myself for inevitable vomiting when suddenly I hear the sound of someone else retching. Looking up in surprise, I see Damien a few feet away, wiping his mouth with the back of his hand. His eyes, full of fear and dread, meet mine, and they go from startled to guarded in seconds.

"You nervous, too?" He gives me one of his trademark smirks.

"I. . .you're going?" I fumble to form a sentence.

"I'll be in the perimeter. Part of the backup in the trees. Outside of the wall. No sewer time for me." He takes a few steps toward me and I instinctively take a step back, which causes him to chuckle darkly in amusement. "Word is you were a ballerina, Newbie. I could totally see it. You're so tiny . . . got that whole delicate look about you. Like I could just snap you in half with my bare hands." He grabs my wrist so quickly that I choke out a gasp, and when he clutches it in a vice-like grip, I can't help the whimper that slips past my lips.

"Girls like you don't belong on the battlefield." Damien's amusement has turned to anger. His grip on my wrist tightens to the point where I feel my knees starting to buckle. My mind is in a thousand places at once, and I can't seem to find my voice. "You just hold everybody back. You get in the way. You make mistakes that get people killed. You're nothing like your dad." That last sentence sends a bullet through my heart, and Damien knows it.

"I just don't get it. He was a great soldier, and then you come along. I bet he's real disappointed in you, and he'd be even more disappointed if he saw you now. You-"

"Damien?" Grace's voice snaps us both back to reality. She's at the back door of the house and doesn't seem to realize the tension in front of her. Damien lets go of my wrist immediately, and I can feel the pain finally start to subside. He gives me a glare, as if warning me not to tell Grace about this, before turning toward the house and walking toward her as if everything is fine. I feel the all too familiar feeling of tears in my eyes, but I go back toward the front yard before they can fall.

Crying seems to be all I do lately, but I try to remember what my mother told my sisters and me time and time again: that it was okay to cry. It was normal, and most of the time, it was helpful to just get all those emotions out. And when we were done crying, we had the chance to realize whatever was the cause of our tears gave us the opportunity to become stronger.

I know I'm not the strongest person here. I'm not the fastest either, or the best shooter, the best hunter, or anything like that. But I'm trying, and I keep trying. I know my parents would be proud. Damien doesn't know my father like I do.

"You good?" Tyler hands me the helmet again when I reach him, and I quickly roll down the sleeves of my shirt before he can see my wrist.

"Yeah." I put on the helmet and join him on the hover, enjoying how the helmet makes everything a little quieter. I close my eyes as we take off, thinking about seeing my mom and sisters again and how happy that would make me, if only for those few moments. I refuse to open them until we've stopped.

TWENTY-SEVEN

I open my eyes again when the hover stops. We are at the edge of the Divide, close to the store I met Tyler in weeks ago. I point to the direction of the sewer and he leads while the others follow at staggered rates to avoid detection from Emigre ships overhead. Once at the cover, Tyler opens it and silently motions for me to lead the way.

When my feet touch the ground and begin to slosh through the water, I instinctively keep my pace slow as I look into the darkness and listen for any Emigre guards or beasts. The group follows behind me, and even though they are trying to be quiet, the water makes it harder to hear. My heartbeat picks up as my nerves rise. Each step makes my muscles tense in anticipation to the point where they feel like they will snap.

After what feels like hours, we reach the cover that leads to the Reserve. We got lucky. Maybe someone died today and the beasts are fed and sleeping. Without speaking, I motion for Tyler to go up the ladder and watch him as he does. He opens the cover ever so slightly, peaking out in the Reserve for when the coast is clear. When he seems satisfied, he whispers for me to find him when I go up.

Even with his success, I can't help but be worried out of my mind. We're here in the morning because that's the easiest time to blend in and see our families. They'll be at their respective jobs, and there will be enough people wandering around that we could easily blend in. But we won't have the cover of the night. I wish more than anything that we could have done this at night, but at night the patrols are more intense. As soon as it's dark, everyone must go to their houses and the doors are locked. It wouldn't have worked.

With a deep breath, I follow up the ladder and open the cover. I notice a guard walking in the distance and wait until some buildings give me cover. When I'm sure no one can see me, I make my move and climb out, lowering the cover behind me. I try to appear as normal and inconspicuous as possible as I make my way toward the row of houses that look the most familiar. I look up ahead just in time to see Tyler notice me and make his way toward me. Nodding to the right, I lead him to where I think my family will be.

Before I escaped, we used to work in the greenhouses. We harvested the crops, which really was a daily job because the Émigrés had some kind of chemical that allowed the plants to fully grow in 24 hours. So in the morning, we would harvest the plants from the night before and then plant the ones to be harvested the next morning. That was it. We didn't have to water them. The greenhouse took care of everything else.

When I reach the greenhouse, I see that they still have an Émigré guard at the front door. I know that because no one has caused any trouble; the Émigrés are pretty lenient in terms of letting us wander around the Reserve as long as the sun was up. Walking around, I wouldn't cause any suspicion, but at a workplace like the greenhouse, I'd have to sign in. Now that I've escaped, I doubt I'm on the list anymore. And I don't think I could just walk in. Unless. . .I could convince the Émigré guard that I was just visiting someone. As long as he or she doesn't see that I don't have a bracelet, they should let me through. They have no reason to believe that I'm not from the Reserve. To their knowledge, no one would bother to sneak back in.

I slow down and wait for Tyler to catch up to me, hoping that the look I give him tells him to follow my lead. I go up to the guard and clear my throat, swallowing hard as I try to appear casual.

"Hi, we're workers from the central market. We're here to visit Abigail Collins." I tell the guard, trying to keep my left wrist out of view even though my sleeve is covering most of it. My breath catches in my throat as the guard turns its helmet-covered head towards me. It seems like too much time passes, and I wonder if the guard sees right through me and we've failed. If it asks for names, what names would I give? If it asks for our specific positions in the market, what would I say? Would it let me speak for Tyler?

"Go ahead," the guard mutters.

"Thank you." I try not to grin, almost running into the greenhouse. I know my family harvests the tomatoes, and those are to the left, towards the back. I lead Tyler through rows of crops, hoping that since the guard let me through, that means my family is definitely here. I keep walking until carrots transition to tomatoes. All I have to do now is find my family and keep my wrist hidden from the few Émigrés that patrol inside the greenhouse.

Up ahead, I can see my mother and Annie working in the fields, and I have to refrain from running toward them. As I get closer, my mother spots me, and her eyes widen as her mouth drops. I hold a finger to my lips for the briefest second, reminding her to act normal or I will get caught. When I reach her, I can tell she wants to embrace me, but she resists and covers Annie's mouth instead, whispering in her ear that she must stay quiet. Annie still hugs me briefly, and I pat her gently on the head.

"What are you doing here?" She whispers to me as I start gathering crops and placing them in the basket. I glance at Tyler to urge him to do the same, and he immediately begins harvesting the tomatoes near him.

"They've taken dad." That's all I say as I try to avoid her eyes.

"What?" she gasps loudly, and I shoot her a warning glance.

"Where have they taken him?" Her voice is now back down to a whisper.

"The main ship," I answer, and I can see her skin pale out of the corner of my eye. "Where's Mary?"

"Still in solitary confinement." She says softly, and I feel my blood turn to ice. "That's the punishment for trying to escape and being captured."

"Where is she being held? I can rescue her."

"Don't." my mother whispers sharply. "Trust me. You-"

An alarm blares loudly all of a sudden, interrupting us. Everyone stops what they're doing, looking around in confusion. But I know exactly what has happened, and my stomach sinks as I search for the quickest way out.

They know we are here.

"Come with me." An emotionless male says and my head snaps up to see the guard from earlier as he grabs my arm. My mouth goes dry. Glancing at Tyler in panic, I watch the color drain from his face. There's no escaping for me. For Tyler. For Alfie. For Rebecca. For Elliot. For Molly. They know we're here and there's nothing we can do about it. Everyone can tell who the intruders are just by looking at our wrists.

I refuse to look at my mother or Annie as I make my way out of the greenhouse to the front gate. I can't let them see me upset. They can't see me accept defeat. By the time I reach the gate, the rest of the rebels are already there, lined up horizontally and facing eight Émigrés who have their strange silver guns at the ready. None of them are wearing helmets, and I can see their eyes, shining violet in the early morning sun.

I see Jacob at the end and my heart stops. He wasn't even supposed to be in here. From what I heard, he was supposed to wait in the woods while Garret brought his parents to him. What the hell had happened? Why was Jacob here and not Garret? I couldn't bring myself to look back at Tyler. As much as I would want him to look like he had a plan, I knew all I would see was him looking angry and defeated.

One of the Émigré guards sees me coming forward and shoves me into the line, placing me with Jacob on my right and Alfie on my left. Tyler gets placed far to my left, where I can't see him. I'm shaking, and unshed tears are stinging in my eyes, but before any of the Émigrés can speak, I feel Alfie take my hand and give it a gentle squeeze.

I know he's holding Rebecca's hand as well, and I assume he's trying to reassure us, along with the fact that he wants the Émigrés to see that we are not mindless targets. We are people. People who feel, people who live, people who love. Even if they see us as obstacles or enemies, we are still people. I take Jacob's hand in mine and squeeze it as well.

There is no time to ask how they knew we were here. There is no time for one of us to pull out our guns, fire, and escape before every surrounding Émigré shoots us down, and our efforts are futile. We stand and wait, wondering what will become of us in the next few moments.

How did you know? The questions build up in my throat. How could you have known? Who messed up? Did someone betray us? Who could have betrayed us?

I watch the guards discuss among themselves in a language I can't understand. One of them, who seems to be the leader, has his helmet off and his violet eyes look at each of us in anger and disgust. A crowd of people is beginning to form, murmuring in confusion as fear etches across their faces. Another guard, helmet on, demands that Jacob move forward. Unable to read lips this time, Jacob doesn't move. The guard demands again.

"He's deaf-" I try to explain before the lead guard steps forward, his eyes darkening in rage. In an instant, he smacks me across the face so hard I see stars.

"Silence! How dare you speak. You humans are all the same.

Despicable vermin who refuse to listen." He snaps. I force myself to stay composed and ignore the pain radiating in my cheek.

"Move!" He commands Jacob, who looks up at me in confusion as my heart beats so fast I feel like I can't breathe. I start to open my mouth to whisper to him. The leader wastes no time. In an instant, his gun is raised, and before I can blink, he fires.

What can only be blood sprays across my right cheek as my eyes squeeze shut, and I can feel Jacob's grip immediately slacken as his body falls to the ground. The second his hand is gone from mine, every nerve in my body turns to ice before lighting on fire. An uncontrolled, unhuman scream of agony tears from my throat. I don't look at Jacob. I can't. I know he is gone.

TWENTY-EIGHT

Jacob is gone. Jacob, the little boy who reminded me of Annie. Jacob, the boy who didn't want to see me sad.

I can feel anger edging out any fear and clouding my thought process. Before I can stop myself and think about the consequences of my actions, I yank my other hand away from Alfie and pull out my gun. Blinded by rage, I aim to shoot at the leader before he can turn to face me. But there is not enough time. There is no way to be quick enough. In the back of my mind, I know this. He knows this as well and immediately points his gun at me.

But something happens before either of us can pull the trigger. Alfie rips the gun from my hand as he tackles me to the ground, and I can hear the leader firing. I can barely see out of the corner of my eye that his laser misses Alfie by inches, and several other lasers fired by the other guards fly over my head. I've landed on Jacob, and I can feel the sadness and anger bursting inside me once more as the smell of grass and blood fills my nose and I can feel his weight underneath me.

All I see is Jacob's smile, his pink cheeks, and his warm brown eyes that exuded happiness. All I hear is his laughter and his voice. All I can feel is his blood on my cheek. It doesn't matter that I barely knew him. It doesn't matter that he barely knew me. They killed an innocent child; a child who knew only of kindness and of good, always winning over evil. I cannot forgive them for what they've done. I have to make them pay, even if it's the last thing I do.

Pushing myself up, my eyes wildly search for the leader as I foolishly ignore the surrounding chaos. Alfie has managed to sink his knife into the shin of the leader and is now trying to wrestle the silver gun away. I can hear Tyler yelling in agony, and my eyes automatically shift to him.

"I promised him I'd protect him! I promised . . . I promised I'd keep him safe!" He's surging toward the leader, gun at the ready, but Elliot is holding him back with all his strength, saying everything he can to get Tyler to calm down. Elliot looks around frantically, as if ready to tackle Tyler to the ground if any guard tried to shoot at them. When he grabs Tyler's shoulders and shakes them, I can see Tyler start to come back to reality and actually look Elliot in the eye, but my anger has nowhere near subsided. The rest of the rebels have started fighting off the other Émigré guards, but all I can think about is killing the leader. I don't care about anything else.

Disregarding all rationale, I step forward and aim at the leader, firing before Alfie can stop me again. I almost want to shout in triumph as a bullet nails him in the forehead and he falls to the ground. My bullet hits him in the cheek seconds later, but it's the bullet fired by someone else that killed him. Surprise, grief, hatred, and relief are all-consuming me, and combined with the adrenaline now coursing through me, I'm seconds away from sobbing and laughing psychotically in the middle of a newly formed battlefield. It's only when Alfie pulls me forward that I remember where I am and that we have to get out.

I search around to see who fired that shot and spot Garret standing atop the wall with his rifle, shooting the guards from above. Now, thanks to him, many of the guards are focused on shooting him down. But with his experience, he's killing them off one by one.

Alfie runs over to help Rebecca finish off two Émigrés, pulling out his gun and leaving the leader's gun in his dead hands. I take the leader's silver gun with my right hand and put the old gun in my bag. As I look for the nearest way out, I run over toward the rest of my allies, gunfire mixing with the sound of Jacob's voice in my head.

A weaponless Émigré lies motionless on the ground to my right, blood seeping through the back of his white jacket. But as I pass him, he springs to life, grabbing my foot. My body slams to the ground and the silver gun flies out of my hands. I look up to grab it as I try to kick it out of his grip, but the gun is too far away. Kicking and pulling myself forward toward the gun, I try in vain to snag my own gun out of my backpack.

I'm kicking as hard as I can, but even when I nail him in the nose and blood runs down his face, he doesn't let go. His violet eyes are filled with a hatred that nearly mirrors the hatred I have for him. I kick harder, but end up missing his face completely. Without warning, I find someone standing over me. I look up to see my mother holding the silver gun, pointing it with shaking hands at the Émigré.

"Don't move!" she tells me, and as I obey, she fires. But strangely, the gun doesn't go off. She pulls the trigger again, but nothing happens. Not wasting any more time, she then runs forward and slams the gun on the Émigré's head. I feel his grip loosen, and I struggle to my feet. She hits him in the head several more times with the gun until he lays motionless on the ground.

"Where's Annie?" I demand, both of us knowing that I would thank her if I had the time.

"Safe. In the house." She keeps her eye out for more guards as I pull out my gun.

"Mary?"

"You don't have time to try to rescue her. You have to go." She's raising her voice at me as another Émigré comes toward us, but this guard is shot down by Molly before I can even aim my gun.

"Come on!" Molly yells at me before running towards Elliot.

"Come with me." I yank on her arm, not ready to leave her here.

"You know I can't-"

"Bring Annie. Come on." I'm begging.

"We have to be here for Mary, and you know it's not safe for us to try to leave right now." Her voice cracks with emotion as she pushes me away.

"I can keep you safe. I pro-"

"Go!" she screams, and before I can protest, she's running back to the house. Reluctantly, I run toward Molly as she meets up with Elliot. Tears are blinding my vision, but I can't stop running. More Émigrés will come soon. As much as I don't want to leave my family, if I don't leave now, I'll die.

TWENTY-NINE

An influx of screaming stops me short. Looking quickly over to my right, I see my mother still running toward our Reserve home, but just beyond her are several creatures running toward us. The gleaming yellow eyes are familiar. The beasts from the sewers.

They run on all fours and are shaped like dogs, but they are even taller and larger than a horse. Their fur is pitch black, their unnaturally long, sharp teeth peeking out of their mouths as they snarl ferociously. My mother is right in their path, and they are much faster than she is, trampling and biting any human in their way. Almost no one is outside their home at this point, but those that remained to try to defend us are being ripped apart by these horrible creatures that seem to have a taste for humans. I run toward her, abandoning Molly and Elliot. I don't know where the rest of the rebels are. All I know is that I need to help my mom.

She sees the creatures and changes her path, going toward the nearest home in the hopes that they'll let her inside. But I know she doesn't have enough time. There is one creature that will reach her before she reaches the door. I have to do something. Taking out my gun, I aim at the body of the doglike thing and fire, hoping that I at least hit it somewhere.

It flinches slightly, so I know I must have hit it, but that barely seems to have hurt it. Luckily for my mother, its freakishly yellow eyes are now trained on me instead of her. With a grunt, it takes off toward me, and I turn back toward the wall and run.

I can hear its panting mixing with my heavy breathing as it gets closer, and as I reach a trash bin near the wall, I can feel its breath on my back. Hopping onto the trash bin, I heave myself onto the wall, but my tired arms refuse to push my exhausted body over, and I can't get a good grip on the wall with my gun in my hand. As the creature slams into the wall and barks just like a dog would, I can feel the wall tremor slightly. I aim my gun at it again and fire before throwing the gun over the wall and onto the safe ground below.

The bullet seems to do nothing but anger the beast more, and it gets up on its hind legs to grab me with its savage teeth. When I look down to see how far away it is from me, I notice a dark liquid, nearly as black as its fur, beginning to pool onto the grass below. It's not some strange, immortal beast. . .it's like a giant dog, I tell myself. If only I hadn't thrown my gun.

The teeth of the beast grip the leg of my pants as I try with all my might to heave myself over the wall, the concrete edge of it scraping the skin of my abdomen. I can feel the creature pulling me back down with its weight, but just as I think I'm dog meat, my pant leg rips and I'm free from the teeth's grasp.

With every ounce of my remaining strength, I heave myself over the wall and drop to the ground, pain shooting up my legs from not taking the time to land properly. I grab my gun off the ground and run toward the Divide just as an Émigré ship from the Divide flies overhead to land in the Reserve, most likely to aid the guards. The pilot doesn't see me as I make it into the trees and dash toward the buildings of the Divide.

As soon as I reach the clearing, I hear the familiar hum of a hover, and within seconds Damien, of all people, is pulled up in front of me.

"Get on!" He yells over the hum of the engine, but I hesitate.

"What about whoever you came with?" I shout back.

"I'll come back for him, just get on!" He reaches out like he's going to yank me onto the back of the hover, then stops as his eyes gaze at something behind me. By the time he screams at me to get down and I do as he says, a laser has flown over us, so close that I can feel its heat. I turn around with my gun ready to shoot, only to see Garret nail the Émigré guard's shoulder over the head with his rifle. Even though the Émigré has a helmet to protect it, it still falls to the ground, and Garret quickly pins it down with his foot and fires at both of the Émigré's unarmored legs before taking its gun. He tries to shoot the guard with the gun, but just like what happened with my mother, it doesn't fire. He takes it with him, anyway.

"Where's Luke?" Damien asks Garret as he reaches us.

"Dead," is all Garret says, his eyes red with unshed tears. Damien's jaw tightens, and he slams his fist down on the ground, cursing loudly. I have no idea who Luke is. He could have been a guard back at the house, but the name means nothing to me. What I really want is to ask Garret about what happened with Jacob, but I know better.

"You're hurt," I blurt out when I notice the bloodstain on Garret's abdomen.

"A laser just skimmed me. No big deal. We should go." He looks around for other Émigrés before starting off toward the woods. I turn to Damien.

"Take him. Not me." I tell him.

"I'm fine," Garret announces to us as he continues walking. I give Damien a pleading look, even though I know it won't do anything for him.

"Whatever you say, Newbie," he mutters, tossing the extra helmet at Garret's back.

"Take her, I'll be fine," Garret protests, facing us and holding up his rifle for emphasis.

"I'm not in the mood to argue, Shaw," Damien growls.

"I'll be okay," I promise Garret, and as if to prove my point, a hover comes toward us from the woods. I recognize Tyler's helmet.

Garret sighs and reluctantly gets on Damien's hover as I begin running toward Tyler. I put my gun in my bag the second I reach him, making sure the safety is on. As soon as I get on and put on the helmet, he takes off, and I have to hold on to him for dear life with the speed he's going. When we go through the Divide, I shut my eyes.

"Don't let go. I have to keep up this speed." He shouts back to me, forcing me to open my eyes again. We're going through the forest now, and I can't help but feel like we're going to crash into a tree. But the longer we ride, the more I feel the adrenaline beginning to fade, and the reality of everything that's just happened comes crashing down. Jacob is dead. My family isn't safe. The false façade of the Reserve is more false than we thought. Garret's hurt. I don't even know if Alfie, Rebecca, Molly, and Elliot are alive. And now the Émigrés will be looking for us. I feel the sobs coming, and as much as I don't want to let them out, I can't hold them back.

I cry into Tyler's shoulder for lack of a better position, and although I know he can hear me and I know he can't be too pleased, he doesn't say anything. The hover weaves and bobs through the trees, and with all the crying I'm doing added to that, I start to feel sick. But before I can ask him to slow down, I feel the hover start to slow down anyway, and Tyler starts to curse.

At first I think the hover has stopped working properly, but the sound of explosions ahead of us tells me that Tyler purposefully slowed down. I look over his shoulder, and although I can't see anything but trees, I know those sounds came from the house. Those ships leaving the Reserve weren't going back to the Divide. They were going to the rebel house. They knew it existed and where it was. I suddenly feel like I can't breathe.

"I'll lead them away. You get off and run." Tyler brings the hover to a halt. Up ahead, I see who he's referring to. A group of Émigré soldiers are up ahead and have just spotted us.

"Why can't we just stay together?" I gasp out, gripping onto him as if to urge him to move the hover again.

"I'd rather just have me get caught than both of us. Just keep running and gather up any other rebels you find and let them know what's happened."

"I'm not getting off." I tell him, trying to make my voice less shaky and more stern, although the fact that the Émigrés aren't just little white blurs anymore is making that impossible. "We're partners."

"That doesn't mean anything now!" Tyler bites back angrily.

"What do you mean?" My tone is just as upset.

"Don't make me force you off, kid," He snaps.

"I'm not getting off!" I hold on to him tighter, not having the slightest understanding as to how someone could be so difficult. He starts up the hover again, and I think I've convinced him. But as he takes off to the right as fast as he can, he turns sharply back to the left, and I can't hold on. I fall hard to the ground, tasting dirt as I hear him telling me to run again. I stand up to watch him ride off deep into the woods.

"Screw you," I choke out, feeling the heavy sobs rack my body again. But I can't stay here. I have to run. I can't go after him now that he's long gone. I can only do as he said and let him lead the Émigrés away.

Making sure nothing fell out of my messenger bag, I take off into the woods toward my right, going as fast as my legs will let me. Despite everything that's happened, I try not to think about anything other than running. I push away thoughts about my family, about Jacob, about Garret being hurt, and about all the other rebels. I just run.

Trying to avoid all the tree roots as best I can, I take a quick glance over my shoulder. No Émigré soldiers are in sight, but I know they can't be far. The ground to my right slopes steeply downward, so I run along the edge of it, keeping up my pace. My legs burn, my heart hammers in my chest, and my breathing is out of control, but in the back of my mind, I can hear my father's voice telling me to keep going.

Suddenly, I see a flash of white coming toward me. I slow down along the edge, fumbling in my bag to get out my gun when I see that it's not white armor but white Reserve clothes. The person stops a few feet from me and I can see that they have on one of the many motorcycle helmets that we use when riding hovers, so I know they're a rebel even though I don't recognize whose helmet it is. I hold up my hands to let them know I'm on their side.

"Émigré soldiers are coming. We think they've taken over the house. We have to run." I pant out, motioning for them to get moving. If they have a hover, that would help immensely, but if they did, they wouldn't be on foot. And the fact that they still have a helmet on and haven't taken it off is a bit odd. "Who are you?" I demand, placing my hand over my gun just in case I am wrong. This person is dressed like a rebel who came on the mission with us, but I don't understand why they're acting like this.

Before I can react, the stranger whips out a silver gun from their messenger back. . .a gun that looks exactly like the guns the Émigré soldiers use. With practiced precision, they quickly aim and fire, and I feel something prick my neck. Reaching up, I don't discover a gaping wound, but rather something small that is protruding out. As I pull it out, I feel my legs starting to give way and my mind starting to slip. I hold up my palm to see what I was shot with as my knees sink to the ground. A silver dart.

As much as I try to fight it, my eyes slip shut and my mind goes blank. I don't even feel the rest of my body hit the ground. Everything just goes black.

THIRTY

I wake up gasping for air as if I've been drowning in the ocean and have finally reached the surface. After everything that happened before I blacked out, I expected to find myself strapped to a metal table, ready to be tortured or experimented on. I could have even expected waking up in some kind of jail cell, or face to face with an Émigré with its silver gun pressed against my forehead, ready to kill me after relentlessly trying to get every ounce of information out of me. Or maybe I would simply not wake up at all, the Émigrés just deciding to kill me while I'm passed out.

I woke up scared out of my mind but ready to fight out of any restraint, ready to take on whatever enemy was in front of me. But instead of a ship's walls, I see the sky through the trees, smeared blood red and fiery orange from the setting sun. The taste of dirt is still in my mouth. All I can hear is the leaves of the trees rustling from a faint breeze. I'm all alone except for the trees of the woods and the steep hill, which I now realize I am at the bottom of instead of at the top. None of this makes sense.

Why didn't that Émigré, dressed like a rebel but clearly a traitor, take me to the main ship? Why would they leave me here? Did I roll down the hill when I passed out, leaving him or her to assume I was dead? Or did they just throw me down here so that they didn't have to deal with me? I didn't understand this at all.

After a quick inspection, I find that my body isn't bruised and everything I brought into my messenger bag is still there. Every part of my body feels perfectly fine. So, they must have brought me down here themselves. But why? Were they trying to prevent the other Émigrés from catching me? Maybe they weren't an Émigré after all. . .but then, how could they fire that gun that no other human seems to be able to use? Who were they?

All of this is too much for me right now. I take a deep breath, standing up slowly and taking in my surroundings again. Taking off my helmet, I listen to the sounds of the surrounding woods. I needed to find another rebel. It didn't matter who. I just need to find someone who is on my side. I know I can't survive out here on my own.

But where would they be? Did any of the rebels from the house escape capture? Are any of them dead? I feel the tears come. Jacob's smile flashes in my mind, and as I reach up to my cheek, I can feel his dried blood on my cheek. Scrubbing my cheeks furiously with my hands, I look around frantically as if a familiar face would magically appear and bring me comfort. But no one is around. Not even the enemy that was chasing me during what feels like just minutes ago.

I want to scream until my lungs give out. I want to cry until I don't have any tears left in me. Go back to the Reserve just to be with my mom. Wander around until I find my old home and go to my room and find the ancient teddy bear from my childhood and hug it until the world isn't scary anymore. Find Mary and never leave her side. Find my dad and never let him go. But I can't. I can't do any of that.

So I walk. I trudge up the steep hill, eyes scanning every direction for a friend or a foe. With footsteps as light and as quick as I can make them, I make my way through the woods in search of the rebel house.

I don't know what I expected to find when I reached it, but when I do, I know I never could have prepared myself.

I come across the small building that I'd seen so many times on my way in and out of rebel territory. It's perfectly intact, still marking the entryway to the rebel house. But the guard I'd seen standing by it every time now lays face down in a pool of his own blood. I walk past him without a second glance, feeling my heart rip apart piece by piece.

The house has been badly damaged by lasers. What was once a large and beautiful home now had chunks of it missing, bricks and glass littering every inch of the front yard. It doesn't seem like anyone that is still alive is here, but I have to check. If there is a rebel that's injured, I need to be ready to help. If there is an Émigré, I need to be ready to fight. No excuses. No hesitation.

When I step inside the house, even the atmosphere is different. Orange sunlight filters through the gaping holes in the house on my left. The lasers have left tears or burn marks on the floors and walls. The air smells like smoke and metal. Every book is off the bookshelf and every pot and pan is strewn along the kitchen floor like the Émigrés shot from their ships in the air and then came inside and tore the place apart.

Right at my feet is a body that I recognize instantly. Even facedown, I know that it's Abe. I imagine him confronting the Émigrés as they stormed through the front door, and when he refused to surrender and instead fought back, they shot him down. As sad as I am, I can't even bring myself to cry. My mind is too scattered, knowing that this is just the beginning.

I squeeze my eyes shut for a moment as I step over him, careful not to make a sound just in case an Émigré is still here, or an outsider has gotten in. Making my way to the kitchen, I search amid the appliances and dishes for any food that I can take with me. Finding some cans of food, I stuff my bag until it can't carry any more cans. I then head upstairs and check room by room to make sure it's clear and there's nothing I could use.

Checking my room first, I find the window busted and the mattresses on the floor. The drawers have all been emptied, their contents piled on top of the mattresses. I find a rain jacket and tie it around my waist, searching the pile for anything useful. I can't find Tyler's solar-powered flashlight, but I find a few other things that belong to him: four packets of Skittles, the Polaroid photographs of him and other rebels, an empty black backpack, and a black moleskin notebook.

I take the backpack and transfer the stuff in my messenger bag to that bag. Carrying around a backpack would be so much easier than a messenger bag. I could actually run fast enough to save my life with a backpack on. Not knowing if Tyler will come back here, or if he's even alive, I leave the Skittles and photographs where they are.

But the notebook intrigues me, and with my curiosity and desperation for a distraction, I open it and take a look inside. I realize very quickly that it's a journal. A date (two days after the invasion, in fact) is scrawled in pen at the top of the page, and below it is a simple paragraph.

"The world has been attacked by aliens. No, that isn't a joke. I found this notebook and figured I'd write about the end of the world. Maybe when this is all over, someone will find it, and it'll become some kind of piece of history. In all actuality, it's just some crap writing from a boy who doesn't know if he's going to get another tomorrow."

THIRTY-ONE

I turn the page, curious to see what Tyler's early days were like. He was an original rebel after all.

"First things first, I avoided being captured. The aliens bombed the most heavily populated cities and then went around capturing whoever they could find. If people resisted, they were killed. So, how did I avoid this? Well, I didn't on my own, that's for sure.

When the aliens first came to the United States, word got around pretty quickly that they were capturing and killing. My parents wasted no time packing and getting ready to run. I got ready with them, willing to do anything to keep us alive. We didn't have that great of a relationship, but I realized they were willing to do anything to keep me alive too. They just had other plans.

They knocked me out and put me underground. Yup. My dad knew of an old tornado shelter in the woods where we were going through at the time, and he figured the aliens wouldn't look there. But apparently, we couldn't ALL hide in there, and my parents knew I would never leave them, so they knocked me out and put me in there. Great parenting.

I'm sure they thought they were saving me, but why we couldn't all hide there I'll never know. Maybe they were hoping to distract the aliens and lead them all far away from me. That's all I can come up with, because when I woke up in that shelter I was completely alone, and when I got out of that shelter I was completely alone. I haven't found them yet."

Skimming over the next few pages, I read bits about his journey. There are paragraphs about trying to find food, water, and shelter. Lucky for him it was so early on that he could find a lot in the stores he came across. There are pages of when he thought he found safety in the basement of a building in the Divide, only to realize everyone was panicking and no one trusted anyone and if he wanted to survive, he could never sleep and just hope that no one tried to kill him. He would lay on the floor with a knife in hand, wary of every shape in the darkness and every noise he heard.

When I get to the part where he finds the rebel house, I stop reading, letting his written words sink in for a moment. Even after reading that entry over once more, I can't even begin to imagine what that must have been like. Still filled with questions, I think about reading the rest of the notebook's contents but decide against it. These words aren't meant for me. They were intended for someone far off into the future to read. Or for Tyler to reread, if he ever wanted to.

Placing the notebook back on the mattress, I go to the next room, which belongs to Kira and Cole. There's has two twin mattresses on the floor, just like ours. Clothes are piled everywhere. Anything that could have been useful to me is no longer here, but I'm relieved that I don't find a body.

Underneath all the clothes, I find a sketchpad that I realize belonged to Kira. Searching through it quickly, all I see are pencil drawings of landscapes. There's a city building, a country field, several of a beach, and even one of this house. The last drawing I find is the one she drew of the full moon above the stream the night Tyler and I followed her.

Not finding anything else, I go to the next room. This is a room that Elliot shared with someone, but even with some inspection, I have no idea who he shared it with. All I can tell is that it was a male, judging by the fact that all the clothes in here are men's clothes. The books have all been grabbed off their shelves and tossed haphazardly in a pile on top of all the clothes that used to be in the closet. I dig out the book of edible plants and the survival guide and shove them in my bag as best I can. Finding some cloth bandages and a pocketknife, I slip those into my bag as well.

I search room after room, finding nothing but clothes and little trinkets of people's lives that are irrelevant to me. The sun has finally set. There are no other bodies, but I don't find any living rebels, either. I walk back into the room I once shared with Tyler and put my mattress back on the bed, sitting on it with a sigh. Taking out a can of beans and a spoon I found in the kitchen that at least looked clean, I eat for the first time in what feels like forever. But it doesn't bring me any happiness.

Sitting here in the dark, with the breeze blowing freely through the broken window, all I think about is how much of a confusing, chaotic nightmare the past few hours have been. Sure, I had been trying to prepare myself for the worst, but when I left the Reserve this morning, I never thought I would end the day alone in the rebel house, with its walls destroyed and everyone captured or dead. I think about Abe again, and the guard out front, and have the urge to search for a shovel so that I can bury them, but I don't move.

All I want is for a rebel to come walking into this house, but all I hear is the sound of crickets chirping and leaves rustling from the breeze. Jacob is dead. Abe is dead. Tyler, Elliot, Rebecca, Alfie, Molly, Damien, Grace, Angie, Garret, Brianna, Cole, Kira. . .if I had to think positively, they are all alive, and gathered together in the woods somewhere, trying to find a new place to live and hide. Maybe some of them are even looking for me. But all I can think is that if they're alive they've been captured. They're either captured or dead. Facing the Émigrés like I have today has left me unable to imagine otherwise. Just because I survived doesn't mean everyone else was that lucky.

The half-empty can of beans falls onto the mattress with a gentle thump, the spoon following after, sliding onto the hardwood floor with a clang. I don't even care. Losing every bit of emotional stability I have left, I curl up on the mattress and do what I do best: cry. I can't even think about the traitor. All I'm able to decide is that I'm staying here for the night. If no rebels come by morning, I'll have to leave. I know it's not safe here. It's not safe anywhere anymore, but I can't keep pretending that these walls will still protect me.

When I don't have any tears left, I just wait for the sun to come up, knowing I won't be able to sleep anytime soon. So I keep thinking. Why me? If I'm the only one alive or not captured, why me? I can't build an army. I can't defend myself against the Émigrés. I won't be able to fight off outsider after outsider. I didn't even set out to save the world. I set out to find my dad.

And the traitor: someone dressed like a rebel but with the gun of an Émigré that they knew how to use. That had to be the person who revealed to the Émigrés where the rebel house was, and it was more than likely that they told them about our plan to go into the Reserve, too. I can't imagine a rebel that would do that. Even if an Émigré threatened to take away everything they had, I don't think any of the rebels would give in. Never surrender. Fight or die. That's how the rebels work.

If it had to be a rebel, it couldn't be Tyler. There was no way he could have looped around, gotten off the hover, changed helmets, and grabbed an Émigré gun all in that short amount of time. At least, I didn't think it was possible. I'd love to blame Damien, but with Grace back at the rebel house during the mission, I highly doubt he would ever put her in any danger. And Molly has her mother and Garret has Brianna.

I refuse to believe the traitor could be Elliot. If he so happened to be, it would shock me to the core, and I'd still deny it. He is too kind, Alfie's too innocent, and Rebecca's too gentle. In fact, the more I think about everyone in that house, the more I can't imagine any of them betraying the rebels like that. Even with Kira being as weird and as cold as she is, I could tell that she liked the people here by the way she looked at them, and even if her brother wasn't here, I'm almost positive she would still be here.

Maybe it was a guard that I had never met. Maybe it wasn't anyone at the house at all. . .it was someone spying from the outside. But then. . .why save me? They had me in the palm of their hand, completely defenseless and unable to run. All they had to do was bring me to the Émigrés. And yet, they didn't. Their hesitation after I told them to run made it seem like they knew me. So who was it?

I feel the overwhelming urge to scream again until my voice can't make another sound, but I don't have that luxury. Instead, I scream in my mind. I shut my eyes tightly and I make the screams loud and shrill so that they drown out anything else. No more thoughts about a traitor. No more thoughts about Émigrés. No more thoughts about the rebels. No more thoughts about my family. Just screams and darkness.

But as much as I try to shut everything out, one thought kept resurfacing. Why had the Émigrés left the house still mainly intact? Sure, they wanted to search it and capture some of us, but after they were done, why didn't they just destroy it completely? Are they assuming that those of us who escaped would come back?

I get up, unable to sit still any longer. With my eyes adjusted to the dark, I do my best to find some clothes that I can change into, knowing that if I continue to wear the white Reserve clothes, I might as well have a spotlight following me around. After finding and changing into a dark tank top and cargo pants that at least fit somewhat, I grab my backpack, ready to head out.

Since no one else has come back to the house, I grab the packets of Skittles and shove them into the side pockets of the bag. I grab the notebook as well, and even head back to Elliot's room and skim around until I find the book he was reading. I take all of this with me in the hopes that I'll see everyone again, but also just in case I never do. Maybe they really are all dead or captured, and in that case, I'll have these things to remember them by. But maybe they knew it wouldn't be safe to stay here and were on the lookout for a new place. I needed to find that place, and if it didn't exist, I needed to find a place of my own.

As I head down the stairs, I make my way to the kitchen and feel around in the dark until my fingers grasp the familiar feeling of the can opener. I shove that in the other side pocket of my backpack, heading out the front door and squeezing my fists as tight as I can as I step over Abe again. The tears come anyway, as they always seem to do. Making my way out into the woods, I prepare myself for a journey alone, however long it may be.

THIRTY-TWO

THE WOODS ARE DARK AND EERIE, BUT I FEEL SAFER HERE THAN I did at the partially destroyed rebel house. I walk quietly but at a good pace, just as I normally would in the woods of the Ruins, listening intently for any sound other than crickets chirping. My gun is in hand, just in case, and I realize now that I should have grabbed more bullets for it. But just as I think about turning back, I hear the unmistakable sound of someone or something quickly approaching me from behind. I prepare myself for the inevitable Émigré soldier or outsider.

"Hey, hey!" A voice that sounds vaguely familiar whispers harshly before I can ready my gun or think to flee. I don't move until I'm able to see the owner of that voice. It's Garret.

"Sorry, I didn't mean to scare you. I just. . .didn't know your name and didn't know how else to approach you." He offers me a small smile, holding up his weaponless hands. His white Reserve clothes stand out in the night, and I can still see the blood on his abdomen from his wound.

"I'm Rachel," I offer him a smile back, letting him think that I trust him. In the back of my mind, I'm wondering if there was any possible way he was the traitor.

"Rachel. Got it." He nods. "I was in the Reserve house scavenging for things when I heard you come in. I didn't know it was you, so I went out the back door and hid outside with my gun, waiting for you to eventually come back out. Then I heard you leave out front so I went around to see who you were and well, here I am." Laughing awkwardly, he looks at me. "You haven't seen anyone else, have you?"

"No, just you," I reply. His face falls. Not wanting to talk about it, I change the subject. "Do you have any bullets? I realized I forgot to grab some. I could just go back to the house-"

"Oh, you don't have to if you don't want to. I grabbed a ton. I'm sure I have some you can use." He assures me, pulling out a handful from his backpack.

"We should probably go back though. For a little bit. I'm sure you want to change clothes." I suggest.

"Right," He looks down at his clothes as if noticing them for the first time. "Totally didn't register that white stands out this much at night."

"Plus. . .." I hesitate, trying not to chase away our forced nonchalance with sadness. "I want to bury Abe and the guard. And anyone else if there is anyone else."

Looking up at him, I see reality hit him again and every trace of happiness leaves his face. He nods again.

"So do I. But we have to be careful. Something doesn't feel right about those freaks leaving the house like that and not coming back at all."

"That was my thinking, too," I follow him back toward the house. Feeling all the questions I have for him gnawing at my brain, I don't hesitate to speak up. "So you haven't seen anyone either?"

"Nope," He shakes his head.

"But what about Damien?"

"No idea where he is. As soon as we realized the house was under attack, we hopped off the hover. He went looking for Grace and I went looking for Brianna. I haven't seen him since."

"You didn't find her?"

"Couldn't get close enough to the house. There were too many of them. I climbed a tree to avoid them and see if I could spot her or anyone else, but by that time most of the soldiers were clearing out of the house and searching the woods. I'd like to think she got out with Grace and Angie."

"I'm sure she did." I try to convince myself and him.

"What about Tyler? Last I saw you were with him." He looks back at me.

"I haven't seen him since we realized the house was under attack." I debate telling him about the traitor. Maybe, just maybe, it was him. But maybe it wasn't, and maybe he might know who it was.

"You got separated?"

"Yeah, we saw soldiers running toward us so. . .he kind of kicked me off so he could divert them away." I wince at the memory, remembering the taste of dirt in my mouth and the harsh words on my tongue.

"Typical Tyler," Garret shakes his head. "Always thinks he has to save everybody. Don't get me wrong, I like the guy, it's just that one day this shit will kill him. If he's not dead. . .he's probably been captured. You said you hadn't seen him since-" He looks back at me again, but I must look more upset than I did before because his eyes widen. "Or, you know, he's alive. I'm sure he's alive. He's definitely alive, and probably headed toward the next base."

"Next. . .base?" My confusion tempts me to bring him to a halt, but we're nearly at the house.

"Yeah. There's another house full of rebels a couple of miles down. You didn't actually think it was just us few, did you?"

"No, but. . .well maybe. . ."

"What kind of army would we be if we only had like 20 people?" He interrupts me, shaking his head. "Plus didn't the fact that most of the people in this house were young and without parents seem a little odd to you?"

"I guess. But I never heard anything about more rebel houses." We reach the yard in front of the house and I feel the sadness weigh me down again. I try to just focus on Garret's white clothes standing out in the moonlight.

"Yeah, because we didn't tell everyone there were more. This house was a decoy house."

"What?" The shock is evident enough in my voice to make Garret stop and turn around, and I'm thankful we've stopped walking. So much has happened and I've had so much to think about that once again my body is starting to feel numb. "What do you mean 'decoy house'?"

"This was the house closest to the Divide, so we figured they'd find it eventually if they ever wanted to go looking for groups like us. We wanted them to think this house was all there was in terms of a rebel group." He's looking at me like there's an apology on the tip of his tongue, but he has nothing to apologize for. It makes sense.

"And you didn't tell people because you wanted to keep it from the Émigrés as long as possible." I think about the traitor again, feeling a chill run down my spine. With Garret standing in front of me, I could make myself panic and say it was him and the mystery was solved, but with the blood all over the front of his shirt, I really don't think it was him.

"We knew word about us would get to the Reserve. We wanted people to know they would have a place to stay if they escaped, but we also wanted them to think it was only this house just in case word got to the Émigrés and they wanted to do something about it." Thinking back to my time in the Reserve, I remember how everyone would say without hesitation that the rebels were barely surviving. . .that they hardly had any food or water and were quickly dying out. I see now that's exactly how the rebels wanted to be viewed.

"It's also a good idea in case a rebel ever betrayed you." I let out a shaky breath, debating again whether or not to tell him about what happened to me. The only person I trust at this point is Tyler if he's still alive. And I want to trust Elliot. But other than that, everyone else could be exactly what I'm afraid of. I want to be completely sure I can trust Garret before I say a word.

"Exactly. We had to think of every sort of possibility." Garret nods, oblivious to all the fear and confusion and sadness consuming me as he turns back to the house.

"Why was Jacob in a decoy house?" I whisper, watching his body stiffen. He hesitates a moment before facing me again, the anguish in his eyes breaking my heart even more.

"Like I said, it was the closest one to the Divide and the Reserve. Pretty much anyone that came from the Reserve would find us first and stay there."

"But he was just a kid. Why wouldn't you consider moving him?" I feel like I'm asking too many stupid questions, but I'm too upset to care. Jacob dying still doesn't make sense to me. He's a kid. A good kid. Things like this don't happen to children.

"A lot of people escaped from the Reserve without bringing their whole family. Even if we told people from the Reserve about other houses, how many do you think would want to go somewhere where they knew they would probably never see their families again?"

I stay quiet, looking down at the ground, knowing he's right. But the questions bubble up in my throat again with the memories of what happened in the Reserve still fresh in my mind.

"Where was the rest of his family?"

"That's a long story-"

"What happened in there? In the Reserve. He shouldn't have been in there. Why was he in there?" I'm nearly yelling at him without meaning to.

"Are you really just going to stand here and bombard me about Jacob all night? Because I hate to break it to you, but I'm really not in the mood." He snaps back.

"I want to know!" I argue exasperatedly.

"Why does it matter? He's *dead*!"

That last sentence cuts like a knife, and we both feel it. A silence falls over us, and I see the pain in his face and the tears in his eyes and I know I look the same way.

"We're both on edge. That's understandable after everything we've been through." He states to break the silence. "But we should go inside and get done what we need to get done."

I nod in agreement, following him inside. We step over Abe as if he's just an object in our way, and that kills me.

"I'll change clothes and then get the shovels and work on burying them. You get the bullets you need from the basement and join me when you're done. And hey," He stops and places a hand on my shoulder. "I'll tell you what you want once we're safe."

"Okay," I try to smile, and he attempts to give one back, patting me on the shoulder.

"Alright, let's get to work."

I head to the basement, discovering what once was a room full of weapons but was torn apart by the Émigrés. From what I can make out, the only weapons that are still here are weapons that are broken. Feeling around in the dark, I look for at least a single bullet. As my fingertips graze over a broken arrow, I suddenly hear Garret screaming my name.

THIRTY-THREE

Taking my gun out of my bag, I run up the stairs, ready to attempt to take on any Émigré or outsider. Realizing Garret is outside, I head out the front door. I see him sprinting toward me from where the guard was, his face full of panic, and that's when I hear it. The sound of an Émigré ship.

We don't even need to speak to each other. One look proves we both know what's happening, and we run off into the woods in the same direction as before. I let Garret lead the way, focusing on my breathing and the heaviness of the gun in my hand in order to stay calm and keep up the pace. The hum of the ship gets louder, but I know it won't see us now. All we have to worry about at this point is if Émigré soldiers are combing through the woods on foot like they were before.

My eyes scan through the trees for any flash of white armor, but my brain keeps imagining the traitor over and over. We reach a gate that looks just like the one the guard stood in front of, and Garret pushes it open and we take off again. I notice the body of another guard out of the corner of my eye, but I don't look over.

Running at full speed for what felt like an hour but was probably only a few minutes, we finally slow down and keep going at an easier pace. Neither of us has spoken, too anxious and too focused on getting away to build up the energy to say something. It's only when my whole body aches and I feel like we're safe that I speak up.

"I can't do this anymore," I pant as I slow to a halt. Garret slows down too, looking back at me.

"What, running? Because you were doing pretty good, but we can definitely stop now." He drops his backpack on the ground as if claiming the land for us, shooting me a grin.

"No, I mean. . ." I stop talking to take a breath and get out my water bottle, taking a long swig as I try to stay composed. "I can't keep doing any of this. I can't keep being a rebel. I can't keep running for my life and watching people die and killing people. I killed two people! Me, killing two people! That's insane . . . I never would have. . ." All the words keep tumbling out, but I can't stop them. And Garret doesn't stop me. "I know the Reserve isn't a perfect place, but I felt safe there in a way. I had my sisters. I had my mom. And now I don't know if they're okay and I don't know if my dad's okay and there are all these other people I didn't even know a month ago that I'm worried to death in and it's all tearing me up inside and . . . I can't do this." I sink to the ground, ready to close my eyes and forget all of this. "I-"

"Alright, that's enough," Garret interrupts me. His dark eyes stare straight through mine. "Haven't you ever felt like giving up before?"

"Well," I gape up at him, caught off guard. "Yeah."

"And what did you do?" He asks me, and when I don't respond, he answers for me. "You kept going. That's why you're here right now. Because every time you ever wanted to give up, you kept going. Why is this time any different? You telling me you can't keep going now, after all you've done?"

"This is different. I never killed anyone before. I never watched someone die." I protest.

"It's not that different. Whether it's a failed test or a breakup or whatever crap you deal with, you take the hit and keep going. You never stopped before. Don't act like stopping now is your best option." He sits down across from me, lifting up his now black shirt and changing the bandages on his wound. It's a larger scrape than I thought, but it doesn't seem to be very deep and it looks like the bleeding stopped.

"You're awfully positive." I smile slightly, hugging my knees to my chest as the chill of the night sets in.

"It makes things easier. Look, this isn't easy for anybody, but just think about how awesome it'll feel when this is all over." He looks up at the stars as if begging them to get us to that point. "You gotta hold on to something. Some kind of hope."

A silence falls over us. I break it once my mind starts to relax.

"We were right about the Émigrés coming back to the house."

"So it seems." He smiles at me again.

"Do you think they destroyed it?"

"Nah, I think it's like you said . . . they're waiting for a bunch of us to come back. Which says to me that a lot of us got away." He leans back against the trunk of a tree, and now I can feel some happiness edging out everything else. The thought of the other rebels being alive and free takes a lot of weight off my mind. I look at Garret again. I don't see a traitor. I see an ally. And I need someone I can trust who trusts me.

"You said you'd tell me everything I wanted to know," I fiddle with the cap on my water bottle. "And I want you to know that there's something I should tell you, too. I think someone betrayed us."

"What do you mean?" His voice is even, and he leans forward with interest. He's not surprised. But why should he be? As he said, he always thought out every possible scenario.

"While I was running through the woods when the house was under attack, I came across someone in a Reserve outfit. They had a motorcycle helmet on, so even though I couldn't see their face, I assumed they were one of us. I told them what was going on, but they just stood there, and next thing I know, they're shooting me with one of those silver guns and I get hit with one of those darts Marcus was talking about. It knocks me out, but when I wake up, I'm still in the woods. They placed me at the bottom of this steep hill and it was like they were trying to hide me from the rest of the soldiers." Just talking about it makes my fists clench and my breathing shake. Garret is quiet, but only for a moment.

"Did you get a good look at the helmet?"

"Yeah, it was black with a black visor and had white lines on the side. It didn't look like anyone else's that I saw. I think it was a spare."

"It was definitely a spare, then." He sighs, rubbing his hands over his eyes.

"Any ideas about who it could be?" I ask quietly.

"No idea," he huffs. "Kinda sounds like whoever they are, they're on our side, doesn't it?" Picking up a tiny rock, he tosses it over my head. I can see that just like me, his mind is thinking about everything and trying to make sense of it all.

"Maybe," I shrug. "But I don't really think so. One second we're fine, and then the next thing we know the Émigrés are onto us and it's like they figured everything out. It was like the flip of a switch."

"Maybe an Émigré guard got suspicious because . . . someone screwed up, and nobody betrayed anybody. I mean, we haven't exactly had the chance to talk to everyone who came with us about what happened in there."

"I don't want to think of the rebels as traitors. You know them better than I do." I admit. "So. . .you mean you didn't get caught trying to help Jacob?"

"No," He shakes his head, his voice getting quiet. "I got in there fine. I found his dad and got him out fine. We had just gotten into the woods when the alarm went off and I ran back to help. That's when . . . that's when I realized that Jacob didn't stay in the woods like I'd asked."

I want to ask him about Jacob. How he got to the Reserve. But Garret was right. He didn't deserve to be interrogated after what he'd just gone through. "Do you think that's why the alarm went off. . .? Because one of the soldiers patrolling the wall found him?" I asked.

"It's possible." Garret throws another rock over my head absent-mindedly. "But he was smart. And fast. And he could climb trees in the blink of an eye. So he might have had nothing to do with the alarm going off, and it was all just the traitor like you said. Or multiple traitors. Who the hell knows at this point?"

"Why would someone betray us? I just don't get it. . ." I bite my lip, trying to think of a reason. We're trying to win this war and take our planet back. Why would someone side with the enemy?

"Maybe the Émigrés made a threat or something. Like they have the family of one of our rebels . . . something that would get one of us to betray all of us, even if we didn't want to. It would probably be a rebel that works as a guard or goes on supply runs, which would give an Émigré the opportunity to confront them without the rest of us knowing. So that narrows it down to. . .." He trails off, his eyes staring intently at the ground before his mouth drops open. "No fuckin' way."

"What? What is it?" I encourage him.

"It's Marcus. If there is a traitor, it's Marcus. He went on that mission that found the ship and he was the only one who had made it back. It has to be him."

THIRTY-FOUR

The idea of Marcus being the traitor makes sense to me and finding some sense in this whirlwind of chaos that these past few hours have been is what I've been craving. But there's some doubt in the pit of my stomach. I have a feeling that in this case, the correct answer won't be the most obvious one. Accusing Marcus seems almost too easy.

"Do you think the Émigrés let him go as long as he gave them information?" I ask, knowing that Garret can sense my doubt. My dad always told me that my expressions and body language practically made me an open book. Whenever I was feeling a certain emotion, everyone always noticed. I was never good at hiding what I really felt. He also knew that I was doubtful, but I was doubtful of myself more than anything.

"I'm sure it went something like that if he is the traitor." He says.

"Well, what do we do about this? It's not like we can start pointing fingers at him." I sigh.

"You're right. Even though I think there are plenty of people who would believe us, we've got no proof. I say we just keep this between us, and then once we have our proof, we do something about it. Like we said, there could be more than one person that betrayed us."

"Sounds good to me." I shake my head in agreement.

"I am going to tell Brianna, though. When we find her." Garret eyes me carefully as if expecting me to object, but even if I did have a suspicion that Brianna wasn't on our side, it's still his decision to make. Not mine.

"That's fine. She is your girlfriend."

"Right. I've known her for almost 7 years. I know she wouldn't betray us and the fact that I've always been with her and she never spoke to an Émigré should be proof enough. Are you going to tell anyone we find? Tyler, maybe?"

I consider telling Tyler if we do find him and he is alive since he's the only other rebel that I can say, with a decent amount of certainty, isn't the traitor. But even though I'm nearly sure he isn't the one who confronted me, what if he's also a traitor? Original rebel or not, he could be on any side he chooses. Maybe he knows now that the Émigrés have his parents, and has been working with them ever since. This gives me the urge to take out his notebook and keep reading, but I know better. If Tyler's working with them, he's smart enough to not write about it.

"No," I say firmly. "There's no one else I need to tell."

"Sounds good to me." He's smiling again. "I can see why Brianna likes you."

"She does?" I'm slightly confused. I'd never spoken to her. Why would she have any opinion of me?

"Yeah. When she heard you used to be a ballerina, she immediately liked you." He chuckles. "Not because she was a ballerina, but because her little sister was. And then when you went to the Divide, she kept talking about how you were a perfect fit here. I totally agreed." I can't imagine someone actually thinking I belong with the rebels when I've felt like such an outcast since the moment I stepped into the front yard of the house. I never even had the intention of staying, but here I am.

"I don't know her well, but I'm sure I'll like her, too," I say lamely, feeling my cheeks flush.

"Oh, you will," He assures me. "She's the best. Kind, intelligent, funny, and the most fashionable person you'll ever meet. Apocalypse or not, she'll look like she's ready to walk down the runway." He's no longer focused on me, his mind wandering to the woman he so obviously loves. "It's funny. . .whenever I think about us as a couple, I always remember how disapproving everyone was of us being together. 'Why is that white boy with that black girl? Are they really together?' Bullshit like that. Even my relatives didn't like it at first until they met her and got to know her. But then the world goes to hell and people actually realize they have bigger shit to worry about than an interracial couple. Nobody bothers us anymore." His smile is so wide now that it looks like it hurts, and he lets out another laugh. He looks like he's trying so hard not to get upset, and yet I can't think of anything to say. A silence falls over us as Garret stares off into the darkness, deep in thought.

"You know what else is bothering me? That if a rebel betrayed us, they might not even be human at all."

"What do you mean?" I inquire as I take in the change of topic, but my mind already has an idea of where he's going with this. I can't believe I've never thought about it before.

"The Émigrés look almost just like all of us, except for their eyes. They have all the technology to get here and overtake us. Why wouldn't they be able to just change their eye color and blend in with the rest of us?" His words send a chill down my spine. Why didn't I think of that before? How could I have been so stupid as not to see that possibility? I suddenly find myself wondering if any of the rebels are actually Émigrés. How did I just trust them so blindly? "I've talked about this with a few other rebels," he continues. "We thought that maybe some people we find in the Divide would actually be Émigrés undercover, trying to make sure that we're dying out like we're supposed to. But we decided to take the risk and just give people a place to stay if they needed it."

"It was just a decoy house anyway, right?" I repeat his words back to him.

"Right."

Now I can't stop imagining the rebels with Émigré eyes. Elliot's light blue eyes, Tyler's dark blue, and Rebecca's bright green . . . all gone and replaced with violet. It's terrifying to even think about, and even though I never knew any of the rebels very well, I find myself feeling like I don't know them at all. If we find them, what am I supposed to do? If I decide I don't trust them, do I just leave and try to rescue my dad all on my own somehow?

"We'll figure this all out," Garret promises, letting out a yawn. I nod, refusing to freak myself out any longer over this. I need to focus on what's happening right now. Food, water, shelter. Look out for Émigré ships and soldiers. Get to safety. Nothing else matters right at this moment.

"You sleep. I'll go ahead and keep watch. I've had enough rest." I tell him, leaning back against the tree trunk behind me and getting a grip on my gun as I remember waking up in the woods.

"You sure?"

"Yeah, go ahead," I assure him, and I smile slightly when he begins snoring in a few moments, obviously exhausted. I'm glad he's able to try to get some rest after a day like this, and I hope he's able to sleep for a while.

My mind quickly flashes to memories of my mother complaining about how much my father snored. She would always start out irritated and would try to stay angry, but pretty soon my dad would be snorting like a pig and hugging her, and she wouldn't be able to control her laughter. I miss them more than anything. I can imagine that my dad might be okay as of right now because I haven't seen anything that proves otherwise. But I left my mom and my sisters trapped in enemy territory as things dissolved into chaos. When I think of how they are now, I can't imagine anything good.

The Émigrés have seen my face. They know I'm with the group that's actively trying to destroy them. And they know I've gotten away. It won't take much to figure out who my family is. They could all be publicly executed as soon as the sun comes up. Along with Elliot's family. And Rebecca's and Alfie's. I realize now that I'm not just out here trying to rescue my dad. I'm fully involved in the mission to save humanity, whether I want to be or not. Because saving my father doesn't mean that this nightmare ends.

The snap of a twig brings me back to reality. Alarmed, my eyes scan through the woods when I suddenly spot movement from behind Garret. I stiffen, immediately sitting up and trying to see what it is. It looks like the outline of a person creeping along to where Garret is snoring. They aren't wearing white, I can tell that much. But as I've learned, this is no indicator of them being on our side. My heartbeat thuds in my ears and my mouth goes dry, but I make the decision to wake Garret.

Just as I start to cry out, I see hands reaching from behind me that quickly place a long strip of cloth in my mouth and yank my head back. As my hands reach up hastily to remove the gag, the person works to remove my gun from my grip and pull my arms down, holding them behind my back.

"I hope you don't mind if we take all your stuff." A female voice whispers in my ear, laughing under her breath. With the taste of sweat and fabric in my mouth and the scent of pond water and smoke filling my nose, I make an effort to stand until I feel the barrel of my gun pressed to the side of my head.

THIRTY-FIVE

GARRET IS AWAKE NOW, RIFLE RAISED AND POINTED AT A BOY holding a crossbow who looks a few years older than me. I turn to face my attacker and see a girl around the same age as me, with the same olive skin and dark hair as the boy. She's grinning down at me, her teeth bright in the moonlight.

"What do you want?" Garret demands.

"Your stuff. Let us have it and nobody gets hurt." The girl speaks for both of them. Outsiders.

"Take it. Take it and go." Garret spits, nodding at our backpacks. I almost want to try to yell in protest despite the gag in my mouth. Without those bags, we'll have no food or clean water. There's no way the next rebel base just happens to be close by. But outsiders don't seem to be known for negotiating.

"Give him the rifle." The girl tells Garret, and with one look at the gun pressed to my temple, he obeys, despite the pleading look in my eyes. With no food, water, or weapons, survival just got that much harder.

The sound of people running through the woods leaves me thinking that we've been surrounded by outsiders and that they don't plan on letting us live. But when I look up at the girl, she looks just as confused as I feel. The second her expression turns to horror, I hear an inhumane snarl as she's tackled away from me by a flash of black fur. It's not people at all that I heard. It's one of the beasts from the Reserve.

The girl's screams, the beast's growls, and the frantic firing of the rifle flood my ears. I rip off the gag and turn toward the commotion. The beast seems to have immediately given up on the girl and is now facing me. I can see the recognition in its eyes. I know now that it was after the rebels that invaded the Reserve. Garret and I are its targets.

As it turns toward Garret and the boy with the rifle, seeming to debate who to go after first, I spot my gun not far from my feet. The girl must have dropped it as soon as she was hit. Looking at the doglike creature, the bullets the boy is firing are hurting it, I can tell that much. But it's not enough to bring it down. Not yet. I lunge for the gun. Everything seems to happen in slow motion. The memory of confronting my first outsider with Tyler comes back to me in full force. Send a bullet between its eyes. That's what I have to do.

The beast turns back to me when it senses my movement, and as my hands grasp the still warm metal of the gun, it leans back on its hind legs to get ready to pounce. It's not that far away from me. I know I can hit it. I take aim and fire, the bullet going right where I want it to. Once again, I am beyond lucky. The beast goes down, but it's not done. I aim and fire again in the same spot, using the last of my bullets.

Finally, it stops moving, and I'm free to breathe again. I can't bring my eyes to look away from the thing. It took bullet after bullet in its side, yet two bullets through its skull is what kills it. And it was looking for us. If it's the same one that went after me in the Reserve, I'm sure it got my scent when it ripped the leg of my pants. But it also recognized Garret. These things may be like oversized, deadly dogs, but they seem to be more intelligent than I'm giving them credit for.

When I look away, I find everyone staring at me. The girl is still on the ground, a fresh scratch across her cheek from either the edge of the teeth or the claws of the beast. The boy has lowered Garret's rifle, and Garret is smirking at me.

"You. . .you saved us," the girl gasps out, looking like she's trying to grasp that this actually happened.

"Not really." I'm just as shocked as she is, but I'm able to form a reply. I'm certain that if that boy hadn't fired all those bullets, the creature would have been much faster, less distracted, and able to take me out before I could do something. And it didn't look like it wanted to waste any time with anyone that wasn't its target. I glance at Garret, trying to see if he realized that it was after us. I can't tell, though. He just looks relieved.

"Thank you." She says, getting up and wrapping her arms around me before I can blink. She's practically squeezing the air out of my lungs, and I'm wondering if she purposely made the hug a bit painful. "I'm Leah," she announces as she lets go of me. "And this is my brother Kieran." The boy doesn't speak, just stares at me before handing Garret's rifle back to him.

"Rachel," I tell her, still feeling wary. Just a few minutes ago, she was holding me at gunpoint. And now she's just finished hugging me.

"Garret," Garret says, but only Kieran looks at him.

"You guys are brother and sister, too? You look sort of alike." Leah notes. I'm about to say no when Garret quickly answers.

"Yeah. We are."

"Do you guys need a place to stay? Our camp isn't far from here. It's not much, but we've got plenty of people. Safety in numbers." Leah offers. It sounds tempting, but we need to get to the next rebel base as soon as possible. Besides, if they were so desperate for food that they would resort to attacking us, it can't be that much better than just being on our own.

"We actually have a camp. We just need to get to it." Garret is purposefully vague. I notice he has his rifle at the ready again. "You guys should head back to yours in case one of those things shows up again."

"Yeah, what the hell was that?" Leah almost laughs in disbelief, looking down at it and taking a few steps back as if it might spring to life again. Come to think of it, with these aliens it could be possible. I step back as well and keep my gun aimed at it before realizing I'm out of bullets.

"A creature of the Émigrés," Garret states the obvious. I'm finally anxious to get away from it.

"Before you guys go, let me give you some of our food," I tell them, taking a few cans from my bag.

"Oh, you don't have to-" Leah starts.

"It's no problem," Garret says. "And let me treat that cut on your face. It'll only take a sec." The two of them step aside toward Garret's pack and he gets to work right away. Kieran comes toward me to take the cans, his dark eyes looking just as expressionless as they did before. I start to hand him the cans one by one when he grips my wrist tightly. I freeze.

"Are you guys rebels?" He whispers so quietly I barely hear him. Knowing that a lot of outsiders harbor hatred against the rebels, I don't answer. He takes this as a yes. "That thing was after you, wasn't it? I saw the way it looked at you and him. You guys did something. . ." His grip isn't harsh, but his voice and gaze are. I swallow hard, unable to speak. He's going to think we've put his people in danger, which we have. His anger will be directed at me. As his eyes bore into mine, I take my free hand and feel through my pack for the pocket knife I grabbed at the house. "Stay out of the woods. Especially at night. If anyone approaches you, say you're from the camp by the river. The Riverbank Camp. Don't forget that."

With that, he lets me go, and I realize he's trying to protect us from the anti-rebel outsiders. He knows just as well as we do that there are plenty of outsiders that wouldn't treat us too kindly if they found out we were rebels, especially if they knew about the chaos we had caused. As he grabs the cans and goes toward Leah, Garret looks my way. I give him a smile to let him know I'm okay, but I'm hoping my eyes convey that we need to talk. Not all outsiders are bad, which makes sense because it seems as though not all rebels are good. But I doubt I'm ever going to blindly trust a stranger ever again. I can't afford to be as stupid as I was when I left the Reserve.

"Thank you for everything." Leah says as she gets up, the scratch on her cheek freshly bandaged. She hugs Garret and then hugs me again. "And sorry for attacking you. No harm done, right?" There's a gleam in her eyes, like all of this was just the kind of entertainment she'd been looking for.

"Right." We answer her.

"Stay safe." She calls as she walks into the woods, Kieran following her.

"You too," I murmur, but they're already too far away to hear me, so quick and quiet. I watch them as they fade deeper into the woods, and only look away when I can't see them anymore.

THIRTY-SIX

"That all happened insanely fast." I blurt out, still in disbelief that all of that wasn't some weird dream, still looking out into the woods to see if Leah and Kieran would come back.

"Tell me about it." Garret lets out a deep breath. "I don't trust them. We should get going." He says, throwing his backpack over his shoulder.

"Yeah, especially with those dog things after us. Did you see the way it looked at us? It was like it recognized us." I struggle to keep my voice low as I follow his lead. Garret nods.

"Nice shot, though,"

"Thanks. I've been shooting at those targets so many times I better have hit that or all that practice would have been for nothing." I see him scanning his eyes through the woods for any danger, and I do the same. If I keep talking and stay focused, I won't have time to think about how afraid I am.

"Do you know where the next base is?"

"Pretty much." He answers, although that doesn't give me the comfort I wanted. "I've only been there once, to get some supplies that we were having trouble finding in the Divide. I know that we keep going west from the rebel house. And we should go past an abandoned barn painted red and falling apart. Then we go north. The base is huge, so I doubt we'll miss it."

"How long do you think it'll take us to get there?" I struggle to keep up with him and keep a lookout.

"Around 2 days." He replies, and my stomach sinks. But of course, it wouldn't be close by. There would be no point in a decoy house if it was.

"I need more bullets," I remind him. Outsider, Émigré, or giant, vicious dog, I want to be ready.

"Oh, right. Give me your gun." He holds his hand back and I hand it to him. Slowing down his pace so that he can pull out the right bullets, he loads the gun for me before giving it back.

"You didn't have anything left. Good thing you killed that thing when you did."

"And it's a good thing those two outsiders didn't try to hurt us after that," I add.

"They've got some morality left in them. But I think it wouldn't have gone as well if you didn't give them some food."

"The boy . . . Kieran. He knew we were rebels. He could tell that thing was after us. He told me that we should stay out of the woods and-"

"I'm not interested in a damn thing that kid has to say." Garret interrupts, walking faster.

"I think he actually wanted to help us. Not every outsider hates rebels, right?"

"Yeah, but how do you really know which ones don't mind us and which ones want to kill us?" He hisses.

"No matter what he feels about rebels, I think he feels we deserve to live. And he has a point." Kieran's argument sounded like an honest one to me, anyway.

"We've got aliens, outsiders, and a bunch of alien dogs after us. I think the amount of danger we're in is pretty much equal, no matter where we are." He mutters. "I'd like to stay out of view of any ships, so I'm staying in the woods."

"Fine," I sigh. There's no point arguing. I understand his side and it looks like he understands mine.

"I think at a minimum, all outsiders don't like us. They may not hate us and want to kill us, but they don't like us. We always have food. Clean water. Weapons. Clothes. They sometimes don't, and it's like we're all hoarding it from them. All they have to do is join us and they'll get their share, but they don't want to join a group with a target on its back who's on a mission that they think has failed before it's even started. I'll never believe one of them is on our side."

"I just want to believe that people are still good," I shrug. We all have one enemy in common. We don't need to be enemies with each other too. Things would be so much easier if we were united instead of divided, but I guess that's too much to ask from the human race. We couldn't do it even if it would save us.

"A lot of them are, in their own way. Problem is, everyone's got a different definition of what 'good' is. The outsiders think they're doing the right thing, we think we're doing the right thing, and I'm sure the Émigrés think they're doing the right thing."

"It would be so much easier if we humans could just work together despite our differences. But that's impossible, isn't it?" I almost want to laugh, but I can't bring myself to.

"Damn near impossible. I've heard there's even groups of outsiders that hate each other. They're more divided than we are."

Both of us are quiet for a moment as we keep walking. My legs are already starting to ache, but when I look up, I see Garret's breathing has started to get heavy. His cheeks are flushed, and beads of sweat dot his forehead. My body is beginning to tire, but I don't feel hot. The sun is down and the woods are almost chilly. Something is wrong.

"Garret, are you okay?" I ask him.

"Yeah, I just need more rest." His voice is strained.

"We can stop-"

"No," He almost yells. "We have to keep going."

We do. But not for much longer. When the woods come to an end and we enter a small neighborhood, I force him to stop at the first house. He hasn't gotten noticeably worse, but I know he's in pain and trying to downplay it. When he lifts up his shirt to check on his wound, fresh blood is seeping through the bandages.

"Dammit," He mutters, pulling out the bandages from his bag as he slumps down onto the porch steps.

"Here, let me help." I'm not good at dealing with blood and injury. I avoid it all I can, even pretending it's not there when it's right in front of me. But Garret is all I have right now. I can't lose him.

"It's getting infected." His voice is nearly void of emotion.

"Do you have anything to treat it?" I ask as I finish bandaging him, trying to keep my voice low in case someone is around. He shakes his head.

"Do you?"

"All I got was more cloth bandages." My stomach sinks.

"Well, shit," He forces out a laugh.

"Let's just stay here for the rest of the night." I suggest, trying to make my voice as light as possible. "In the morning, we can look around for something to help you."

"If there is anything." He sighs.

"Hey, what happened to Mr. Positivity?" I crack a smile, but I'm also trying to keep it together. I need him to be positive right now.

"He's still here," Garret assures me. "It's just hard to imagine finding good medical supplies this late in the game. I'm sure everything's been picked clean by now."

"We'll find something." I insist, opening the door to the house and getting my gun out. I'm ready to search for anybody hiding in here, but I don't have to look for more than a second. Illuminated by their own flashlight pointed in my direction, a pair of green eyes meet mine. I know those eyes. My mouth goes dry, but I manage to croak out his name as I lower my gun. Ross.

Ross Michaels. The older brother of my best friend Callie. The boy I'd had a stupid crush on for so many years. The boy who called me Braceface when I got braces and then pretty much didn't know I existed when I got them off. The boy who practically lived in sportswear and was always, always on his Xbox. He was here. And Callie was not.

"Well, if it isn't Rachel Collins?" He's smiling, but it's not the smile I remember. I realize right away that he's angry, and I bring my gun back up.

"Where's Callie?" I take the risk of asking him. He starts to laugh and hold up a gun of his own, and I hear Garret ready his rifle next to me.

"Funny you should ask." His face flicks back to anger in an instant. "She left not long after she heard a rebel named David Collins had been captured by the Émigrés. She found out he was at the camp by the Reserve and figured you would be there. And she left. I mean, I can't believe how fucking stupid she is sometimes! What if you weren't there? What if David Collins wasn't the David Collins she knew? She would risk her own life. . .leave her own goddamn family. . .to see you."

On one hand, his words bring me relief. Callie was alive. Callie was safe. But she was also the same girl I had remembered. Impulsive. Spontaneous. Loyal. Of course, she would drop everything to look for me. She wouldn't think about her own safety or if the information she got was true, she would just leave. And she had just unknowingly walked right into a warzone.

"I've been looking for her everywhere." Ross goes on, sounding borderline hysterical. It seems as if these years since the invasion have taken a toll on his sanity, and Callie was the only thing keeping it together. Now that he doesn't have her, he's losing it. He's slouching forward, his body shaking as his eyes nearly bulge out of his head. Prominent dark circles under his eyes, hollowed cheeks, untamed curly hair. This is far from the prep-school varsity lacrosse captain, I remember. "My parents told me not to come after her. That she would come to her senses and come back. But she hasn't. So now here

I am, out of water. Almost out of food. Hiding from aliens and psychopaths. . ."

"I was in the Reserve," I speak up softly. When he looks at me without speaking, I continue. "My dad left to join the rebels two years ago. My mom told me not to look for him either, but a few days ago, I left. I've been looking everywhere for him, too. I . . . sort of understand what you feel. I think that . . . I think maybe it would be best for both of us if we teamed up to get them back." I choose my words carefully, but I'm worried that I'll set him off no matter what I say.

"I can't help you with your dad." He growls. "As far as I'm concerned, your dad is gone." His words hit me like a blow to the stomach. I feel my eyes begin to water, and I don't even feel relief when he puts his gun down. If I tell him that there's a possibility that Callie might have been captured just like my dad, he'll demand a reason why. And the reason is because of what we did in the Reserve. He'll only get angrier. He won't be reasonable. Not without her.

THIRTY-SEVEN

"Look, we're not your enemy here," Garret says, still keeping his rifle trained on Ross.

"Yeah? Who the hell are you, tough guy?" Ross spits.

"I'm a rebel. Just like you." Garret keeps his voice even, masking the pain he's in.

"What're you doing out here, then? Helping her find her dad?"

"Something like that. I'm looking for someone too."

"Well, isn't that nice?" Ross laughs again. "Everyone's looking for somebody."

"We just need to get to the next base. The one by the red barn." Garret tells him.

"Real specific." Ross rolls his eyes. "The one owned by Ralph Peterson." Garret's tone gets icy, and I give him a tiny nudge on the shoulder.

"Amazing. That's where I just came from!" Ross's false grin is back. After all these years, his sarcasm and fake enthusiasm are still as present as ever. It's the only sign that he's the same guy from my childhood.

"Would you consider going there with us? Maybe Callie went

back." I suggest, thinking about my options. He knows exactly where the base is, and we could use the safety added by another person.

"And maybe she didn't. I'll keep looking for my sister, thanks. Get someone else to be your tour guide."

"We can give you food and water." I offer, pointing at our packs.

"That would be nice, but don't bother. I'm still not going to take you there. Not until I find her."

In the back of my mind, I feel like I should be looking for Callie, too. The only reason she left the safety of the base was so she could find me. And she's my best friend. So, do I move forward and work to rescue my dad? Or do I hold back and look for Callie?

"I know this isn't what you want to hear, but I've been around that house for a while now. I was just there earlier today. I haven't seen her." I tell him.

"Just consider the possibility that she may have gone back." After a long pause, he lays back on the couch.

"Fine. We'll leave tomorrow morning." He glares at us. I breathe a sigh of relief as Garret lowers his rifle. "You two lovebirds can sleep upstairs. It smells like dead people."

"Thanks," Garret scrunches his face into a fake smile of his own. He leads the way upstairs, and we discover two bedrooms. It smells gross, but thankfully, there are no dead people. "I'll take one bed, you take the other. You need anything, just holler." He yawns.

"Are you okay?" I ask him again. I don't hide the fact that I'm worried, but I do everything to keep from sounding like I pity him. It's the last thing he'd want. He looks down at me, patting me gently on the shoulder. I consider hugging him, but I push that thought away, knowing that it might hurt him. It's just that I've barely even trusted him for a few hours, but I already can't imagine this world without him.

"We'll work on it in the morning. Who is that guy, anyway?" He quickly changes the subject.

"He's my best friend Callie's older brother." I keep my voice down to a whisper. "Weirdly enough, I used to have a crush on him."

I figure I could try to lighten the mood at least a little, and thankfully, Garret laughs softly.

"You sure know how to pick 'em." With that, he says goodnight and goes into his room.

I smile for a moment as I go into mine. When I open the window to air out the smell, I can see that the sun is starting to come up. Taking off my backpack, I collapse back on the bed, my body exhausted.

But sleep never comes. All I get is vivid replays of everything I'm trying to forget. Mary being taken away by Émigré guards. Jacob dying. Leaving my mom and Annie behind. The vicious Émigré beasts that tear people apart with their long, pointed teeth. Everyone I thought I could trust staring back at me with violet eyes, raising silver guns to my head. I know that if I do manage to sleep, I'll probably wake up screaming. And it doesn't even matter because everyone around me has less sanity than I do. As much as I want this to all go away, I know that even if humanity won this war, and I was still alive, I would never recover.

Sunlight starts to trickle through the windowpane as I try to get myself to doze off. But every time I start to slip away, something jolts me awake. Sometimes it's because I think I hear my mother screaming, but she's obviously not here. Other times it's because I think armed Émigré soldiers are standing over my bed, but when I open my eyes, nothing is there. Eventually, I just stay awake, curled up on the bed and staring at the wall next to me.

My heart breaks when I imagine Callie feeling what I feel. How panicked she must be, alone out there, desperately trying to find me. Imagining me being tortured, or dead. Add that to all the other things I'm sure she's been through that have caused her pain and kept her up at night. But she had to have realized that it was useless to try to find me, especially on her own. She had to have gone back. It's the only hope I have.

I hear footsteps downstairs, and I know Ross has gotten up. It sounds like he's coming up the stairs to our rooms, but I don't feel like moving. He opens a door. . .Garret's door, and says words that just sound like mumbled gibberish from where I am. Then he opens the door to my room.

"Get up," He mutters.

"I'm up," I tell him, still staring at the wall, still not moving.

"Well, get out of bed. Your man needs you." That's all it takes to get me going, not caring enough about Ross's remarks to correct him. I'm in Garret's room in seconds. He's ghastly pale, covered in sweat, and his breathing sounds worse than before.

"Hey," He greets me weakly. I can tell he's in more pain, but he makes himself sit up as if to put my mind at ease. All that suffering throughout the night and he didn't even bother to call out to me.

"Hey yourself," I try to keep my voice positive, sending him a smile. But inside I'm breaking, and I can tell he knows it because he takes my hand and gives it a small squeeze and tells me he's fine, even though we both know he isn't. From stranger, to ally, to friend, all so quickly . . . and now, if I can't find anything to treat him with, that will be taken away.

"We need to get him something to treat his wound," I tell Ross, who's still standing in the doorway.

"We?" He scoffs at me.

"Yes, 'we'. Now let's go. Stop wasting time." I say, giving Garret's hand another squeeze. It's like fire in my palm. "We'll be back soon."

"Stay safe," He manages to tell me as I leave. Thankfully, Ross follows me out. I can tell he isn't happy about it, but I can't find the motivation to care about what he feels at this point.

"Lead the way." I sigh as we walk out the door.

"To where, exactly?" He snaps.

"Anywhere where you think we'll find something that will help him," I state the obvious. With a groan, he drags himself forward and takes us down the neighborhood street. We pass house after house, the only sound coming from him complaining that if I didn't exist, Callie never would have left.

"Just so you know, there are alien dogs out there. Huge, ferocious dogs that'll rip your face off with their teeth."

"Alien dogs?" He looks at me like I've gone insane, then seems to consider the possibility.

"Believe me, don't believe me, it's up to you. But I'm pretty sure they have an excellent sense of hearing." That finally shuts him up.

It looks like he's actually going to help me, so as we walk, I skim through the pages of the survival guides I found at the rebel house, trying to see if they can help. If we can't find antibiotic ointment, they suggest rinsing it in a saline solution, or even urine if we're desperate. Then, since it's not deep, keep re-bandaging it with clean bandages.

I find myself wishing that my parents were here. Either one of them would know what to do, I'm sure. Even Elliot would probably know, but he's not here either. Maybe, by some miracle, we could stumble across a doctor. Someone with some knowledge about this kind of stuff. As if to humor me, up ahead I can spot a man running toward us. I shove the books away and take out my gun just in case, as he yells something I can't understand. Ross and I come to a halt as the man bolts toward us, and as we point our guns in warning, I see that he isn't armed. He holds up his hands as if to surrender.

"Please, please help me! My baby. . .my son. . .we're desperate. Please!" His eyes are wild, his hands shaking. I should be thinking 'danger', but I feel a tug of compassion. As the man gets on his knees to beg, I don't move. How can I find it in me to threaten someone that has a child they're trying to keep alive? An innocent child doesn't deserve the pain and difficulty of this world. The man's eyes fill with tears. My gun is up only for defense. I'm about to ask him what he wants when Ross fires, sending a bullet straight through the man's skull.

THIRTY-EIGHT

Shock. Anger. Fear. So many emotions run through me at once that I almost drop my gun. The man's lifeless body crumples to my feet, and my legs go numb.

"H-how could you?" I gasp out, glaring at Ross. His face is completely calm until he hears me, and only then does his anger return.

"How could I? How could you not?" He yells back.

"He wasn't armed!"

"Oh, really?" Ross pulls out a knife from the man's back pocket.

"We clearly had the upper hand. We had no reason to kill him." I protest.

"We had every reason to kill him."

"He needed help!"

"For what?"

"For his child-"

"What child?" Ross throws his arms in the air, waving his gun around as if to show me how alone we are. "What kind of father leaves his child, even if it's to get help?" I'm silent for a moment. He has a point, but I know I do too.

"Maybe the baby is with the mother."

"No wedding ring."

"Maybe they weren't married."

"Maybe there is no child. Maybe he was looking for the only way he thought he would ever be able to overtake us." Ross's face is red from shouting at me.

"So, what? He lies about having a baby so that he can get. . .food, or whatever. And we give it to him. Big deal! We didn't have to kill him." I emphasize every word in that last sentence.

"I'm sure they don't teach you this in the Reserve, but out here, it's 'shoot first, ask questions later'. If you don't do that, you're dead." He sneers at me.

"No, that's not how everyone out here operates." I snap, just knowing that most of the rebels I met would never think that way. They wouldn't have shot right on the spot. They would have waited until they knew for sure the man was a threat.

"Yes, it is!" He argues. "Sorry to burst your bubble, but not everyone in this world is a goddamn ray of sunshine. I've heard about these things happening before. Outsiders claim they have children in order for you to get your guard down. Or they use their children to lure you. Plenty of them know how to put on an act. It's an easy way for them to get what they want if they don't have guns."

"If he pulled that knife on us, we could have easily shot him down. Two against one. He wouldn't risk that."

"So then he leads us into an ambush and then we die." Ross shoves me aside. "So you need to get your stupid supplies and get back to the house before somebody comes looking for him." He crosses the street to a supermarket, and I follow without any further arguing, half tempted to pick up one of the rocks on the side of the road and hurl it at him as hard as I can. I kind of want to tear down every building around here to find the supposed baby, but I know it's no use. Even if I'm right, I have a lot of other people to worry about, as well as myself. Rebecca's words echo in my head: You can't save everybody.

As expected, we find nothing. And by that I mean I find nothing. I searched the whole store while Ross stood guard at the door. I do manage to find a jar of salt, though, and I take that with me. Even with that, I don't really see how it's going to help, but I'm no expert on things like this. If a book says it'll help, I'll take the chance.

Ross and I don't speak on the way back. The sun is nearly overhead now, baking the asphalt below us. Taking out my water bottle, I drink slowly and conservatively before handing the water to Ross. He, of course, drinks too much before wordlessly handing it back. Water; yet another thing to worry about. All I have left is this bottle, since I stupidly didn't think to look for any more at the rebel house. All I can hope for is that Garret has plenty, and whether he does or not, I hope we find a source of water soon.

I'm also worried about an Émigré ship flying overhead or one of those dog creatures jumping out at us. Not only because I'll have to run or fight for my life, but because Ross will know something's up. If we survive, he'll tell me he's never seen the ships this far out, or that he's never seen the creatures before, yet I somehow knew how to kill one. And I don't know what explanation I could give other than the truth.

"You have no idea how much I hate you right now," Ross mutters as the house gets within view up ahead.

"Gee, thanks," I reply dryly.

"Truth is, I wasn't even going to leave with you guys. I was gonna steal your shit while you slept and then bolt. But if I hurt you, then I hurt her. She'd never forgive me if something happened to you because of me."

"Why don't you just lie to her, like you did to us? Can't be that hard for you." I say as we walk into the house.

"That's the problem. I can't lie to her." His voice is raw with sincerity.

"There's hope for you yet, Ross Michaels." I snort, using his trademark false enthusiasm against him.

"When'd you get that mouth on you, Collins?" He hisses from behind me, following me up the stairs. "You used to be quiet."

"And you used to be reasonable." I bite back, walking into Garret's room. He looks the same as before, and I don't know if I should be relieved by that.

"He givin' you trouble?" Garret manages to get out, glaring at Ross. "Because I don't care if I'm on my deathbed. . .I'll shoot your brains out."

"I'll kill you before you can even get out of bed, asshole," Ross walks forward, but I step in between them.

"Enough." I hiss. "Get out."

"No thanks," Ross smirks. "If he dies, I want a front-row seat." Neither of us gives him the satisfaction of a reaction. I turn to Garret, readying myself to help him all I can. Placing my hand on his forehead, I check his temperature like my mother used to. He's burning up.

"Have you been staying hydrated?" I ask him.

"No, mom," He sighs, giving me a playful half smile. It only makes me think of my mother even more, and I have to take a moment to pull myself together.

"Well, stop being an idiot and drink up," I tell him, digging his water bottle out of his backpack and taking off the cap. He has this bottle and one more. I put the opening to his mouth and let him drink as much as he can. "I'm not really sure how to rinse your wound with a saline solution, but-"

"That's okay, I can do it." A familiar voice says, and I whip around to see Grace standing in the doorway, Brianna right behind her.

"Brianna!" Garret's face lights up so much he almost looks healthy. She gasps before grinning and laughing, running up to him. She takes both of his hands in hers and gives him a brief kiss on the lips.

"What the hell happened to you?" She looks him over, her smile faltering.

"I got skimmed by one of those lasers, and it's getting infected." I can tell he's working as hard as he can to make his voice sound as strong and as normal as possible for her.

"I can help treat it," Grace speaks up again, smiling softly at all of us.

"Yes, she can help you. I'll let her get to work." Brianna kisses him again before stepping aside.

"How did you find us?" I ask them as Grace makes her way toward him.

"We saw you and, uh, that guy," Brianna looks briefly over at Ross, who looks like a deer caught in headlights.

"Ross," He mumbles, waving awkwardly.

"Right, Ross . . . and we followed you inside. I didn't know who else was here, but this is better than anything I could have hoped for." She beams down at Garret, and I can't imagine the relief she feels, even if he is hurt.

"I'm gonna go throw up now," Ross leaves the room, but we barely notice.

"Damien was with me for a while," Garret tells Grace. "I'm sure he's fine." She nods slowly, her smile tight as she gently takes off his bandages and gets out the first aid kit I remember Elliot having back at the house.

"You guys went back to the house?" I glance at Brianna.

"Only once. Very briefly. We just got a few things and left. It was just me and Grace. We were with Angie and the others, but we got separated by a bunch of Émigré soldiers coming in. Ever since then we've been circling around the house in search of other rebels, but haven't found any." She says.

"We must have just missed you. Garret went back to the house, too. That's where I met up with him."

"Must have." She shakes her head as if this is all just a dream. "We weren't close to the house because we were afraid more soldiers would come up. But we kept around it just in case we spotted any rebels. When we saw nobody for long enough, we moved on to the base."

"So you know where it is?"

"Yeah. I went with Garret a few months ago."

"You two should get going, then," Garret says, meeting my eyes. "We don't have a lot of time." I know exactly what he's talking about. Soldiers and creatures are after us, surely closing in if we keep staying stationary.

"Brianna, you stay with Garret," I tell her, not having the heart to separate them. "I can go with Ross."

"I don't want him around you." Garret makes his voice louder.

"It's okay," I come up to the side of the bed, taking his hand again. "He won't hurt me." I give it a squeeze before letting go, trying to ignore the stinging of tears in my eyes.

"He better not."

"If he does hurt you, I'll kill him myself," Brianna yells loudly enough for Ross to hear when she sees that he's no longer in the room.

"Keep fighting." I try not to plead at Garret, keeping my voice neutral.

"You know I will." He smiles again, and I try to do the same.

I say goodbye to Brianna and Grace before my emotions can take over. Both of them hug me and tell me to stay safe, and then I'm out, grabbing Ross and dragging him out the door. We walk in silence once more, just the way I like it. It's hot, we're low on water, he despises me, but I don't care about any of it. All I do is think about Grace making Garret better, and the three of them going toward the base not long after us.

It doesn't take long until we're in the woods again. The heat is less harsh here, and I'm finally starting to relax. I clear out the memories of today and just focus on the ones that make me happy. Mary skipping out on 'the party of the year' to see my ballet recital. Annie saying my name right for the first time and saying it with such happiness. Callie and I riding our bikes in circles around the cul-de-sac, foolishly trying to eat our ice cream cones at the same time.

Unfortunately, my bliss doesn't last long. Ross starts demanding water, and that sets us off into another argument when I say we should conserve it. All I get is a sip when he snatches it from my hands and selfishly gulps down the rest of it. We spew hateful words back and forth until we're both starving and exhausted. The sun is setting, and I realize how long it's been since I've eaten and since I've slept as I collapse on the ground, feeling like I'm going to vomit up what little water I've consumed.

Eyes heavy and burning, I take out a can of tuna and force it down. It only makes me more thirsty, and I lay down in order to get some sleep and not think about it. Ross and I haven't even established who's keeping watch, but I'm so exhausted that sleep takes over before I can fully form a thought about the alien dogs that are after the rebels. When I wake up, groggy and dehydrated, the sun is back up and Ross is awake and keeping watch, his eyes just as paranoid as when I found him.

We walk again in silence, too thirsty to speak. It seems even hotter today, but I could be imagining that. Nothing comes our way. No Émigré soldiers, no alien dogs, no outsiders. I haven't even seen any regular animals, like rabbits and squirrels. It's like the heat has made it impossible for any living thing to do anything.

Sometimes, the heat makes my eyes play tricks on me. One minute I think I'm seeing my mother, the next minute it's just some tall grass blowing in the hot breeze that gives no relief. Then I think I see my father, but when I blink, he's gone. The worst is when I think I've spotted water, and I perk up just enough to see that it wasn't water rippling up ahead that I saw, but the heat causing the air to sizzle.

Night falls once more, and this time I keep watch. Nothing out of the ordinary happens. It's all too good to be true. Maybe they've seen how pathetic we are and don't want to waste their time, preferring that we just die off on our own. When we go forward the next morning, our pace is so slow that even the slowest and weakest of children could probably overtake us.

We've walked for so long that I'm not even sure Ross knows where we are until we pass the red barn that Garret was talking about. Ross continues to lead the way, and I'm praying that we come across a stream or that it starts raining. But all the land we pass is dry as a bone, and there isn't a cloud in the sky. I can barely swallow, and I'm so out of it that I barely notice movement behind a tree ahead of me. But then, whatever is behind it steps out into the open. I see the unmistakable tousled mess of chestnut hair as an unforgettable pair of dark blue eyes meets mine.

THIRTY-NINE

"Tyler. . ." I breathe, almost not believing that I'd finally found him. That he's actually real and in front of me. Maybe he's just a vision. Maybe I'm still just that out of it. But when I hear Ross mumble and raise his gun, I know he's really there. Without even thinking, I'm running up to him as fast as my legs can carry me, the memory of him leaving me far back in my mind. He's alive and free, and surely there are other rebels who are also alive and free. I throw my arms around him. His body stiffens in surprise. But unlike what I expected, after a moment, he embraces me back.

"Rachel," he laughs in disbelief, clutching me as if he can't believe I'm real, either. As if he'd been worried that I'd been captured. Or that I'd been killed. For the first time since meeting Tyler, I realized I actually had a friend. I'd had a real friend in him all along and I didn't know it. Or I didn't want to believe it. But as good as it feels to have found someone so familiar and to know that he was okay, I can't help but notice the scent of soap on his skin, knowing that, on the contrary, I smell like sweat and dirt.

"So, you made it to the other rebel base," I state as we pull away, feeling even more relieved when he nods. The thought of finally getting a bath almost edges out everything else, but not quite.

"It's not too far from here. I can take you guys. How are you? Are you hurt? Do you need anything?"

"Water," is all I say, and he gets it out in seconds. I drink way too fast, trying to refrain from sighing in relief, but I can't help it. Not slowing down, I end up choking and sputtering water all over myself. I'm a mess, but too drained to care.

"I was really angry at you, you know. I still am." I add as I hand him back the water bottle, amazed at how good I feel now. It's like I'm snapping out of a daze, my whole body coming back to life. "It may not seem like it, but I am." All of my anger is just getting edged out with the relief I feel to have him in front of me and to have water back in my system. But I can feel some sadness coming back.

"I know. I'm an idiot." He shakes his head, and I'm thankful he's not being sarcastic. He looks like he's genuinely frustrated with himself and thinks he made a mistake.

"You just left me." I look up at him, although he doesn't meet my gaze. "You didn't listen to anything I had to say and you just-"

"COLLINS!" a voice bellows, and I turn to find Alfie, Rebecca, and Elliot running toward me, grinning from ear to ear. Happiness bubbles so quickly inside of me that I find myself laughing in relief and joy. I run up to meet them and they all hug me at once, almost knocking me over.

"Oh, great. More people." Ross mutters, and as the group lets go of me, I see him give a fake smile. I shoot him a glare, stepping between him and the other rebels.

"Who's this?" Rebecca speaks up hesitantly.

"Guys, this is Ross. He's from the rebel base we're going to. Ross, this is- " I start, but he interrupts me.

"I don't care about them." He rolls his eyes as he continues walking.

"Glad to see you made such a good friend." Alfie doesn't bother to keep his voice down as he speaks to me, and I don't hide my laughter.

Ross keeps going, and I let him go, not wanting to deal with him any longer. The lighthearted mood fades when I tell them about Garret. But I also tell them about Brianna and Grace being alive and helping him, along with the fact that the dogs from the Reserve are after us, and we don't waste any time getting to the base. After walking for what seems to be around 20 minutes, I can see some guards up ahead. I know we're close.

"Give me your gun," Tyler whispers as he suddenly walks up next to me.

"What?" I look at him in confusion.

"You still have it, right?" He holds out his hand.

"Yes," I don't hand it over. I'm not in the mood for him telling me about how I shouldn't have a gun again.

"Well, if you want to keep it, give it to me. You weren't with us when we left, so they're going to search you and take any weapons they find." He looks sincere, and with a sigh, I reluctantly give it to him. A few moments later, two guards meet us halfway.

"Welcome back," the male guard says, waving them through but holding his hand up to stop me. The female guard checks every inch of me before digging through my bag and confiscating my knife.

"Sorry. You understand, right? It's just for now." She offers me a small smile but doesn't wait for my response. I hurry after the others, who decided to wait for me. Ignoring Tyler, I walk beside Elliot. I don't want Tyler to think that helping me out like he did just now means that he's in the clear for leaving me behind. He has to know from me that he shouldn't have done that.

This new house is even bigger than the last one, bustling with people who are all busy with something. Some are throwing knives and shooting guns at targets, just like we used to. Others are practicing hand-to-hand combat. There's even a group of children playing tag, one of the adults shooing them away from the training ground when they get too close. Seeing even more people inside the house, I can't hide my smile. This is what an army looks like. This is what a home looks like.

"Don't you want this back?" Tyler asks me as he taps my shoulder.

"Who, me?" I turn around, attempting to look baffled. "Are you sure I'm responsible enough?" My voice is full of sarcasm.

"Yes," He responds as he hands me the gun. "I'm really sorry, Rachel. I truly am." His eyes look like they're pleading with me to believe him, and it catches me a bit off guard. I slow down just enough so that he's walking beside me.

"I forgive you. But don't be surprised if I'm angry for a while." I tell him before running to catch up with Rebecca and have her show me where I can take a bath. I don't know how long I can avoid Tyler in a place like this, but I'll do my best to try.

FORTY

After bathing, I feel better than I have since I was at the Reserve, where warm showers were always at our disposal. I get new clothes to change into, clean water to drink, and even some crackers and peanut butter to snack on while Rebecca shows me where I'll be sleeping. It's just a mattress in a room full of other mattresses already claimed, but I'm relieved to know I'll only be sharing this room with other girls. It's like I've been offered a free stay at a five-star luxury hotel.

She also introduces me to the owner, Ralph Peterson: a tall, broad-shouldered man with a long beard who shakes my hand with a firm grip. Then I'm free to sleep. When I do wake up, it's because Rebecca wanted to let me know that dinner was ready for anyone who wanted it. Still hungry, I head downstairs and fix myself a plate of meat and vegetables, also making sure that I get a huge glass of water. I take my meal and go back upstairs, avoiding any possible interaction with Ross or Tyler. To my surprise, a young girl is already seated on the mattress next to mine, picking at her food.

"Hello," I say cautiously, sitting on my mattress. She looks at me and then grins.

"Hi! You're new." She looks older than Annie. . .more around the age of Jacob, maybe even older. And I can already tell she's much more extroverted than the both of them.

"Yeah, I'm Rachel. What's your name?"

"Ava," she replies, eating a tiny piece of meat.

"Do you always eat up here by yourself?" I ask her, looking at the rest of the empty mattresses. Memories of Jacob hit me like a train, and I mask the shudder of sadness in my voice by pretending that the food I'm eating is too hot. Trying to avoid people and eat my meals alone always seems to have me end up talking to a kid. A kid who deserves so much better than the world the Émigrés have given them.

"Not always. My friends don't like eating up here, so they eat down there. Sometimes it's too crowded down there, though. I like it up here. If my mom's not busy, she joins me."

"What would your mom be busy with?"

"She teaches. Lots of things. And she helps cook the meals."

"Impressive," I say, taking a moment to eat more of my food. I notice that Ava's wearing a pink cotton dress, and has a light pink ribbon in her hair. Both are a little dirty, which is expected, but they still remind me of pre-invasion life. I haven't seen colorful clothes in years. "You like pink?" I give her a smile.

"Yup, it's my favorite!" She nods enthusiastically.

"I like pink, too," I tell her, which motivates her to get up and abandon her food. She walks over to one of four dressers in the room, pulling out a small pink bag and getting out a ribbon that matches the one in her hair.

"Here," she proclaims, handing it to me. "We can be twins!" That earns a laugh out of me, but I tie it in a bow in my ponytail without hesitation.

"Twins," I smile, and to my surprise, she hugs me.

"I like you. Not all the older girls are this nice to me." She says as she lets me go. My heart sinks.

"Well, they should be," I assure her, but she just shrugs.

"It's okay. I have my friends, and they have theirs. Oh, you should meet them!" She gets up again, pulling me up.

"Okay," I laugh again, hurriedly finishing my food as she drags me out. We've only just stepped out the front door when Ross cuts me off.

"We need to talk." He demands, glaring down at Ava as if she were the cause of all his problems. Ava doesn't seem to be affected by it at all, though, and I decide I like her, too.

"Later," I tell him, already knowing what this is about. If he's still angry, it's just as I feared. Callie isn't here.

"No, now," He growls, gripping my arm so tight I let go of Ava's hand.

"Ava," I keep my voice calm and light. "Why don't you go meet up with your friends? I'll join you in a bit."

"Okay," she says, and I hear her run off. As soon as she's gone, Ross lets go.

"Callie's not here." He confirms what I already suspected.

"What do you want me to do about it?" I take a step back.

"I don't know!" He's yelling again. "Maybe you could-"

"Ross Andrew Michaels!" A female voice shouts, making him immediately go silent and pale.

"Mom," Ross says quietly as Mrs. Michaels marches up to him.

"How many times do I have to tell you not to leave our sight? Your father and I are already missing one child. We don't need to be missing two again. You can't just go running off like that!" She lectures, oblivious to me standing there. "You keep running off as if this family hasn't been through enough."

"But Callie," Ross starts, but Mrs. Michaels isn't having any of it as Mr. Michaels approaches us.

"We're working on getting a team together to find her. I told you. We're going to find her together!"

"Yeah, well, if it takes you any longer, don't be surprised if she's dead!" Ross storms off, leaving Mrs. Michaels sighing in frustration as her husband rubs her shoulders.

"Jim, could you get him?" She tells him, and I can hear the sadness in her voice even as she sees me. When he leaves, she embraces me.

"Hello, Rachel," she greets me, and nostalgia hits me so hard I'm nearly in tears.

"Hi, Mrs. Michaels. I'm so sorry about Callie." I tell her, and she nods, knowing I mean more than that. Her eyes and hair match Callie's so perfectly that it feels like I can't get enough air in my lungs.

"That's my daughter, always doing things without thinking." She lets out a shaky laugh. "I'm glad you're safe. How are your mother and sisters? I haven't heard anything about them."

"They're okay," I reply. Maybe it's a lie, maybe it isn't, but she doesn't need anything more to worry about.

"Good. I hope they find your father soon. Excuse me," she heads off to find her son, leaving me standing alone in the front yard.

I know exactly what I need. A distraction. Anything to take my mind off things. Some kind of job would be nice. Like back at the rebel house, when I would clean even when there was nothing left to clean. A distraction and a way to help out, all in one. I don't see Ralph anywhere, but I think I know where I can find something. Going back into the woods, I keep walking until I find the guards from earlier.

"Hey," I call out to them, making sure I'm walking loudly enough not to startle them. "Is there any way I could help guard this place? I want to help out."

"Can you shoot?" The girl says in an almost bored voice.

"Yes," I reply. I don't tell them that my skill level is under par, though.

"Sold." She says, practically ready to break out into a run back to the house before the male guard stops her.

"We confiscated your weapons for a reason. You're new here. We don't exactly trust you, right Erin?" He stares angrily down at the girl.

"Whatever," she rolls her eyes.

"Well, if you guard with me, you can make sure I don't do anything stupid," I tell him. His eyes narrow as he seems to consider this. After all, I did come in here with bona fide rebels that at least somewhat trusted me.

"Fine. Don't make me regret this, uh. . ." He's waiting for me to say my name, I realize, so I tell him. "Rachel. I'm Chris. You can start tomorrow morning at dawn." The girl groans loudly at the fact that I won't be relieving her of her current shift. But to my surprise, she casually slips my pocket knife back into my hand before I leave.

FORTY-ONE

I find Ava again, and she introduces me to some girls and boys around her age, but I'm not really paying attention, my mind elsewhere. Pushing that aside, I play duck-duck-goose with them for a little while, before deciding that I should do some training. I don't know when anyone plans on leaving to find the mothership, but knowing all the danger that looms overhead, it has to be soon.

Of course, it seems like everywhere I try to go, Tyler is there. When I go to the targets, he's there throwing knives. When I check out the area of dirt where they practice combat, he's practicing against a guy close to his height and weight. Even when the sun sets and I go out back to find somewhere to relax, he's there, talking to the guy he was fighting with earlier. I almost think he's doing this to spite me, but each time, he never noticed me before I left.

Thankfully, I finally run into Elliot, who I realize I'm eager to talk to. We have to go into the woods if we want privacy, and we end up just sitting with our backs against a tree with a trunk wide enough to support us both.

"So, how have you been?" He asks me.

The response 'good' automatically comes to my lips after years of unintentionally perfecting the bland art of small talk, but he and I both know how pointless of a lie that is. I tell him about everything that happened the moment I left the Reserve after Jacob was killed. Everything except for the traitor. I want to tell him so badly, but I know that if word gets out, things won't end well. It's not that I think he'd go blurting this out, but I promised Garret I wouldn't tell anyone else.

I find that I do still trust Elliot. Maybe it's the wrong choice, but I don't think he betrayed us, and I can't imagine his blue eyes suddenly morphing into violet or anything like that. But I can just imagine him wanting to tell the other rebels from the house about the traitor, maybe even trying to figure out who it is on his own. And then somehow, other people overhear, and panic breaks out. Elliot's smarter than anyone I've met since I first joined the rebels, but he can't control what people hear and how they react.

"How have you been?" I ask when I'm finished catching him up on what happened to me.

"Well, Molly and I got out of the Reserve fine, but when we saw that the house was being attacked, we abandoned the hover and came straight here. We didn't have any problems. No outsiders, no Émigrés, no dog creatures. We were just low on food and water."

"You abandoned your hover? Why?" It seems like the most counter-productive decision, abandoning the one thing that would get you to your destination faster.

"We always suspected that there would be some kind of tracking device in them, like there are in the ID bracelets you get at the Reserve. That's why we didn't store them near the house, and why I've found out they don't use hovers here. Maybe they do have trackers in them, maybe they don't. We didn't want to risk it."

"But if they were tracking them, they could have just attacked the house a long time ago."

"My train of thought is they didn't think they had any reason to," He begins. "Until-"

"Until we showed up in the Reserve and they thought we were

trying to revolt." I finish, and he nods. "How do you think they figured out we were there? Did you see anything that would have given us away?"

"No," He shakes his head. "I already talked to the others. Everyone here seemed to be really shocked that we got caught because before that alarm went off, everything was fine."

"Who all is here?" I ask, realizing I never made the effort to see who made it and who was still missing.

"Besides me, there's, as I said, Molly, and then Tyler, Alfie, Rebecca, and Damien." That means Marcus, Angie, Cole, Kira, and anyone else from that house are still missing.

"Damien? I haven't seen him at all." I state.

"Apparently, he tore up the woods looking for Grace. When he couldn't find her, he just assumed she came here, so he came here as fast as he could. I think he hardly ever ate, drank, or slept. He's still recovering and was actually getting ready to go back out to look for her when we found out from you that she was okay and would be on her way."

"I hope they make it." I admit.

"I think they will. Even with Garret hurt, Brianna can make up for whatever he lacks. And Grace can easily take care of them both." Elliot says confidently. After a few moments of silence, I turn to hug him.

"I missed you," I say.

"I missed you, too," He smiles at me.

"Did you get to see your parents in the Reserve?" I want to know that the mission had at least one positive thing for him.

"I did." He assures me. "When the alarm went off, I made sure that they promised they'd stay in their house and wouldn't leave no matter what. I don't know if they followed that, but generally, they trust my judgment."

"What do you think is happening to our families right now?" I can barely ask the question. But I feel like if Elliot is thinking positively and says they're fine, my mind will assure me they are because

I'll tell myself he's smart, so he must be right. Except he doesn't pretend for me.

"I don't like to think about that." He says, forcing his smile now. "Let's go back to the house."

When we go back, I see that no one's really at the combat section anymore, now that the sun is almost completely down. I take the opportunity to get some training, and the two trainers, Travis and Maria, don't cut me any slack for being a beginner. I practice with Rebecca, learning the best way to utilize my body when someone tries to attack me. I'm quick and I have endurance, but I lack strength, so my best bet is to go for fast, hard strikes in my enemy's most vulnerable areas, like the groin and the stomach, and even the backs of the knees. We work for a long time, only calling it quits when we can no longer see in the darkness. Eager for more rest, I go back to the room to find Ava and a few others already there, fast asleep. I quietly get to my mattress and let the sleep pull me under once again.

I don't remember having any nightmares, but when Erin comes to shake me awake, I'm covered in sweat and breathing heavily. Luckily for me, though, it doesn't seem to have woken anyone else up, including Ava.

"Up and at 'em, princess," She yawns before crawling back to her mattress and promptly falling back asleep. I head out into the woods, not bothering to change clothes for fear of waking someone else up. When I get to the gate I'm supposed to guard, Chris isn't there yet. I wait patiently but nervously, taking out my knife. The sun has lightened up the woods by the time I hear someone coming. When I turn around, it's not Chris I see. It's Tyler.

"Where's Chris?" I demand, not hiding my anger.

"Don't look at me like that. It's not like I want to be here." He scowls at me, handing me the gun that Erin had. "Guess Chris and Erin decided to both take the day off."

"Guess so." I refuse to look at him now, training my eyes on the woods up ahead. It could be worse. They could have sent Damien or Ross.

Neither of us says anything, but as the minutes pass, I realize just how boring this job is when no danger is present. No wonder Erin was quick to leave. There's nothing interesting about staring into the woods, waiting for something to happen. I start counting the number of trees past the fence, only getting to 6 before Tyler speaks up.

"What happened to you? I mean, after I left you." He asks uncomfortably.

"Oh, nothing really," I answer vaguely, still not looking at him.

"I heard what you said about finding Garret and killing one of those alien dogs, but I know there's more than that. Something happened, or more than one thing happened. I don't know. But I can see it in your eyes and it's worrying me." To be completely honest, keeping all these things that only Garret knows from everyone else is eating me up inside. I'm half tempted to blurt it all out anyway, but it's not Tyler I want to tell it all to.

"What you're seeing," I begin in a measured voice. "Is me being angry at you, still, and worrying about Garret, along with Grace and Brianna. That's all."

"You sure about that?" His voice is practically oozing from the fact that he doesn't believe me.

"I'm positive," I say firmly.

"Then how'd you end up with Ross? What was he doing out there?" There's so much that happened between the moment he kicked me off the hover to the moment I got here that I wonder how long I can actually keep this stuff from him, and if it's actually worth it. He'll probably catch on, eventually. Nothing gets past him.

"He was looking for his sister. We found him in the first house we took shelter in."

"And he just brought you back without her?"

"Alright, listen," I snap, finally looking at him. "A lot happened. It's none of your business. But if you're really that nosy, Ross is my best friend's older brother. She left here looking for me after she heard the Émigrés had my dad. No one knows where she is, so he hates me. Happy?"

"I'm sorry," He says again. I don't need his pity.

"Yeah, I heard you the first time." I roll my eyes, looking back at the woods again. He knows there's more to my story, and there is, but I won't tell him.

"Look, I haven't been treating you like I should have. I know that now." He lets out a deep breath before continuing. "I felt like I circled that house a million times looking for you. I thought maybe you'd found other rebels and made it here, but when you weren't, we all wanted to go out and find you and the other rebels. But people assured us that if we stayed put, you guys would start showing up soon. That day we found you was the day we couldn't take it anymore and decided to go looking for you guys."

"The hell's wrong with you, Forester?" Chris's voice shouts as he comes up to us, confronting Tyler. "You practically begged me for my spot and insisted that you would do a good job, and I come here to check on you only to see you running your mouth and not paying attention to a damn thing. Are you sure you even have the brains to do this job?" I do everything I can to hide my laughter as Tyler's cheeks flush.

"Yes, sir," Tyler keeps his voice strong.

"Idiot," Chris mutters under his breath before walking away. "If I catch either of you two fooling around again, you can forget about ever guarding this place!" He calls out to us. When he's finally gone and I look at Tyler again, I can't hold in my laughter any longer.

"I thought you said you were forced to be here," I smirk at him. He just frowns at me.

"I guess we both tell lies to each other now." His voice is cold, and he goes to his spot at the other end of the gate. This time he's the one not looking at me.

FORTY-TWO

As my shift goes on, I think about when I first saw Tyler in the woods the other day and he gave me water. I was so certain he was a friend. I was so blissfully happy and relieved and ready to start functioning normally. But then reality comes back and I just want to be as far away from him as possible. Are we friends? There are things he's done for me that suggest we are, but I've done nothing for him. All I have to show for it is being upset at the thought of him being dead and being happy to find him alive.

In the grand scheme of things, it doesn't actually matter if we are or not. It won't determine the fate of humanity, the fate of my family, the fate of me. It won't put an end to Émigrés or outsiders. But for some reason, I'm still curious. The old me would have called everyone I met my friend. Now I'm not even sure if I have any actual friends here other than Elliot, possibly.

Whatever Tyler is to me, I'm starting to understand him. When people hurt me, I push them away. I think it's a pretty natural response to protect yourself from getting hurt again. But he pushes people away before they even have a chance to hurt him once. He doesn't even want one scratch and will do anything to keep it that way, but eventually, he'll get hurt, anyway. That's the way life is.

I remember how much it broke him to see Jacob die. It hurt him more than it would ever have hurt me. It was clear as day on his face and in his voice. How in the world could he have been the traitor I saw? How could I think I couldn't trust him? I can be angry all I want at what he's done, but that's no excuse to label him a traitor. I clear my throat to get his attention.

"I have some stuff of yours. That I got from the house." I keep my voice low and my eyes straight, just in case Chris is hiding in a tree or something ridiculous.

"Like what?" I hear him mumble.

"Skittles. And your notebook."

Silence.

"Don't worry, I didn't-" I start, but I hear footsteps and immediately shut my mouth.

"Looks like you two aren't completely worthless. You're done for the day, free to go." Chris says as he and Erin take their guns back from us. We walk back side by side, and when we're out of earshot, I speak again.

"I didn't eat any of the Skittles, and I only read the beginning of the notebook. Your photos are in there too." I dig his stuff out of my bag and hand it over. He stares at them for a few moments before putting them away, and I have no idea what he's thinking.

"You better not have read it all. I don't say very nice things about you." I can't tell if that was a joke, but neither of us are angry anymore.

"I don't know if you're being serious, but now I want to read it all," I admit with a small laugh.

"Guess you'll never know." He smirks, zipping his bag up tightly for effect. And I know that just like at the rebel house, he'll keep it somewhere safe. Where I'll never find it unless I tear the place apart. "Thank you, though. You didn't have to do that."

"It wasn't a big deal." I shrug. "I got Elliot's book, too. Since no one showed up, I figured I could bring people's personal stuff back to them if I found anything." Without a doubt, he knows those items would have also been a way to remember them if they were dead. We're approaching the house now, and I can see Damien walking out the front door, looking exhausted but still having the energy to launch some fresh insults our way.

"Ah, my favorite pair of idiots. Nice ribbon, Newbie. Did your mom pick it out for you?" His way of insulting is so childlike that it doesn't even dent me, even with my mom probably in danger in the Reserve. It's exactly like the way Mary used to tease me when we were younger and not as close, so I respond like I always would have with her.

"No, I stole it from you. I hope you don't mind." My tone is good-natured, unlike his hostile one, and he rolls his eyes in response as if he can't stand the sight of us. He walks off without another word to wherever he was headed in the first place. Seconds later, Molly runs out the door, tears streaming down her cheeks despite the smile on her lips.

"What's going on?" Tyler asks her, but she doesn't answer, just keeps running.

We turn to see where she's going and my stomach catches at the sight. Up ahead are Cole, Kira, Angie, and. . .Marcus. Just seeing him sends a chill straight down my spine. Tyler goes to meet them, but I can't move. I can't take my eyes off him, and it's like my mind is tele-pathically demanding him questions I'd never dare to ask out loud. Was it you? Did you betray us? Why did you do it? How could you possibly do it? If you did, do you know you caused the death of an innocent child and so many others? What did they have on you that made you do it?

Molly's embracing her mother as Damien and Tyler greet Cole and Kira with smiles and hugs. Tyler shakes Marcus's hand and they pat each other's backs. I'm reminded of how much I'm keeping from him. Cole meets my gaze and nods at me, and Kira offers a smile which I'm sure is a rarity, but I can hardly smile back. The second I lock eyes with Marcus, I force myself away from my dazed thoughts and go inside the house.

I find Elliot and give him his book, relaxing a little at his surprise and elation. He thanks me repeatedly, and it gets easier for me to act like everything is fine, but something in my gut says that whatever amount of time we thought we had before the Émigrés closed in has dramatically reduced. There's no sense in keeping what I know from him and Tyler anymore. I decide that I'll tell them both tonight, when the sky gets dark and things quiet down, and we can finally get privacy. I don't plan on telling anyone else, knowing that it's up to them if they trust anyone enough to tell them.

Maybe I'm overreacting, and Marcus has nothing to do with what's been happening. I should have known how I would react if he ever showed up here, but a part of me was hoping he would never show up, and I could assume he was captured or dead. I could assume, with some confidence, that he isn't who I have to be afraid of. I wish Garret was here. He would understand exactly how I feel and talk me out of doing anything stupid. He would probably tell me it was okay to tell Tyler and Elliot, because I know he trusts them. And he's the only person here who has any idea what these past few days out in the Ruins have been like for me.

FORTY-THREE

AFTER SPENDING SOME TIME ON MY MATTRESS, TRYING TO SHUT out the snores of other girls napping or their hushed conversations, the house feels like it's suffocating me. I go out to get some air, almost instinctively glancing at the sky to see if any ships are flying overhead. When I bring my eyes back down to earth, I see Ross up ahead, looking like he's trying to take his mind off of things by flirting with a girl. He's got his arm around her, oozing the confidence I remember him having before the invasion. When I get closer to them, I catch their conversation.

"I'm in the mood for some Chinese takeout, if you know what I mean." His voice is so arrogant it's nauseating.

"For the 800th time, I'm Japanese and not interested, you moron." She snaps, and without hesitation, she elbows him in the stomach. He lets go of her, doubling over and letting out a stifled groan.

"Thank you for that." I can't help but say to her as she walks by me. She grins, giving me a nod.

"No problem. Does he bother you, too? I can give him a kick where the sun don't shine if you'd like."

"No," I shake my head while a laugh slips past my lips. "He just hates me."

"Well, anyone Ross hates is a friend of mine." She says sincerely, but with a playful smirk, holding out her hand. "I'm Olivia."

"Rachel," I tell her, shaking it. Ross walks by us, muttering under his breath until Olivia gives him a look that silences him again.

"You know, if you're looking for any kind of hair or body products, I've got a ton. Well, my friend Alana and I do. Shampoo, conditioner, different scented soaps, even a few bottles of nail polish that haven't completely dried out yet." She winks at me before heading off into the house as I tell her thanks.

It's interesting. Some people scavenge candy. Some scavenge books. And others scavenge beauty products. Whatever they can find that will give them a sense of comfort and normalcy. What would I scavenge? All I really miss besides family and friends is ballet, and I haven't exactly stumbled across a dance studio.

I walk around the territory, pretending like I actually have somewhere to be, even though I'm just exploring. There's so many people here that I don't think I could remember all of their names, even if I actually tried. By now, I'm sure word's gone around about what happened in the Reserve, and plans are being made. I'm surprised Ross hasn't confronted me again. Maybe he doesn't know, but I doubt that. Releasing all his anger on me must not be enough anymore.

"What'cha looking at?" Ava's voice interrupts me, and I look down to find her marching forward.

"Just the house. This whole place, really. It's huge." I admit, falling into pace with her.

"That's the way my dad wanted it. He always thought something like this would happen, and he was right." She says proudly. I don't need to be told in order to make the connection that Ralph is her father.

"What are you up to?" I ask her.

"We're playing hide-and-seek. I'm the seeker."

"Well, I better leave you to it." I smile.

"Ok, see ya!" She runs off.

I continue to walk around, clearing my head and taking everything around me in. It's a bit funny for me that I seem to move from one enclosed space to another, always assuming that it's where I'll stay and have at least some safety, and always having that proved wrong. I can't allow myself to get comfortable here. No matter how perfect this place seems, with its frolicking children and army of guards, there is always a flaw. I have to be ready to bolt when the danger unveils itself.

I know what I have to do now. I go to the room I share with other girls and pack my bag. Food, water, my weapons, and anything first-aid related that I can get my hands on. This time I'll be ready at a moment's notice. When it all goes to hell, I can take off and have everything I need. The surrounding girls don't pay any attention, but when someone calls my name, I stop packing and look up.

"There's something I should have told you when we spoke earlier," Elliot says quietly as he stands in the doorway. I must look confused and worried because he quickly adds to that when I go up to him. "It's nothing major. I just didn't think it was important until now. But no one else can know about it." The last sentence is a whisper.

"There's something I should have told you, too." I admit, walking with him. "I also want to tell Tyler."

"He's off on a run. Not a supply run, just a training run. I've already told him what I'm going to tell you."

We get to the tree we met at before, and Elliot gets right into it as soon as we sit down.

"You know those silver guns the Émigrés use?" He asks, and I nod. "I've never even touched one before, and neither has anyone in the rebel house. At least as far as I know. But at the Reserve, I grabbed one as a last resort and fired it at another soldier. It worked perfectly for me."

As soon as those words slip past his lips, my world starts to crash. I couldn't use that gun. My mother couldn't. Garret couldn't. We'd all established in our minds that no human could. But the traitor could. This is exactly what I've been trying so hard to deny. I told myself over and over that Elliot was my friend, that I could trust him, that he would never do this. Was I really that wrong?

"I didn't think there was anything unusual about that." He continues, and he's gauging my reaction, so I have to do everything in my power to stay as composed as possible despite my pounding heart and the aching in my chest. "But then I talked to some other rebels about what happened in there. Damien said Garret wasn't able to use an Émigré gun. Tyler told me that he saw you couldn't use them and neither could your mother. I don't know exactly what this means, whether it's a malfunction or something else entirely, but we could use this to our advantage if we could get a hold of those guns again. Unfortunately, I don't still have that gun, because I put it up at the last minute to defend myself from one of those dogs, who bit it and then tossed it to the side. I only got away because an Émigré soldier was knocked into it and it was interested in eating them rather than me for a few moments."

"Those dogs. . .they ate Émigrés too?" It's the only sentence I can allow myself to speak. It was just a malfunction, I tell myself. A malfunction. A harmless mistake. Malfunction. But what if it wasn't? What if he's just telling me this because he knew I'd find out eventually, and it would have been suspicious if I didn't hear this from him? No, don't panic. Breathe. He will notice a knitted brow, a flushed cheek, a sheen of sweat on the forehead, a look of fear in my eyes. Breathe. Think of home, real home. Mom, dad, Mary, Annie.

"Yes. They seemed to be starved beyond imagination." Elliot's voice sounds far away, and I struggle not to slip away like I did at the Divide.

Deep breath. Calm thoughts. Speak.

"The one that attacked Garret and me. . .it wasn't like that. It wasn't hungry. It was like it was looking for us to destroy us, and that's it. It didn't care about anybody else." I tell him, my fists clenched so tight behind my back that I think my nails might have pierced my palms.

Friend. Ally. Human.

Traitor. Enemy. Alien.

"Maybe they don't let their prey get away. Maybe the Émigrés have full control of what they do. I don't know." Elliot sighs before looking at me. He doesn't even look the same in my eyes anymore. A face that once seemed so young and friendly looks completely foreign and untrustworthy now.

Marcus. Think of Marcus. The one we knew we could point fingers at. It's him, it has to be him. It won't hurt if it's him. Maybe we all pulled the trigger wrong and Elliot just happened to figure things out like he always does. Maybe I'm just overthinking myself to the point of insanity, and that's what will destroy me. What if I'm wrong? What if I'm right?

"What is it you wanted to tell me?" He interrupts my thoughts, looking at me expectantly. With no control left, I stammer.

"Oh, um," Is it the right move to tell him, or not tell him? If he was the traitor, wouldn't he expect me to tell him? I shouldn't feel thankful when I hear the snap of a twig behind us, but I do. Someone or something isn't as quiet as they should be when they sneak around. Our eyes widen in shared surprise as we peek around the tree, but nothing is there. "We should go. It can wait." I tell him, and to my relief, he agrees and follows me out.

I'm now desperate for someone to confide in. I want Garret and Brianna more than anything in the world, and I would beg to have Callie, but with none of them here, I would settle for the one person who doesn't fit the bill as a traitor. Tyler. My luck runs out though because I can't find him. And no one seems to know where he is at the moment.

It hurts for me to feel like I can't trust the other rebels, but would they blame me if they knew? If the traitor is Elliot, it's possible that Alfie and Rebecca might be on his side. It's possible that anyone could be, but I feel like I can rule out Angie, Molly, Damien, Grace, and Tyler because of how long they've been in the Ruins. They've been on the run since day one and helped establish the group that would work to bring the Émigrés down. All they have left is each other, whereas the others have loved ones confined in the grasp of the Émigrés.

I need answers to all these questions swimming in my head, but I know I'm not going to find any right now. The rest of the day slips through my fingers, and I vaguely remember eating meals and not finding Tyler. It's getting late. I'm supposed to be in bed to get some rest before my shift. Going toward the bedroom, I prepare myself to have nightmares about violet eyes, only to see someone blocking the doorway.

It's Grace.

I'll never get enough of this feeling of relief. . .of temporary happiness that blocks out everything else. I embrace her and Rebecca gives her a mattress near mine. Brianna appears from out of nowhere and quickly follows suit, hugging me even though we barely know each other.

"Took you guys long enough. Where's Garret?" My smile falters as I actually take a moment to look into her eyes. Bloodshot. Vacant. Still filled with tears. And I realize Grace and Rebecca look that way too. "Oh. . ." That is all I can manage to say, and I'm hugging her again. She doesn't need to say a word. He's dead.

FORTY-FOUR

I FEEL LIKE MY HEART IS BEING YANKED APART. SOBS BUBBLE UP in my throat, but for some reason, I can't seem to release them. Garret didn't just know how to survive out here. He thrived. Through his skill with his weapon, we were able to escape the Reserve relatively unharmed. And he made sure that meat was always on the table. He respected me before I even fired a shot. Anyone would think someone like him would die in a blaze of glory on the battlefield. Not by some scratch that his body refused to heal.

Blocking out everything else so that I can just grieve isn't something I have the time for anymore. There's so much that I still need to worry about. I try falling asleep on my mattress, but all that ends up happening is my sobs start to break free when I need to be silent so the others can sleep. The last thing I want to do is keep everyone up, especially Ava, so I go outside again, making sure to bring my bag.

I'm a mess, nearly crashing down the stairs and out the front door as tears blind my vision. A flash of yellow-green goes past my eyes as I make my way to the yard, and I panic. My gun is out, ready to confront something alien but only finding a firefly. It's nothing to worry about, yet I'm shaking and my heart is pounding so loud and so fast it's all I can hear. Until the bark of a dog pierces through the air.

The alien dogs are back. They've gotten in. Probably killed all the guards by now, and they're ready to kill me. I ready my gun with unsteady hands, blinking my eyes rapidly to clear them from tears.

"Turbo! Turbo!" a voice calls, and my eyes scan the darkness. Confusion and fear make my heart feel like it's going to explode. Suddenly, a normal dog comes running out of the woods, followed by Olivia. She calls the German Shepherd to her, calming it down while I try to calm myself. A dog. A goddamn pet dog. From Earth. And I almost shot it.

"What the hell is that thing doing here?" My voice snaps out, and I have to remember to lower my gun.

"Sorry about that," she says, petting it. "He doesn't usually get like this. You must have freaked him out, right, Turbo?" She coos. "He's the Peterson's dog. They've had him for years. He normally stays with Ralph, who guards up there. But he greets me when I go to take Ralph's place." The dog is still looking at me, and after a moment, Olivia looks at me too. "What are you doing out here?"

"My friend's dead." My voice doesn't even sound like my own.

"Oh. . .I'm sorry to hear that." Her voice is soft, her eyes concerned. I notice some outdoor furniture and take a seat, allowing my body to just shut down. I curl up as if to distance myself as far away from the dog as possible, unable to deflect the memories it stirs up in me. "Would you like me to stay with you, or would you rather be alone?" I'd like the company to keep me from feeling so empty, but tell her I'd rather be alone because I don't want to drag her into this. I barely know her. She doesn't need to deal with my problems.

I'm left alone, but only for a few minutes, it seems. Then I hear someone take a seat in the chair next to me. I lift my head out of my arms and see Alfie. For the first time since I've met him, he has to force a smile.

"Can't sleep?" He asks quietly.

"Yeah," I answer, clearing my throat as if to rid the sadness from my voice.

"Me neither."

"Where's Rebecca?" It's a stupid thing to ask, as if there can't be one without the other, but I ask it anyway.

"Comforting Brianna." He answers. We sit in silence until I realize he's trying to hand me something. It's a bracelet woven out of black string. "Here," He says, tying it on my wrist. "I know I promised a grass bracelet, but I've found better material. All of us from the O'Brien house will have one." I don't know what to say, except a muttered 'thank you'. I'm once again reminded of how I've become a part of this group, even though I never intended to be. And with that, I know how much it will hurt me each time we lose someone.

I find that my sadness is being overtaken by fury. There are no tears for me to cry anymore, only a clenched jaw and clenched fists. My teeth are pressed together so hard I have a brief thought that they might somehow start to crack. I can't let any other rebels die. I can't let any other civilians die, either. This war has to end, and sitting around waiting for others to fight isn't going to cut it for me anymore.

"Aw, y'all got matching bracelets. How cute." A girl's sarcastically sweet voice interrupts us. I look up to see a girl with wavy blonde hair sitting across from me. "The O'Brien house. Like your own little club." Her hazel eyes gaze at us in amusement, either oblivious or uncaring to the state we're in. I'm guessing the latter, quickly feeling defensive and angrier.

"Do you need something?" I spit, giving her an icy look.

"No, just getting some air," she says nonchalantly. "I'm Alana, by the way," The name is familiar. Olivia mentioned it. But Alfie and I are in no mood for this, opting to stay silent. An elderly man hobbles into view, further proving that in a place with this many people, you can never get some privacy. Not unless you submerge yourself deep into the woods.

"Annabelle!" He gasps, and I realize he's looking at me, gripping the arm of the chair I sit in. It's as if he thinks I'm someone else. Age has taken a toll on his mind. "Annabelle, where's Rose? I have to find Rose. Rose said she'd meet me at 6 o'clock on the dot and never showed up. I'm so worried. I went to her house-"

"Oh, piss off, you old shitbag! No one knows where your damn Rose is!" Alana yells loudly enough to earn some shushing and scolding from inside the house. She just laughs, looking up at the sky. "If I ever get like that, just shoot me."

I want to comment right back, but all I can think about now is how if I kept losing memory like that, I might be able to find peace in the world we're in now. I'd probably forget about Jacob's death, and Garret's. I might not even realize Earth had become so damaged by an alien invasion. It might be hell to forget so much and lose that much, but it could be bliss in comparison to what I feel now. If I lost my family, I would beg to forget it all if I didn't lose the will to live.

"You know, I came to talk to you because you've got that ribbon in your hair," Alana says to me, grinning. I stare at her blankly. "My little sister, Ava, has a bunch of ribbons just like that. I'm glad you've managed to find time to become friends with children." Her tone is mocking, her eyes sharp and mischievous.

When I continue not to talk, Alana gets bored and leaves, relieving some of my agitation. Alfie goes back inside to try to sleep. I try to get some rest out here in this chair, but I don't know how many hours I manage to get before the sun starts to rise and Tyler is shaking me awake for our shift. Images of my family fading away still linger in my mind from the fragmented nightmares I had.

"You okay?" I feel like it's polite to ask as we walk to our post.

"No," His voice is more detached than I've ever heard it. "You?"

"No." We know the other is far from okay, but for some reason, speaking makes things seem normal.

Like most moments where I'm in one place, I feel like I'm wasting time. I tell Tyler about the traitor, not excluding a single detail. I tell him that Garret and I suspected Marcus, and I let him come to his own conclusion about Elliot. He seems convinced it's Marcus, and if he was angry at me for holding out on him, he doesn't show it. Maybe he thought this made us even.

Our shift is nearly over when we spot someone running toward us from beyond the fence. Guns raised, we try to see who it is. Black clothes. Olive skin. Long black hair. As she gets closer, I realize it's Leah and I lower my gun, letting Tyler know who she is but allowing him to keep his gun up. From her expression, it seems like she recognized me and that's why she came running.

"Rachel!" she gasps as she stops in front of the fence, holding up her hands to show that she wasn't holding a weapon. "I knew that was you. What the hell are you doing here?"

"This is the camp we said we were going to." I don't doubt that Kieran told her that Garret and I are rebels.

"Well, you need to evacuate anyone you can, because my camp is on its way here. They're planning to attack. We've been scoping this place out for almost a week." Leah's exasperation is convincing me. She genuinely looks like she wants us out, because she can't control what the others in the group do.

"How much time do we have?" Tyler demands, seeming wary but not wanting to take chances.

"20 minutes tops."

"Why are they attacking?" I ask.

"We've spotted Émigré ships for the first time since the invasion. They've driven us out of our camp and we have almost nothing. We're only attacking to get what we need, but Kieran and I knew you and your brother were rebels. Those ships are looking for you, and if you survive our group, you'll have to survive the aliens too. It's better if you don't stay in one place." Her words fly out so fast I barely catch them, and she's about to take off running.

"Wait, Leah!" I call out, halting her. "Make sure they spare the children. Spare as many lives as you can, but especially the children."

"Our group doesn't kill children. We're not savages." She says firmly, glaring at me.

"Then make sure they still have parents when this is over." Tyler snaps. "Don't kill if you don't have to. Drive them out."

"You know some of your people are going to have to die, right?" She steps toward him, only allowing the fence to be the distance between them. "There's no way you're going to convince everyone to just up and leave. Some people stay and fight and defend. And there's no way we're getting in without killing some guards, at least. And I can't convince like 50 starving, angry people to just turn around and sit on their asses."

"This'll be your way in." Tyler opens the gate. "Spare as many people as possible, and protect the children." With a frustrated sigh, she nods and runs off.

"I doubt any of these parents will leave this place with their children," I say worriedly as we waste no time getting back to the house. "They're probably convinced they can defend this place."

"Maybe they can," Tyler responds.

"But we don't know what we're up against. And I don't want any of these people to die."

"Me neither. That's why we'll stay and fight." I like that idea. Running feels cowardly. I'd never forgive myself if I ran. "We'll send a bunch of people over to that gate and stop them right there before they can get in. I take it they're outsiders?"

"Yup." In my panic, I'd almost forgotten he doesn't know Leah. "Garret and I met them in the woods when that alien dog attacked us."

"And I'm guessing he told them you were related."

"He did." My heart tugs at the memory, but I have no time to grieve.

When Chris and Erin approach us, we hand back the guns and keep going at the same pace, ignoring their questioning looks. We split up once we reach the house, trying to warn as many people as possible as to what's coming. But I've only just approached Elliot when two men come up to him and grab him, tying his hands behind his back. I'm so shocked I freeze in place, only snapping out of it when he shoots me a desperate look.

"Hey, what's going on?" I yell, marching up to them. "What are you doing?"

"This boy is a traitor." One of the men says simply as they drag him away, putting a gag on him so he can't speak. My stomach drops. Someone did hear me talking to Elliot. And someone may have heard me talking to Tyler this morning.

FORTY-FIVE

"Says who?" I still demand, refusing to let them get away. I have no proof it's Elliot, so neither do they. Sure, I don't trust him, but I also don't want him taken away. There's a chance he could be just as innocent as I want him to be, and now, with him in the hands of someone else, I'm realizing that.

"Says me." Ralph approaches the group, leading us all the way to the other side of the spacious front yard, to a place where I've never been. There's a wooden post, and hanging off of it is a noose.

"What proof do you have?" My yelling is more frantic now.

"My daughter told me everything you O'Brien rebels have been trying to keep from us." Alana. Alana's been spying. Her amusement at my grief, her idea that our group was somehow disconnected from theirs, as if because Alfie made bracelets we thought we were better than them. And I'm sure Alana always gets what she wants. She seems like that type, and Ralph seems like that type of father. And she wants us out. Maybe when she first overheard us it was an accident, but it's clear that to her we don't belong here.

"And, so what? You just hang people for that? How stupid are you?" This man is out of his mind. He shouldn't be a leader of rebels.

He shouldn't be the father of a girl like Ava. "We need people. We need numbers. Be rational."

"Will someone shut her up?" Ralph groans.

"Gladly." I hear Ross's voice before I see him. When I do see him, his fist connects to my face so hard my world spins and I find myself on my knees, head pounding. A gag goes in my mouth. I'm forced onto my feet before I can recover. "Guess what, Collins? My parents left to find Callie WITHOUT ME." He's screaming in my ear, causing my head to throb harder.

Serves you right, I think to myself, trying to ignore my head and focus on my surroundings.

"And now they're all probably going to die because you fucking idiots pissed off the aliens." A blow hits my back and I cry out in pain, feeling him tie my hands behind my back.

"Easy, Ross," I hear Ralph scold him, but he doesn't do anything to stop Ross. People are starting to gather now. As I feel my hands being lifted into the air, my body soon following after, they start to break out into arguments. I'm hanging from a tree now, my arms stretched back so far I'm afraid they'll pop out of my sockets. Ross is grinning up at me, and I lift my body up just enough so that I can kick him in the face. Blood pours from his nose.

"You bitch! I'll kill you for everything you did! I'll kill you!" He has to be restrained, and I take some satisfaction in that.

"You said you wouldn't do this, Ralph. We had a vote! Hanging is not a form of punishment here anymore!" A middle-aged man shouts, surging toward us before two more men hold him back.

"I've said it before and I'll say it again," Ralph says, putting Elliot below the post. "My house, my rules. You don't like it, you leave."

"That's not the way things work. We had an agreement." A woman yells.

"They're just kids!" A man screams.

"They betrayed us."

"How do you know?"

"Where's your proof?"

"There should be a trial!"

"Just kick them out, force them to live on their own."

"If they're working with the aliens, we can't afford to take any risks."

"This is stupid. You're all stupid!"

"Let them hang, so everyone knows what happens when you betray the rebels."

"Hang them!"

"Free them!"

"HANG THEM!"

"FREE THEM!"

I see Rebecca and Alfie, and I try to convey with my eyes that they should leave. It seems like Ralph is intent on hanging Elliot. I don't know what he plans to do with the rest of us, but I'm sure punishment is in the cards. I don't think he intends on hanging us, but hanging one on just mere speculation could mean he's crazy enough to hang us all. If he always expected that something like an alien invasion would happen and spent all his money preparing his house, he's surely the type that lets his paranoia overtake his logic. Sure, he was right, but this house had to have been constructed long before the mothership first showed up.

Rebecca looks like she's trying to reason with Ralph. I can no longer hear what anyone is saying since the crowd has gotten so big, but it doesn't look like it's working. Ralph is shaking his head, looking angrily at her. She doesn't back down, never taking her eyes off his as she keeps arguing back. I see Olivia arguing with Alana, looking like she's ready to cut me down herself with the knife she's holding. Then, several things happen all at once. I lock eyes with Tyler and Brianna as they enter the crowd. Ralph grabs Rebecca, Alfie starts yelling and pushing him away, the noose is placed around Elliot's neck, and from somewhere in the distance, a gun fires. And then another.

The outsiders are here.

An eerie silence falls over the crowd as confusion breaks out, and then, the pandemonium that was once directed at Elliot and me is now directed at the chorus of gunshots. Whoever was holding me up with the rope lets go and I slam to the ground. Olivia is by me in seconds, cutting the rope away to free my hands and pulling the gag out. We run over to Elliot wordlessly, seeing a man I vaguely recognize working on setting him loose, fighting off anyone who opposes him. When Elliot is free, we join up with Alfie and Rebecca and run until we find Tyler and Brianna. Together and free, we run.

I run toward the house, only dimly aware of Olivia yelling at me.

"What are you doing? Go! Leave! You guys have to go!" Of course. We can't stay and fight like we planned. Even if the rebels win, who knows what they'll do to us?

"We need to grab our stuff!" I tell her, going inside, almost colliding with a rush of people storming out with their guns in hand.

"I'll cover for you guys." Olivia's eyes get focused as she holds a knife in each hand. I make a mental note to find a gun for her. "What's going on, anyway? Any ideas?"

"Outsiders," Tyler answers her.

We split up to grab our bags, and I'm thankful I took the time to pack mine. I dash up the stairs, go to the girls' room, and grab it. Out of the corner of my eye, I see Ava curled up on her bed, surrounded by her girlfriends. Her eyes are full of tears, confused and scared.

"Ava." I kneel down for a moment, seeing Brianna pack her bag and explain things to Grace. "I need you and your friends to stay here, okay? Don't leave this room. Everything's going to be okay."

"Okay," she whispers, seeming to trust me. Without any more time to waste, I head out. Once outside, I meet up with the others at the top of the staircase, hearing Brianna, Grace, and Rebecca behind me. Damien has joined us, but I don't see Molly, Angie, Cole, Kira, or Marcus. I'm about to ask if anyone knows where they are when I see Ralph making his way through the front door.

I know he's looking for us. The others know it, too, and Damien ushers us into the nearest room. Alfie's talking about jumping from the window when I take a peek out the doorway. I catch Ava's eyes as she looks out from the girls' room. She's smart enough to notice the fear in my eyes and smart enough to see her dad marching angrily toward Olivia. When Ava lets out a bloodcurdling scream, I think we're done for.

I expect her to point at us, to rat us out, just like Alana did. But she does something completely different. She dashes back into the girls' room, screaming her head off. Ralph is yelling her name in a panic, running up the stairs and into that room. In an instant, all his concern has shifted to her. We're free to escape.

All of us sprint down the stairs and out the door, trying to keep our footsteps as quiet as possible until we're out of the house. With Olivia with us, we take off toward another gate, away from the one the outsiders are using to get in. Damien is leading the way, telling us he knows where another one is since he started guarding there this morning. Grace is saying we should go back to find the others, but Tyler says we have no time. We can only hope they caught on and got out.

I'm just about to protest, knowing that it's pointless but wanting the others to be with us anyway when I spot Chis and Erin approaching us, guns in hand.

"Freeze!" Chris yells, his eyes trained on Elliot. But we get lucky again because Erin takes the butt of her rifle and slams it on the side of his head.

"Go!" she yells as he crumples to the ground. We may have enemies here now, but we also have allies.

We're running through the woods now, past the gate and into unknown territory. The sound of gunshots is fading. The sound of our breathing and our footsteps get louder. My head is pounding still, but I reach up to make sure my withered, light pink ribbon is still tied in my hair. Despite everything, when my fingers brush across it, I smile.

FORTY-SIX

WE SPRINT THROUGH THE TREES, AND I FIND MYSELF wondering if we're all more focused on what could be behind us rather than what we could come across. The woods don't fail to remind me of my encounter with an alien dog, so as we run, I keep my eyes peeled for anything that would attack us. I can't hear anything other than my pounding heart and the sound of all of us panting as our feet hit the ground. Relying heavily on my sight, I scan through the tops of the trees just in time to spot movement.

"Up in the trees!" I manage to yell. As if to enlighten the others as to what I mean, a knife whizzes past me, nearly nicking my cheek. The person jumps, dropping to the ground as I raise my gun, and as we come to a halt, more people drop from the trees until we're surrounded.

Judging by the looks in their eyes when they see us, they're outsiders. I assume they positioned themselves out here to stop any rebels from escaping. A man with an axe. A woman with a knife bigger than any I've ever seen. Spears. Crossbows. But no guns.

"You sure this is a fight you want to make?" Damien calls out when he realizes the same. I point my gun at a woman with a spear, and she smirks.

"Pretty damn sure." She says in response.

I have no idea how they could look so confident with what little they have, but before anyone can pull a trigger or launch a spear, someone is yelling for us to stop. Kieran storms into view, crossbow in hand.

"Let them go. They're not with the rebels." He says firmly, glancing at me for the briefest second.

"How do you know?" someone demands.

"I saw them being tied up. They were about to be hung." He assures them.

"Hung for what?" The woman in front of me asks. "That doesn't prove that they're not rebels."

"I heard them say it was because they snuck in to steal shit. Take it or leave it, but they're not who you're angry at." Kieran glares at her.

"You sure about this?" The man with the ax growls.

"Yeah, I'm sure. Let them go. You're wasting time." Kieran remains adamant, but I can tell we're not in the clear. The outsiders are eyeing our weapons and bags with greed. They may not see us as an enemy, but they do see us as an opportunity.

"Hand over the rifle." Demands a young man with a crossbow, aiming it at Damien.

"You're joking, right?" Damien laughs easily.

"There's plenty of weapons at the base." Kieran nearly shouts. "Let them go and get back into position."

"We don't take orders from you. Remember?" The woman in front of me grins.

"Nah, let them go." An older woman with graying brown hair says nonchalantly. "I'd rather deal with some actual rebels with better weapons. If what you're saying is true, boy." She gazes at Kieran with such intensity that even I feel nervous.

"It's true." He promises, refusing to let his voice or body language give him away. All at once, the outsiders follow the lead of that woman, climbing back into the trees until Kieran is the only one left on the ground. I open my mouth to thank him, but he quickly puts a finger to his lips before nodding and heading back to the base. My gratitude is still at the tip of my tongue when he disappears.

Our rebel group takes off without a word, only stopping when we're as far away from the base as we can manage. Then we walk. Woods melt to fields, then to small neighborhoods, and then back to woods again. As we pause to take a breath, all the questions come out. Alfie asks who Kieran was and how he seemed to know me. Almost everyone asks all at once why Elliot was being hung and why I seemed soon to follow. Soon, everyone knows everything, and nothing is a secret anymore.

"Well, no wonder they thought you were a traitor," Olivia huffs at Elliot, pacing anxiously. "We had an incident last year where Ralph claimed someone had been working with outsiders. He hung him without consulting any of us, but it turned out he was right. The whole base has been divided on the issue ever since."

"Pretty stupid to trust Ralph's judgment, if you ask me," Alfie mutters.

"Maybe if you morons hadn't been gabbing about this stuff so much, we wouldn't be in this mess," Damien yells.

"It's not our fault that someone was snooping on us when we were trying to talk privately," Elliot says defensively. I can see the way the others look at him now, and I can tell they trust him less as well. If he's innocent, I can't imagine how cornered and helpless he must feel. He can argue and defend himself all he wants, but he knows it won't change what anyone thinks with what we already know.

"Who'd you even see, anyway?" Damien confronts me, stepping forward. "Do you have any idea at all? You can say Marcus and you can say Elliot, but just in case you've gone completely brain-dead, they're two completely different skin tones and heights."

"You think I haven't thought of that?" I don't shy away. "I've replayed the scene in my head thousands of times. The person was wearing a helmet and gloves. I didn't see any skin. And while I don't think their body matches Elliot's from what I remember, it all happened so fast. The person was standing on elevated ground and they were about 10 feet away. Before I could think up who it was, I blacked out." I feel Elliot's eyes on me, and I know I can't look at him. His expression will break me, whether he's angry, sad, or disappointed.

"And what if you're lying about all of it?" Damien keeps going.

"Alright, that's enough," Tyler snaps.

"I'm just saying!" Damien throws his hands up in frustration. "One of you could be working with those aliens, and that makes the rest of us completely fucked. It makes me sick to think about it."

"But we don't know anything for sure," Rebecca says firmly.

"So, what do we do, then?" He shouts. "Interrogate Elliot? And what if Rachel's lying? She showed up right when things started to fall apart and was real intent on going to the Reserve."

"Shut up!" Tyler's voice gets louder. "You don't know what the hell you're talking about." I'm suspecting another fight between them, so I put my hand on Tyler's shoulder and tug him back, trying to convey that it's not worth it. Grace senses the same and laces her hand in Damien's.

"You know I'm right to be suspicious." Damien bites back the same moment Tyler shrugs my hand away.

"Yeah? Well, she may have suspected you, but she never acted on it. Like any sane person, she wanted to wait until she had some solid proof." Tyler's quick to reply.

"Arguing isn't going to get us anywhere," Olivia interjects, rolling her eyes.

"And who the hell said you could come along? Don't you have your own team to go back to?" Damien doesn't hesitate to get her involved in the fight.

Soon, everyone's either arguing or trying to calm everyone down, and we're just one huge group of chaos. If we get any louder, we'll surely attract some unwanted attention. I try to speak up, but my voice just gets lost in the shouting.

"Guys? Guys! Listen for a minute!" I'm yelling at the top of my lungs, but the only person who turns toward me is Tyler. Seeing that I have something to say, he takes a stab at trying to quiet everyone down, but that only makes Damien get angrier, and the yelling gets worse. Fed up, I raise my gun in the air and fire once. Mouths close and eyes lock onto me.

"Thanks for making me waste a bullet," I hiss, and no one says a word. I'm the quiet one, the shy one, the young one, the tiny one, and I've just stunned them all into silence. Almost just as surprised as they are, I swallow hard before I speak. "As far as we know, we're what's left of the O'Brien house. The Peterson house doesn't want anything to do with us, for the most part. We have no army, but there are still rebels on that mothership. So, what the hell are we going to do?"

FORTY-SEVEN

I'VE STATED THE OBVIOUS, BUT IT'S CLEAR THAT NOT EVERYONE here has thought of that yet. With a lot happening in such a short amount of time, the last thing on their minds was what our purpose is now. We all want to find out who betrayed us, but if we focus solely on that, we risk losing everything else we were fighting for.

"I guess we just focus on the priorities," Rebecca sighs. "Food, water, shelter, safety. The basics. And while we do that, we work our way toward the mothership."

"Do you guys know where it is?" Olivia asks.

"Only Marcus knows. Or, well, he told Angie," Alfie begins.

"No, I know where it is. I mean, I have a good idea of where." Elliot interrupts, and I feel another ache in my heart as some of the group look at him warily. If I'm wrong about Elliot, I'll spend the rest of my life apologizing. "When I was tending to Marcus's wounds, I watched them map out where it was."

"I know where it is, too. I saw the maps as well." Brianna says, giving Elliot a smile that seems to make him feel like less of an outcast. Damien looks like he's going to spout off again, so Grace speaks up.

"The sun's going to start setting in a few hours. Let's set up camp for the night."

We agree silently, claiming the ground as our own. Tyler approaches me, eyeing me with concern, and I know Ross must have left me with some visible marks. His eyes shift to my forehead and zero in on the right side.

"Who did this to you? Was it Ralph?" His voice is low, but I still sense the anger. He moves his fingers toward my head and then decides against it, lowering his hand. I touch the skin myself, finally having the time to inspect it. I wince. Definitely a good bruise there, but no blood. I'm sure my back is the same.

"It was Ross," I reply. His jaw tightens, but he doesn't make a comment. Olivia does instead.

"Somebody's gonna get so fed up with him they'll kill him without even thinking about it."

We sit around talking in small groups, eventually eating some of the food we have. I make a point of sitting by Elliot and force myself to get over my paranoia and talk to him.

"I'm sorry. I feel like all of this is my fault. I jumped to conclusions without any real proof."

"It was a valid assumption, based on what you knew." Elliot shrugs, but I can see the sadness in his expression.

"I suspected Marcus, too, but I never wanted to start accusing either of you of something I had no proof of."

"People hear things and people panic. We can't control that. Rachel, I'm not mad at you. I understand your side. I'm just frustrated because I still don't understand why I could fire that gun. The odds are stacked against me."

"I don't want them to be stacked against you. I know that the way I see you, you would never betray us. And even if something happened, and they threatened you and you had no choice but to give up, I'd like to think you'd tell one of us." When I say that, he smiles softly.

"You have more faith in me than most people would, knowing

what you know. I'm not even surprised you befriended some outsiders."

"Uh, I wouldn't say I befriend them." I let out a dry laugh. "They probably felt like they owed me, and now we're even."

"You're an easy person to like." He shrugs. "Kindness goes a long way."

"We should split up to check the area and make sure we're alone," Brianna announces when she sees that most of us are done eating. "If you find an empty house or any place we can stay, come back to tell the rest of the group. Watch out for demon dogs."

"Demon dogs?" Olivia makes her way toward us again. Even though she's not introverted in any way, I seem to be the most familiar person to her, and naturally, she finds it easier to talk to me.

"I think she means the alien dogs we've run into a few times." I clarify, feeling a tug at my heart again because it was probably Garret who started calling them that.

"I like it," she smirks. "It's got a nice ring to it."

"Are you going to go back to the Peterson base?" Elliot asks. "Not that you're not wanted here, but because I'm sure you were there for a long time." He adds quickly, giving her a friendly smile.

"I'm not going to go back there. If they all happen to survive after the attack, they aren't going to be too happy with me." She acts like it's not a big deal, but I can tell from her eyes that she's a little upset. I don't blame her. In a split second, she made a decision and ran for her life. Now she's got nowhere to go back to, and she doesn't know the fate of the people she cares about. I can definitely relate to that.

"Hey, if you don't want to stay behind while the others have a look around, you can go with Tyler." I offer as people start pairing up, just like at the old rebel house. With the accusations against Elliot and the fact that Molly isn't here, I have a feeling he'll be one of the people staying behind, and Olivia might not want to be around him. And she might be like me, wanting something to do to take her mind off things.

"That's okay," she shakes her head. "I can stay back. I wouldn't want to intrude on you two or anything."

"Why would you think you'd be intruding?" I give her an amused smile as Elliot chuckles.

"Oh, um, I thought maybe you and Tyler were related or something." She laughs awkwardly. "You guys seemed close."

"Not related," Tyler says as he approaches us. "Not close either. I hate her." He fights off a smile as I roll my eyes.

"He's such a joy to be around," I tell her, my voice full of sarcasm.

We say goodbye to the others as Brianna tells us to go north. Olivia, Elliot, Damien, and Grace stay back. Alfie and Rebecca go south. Much to everyone's dismay, Brianna insists on going west herself, even if it means going alone. No one goes east, since that will just take us back toward the Peterson house.

Tyler and I walk through the woods at a steady pace, and it almost feels like we're on guard duty again as our eyes search through the trees. Going this direction, the woods don't seem to end up for miles. I don't see a single house or any sign of civilization, except for some randomly discarded cans that we decide look too old to be recent. When the trees do let up, we're approaching the edge of a cliff that looks over a lake.

"This reminds me of the place I used to go to in Michigan," Tyler says quietly as he steps closer to the edge. I stay back, knowing that this cliff is high enough to elicit my fear of heights. "This is nowhere near as high as the cliff by the rebel house, and if you were to jump off it, you'd just land in the water. Looks deep enough to be perfect for cliff diving."

"You're not going to jump off, are you?" Fear makes my voice shake.

"Of course not," He looks back at me. "I'm going to go down to see if it's deep enough first." Walking along the edge of the cliff, he starts to work his way to the lower ground. I follow, but still keep my distance from the edge until we're not as high up anymore. Once we reach the shore, he slides off his boots and clothes until he's in just his boxers, setting his bag and gun aside before slipping into the water.

I debate whether to join him. It's hot enough outside that the water would feel extremely refreshing, but the sun is about to set, and once it's down, I'd be freezing. Plus, I don't really feel like stripping down in front of Tyler. I stay on the shoreline and wait for him to come back. It only takes a few minutes before he's sloshing back onto land.

"It's definitely deep enough." He puts his stuff back on and walks up toward the cliff.

"Are you going to jump off it, then?" I follow him again.

"Maybe tomorrow. I'll bring the others down here, too. It'll be fun. Will you jump?"

"No," I almost laugh. "I'm afraid of heights."

"Fair enough. I'm afraid of drowning."

"What?" His admission catches me off guard. "But you just. . .swam all the way out there. And checked how deep it was. And you make it seem like you cliff dive all the time."

"Well, it's not like I'm so afraid that I can't even go in the water, but I do think about it every time I'm in the water. It's why I try to keep my head above water as much as possible. If I'm underwater too long, I start to panic."

"But you still go in the water, anyway. That's pretty impressive. I never do much to combat my fear of heights." It sounds strange to say, considering I've dealt with dead people, ferocious alien dogs, gun-toting Émigrés, and I've even killed people. Yet the only time I dealt with heights was whenever I jumped from the Reserve wall or climbed a tree to get over it. Put me in front of the enemy and I'll do my best. Put me in front of a ledge like this and I'll freeze.

"If it makes it any better, I promise it's not as high as it seems," Tyler says as we get to higher ground. I look over at the cliff.

"If I go check it out, you better not push me in or anything stupid like that," I snap, giving him an icy look.

"I would never. I'll just stand right here." He holds up his hands as if to claim innocence, and for some reason, my mind flashes back to the man Ross shot. Squeezing my eyes shut for a second as if to clear the image from my brain, I wonder if my mind will always be like this. If the war keeps going and I'm still alive, it could get to a point where everything that happens to me brings up a terrible memory that consumes me.

I walk toward the edge, trying to block out everything else. Thankfully, my fear of heights takes care of that. Feeling adrenaline course through me, I force myself to stop only when I'm inches from the drop. Looking over, I can see the dark blue water below, and the height makes me dizzy enough to step back. The world almost starts to spin, and I know that this is as close as I'll ever get. I go toward Tyler again.

"Too high?" He asks.

"Too high." I nod.

He nods back, and we start to make our way to where the rest of the rebels are. By the time we reach them, the sun will probably be down, but we both decide to split up a bit as we head back, trying to cover more ground to see what we can find before dark. We make sure that we aren't too far away from one another, and once we think we're close enough that the other one will be able to hear us if we call out for help, we get to work.

Despite being alone, I find that I'm pretty calm. With my gun in my hand and Tyler a few yards to my left, I feel like I have a chance no matter what happens. But we're not even halfway to the other rebels when I hear a sound that makes me freeze. It's coming from Tyler's direction, so I think that maybe he found something or started running for some reason. My muscles tense as I hold my breath and listen closely.

The sound that follows is one I know all too well, even if I've only heard it once. It sounds like multiple pairs of feet smashing through the woods, yet the faint snarling and panting proves that once again, it's no ambush. It's demon dogs.

FORTY-EIGHT

MY FIRST INSTINCT IS TO SCREAM FOR TYLER AS LOUD AS I CAN, hoping he knows the demon dogs are here and that they'll be diverted toward me, but his scream comes first. It's a scream of pain so loud that I can barely hear the growl of the beast that follows it, and a chill of utter terror runs through me. This isn't like when I was in the Divide and I heard a scream and couldn't tell who it was. I know it's Tyler, without a doubt, and it tears me apart so much that for a second I don't move. His second scream snaps me out of it, and I run toward the sounds as I imagine Tyler being ripped to shreds by the long, pointed teeth of the demon dogs before I can reach him.

When I get to him, he's on the ground and one demon dog is on top of him. There's blood on his left leg, and he's got his backpack up as a last resort to protect himself, probably not able to aim his gun at the right place before he got attacked. The beast is just sinking its teeth into the bag and his arm when I get there. The bite ensures that Tyler doesn't even notice I'm there as he cries out in pain.

Blocking Tyler out, I focus solely on the demon dog and what I know. Saving my bullets for when I get a clear shot at its face, I launch my pocketknife into its side. I know it'll do next to nothing, but it's enough for the thing to realize I'm there and maybe release Tyler from its jaws. It lets go of Tyler's arm slightly as turns its pointed ears toward me, and I take this opportunity to use one bullet. Knowing that my aim isn't that good, I shoot its side instead of its face, hoping that the pain and the noise will bring it to me and also alert the other rebels that something is wrong.

It works. The yellow eyes are trained on me, and to my surprise, it doesn't show the recognition that the first demon dog did. It doesn't know me or Tyler, so it has no problem letting him go and coming after me. I take aim at the head and fire quickly, but I end up nailing it in the eye. It falters, yelping in pain and shaking its head wildly. I try to aim for the head again, but it's almost impossible. Before I can get a good shot off, it throws its head back and roars so loudly that I feel it shake my bones and its hot breath, reeking of warm blood, hits me full force.

Just like that, I realize that this is no lone wolf. It's a member of a pack. Off in the distance, I hear howl after howl, four in total. Then I can faintly make out the sound of them running toward us. Tyler's been given enough time to muster up the strength to grab his gun and take a shot. He manages to hit it right on the head where it's most vulnerable, and all we need is one more shot to finish it off. I take it, and that's one dog down.

We know more are coming, hearing them smash through the woods. As long as they are focused on us, the other rebels are safe, but we can't take on a whole pack and expect to live. I yank my knife out of the skin of the demon dog, noticing for the first time that they don't actually have short, glossy black fur, but smooth reptilian-like skin that gleams in the fading sunlight. When Tyler and I make eye contact, it's clear that we are both on the same page. Taking off back toward the cliff, we hope to lead them away from the other rebels. It'll only be a matter of seconds before they're breathing down our backs.

Whatever happened to Tyler's leg, it's slowing him down enough that even I can easily keep up with him. He runs with a slight limp, occasionally grunting in pain as we run. Hoping that we can continue to outrun them, I try to turn away from the upcoming cliff, but out of the corner of my eye, I can see a demon dog in the woods on my left, curving toward us as it surges through the trees. Even in the bluish light of early night, I notice the other dog coming in on Tyler's right, and I can hear the one behind us. We're almost completely surrounded. The only direction we can go is forward. Toward the cliff.

I force myself not to think about the feeling of my feet hitting the rocky ground beneath me, knowing that in a few more steps there will be nothing below them but air. Quickly putting the safety on my gun, I fumble to try to slide it into the side pocket of my backpack. Once my hands are free, I grab Tyler's hand in mine to keep him going and keep me calm. He squeezes it so tightly that I'm able to ignore my pounding heart. I hurtle off the edge without even thinking about it.

The feeling of being suspended in the air puts my stomach in knots, but the lake water rushes up to meet us fast enough so that I barely have time to be afraid. My body smacks into the water, almost knocking my breath right out of me. The impact causes Tyler and I to let go of each other, and I'm tempted to open my eyes. Knowing how murky the lake water is, though, I decide against it. I just swim upward, driving myself to get to the surface.

When I reach the surface, I look around desperately for Tyler. Not seeing him anywhere, I start to swim around, waiting for him to come up. I glance upward just for a moment to see what happened to the demon dogs. They're crowded by the edge of the cliff, looking down at me and snarling. Now that they've spotted me, they start to run along the edge of the cliff toward the shoreline. We don't have much time before they greet us again.

As if on cue, Tyler emerges from the water, gasping for air. I swim toward him and urge him forward as he hisses in pain. The water around him is stained red. My mind pushes it aside and thinks only of the demon dogs as we trudge onto the shore. Taking out our guns and turning the safeties off, we're able to shoot them down before they can reach us because of the fact that we're waiting for them and working together. All we needed was an edge. With them unable to go anywhere but straight toward us, no longer protected by the trees, we've got it.

An eerie silence now falls over the area as four dead demon dogs lay in front of us. All I can hear is the sound of our heavy breathing and the water lapping at our feet until Tyler lets out a frustrated, pained yell. He surges toward the closest demon dog, firing bullet after bullet into its skull.

FORTY-NINE

"Tyler!" I go toward him. "Tyler, stop! It's dead. You're going to waste all of your bullets. Stop!"

But he doesn't stop until the gun is empty. Tossing it aside like it's a piece of trash, he throws his backpack onto the ground.

"They don't even fight us!" He screams. "They don't even bother fighting themselves, they just send out fucking dogs to do their work for them!" He looks back at me, his eyes red with unshed tears. "But yet they can kill a kid. A defenseless kid. They're cowards. Monsters. All of them!" I catch him before he collapses to the ground, holding him to me as he shakes with sobs that don't come out. I try to avoid his injuries, only seeing the blood on his long-sleeve shirt and pant leg.

"We have to get back to the others and treat you." I say, trying to keep my voice from breaking. He lets out a laugh that's somehow free of emotion, and that's when I realize where a lot of his anger is coming from. He doesn't think he'll survive this.

I pull up the sleeve of his shirt, revealing deep bite marks that are still oozing blood. It looks extremely painful and knowing that his leg is much worse than this, I find my eyes beginning to fill with tears.

When I look back at him again, his eyes are dead as he stares at his wound.

"Tyler," I speak up, as if trying to rouse him from a nightmare. "Let's go back to the others and make sure they're okay." I'm hoping that this will give him more motivation to get going than trying to treat his injuries would, and it looks like I'm right. He gets up, grabbing his backpack and refusing to let me carry it for him. I retrieve his discarded gun, and as I make him lean on me for support, we move forward.

The sight of the dead creatures, with their strange yellow eyes unblinking and their long, pointed fangs poking out of their jaws, makes me angry as well, and I force myself not to look at them as we pass. We move agonizingly slow, easy prey for anything and anyone lurking in the woods. By the time we reach the rebel campsite, the sun is down, and we're shivering to death in our damp clothes. When we let ourselves flop down onto the ground, I barely make a mental note that everyone's here except for Brianna and Olivia.

Elliot sees the blood on Tyler and immediately goes to work with what little he has. Grace helps me take off my damp long-sleeve shirt that I had put on for morning guard duty, and I slip on my windbreaker that I had shoved into my backpack. I take off my damp shoes and socks but leave on the pants. Although they're soaking wet, they're all I've got, and it's not like anyone managed to grab extra pants when we left the house so quickly.

"Where are Brianna and Olivia?" I say as Grace offers me her socks to keep my feet warm.

"They went looking for you guys," Alfie explains. "What happened?"

I tell them everything, and the surrounding air grows grim as people take in Tyler's injuries. Even Elliot looks like he thinks Tyler won't make it. If Garret could die from a laser skimming his chest, Tyler could definitely die from two deep bites from a beast. To lighten the mood, Elliot mentions that he thinks these demon dogs might mean we're close to the mothership, and he even assures us that the bites didn't break any of Tyler's bones, but Tyler just laughs that emotionless laugh that shatters my heart and makes me want to hate him at the same time.

Brianna and Olivia eventually return. Damien and Brianna offer to guard during the night and suggest that we all get some rest. As everyone attempts to get some sleep, Rebecca gives me her jacket to use as a blanket as she cuddles up next to Alfie. I give it to Tyler, laying down next to him as I hear his ragged breathing. Taking his hand in mine just like I did earlier, I try not to cry.

"I'm sorry I couldn't get to you sooner," I whisper.

"Don't be," He manages to say.

"Don't die," I demand, not caring how stupid it sounds. I almost expect him to laugh again, but he doesn't.

"I can't. . .promise that," He sucks in a breath as another wave of pain hits him. I find myself missing Garret's optimism. If Tyler won't be optimistic, I'll have to be positive for both of us. I should have expected that.

"Well, don't give up, then." My voice sounds angry, and I work to soften it.

"Okay," He says.

"Promise me that."

"I promise." He squeezes my hand again, and this time I squeeze back.

I try to fall asleep, but I know it'll never happen. I'm too afraid that if I close my eyes, he'll be gone the moment I open them. And I know now that if he was gone, I'd lose it. Even thinking about it now brings me close to tears. At some point in these past few days, he crept up under my skin and found a place in my heart. It may not be that hard to accomplish, but it certainly means more pain for me.

That's why it's no surprise that Brianna would stay up to guard. She'd just lost Garret. I can't imagine what kind of nightmares she would go through if she tried to sleep. Tyler has dealt with death so many more times than I have, and since I've only known him for a few weeks, he would be able to recover if it was me who died. Sure, he would be wracked with guilt, and he would be sad for a little while, but he would move on. He always does.

It's different for me. When I left the Reserve, he was the first face I saw. When I passed out in the Divide and woke up, he was the first face I saw. When I was wandering in the woods of the Ruins with Ross, dehydrated and exhausted, he was the first face I saw. He's always signified that I was safe. That I wasn't alone. That I was going to be okay. With him gone, I would lose all of that.

Thinking back, I remember when I thought I hated him. We argued as much as I used to argue with Mary. I always thought he was holding me back. I thought he was selfish and rude and judgmental, so I didn't even care that I was trying to force him to be my partner. It didn't matter if it inconvenienced him or upset him. I had to find my dad.

And yet, when I thought it was him that was screaming in the Divide and I ran out into the line of fire without caring about what happened to me, I knew he mattered to me. I tried to deny it then, but I think that's when it all started. He can be mad at me all he wants, and I can be mad at him all I want, but I care. I do care, even if I don't want to, and that's what will ruin me.

I sit up when it seems like Tyler's fallen asleep and hold his hand in both of mine, keeping my eyes peeled for any danger. Glancing briefly at the others, it seems that no one else is getting any sleep either. Whether they're worried about Tyler, demon dogs, or something else entirely, they're being kept up as well.

When the sun rises, everyone else rises too, confirming that none of them slept much, if at all. Elliot goes to work changing Tyler's bandages. The second Tyler's hand slips away from mine, I think of Jacob letting go of me when he was killed. I immediately take his hand again once Elliot's done, as though he'll be alive as long as his hand is in mine. He actually gives me a smile, and things seem like they might be alright. Until a group of white-clad figures emerges through the woods.

I let go of Tyler's hand and step in front of him, barking at him to stay down when he tries to get up as well. We all grab our guns and raise them in an instant, and I feel my stomach sink as I recognize the white armor. There are three of them approaching us with their silver guns raised. The demon dogs must have led them right to us.

But to our complete shock, they lower their weapons when they get closer. As they do so, they remove their helmets and hold up their now weaponless hands. Confused, we wait until we can see their faces. I almost drop my gun when I recognize one of them. Brown eyes. Dark brown hair shining in the early sunlight. I can't hide my smile as joy swells in me.

"Dad," I blurt out as tears fill my eyes and I take off toward him. He grins back at me, alive and healthy. Better off than me, in fact. The tears fall as I launch myself into his arms, gripping onto him with all my might. Everything I'd done, everything that had happened to me, everything I'd risked my life to do, was all worth it.

"Hey, Ray Ray," He chokes out, calling me by a nickname that I haven't heard in years. All of a sudden, I'm his little girl again. "What are you doing out here?"

"I came to find you," I tell him as we pull away. Now he really looks at me, and I have a good idea of what he sees. His little girl grew up way too fast, her starved body covered in dirt and blood. He remembers a girl who's no longer here.

I want to tell him everything. I want him to know that Mary's in solitary and Mom and Annie might be in danger. He should know that I killed two people. Outsiders, but people nonetheless. I've let everything fall apart just to find him. And it's not his fault, it's all mine. No matter how he feels about me after he knows everything, it's worth just having him alive and well in front of me.

"How did you guys escape?" Damien asks, and I suddenly remember the other two people here. It all starts to come together. If the other rebels know them, they must be the other men who were captured by the Émigrés.

"There's something you guys should know," one of the men says vaguely. I look back at my dad, who looks as though he knows I'm not going to like what they're going to say. As though he has something to apologize for. My mind jumps and I take a step back. Is he the traitor? Did my own father betray us all? Are all of these men traitors?

"What is it?" Brianna demands when no one has said anything for a moment. Then we see another white armored figure come through the woods. When they reach us, they remove their helmet, and I almost expect it to be Marcus, but it's not. To my complete surprise, it's Cole. He defensively keeps his gun up as he looks at all of us, and with the sunlight streaming through the trees, I can clearly see the color of his eyes. They aren't blue like I remember.

They're violet.

FIFTY

No one speaks. In fact, I'm pretty sure no one moves. A stillness falls over the woods as Cole allows us to take him in, still holding up his silver gun in case one of us decides to send a bullet his way. But I barely think about shooting him. My thoughts are all jumbled by shock. I even momentarily forget that my dad is next to me, and when he puts a comforting hand on my arm, I jerk back.

Those eyes. Those hauntingly violet eyes have always instilled fear in me. They've been the beacon of danger, the only noticeable difference between us and them. They plague my nightmares and even my daydreams. They mean death and destruction, and yet one of their owners is standing right in front of me, having just given me back my father.

I remember Garret and me talking about the possibility of an Émigré changing their eye color so that they could blend in with us. That never sounded far-fetched; they have the technology to do more than we've probably even imagined. But I could never come up with a reason as to why they would bother. They've always clearly had the upper hand. They have no reason to hide, and every reason to want us to know exactly who is destroying and controlling us.

"You realize what this must look like, right?" Brianna speaks up slowly, as if trying to find her voice. Cole nods once. "Care to explain?"

"I will. But first, I'm going to need everyone to put their weapons down." Cole says, and we all comply without protest, still in shock but also knowing that his weapon is more powerful than ours. Cole takes a deep breath before he begins.'

"Yes, I am what you call an Émigré. I'm not human and I never have been. I'm from a planet called Kofal, and my people are called the Kofali. As you may have heard from the Reserve, we came here after destroying our home planet with nuclear war. It was my mission . . . my chosen mission, to uncover any sort of rebel facilities and monitor them closely. It was my job to make sure no human group ever grew too strong and to report back to my people if you guys ever decided to attack.

"But I need you to understand and believe that I am on your side. I know it doesn't seem like it, but I promise you that I am. There is a group of us. Of my people. We have never liked the way our leaders did things. We never liked the plan to take over this planet. We never wanted humans to die. They're here to kill you all off once our people no longer have any use for you, but my group is determined to make sure that doesn't happen."

"And how the hell do you expect us to believe that you're on our side?" Olivia speaks up, not as attached to him as the rest of us are.

"My resistance group petitioned to allow the rest of your people outside of the Reserve to live freely. We argued that you would never become a threat and promised to monitor the Ruins to ensure that. Our leaders only agreed because they assumed you would die out eventually and didn't want to waste any of our people trying to kill off the rest of you. My group worked to ensure that all of our reports convinced them that you were nothing to worry about, even if we weren't actually monitoring the entirety of the human population left in the Ruins.

"What you need to know is what my people have done to the humans they've captured. They've been testing a new method of what you would call brainwashing. They wipe away memories and manipulate the humans into becoming soldiers for us. Or workers, if they don't want to fight. It's their choice, which makes our people seem like the good guys and the humans of the Ruins seem like the bad guys. It's working better than they could have hoped. I don't have much power to save humans from that fate once they've been captured, but I worked very hard to make sure that didn't happen to these three men of yours here. They have all of their memories, and they know everything I have to say."

"Why didn't they just do that to everyone?" Rebecca asks, and it seems as though the rest of us are starting to take everything in and find our voices.

"It's a very time-consuming process. They wanted to do it to everyone, but as you can guess, that hasn't been done yet. They don't want any of the brainwashed humans to find out that others of them are being brainwashed, so the slow procedure is also very secretive. And our people have come to a consensus that they would like to live in harmony with some normal humans. By that, they mean they want some human workers that aren't brainwashed, but our resistance group wants you all as free as you were before we came here."

"If you were looking out for us, why did it seem like your people knew we were coming to the Reserve?" Damien snaps. Cole's face grows somber.

"Kira felt as though she had to report something. She thought that if you guys were found out, they would find out what our goals really are, and then our efforts would be worthless. Without our help, we're afraid that the rest of the humans wouldn't be able to survive for much longer."

"So, Kira's an alien too?" Damien sounds like he's working to keep his voice low.

"Yes."

"Some of our people died because you did that." I end up blurting out what I think, my tone accusatory. We could have been in and out of the Reserve just fine if Kira hadn't said a word. Jacob would be alive. Abe and Garret would also be alive, and the rebel house would still be inhabitable.

"I know, and I'm sorry. I truly am." He sounds sincere, but I only find myself getting angrier.

"Where is Kira?" Asks Damien.

"With the others. Molly, Angie, and Marcus."

"How did you find us?" Alfie sounds like he already knows.

"I'm the one that gave you the string for the bracelets. They've got the same tracking material in them that the bracelets of the Reserve have." Cole explains, and only then do I realize all of us except Olivia were given a black string bracelet from Alfie and wore it without question. My anger, which was once at a simmer, is starting to boil.

"How did your group have that much influence without getting caught? Wouldn't it be bad if they knew your motives were to help us?" Brianna inquires.

"Yes. But Kira and I are descendants of the . . . supreme leader, I guess you would say. Or queen. She listens to us more than she would anyone else. My real name is Kovet, and hers is Kaihri. "

This shocks me even more, and it seems to have that effect on everyone else as well as I hear them murmur under their breath. If he's telling the truth, it's insane to imagine that the son and daughter of our enemy's leader would be on our side.

"And she was okay with sending you out here?" Grace speaks up.

"She knows we're capable of taking care of ourselves. Plus, not to offend any of you, but among our people, humans aren't considered dangerous. The only thing we have to worry about is the darthra we send out. But as long as I have my gun, one blast in the head will destroy it." I have no idea what darthra are, but if I had to guess, that's their term for the demon dogs.

"Are there any more of you here?" Tyler speaks up with a gasp of pain, and I turn around, suddenly remembering he's hurt badly. His voice is weaker than it was last night, his face covered in sweat.

"Not anywhere near here, no. The others are scattered across the country." Cole, or whatever his name is, says, stepping forward when he notices Tyler's injuries. "Darthra bite?" He asks.

"What?" Tyler looks up at him in confusion, his face pale. I immediately remember Garret looking just like this the last time I saw him. "Something bit me, yeah. One of your dogs."

"Right, sorry. We call them darthra." He goes to grab something from his bag and pulls out a needle. For whatever reason, I panic. All I can think of is the darts that rendered me unconscious. Grabbing my gun off the ground, I quickly step between Cole and Tyler.

"Get away from him," I snarl as he also takes out a silver can. My mind imagines him torturing Tyler, making his pain worse so that we know what he's capable of. Even if I try to think positively, I can only imagine him attempting to do what we've already done to help Tyler. More bandages won't help. Some antiseptics won't either, not at this point. He needs professional medical treatment, which is something that even the rebels have found hard to come by. I don't think anyone that happened to have the right skills to treat Tyler's wounds would also have the right supplies to do what they need to do. So even if all he wants is to make Tyler's inevitable death easier, I don't trust him.

"Yeah, what the hell are you doing?" Elliot shouts, sounding angrier than I've ever heard him as he grabs his gun too, standing by my side. I momentarily remember all the blame he's gotten all because of what I thought he did. I was wrong, and he paid for it. This only adds fuel to the fire of my emotions.

"Rachel, relax. He has stuff that will help." My dad says soothingly, but I barely hear him.

"I said get away!" I yell when Cole keeps walking toward us. I step toward him, gun held steady.

"Tell us what you're doing," Rebecca demands as my dad attempts to get me to lower the gun. I slowly oblige, only because my heart will always trust my father. But my rage at Cole is still very clear.

"I'm going to treat him," Cole says, obviously. "Darthra bites aren't to be taken lightly." His shoulder slams into mine as he walks past me, as if wordlessly telling me to piss off. My dad's staring at me, and I can guess how I must look. Deranged. Hostile. Broken. Not the girl he left behind.

FIFTY-ONE

COLE INJECTS THE LIQUID IN THE NEEDLE INTO A VEIN IN Tyler's arm and then sprays a liquid on his injuries. Tyler gasps in pain again, and I'm at his side in seconds, taking his hand once more as if it's the only thing I know how to do. Elliot grabs his other hand, ready to help him through any pain. Cole takes out a jar and starts plastering a thick blue paste onto Tyler's wounds. I get a whiff of what smells strongly of bleach and eucalyptus before his skin seems to sizzle, and the only scent in the air is burning flesh. Tyler cries out and squeezes my hand so hard that I have to bite my lip to refrain from making a sound.

Tyler's screams seem to go on for hours, but then it's over abruptly, and he doesn't make a sound. Cole rinses off the paste with water from his own water bottle, and all that's left of the bite marks on Tyler are scabs on his skin. Intense-looking scabs, but just scabs and nothing more. When he lets go of my hand, I feel the blood start to flow back into it. He sits up, then stands, the color slowly returning to his face. Surprised but seemingly healthy, he grins at his soon-to-be scars. Our group is quiet once more as Cole steps back. Only Damien breaks the silence.

"I'm hungry. Brianna and I will go hunt." It seems like the most random thing to say, but when I look at Brianna, tears are streaming down her face. I can only assume what she's thinking. This should have been done for Garret.

Damien gently leads her away, and the rest of our group takes that as a sign to try to pretend like things are normal. I can tell everyone has a million questions on the tip of their tongue, but they also want to get over the shock and process everything we've just heard and seen. We open up some cans of food, offering some to Cole as a way of saying thank you. His violet eyes still unnerve me, but I can see what looks like sincerity in them. Any emotion that isn't hatred is an improvement from what I've seen.

I embrace Tyler briefly, relieved that he seems to be okay now. The thoughts of him dying on me are still fresh in my mind, and it will take some time before they're gone. I don't want to go through that again, where I'm about to lose one of the rebels, and I feel like I should have saved them. The other rebels take turns embracing him and inspecting his new scabs as I sit next to my dad.

"Was it you?" I ask Cole, and when his violet eyes look at me, I have to force myself not to look away. "Was it you I ran into in the woods when your people took over the rebel house?" I still remember the traitor as if it all happened a few hours ago. Someone was pretending to be one of us, and when Cole nods his head, I find that I believe him but feel no relief in knowing the answer I've been searching for.

"I thought you were trying to take me away, or kill me, but you saved me. Why?"

"Why wouldn't I?" He answers, and only then do I realize the others have gone silent and stopped moving. Everyone is listening as he continues. "Like I said, it was never my intention to hurt or kill any of you. I wanted you all alive." The memory of being shot with the dart and waking up alone at the bottom of the hill replays in my mind over and over. I now have a face and a name for the person. . .the alien behind the mask, yet I still don't feel any better. This doesn't change the fact that Jacob, Abe, Garret, and so many others that I never met are dead.

When he doesn't say anything else and starts eating his food, the rest of us soon follow. Some are still completely untrusting of Cole, like Olivia, Rebecca, and Elliot. I can see it in their expressions as they stare at him while they eat. Others, like Alfie, Tyler, and Grace, look ready to accept him. Maybe not with open arms, but without guns pointed at his face.

"They didn't do anything to you, did they?" I ask my dad, studying him as if I'd never seen him before. Everyone else has started their own conversations, no longer listening to me. I notice that none of them are talking to Cole, but I'm sure they're all talking about him, even as he sits a few feet away. The other two men seem to be explaining to them what my dad is explaining to me.

"You mean like torture me? No. Cole made sure nothing happened to us. Since there were only three of us, he was able to do that without anyone else noticing or caring. He just told us to do as he said and not mention anything of our past." It's only been a year since I last saw him, but it feels like we're trying to reconnect after an eternity. We barely make eye contact. Our voices have a forced casualness to them.

"And you trusted him?" I raise my eyebrows.

"Of course I did. What choice did I have?"

"What have you been doing all this time?" I start fiddling with a blade of grass under my fingertips now that my can of beans is empty. It seems like I've eaten beans so many times that they just taste like flavorless mush to me now.

"Training to become a guard. What have you been up to? You got out of the Reserve fine?"

"Mary diverted the guards to let me escape. I found the rebels almost right away."

"That's my lucky girl." He gives me a genuine smile, and I feel like I'm back home, waiting for him to tell me the punchline of some corny joke he heard somewhere and just couldn't wait to tell me.

"Mary's in solitary," I say, not allowing myself to give in to nostalgia and comfort. As soon as I get happy, something takes it away.

"That's the punishment for getting caught." He states simply, although his face falls.

"Yeah, well, I didn't know that. Otherwise, I wouldn't have let her help me." I guess I never paid much attention in the Reserve. Outside of my family, I only really talked to Tina. But I knew how other people escaped. I asked around, and there were plenty of rumors.

Yet I was always under the impression that if you did get caught, you were just detained for a few days. Or maybe you'd get one of your three daily meals taken away, which is the punishment for taking more than your share of food. Annie often attempted to do that, trying to snag an extra apple or two before I smacked her hand away. She would try to argue that no one would ever know, but I assured her they always knew. No one gets away with taking more than their share inside the walls.

Being detained. Getting a meal reduction. It's not something anyone would want, but it's better than execution or weeks, even months, of solitary confinement. The thing was, people rarely tried to escape. It wasn't common. We had food, water, shelter, showers, beds, clothes. Our lives were controlled but relatively comfortable, so long as you did your work and followed the rules.

Only those who strongly believed the humans in the Ruins had a fighting chance to take back the earth attempted to escape, and most of them went at it alone. On the positive side, most of them made it, and by that I mean they made it to the Divide. Anyone that didn't make it was no one I ever knew. I should have just gone alone, but Mary was so intent on making sure that I had an easy escape.

"She knew the punishment could be severe, I'm sure. She would have helped you regardless of what the punishment was."

"Which is why we have to get her out."

"We will." He promises. I pause, thousands of thoughts going through my head.

"If you're going to be a guard, will you kill people for them?" I suddenly feel as though my father is just a piece that Cole is using. It makes me uncomfortable to imagine him under the control of someone else. When the strongest and bravest person you know comes to be some expendable object that someone else is in charge of, you start to wonder if you've ever been right about the people you put your faith in. You can convince yourself that you know them and the person controlling them does not, but it doesn't change who's the puppet and who's the puppeteer.

"No. Cole made sure we would only guard inside the ship. No human intruders ever get in there."

I want to ask him about the ship. What it's like. What he sees. What he knows. But I realize that the whole time we've been sitting together, he hasn't opened the can of food I offered him.

"Why haven't you eaten anything?" I expect a simple reply, like he's not hungry, or he doesn't want to waste our food. Instead, he frowns.

"I can't stay." He says. I feel my heart crumble.

"What do you mean you can't stay?" My voice is hollow.

"None of us can stay. It's not just Cole who has to go back to the ship. If we all don't go back, they'll think something's wrong and send forces out to our location. We don't want any of you to be caught up in that."

"So you're just going to try to find me every now and again so you can visit me and give me updates or something?" My tone is angry, but I don't hide it.

"I don't think we can keep coming out here. It was already a risk for us to travel this far from the ship."

"How far away is it?"

"A few hours, if you walk."

"So you're just going to leave me again?" My voice falters, and I see his eyes fill with tears. In all my life, I've only seen my dad cry twice. Once when his dad died, and once when he left us a year ago in the Reserve. I fully understand now, just how much it hurts him to leave us . . . to leave me.

"I would never have left if I hadn't thought I was leaving behind four strong ladies. You're all capable of surviving without me. You all have courage and strength and perseverance that impressed me every day before I left. It may upset you a lot when I leave. . .I know that. But I also know that you will be just fine. You're a Collins. You're my daughter, and you've grown in ways that I can't take credit for. I'm so proud of you." He embraces me and I find myself crying, my tears bouncing on his armor before sliding off.

"I've killed people," I whisper, feeling so much guilt and shame for not being the girl he knew.

"So have I." He murmurs back. "This is a war, after all. But I promise that when things get better, I'll make sure you're happy. That you can recover. We'll do all the things we used to do. Friday night pizza. Saturday night ice cream runs. Sunday morning pancakes. Everything."

"Dad, you're just talking about food-related things. . ." I laugh through my tears, and so does he.

"You know me." He pulls away, and I see Cole and the other men getting ready to leave. Once again, I find happiness only to have it taken away. I need to get used to this. Be happy with what I was given and ignore the sadness when it's gone.

My dad hugs me again, kissing the top of my head as he says goodbye. Then he's walking away from me toward the rest of them. I still don't understand any of this and have no idea what to make of it, but that hardly matters due to the pain of watching my father leave again. For a brief moment, he was here with me. But like everything good in my life, he was gone too soon.

Cole is saying that he came to us and explained everything because he wants to start building a human army inside the ship. An army that isn't brainwashed, since apparently, they have very few of their own people on their side. He claims he will return again tomorrow and reunite us with the other rebels, and while it sounds nice, in my mind, it's all too good to be true. I don't know what to think, given all Cole has supposedly done for us, along with who he claims he is.

"If anything happens to these men," I say to Cole, my voice threatening. "I will find you and kill you myself. I don't care what weapons you have. I'll kill you."

"I think we can all second that." Tyler nods, all six of us staring him down with cold eyes. Cole nods again, understanding. And then the four of them are walking away. The sight of my dad getting further and further away rips at my heart piece by piece. He doesn't look back, maybe to make it easier, but I find myself wishing I could just meet his eyes one more time. I'm terrified I may never see him again.

I know I'm crying my eyes out, but I don't care. Having my family alive and together means more to me than finding out all the answers. Someone tries to turn me toward them to take me into their arms and comfort me. When I see the scabs, I know it's Tyler, but I gently shove him away before I crumble to the ground. I don't want to be in anyone's embrace except for my father's, and anyone else's arms will just have me wishing they were his.

FIFTY-TWO

I PULL MYSELF TOGETHER QUICKLY WHEN I HEAR SOMEONE rummaging loudly through their backpack. Wiping my eyes, I turn around to see Elliot pulling out a knife and hastily trying to cut the black bracelet off.

"What are you doing? Keep it on," Tyler grabs his arm to get the knife away, but Elliot yanks his arm free, glaring at him.

"You really think we can trust him?" He goes back to work at cutting it off.

"Yes!" Tyler tries to take the knife back again, but Elliot holds it behind his back. The two boys stare each other down. "He saved the three rebel men we thought we lost, he saved Rachel, and he just saved me. You saw it."

"What I see is someone who really wants us on his side. And that side may not be ours at all. He felt the need to track us, Tyler, just like they do in the Reserve. So, we're his prisoners now? His little pawns he can move around wherever he wants?" Elliot counters.

"But I think he might be our only way of winning this war," I say. "It seems like every day we're seeing more and more of what the aliens are capable of."

"She has a point," Alfie nods. "I don't think we're going to make any progress by trying to build up another army and then attempting to barge onto the ship. It seemed like we had a chance before, but that was when we only knew of the laser guns. Now that we've seen the darts and the dogs, who knows what else they have?"

"You sound like an outsider." Rebecca narrows her eyes at him, and Alfie grits his teeth.

"Cole says they're brainwashing people, Rebecca! We can't keep acting like we have a chance when we don't. They're finding ways to take us out and expand their army, and we just keep falling apart."

"Outsider talk. You sound just like them." She says again.

"But he's shown us that he can help us. Multiple times." Tyler points to his scabs as if she's gone blind.

"This is bullshit," Elliot snaps. "You're all so quick to trust him, with his purple eyes staring right at you, yet you were ready to throw me under the bus. I was about to be hung because you thought I couldn't be trusted!" He glares at me only for a moment, but it's like his words have wrapped around my neck, squeezing the life out of me. I don't say another word, although the word "sorry" repeats in my head until it sounds like a chant.

"I'm with Elliot. I don't think we should trust him." Grace brings up, her normally quiet voice much sharper and firmer.

"Well, you don't speak for the group," Tyler says.

"Neither do you," she snaps, silencing him.

"So, what do we do?" I ask quietly, not used to seeing us so angry and in disagreement with one another. "Do we stay and wait for him, or do we leave?"

"Leaving is an option for you?" Rebecca raises a brow at me, knowing I've just been given a way to be with my father, the sole reason I left the Reserve. They all know I didn't leave to help fight in this war. I left to find him, and now I can have him back. But what they don't yet seem to know is how much being outside the Reserve walls has changed me. How much being with them has changed me. I can't leave my dad, but I can't leave this group either.

"I want to go where the group goes," I tell her. "I think whatever we decide, we should decide together. And then we should stick together. We're strongest that way."

"What are we debating?" Damien calls out tiredly, and we turn to find him and Brianna walking toward us, lugging a dead darthra that they tied onto a thick fallen branch. We rush to help them, bringing it back to camp and easing it onto the ground. I immediately step back from the creature, its yellow eyes and sharp jaws too familiar and still unsettling. "Figured we may as well try to eat one of these." Damien shrugs. "So, what are we debating?"

"Whether to leave or stay." Grace replies.

"That's easy. Leave." He says, and I'm not surprised he doesn't trust Cole either.

"Why don't we eat first? We should think this over." Brianna suggests.

No one argues. Damien gets to work attempting to skin the darthra, cursing at its thick hide. I almost bring up the fact that darthra skin can take an insane amount of bullets but decide against it, especially when Damien starts to get the hang of it. The body is skinned. The head is cut off and put aside. Brianna and Damien keep working until a fire is built and we've got meat roasting on it.

I turn away when Damien starts joking about wearing the head as a mask, and I see Elliot walking into the woods. Hurrying after him, I almost trip on some tree roots as I ask him where he's going.

"I'm going for a walk." He replies. "Do you trust me enough to do that?" His tone is mocking and takes me back. Speechless, I watch him walk away. I thought he understood why I was suspicious of him, but maybe it still angers him that I would lose faith in him so quickly.

"What's going on?" Tyler's voice startles me.

"You should go talk to him," I say, turning back toward camp.

"What? Why do you want me to talk to him?" He asks, and it's clear he knows why Elliot's upset but doesn't understand how he can help.

"Because you're the only person that knew everything I knew

and still believed in him." I start to walk back, but he stops me, placing a hand on my shoulder.

"Hey," He lowers his voice a bit, and for a second I think he's going to attempt to comfort me about my father. My father leaving again is something I don't want to think about, so I almost try to wiggle out of his grasp when he keeps going. "I never got to tell you this before, but thank you for saving me back there. The other night. I would have been a goner if it wasn't for you." He actually smiles at me, and I start to think he might be proud of me, along with being grateful.

"You would have done the same for me." I smile back. He would have done it for anyone, and I'm slowly realizing that I would, too. Our group is no longer the people who run to safety in the face of danger. We run straight to the danger, regardless of our fear.

"I would have tried to, yeah," He laughs.

"How are your scabs?" I glance briefly at them.

"Fine. I'm not in pain anymore. They just itch. Cole let me keep that jar of blue stuff. He said it'll heal pretty much anything, as long as there's not something like a bullet stuck in you."

"That's good," I find my mood lifting.

"If only he also had something to dry off our stuff." Tyler jokes and I realize I hadn't even noticed that my shoes were still soggy.

"If only," I agree. The air is hot and humid, though, so maybe our stuff will be dry soon enough.

"Go after Elliot. And be careful. Please." My eyes scan to make sure he's got his gun, which reminds me to get more ammo from Brianna. Assuming she took all of Garret's stuff.

"I will." He nods. I'm worried, but I know he can take care of himself.

"Do you have ammo?" I add quickly before he leaves.

"Yeah, Rebecca said she loaded both of ours last night." He says. I check my gun and see that he's right.

Heading back to camp, I find Rebecca and Alfie arguing. A new slab of meat is on the fire, tended to by a worried-looking Brianna.

Olivia is finishing off her share of meat, glaring at the fire. Damien and Grace are gone.

"Where are they?" I ask, wondering if they went to haul back more darthra. It's doubtful, and my stomach sinks as I start to piece everything together. I can only imagine that some kind of argument ensued and made Damien and Grace angry enough to walk off.

"They left. They think Cole is going to come back and kill us." Alfie rolls his eyes.

"Which could happen!" Rebecca insists.

"He could have killed us the second he found us!" Alfie argues.

"I'm with blondie on this one." Olivia stands up. "I don't think we're in the clear yet. He's one of them."

"So, you just let them go?" I don't hide my disbelief.

"I didn't want them to," Alfie begins.

"It's their choice." Rebecca snaps.

"We're better off together!" Alfie hisses back.

"Guys, we can't just let them leave," I say, looking worriedly out into the woods. "It's dangerous out there."

"It's dangerous everywhere. They'll be back." Brianna insists, but even she doesn't seem convinced. "They'll be back." She repeats more firmly.

"I'm going after them," I announce, slipping off my windbreaker and sliding on my shirt from the other night. It still feels slightly damp, but I can deal with it. Throwing my windbreaker into my bag, I get ready to talk off. I think about going back to find Tyler to get him to go with me, but I feel like that'll just waste time. "Will one of you tell Tyler where I'm going? And tell him I'll be back soon. If I don't find them quickly enough, I'll just come back." I don't know if the whole partnership thing still stands anymore, but I do know he won't be happy at the idea of me wandering out there alone. It's not that I need his permission to leave, but after almost losing him once, I don't want him tearing through the woods by himself just to find us.

"I'll go with you," Olivia says, grabbing her knives.

"Great," I smile at her. There's some relief in that. I won't be alone.

"Tyler will be fine," Brianna says, as if reading my mind. She gazes at Olivia. "He said you never miss with those knives."

"I try my best." Olivia laughs, blushing slightly. I think of the darthra, and how I promised myself back at the Peterson house that I'd get her a gun, but I never did.

"Can she borrow one of your guns?" I ask, and Alfie hands her his gun without hesitation. Finally, feeling like we're prepared, we take off.

FIFTY-THREE

Despite the sun shimmering down through the trees, I hear a rumble in the distance behind us that sounds like thunder. After everything I've seen, I wonder if it's something else. Picking up my pace, I glance briefly at Olivia, who looks just as wary as I do. Another rumble follows, louder this time. It sounds enough like thunder, but the sky above me is clear. We move even faster without a word.

The trees fade away until we're walking on a road. I feel the heat of the asphalt under my shoes as another rumble sounds, loud enough to shake the ground. Large raindrops suddenly fall hard and fast, soaking us instantly. As the rain hits the hot road, steam rises up around our legs. The humidity causes my wet clothes to cling to me, and I struggle to keep my eyes peeled through the sudden storm. There's still some sun lighting the way, but the rain is so harsh it's hard to see through. Clumsily attempting to take my windbreaker out of my bag and walk at the same time, I yank it out and hastily hold it over both of us so that we don't get as wet.

"This is just what I wanted!" Olivia remarks sarcastically, having to shout over the rain. That earns a laugh out of me, which eases my nerves.

Lightening cracks. Thunder demands to be heard. And then it's over just as quickly as it began, leaving a trail of steaming asphalt in its wake. We've come across a small town now, the low fog giving it an eerie feeling despite the fact that all the buildings remain intact, illuminated by the sun that has come back out. This town was never bombed, nor had it ever had lasers fired upon it. It was too small to suffer from such a fate and become a part of the Divide. As I put away the windbreaker, I have a good look around.

No Émigré ships sweep through the skies. No humans besides us walk through the empty streets. Broken glass litters the bottoms of windows, and doors hang open, some off their hinges. . .but other than that, this town almost looks normal. Small businesses with the signs still visible. Gas stations with cars still parked in them. Apartments with different types of lawn furniture and plants on their balconies. I almost smile. If it wasn't for the silence, I could easily imagine pre-invasion life here.

"How's this sound?" I stop in front of an ice cream shop, and Olivia stops next to me. "I take the left side, you take the right side, and we meet in the middle." It's the same strategy I had at the Divide, except I feel much safer here.

"You really think they'd stop here?" She asks, looking around.

"It's nice enough," I shrug. "I don't think it would hurt to look, and we could find something useful. But be careful. There could be other people here."

"Right," she nods.

"Hey," I stop her for a second. "I know our group might not exactly be the type of people you would have risked your life for, but I just wanted you to know I'm really glad you're here."

"Thanks," she grins at me. "I'm glad to be here, though. All I've wanted to do since the invasion started was fight back, and now it looks like I'll get the chance." She heads off to my right, faintly slipping away in the thin fog.

Going off to the left, I take quick peeks into every building. Fast-food restaurants and family businesses. Dry-cleaners. Bars. All empty. Nothing to scavenge either, as though even survivors have had their fill of this place. There's a large stain of blood on the wooden floor of the ice cream shop, but other than that, it looks like no one has been here for a long time.

Another rumble of thunder shakes the earth a bit as I start towards one of the apartment complexes. I'm nearly at the doorway when the sun is suddenly blocked off by a cloud and the rumbling gets louder. With a jolt of panic, I quickly realize this wasn't another storm. Dashing inside, I cower down below a window, hesitantly peeking over to see what's in the sky.

The hum is almost deafening; the ground vibrating below me and causing my teeth to rattle. I'm expecting an army of Émigré ships just like the ones that patrol the Divide, but all I see is one. One ship, larger than any I've seen yet. It's still blocking out the sun as it moves slower than the ones I'm familiar with.

It shows no sign of stopping or landing, moving along at a steady pace and never changing altitude. Curious as to where its destination is, I work my way up the stairs in the apartment, sprinting until I can't go any higher. Running into the nearest open room, I look out the window. Off in the distance, I spot what looks like an extremely large white building. But as I continue to stare at it, I see that it's actually a ship. A massive ship on the ground, that the ship in the sky is headed straight toward. It's the mothership.

My father was right. It's not too far away from us. We could walk for just about an hour or so and we'd probably walk right into their first line of defense, which seems to be guards from what Marcus said. But I'm guessing they have plenty of darthra lurking around to try to pick us off before that.

The ship in the air is finally far away enough for my ears to start recovering. They ring as the ship gets smaller and smaller until I can't see it anymore. I gradually bring my gaze away from the sky and look at what's in front of me. To my surprise, I notice that the wall of the building right across from me has been painted. It has some kind of graffiti on it, and the ladder the person must have used is still against the building.

"VICTORIA AUT MORS" is painted in a dark, almost blood-like red at the top. On one side of the building are figures painted in black combat gear. On the right are figures painted in white armor. I can tell that this is supposed to show rebels vs aliens, but what's interesting to me is that as I look down, the rebels fade into a cloud of black smoke until all I can see are what looks like black wolves. The Émigrés, on the other hand, fade into white smoke, and then all that's left is sheep.

We're wolves, and they're sheep? I guess that's a nice way of thinking about the rebels. We can fight like a pack and fight on our own, just like wolves and just like their darthra. But I'm not sure why the Émigrés would be compared to sheep. Maybe the artist just used sheep because the colors matched and they wanted us to look like we have the upper hand. Wolves hunt sheep, we hunt Émigrés. . .or something. Admiring the work for one last moment, I make a mental note to tell the others about it.

Jogging back down to the first floor of the apartment, I take a look at the building again as I step outside. There's a paint shop two buildings down from here, so it's no surprise where they got their paint, but how they managed to find the time to paint something like that when the world is like this is beyond me. I turn back toward the other buildings, noticing that the light fog is starting to fade, although the air is still hot and sticky. Up ahead, I spot Olivia walking toward me. As I walk up to meet her, I notice the fear in her expression.

"What the hell was that?" She looks up at the sky again, and so do I. Nothing's there, and I can't hear another one coming.

"It was like the Émigré ships that patrol the Divide, but much bigger. I don't know what it was doing, but I saw that it was going toward the main ship." I respond.

"Figures. Those other guys said it was nearby." She pauses, seeming deep in thought. "You know, a couple of days ago, we heard a sound like that. We thought it was thunder, but it went on for too long. It wasn't close enough for us to see anything, though. Now that I think about it, that must have been the day after you guys said you got caught in the Reserve."

As her words sink in, my thoughts start to come together, and I feel like ice has suddenly been pumped through my veins. That ship was going to the Reserve from the mothership after we got caught and all hell broke loose. And now it was finally going back. Was it transporting people? My mom. Annie. Mary. Now I'm even more desperate to find them or find out what happened to them, but I feel like I'm even further away.

"You okay?" She interrupts me, looking at me with concern.

"Yeah," I nod. "It's just that whatever it is can't be good."

"Of course," she sighs in agreement. "I take it you didn't find that couple?"

"Damien and Grace?"

"Yeah, I didn't either. No signs of life. No nothing. Did you find anything interesting?"

"Actually," I begin, but I'm cut off by a distant scream. We both freeze, listening intently as if we may have just imagined it. But when I hear the scream again, I know.

Grace.

FIFTY-FOUR

OLIVIA AND I RUN THROUGH THE TOWN, WAITING WITH DREAD for another scream that would help us find Grace, but it never comes. I once again prepare myself for what we might come across; Darthra, Émigrés, outsiders, or something new. There's still a feeling festering in the pit of my stomach that says we may be too late, but I hold on to the hope that we will find them alive. It's what Garret would do, and my father would think that way, too.

The air is still quiet, except for the sounds we make as we tear through a suburban neighborhood. The houses all look almost identical, lined up side by side. Their once perfect lawns are now covered in weeds, the grass stretching higher toward the sky. Olivia is faster than me, so I let her lead, but I don't dare separate from her. Losing one just to find another won't help anything.

The scream sounded far away, so I have no idea if we were close. I debate whether to search the houses, but Olivia doesn't stop, so I don't either. We were able to hear her scream because she was outside, and whatever caused that scream would probably be something we'd see for ourselves. I try to keep my breathing down to try to hear any kind of commotion.

We're in a small patch of woods when I hear crying. I know Olivia heard it too as she bolts to the right. Following a narrow, clear walking path, the damp ground slopping noisily under our feet, we come across Grace kneeling on the ground. It looks like they're surrounded by bags and piles of clothes, but I don't see anyone else. Or any demon dogs. Damien, who was hunched over comforting her, snaps upright and points his gun at us, only lowering it when he recognizes us. There are no insults or anger thrown our way, and nothing but sadness in his eyes. When I look down at the ground, I see why. In my panic, I failed to fully notice what was around me, only searching for Grace and focusing on her. The piles of clothes on the ground aren't actually piles of clothes. They're bodies.

"I was just. . ." Grace begins, gulping away her sobs. "We were walking and arguing. We didn't even notice, and I tripped and landed on one of them. And then accidentally rolled off onto another one."

I walk forward as if in a trance, taking in the scene in front of me. Blue eyes stare back at me. Then brown. All unblinking, all human. Some look as young as Elliot. Others are probably as old as my father. Each one of them either has a gash in the head, neck, or chest. Very precise work, which only could have been done by Émigrés or outsiders. Both possibilities immediately put me on edge.

"My guess is outsiders. All of their bags are empty, for the most part. And there are remnants of a fire over there. This was a camp of survivors that got attacked. And recently, too." Damien tells us.

"They must have been living in those houses, only coming out here to cook and convene." Olivia guesses.

"What could I have done. . .if we were attacked?" Grace is crying again. "How could I have helped you? They were right. We should stay with them, even if we don't agree. That's how we're stronger."

I notice the closed eyes of the girl beneath my feet twitch slightly. Nearly jumping backward in shock, I quickly bend down to see if she's still breathing. Putting my hand under her nose, I feel nothing. But I remember learning how to check for a pulse in Health class back at school, so I do that, placing my fingers against her neck, careful to avoid the wound on the other side, near her collarbone. I feel a weak but noticeable pulse.

"Guys!" I shout, before remembering I should probably keep it down, considering the fact that we now know there are outsiders around. "She's still alive."

The others are by me before I can blink, and it's like they've gone into rescue mode. Damien tears out a spare shirt from his bag and wraps it around the girl's neck as Grace lifts her honey blonde curls out of the way and feels for a pulse as well. She nods to Damien, who immediately picks the girl up as if she didn't weigh a thing.

"Check the others. See if they're alive. Then follow us back to the camp." Damien orders before he and Grace start running back to the neighborhood. Olivia and I do just that, and I try to get over my fear as I check for pulses from those with their eyes still closed. We check and double-check, but none of the others are alive.

"Do you remember the way back?" I call out to Olivia as we dash back through the neighborhood.

"Sort of," she says back, leading the way to the town. Once surrounded by the familiar buildings, I spot the ice cream shop and momentarily remember the rebel artwork on the side of the building by the paint shop. Then I think of the girl, barely in her teens and clinging to life, and I push myself until I'm side by side with Olivia. Thankfully, no ships glide through the air this time as we head back to the road we think we came here on.

Damien and Grace are just ahead of us as we follow the road. They seem to know where they're going, having not gotten caught in the storm right when Olivia and I did. That's the only reason I'm not sure if this is right, because the rain was so hard I could barely see where we were. When they veer into the woods, I make a note of the spot and then head in when we get there.

We manage to arrive at the camp seconds after Damien, who had been slowed down trying to carry the girl and not disturb her injuries. The others are all there, looking at us with a mixture of surprise and confusion.

"Tyler," I manage to gasp. "She's hurt. She needs that blue medicine." Catching my breath, I watch as he zaps into focus and takes out the jar. He also has the spray that Cole used on him. Damien lowers the girl onto bedding made of jackets that Brianna and Rebecca have hastily made, and Tyler gets to work. The girl slightly opens her eyes as he sprays her wound. In the sunlight, they are a brilliant bluish green that reminds me of my mother.

"Hey," Tyler says softly to her, offering her a kind smile. The girl is struggling to hold on to consciousness as Tyler brushes her hair back from her face. I back away to give her space, and the other rebels do the same. "This next stuff is going to really hurt, but I promise it'll help. Just hang on." He tells her, and he begins applying the blue paste with his right hand while holding one of her hands with his left hand, just like Elliot and I did for him.

The girl grimaces and gives a small whimper, but it's clear she's much too weak to respond to the searing pain she's probably in. Tyler notices this, and his face falls. When he finishes applying the paste, he slightly lifts up the hem of her dark shirt to reveal a deep abdomen injury. I can't hide my gasp as I look away, suddenly feeling overwhelmed with sadness.

When I look back, Tyler's doing the same process to her other wound as she tries to watch him. I come forward, leaning down and taking her other hand in mine. She looks over at me, and it almost looks like she wants to say something, but can't. My guess is she wants to thank us, so I just smile and give her a nod to say that I understand.

Tyler finishes his work, and the scent of burning flesh and medicine begins to fade. He's quiet for a few moments as he holds the girl's hand. I can hear her breathing, ragged but extremely faint. Then, his smile is back, and he begins to speak.

"My name is Tyler. That girl on the other side of you, her name's Rachel. We're all part of the rebels, fighting to end this war. I promise you that you're going to be okay. You got that? You'll be okay. We've got fancy medicine, the best in the world, stolen from the aliens themselves. It saved me, and it's gonna save you." His voice is so gentle, full of sincerity. From the girl's eyes, it still looks like she has something to say, but she can't say it. I wonder if she wants to say that she's a rebel, too. That there are more of us. Or that she's not a rebel, but she hopes that we'll win. There's a million things that could be on her mind right now, but Tyler's intent on taking her mind off of the pain she's still in. I brush my thumb across her hand in a way that I hope is comforting.

"It's a nice planet we've got here," He continues. "Beautiful, really. I feel lucky that I've gotten to live on it. There's this place in Michigan that I used to go to every summer. . ."

I feel tears starting to sting my eyes as he murmurs about the trails and the lake, going into vivid detail even more so than he had done with me. He wants to take her mind away from it all, but not because she killed someone. Because she's going to die. And there's nothing any of us can do about it. Not even advanced alien medicine can save someone who's lost as much blood as she has.

There's a faint smile on her lips when her eyes stop blinking, and we can't hear her breathing anymore. The tears spill over as I let her hand go. Every death gets to me, whether I want it to or not. Tyler releases her hand and then closes her eyes, looking at her with an expression I can't place.

FIFTY-FIVE

"We should bury her. . ." Grace's voice is a whisper.

"With what?" Brianna asks, wiping her eyes.

"We can find something." Damien comes forward, slowly lifting the girl up and away from us. He's the only one of us who doesn't show his grief at this moment, choosing to just act instead.

Time seems to slow down a bit as I continue to stare at the spot where the young girl once was. Her death nearly affects me in the same way as the deaths of people I knew, because as of right now, I can't seem to fully grip reality. Another life is gone, yet the sun still shines overhead. The birds sing, the cicadas buzz, and the air still feels thick and heavy with heat. It's glaringly obvious how even when your life ends, the world doesn't stop. The sun will come up the next morning. Another day in another year. It'll be no different when I die, which could be terrifyingly soon, and it's all weird to think about. Even if I lose someone again and my world is violently flipped around, life won't stop to wait for me to recover.

"I'm sorry about how I acted earlier," Elliot's quiet voice snaps me back into the present moment, his eyes grim and unsure. "It was childish and uncalled for."

"It's okay," I clear my throat. "I deserved it."

"No, you didn't, I just let my anger get to me," He insists.

"Yes, I did deserve it. We both know it." I snap before he can say anything else. "Let's just move on. If you'll excuse me, I haven't slept in a while and I'd like to get some rest." Softening my voice, I attempt to give him a smile to let him know that I hold no hostility towards him. We're all going through a lot. And besides, no one ever said we had to be friends. All we need is to be able to work together.

I go to where I attempted to sleep last night, using my backpack as a pillow. It's uncomfortable, but it'll do. My eyes feel heavy and my body aches, but I know it'll take a long time for me to fall asleep if I do at all. With my eyes closed, all I see is what the girl looked like when she passed away. Her beautiful eyes zapped of life. I don't even know her name.

"Hey," Tyler speaks softly, and I think he's trying to wake me for some reason, so I gladly open my eyes to rid them of images of the girl I couldn't save. But he's not speaking to me. Elliot stands next to him, a worried look on his face.

"I need to speak to you. Alone." Elliot murmurs. I shut my eyes again when his gaze shifts down to me, knowing that this conversation isn't meant for me to hear. But I'm curious, so I work to listen in.

"What's wrong? Is everything okay?" The confusion in Tyler's voice is clear.

"Everything's fine, for now. I just need you to hear me out on something."

I can hear them walking away, and neither of them says anything else, but I have an idea what this might be about. Elliot is still certain that it's not safe to stay, that we can't trust Cole. And if he can't convince the whole group, he can try to convince the person that he trusts the most. My heart sinks. He knows I'd never leave. Not with my father under Émigré control. Elliot doesn't need me, and that's fine. Problem is, I think I need him, and Tyler too.

I've come to care about these rebels a lot. And over this short period, I already can't imagine fighting this war without them. If any of them left, I'd think about them every day. Even now, it's hard for me to wrap my mind around the fact that Garret is gone, since I didn't see him die and I never saw his body. My mind shifts back to him consistently, and I almost expect him to come walking through the woods to join us, his hands full of freshly hunted rabbits and squirrels.

If I can't handle losing Garret, how can I handle losing Elliot and Tyler? I've tried to stop caring about them multiple times, but I can't deny how much I want them alive and by my side. On the positive side, if they did leave, I'd have Olivia. She seems like a great addition to the group. . .smart, agile, determined, and nice enough. Even with the two couples and a heartbroken Brianna, I could probably manage if Olivia was with me.

With all these thoughts running through my head, I've forgotten to even pretend to get some sleep. I spot Damien coming toward me, his mouth in a thin line and his eyes unreadable. Looking around me, I wonder if he means to find someone else, but no one is near me. He apparently wants to talk to me, although I have no idea what he could possibly want to say.

"Remember how I said the bags of those people were mostly empty?" He says when he's almost reached me. I nod. "That girl had a hardcover notebook in her bag. I figured if she was alive, she might want it, but since she's gone, I took a look at it." I still can't place this expression or determine what this has to do with me. Looking up at him in confusion, I watch as he holds up a notebook and opens it.

A handful of Polaroid photographs spill out onto the soil right in front of me, reminding me of the photographs that Tyler kept in his notebook. I'm wondering if these pictures will also be of her friends and family and if she happens to know someone I know when I take a good look at the first photograph. It's not a person, per se. It's graffiti, just like I saw on the building in that small town. Yet this is no face-less, nameless rebel or alien. It's Garret, painted on the wall clear as day.

This art is different from the art I saw earlier, though. Whoever painted this was a different artist, and they didn't have any actual paint on hand. One color was used to bring him back to life, and judging by the looks of it, it was made with whatever they could find and might have already washed off in all the rain we've had. And the work isn't massive, only stretching up a few feet high. But the message is clear. Garret is a symbol.

"THE REVOLUTION HAS BEGUN" is painted above him, in the same muted navy color used to paint him. He looks so stoic in the artwork that it almost takes me back. Whoever painted him either knew him or. . .now that I look at it, the building he's painted on is familiar. It's in the Divide, right outside the Reserve. In fact, it's the convenience store I went into after my escape. The place I met Tyler.

"Look at the others," Damien interrupts my hectic train of thought, and I tear my eyes away to move on to the next photograph. All it takes is one glance and I can't breathe. It's me, painted on another building, in the same color, with the same words above my head. The artist painted my hair down and made it much longer than it actually is, and my lips look much fuller, but it's me. Not as accurate of a portrait as Garret's, but it's all starting to make sense. People in the Reserve saw us get caught. They saw us about to be executed. And they saw us fight back. They think we were there to free them.

Alfie is in the next photograph, painted on another building just like Garret and me. The artist gave him too many freckles, yet his eyes are so angry it sends a shiver through me. On that day I didn't even notice his expressions, and I'm sure I must have looked like a deranged animal, but the artist chose to paint us in a much better light. One that would get people motivated. The last photo brings the familiar sting of tears to my eyes. Jacob, his eyes full of fear, tears on his cheeks, blood on his temple, and his hands up in surrender. The words above him are different, reading "THIS ENDS NOW".

We are symbols. We, who only entered the Reserve as a practice run to see our loved ones, have apparently shown these people that the human race has a chance. That the war has officially started, and we are all somehow unified and ready to fight. We have unintentionally given them hope. With trembling hands, I set the photos down, although I can't tear my eyes away.

I imagine people leaving the Reserve by the hundreds, smiles on their faces as they think they now walk toward a better life and a fighting chance against the alien race that has controlled us for two years. To them, we are their leaders, ready to give them orders and help them end this war. To them, we are strong, undivided, and fully capable of victory. They don't know of darthra. Of outsiders. Of the rebel body count. They're walking to their deaths, and they have no idea.

They think we can save them. How much will it destroy them to find out they're wrong?

FIFTY-SIX

I can't wrap my mind around the fact that my face is painted somewhere for survivors to see. The idea of people imagining that I'm proof that they can make it or that I could somehow help to lead them is unfathomable to me. In fact, I almost feel nauseous. All I can do is hope that anyone who's seen that knows better than to assume that I'm someone to look up to or a sign that they can be saved. I'm just a girl who was looking for her father and got caught up in the war.

Damien mutters something about how those paintings may as well put a bigger target on our backs, giving the Émigrés more incentive to hunt us down and kill us like they planned. He then gathers up the photos and walks away, leaving me unmoving and still staring at the ground. I only snap out of it when I hear footsteps again.

"Hey," Tyler says as he makes his way toward me, Elliot nowhere near him. "Thought I'd try to get some rest as well."

"You could use some rest," I agree, nodding. I refrain from telling him about the photos and confronting him about possibly leaving. It can wait until after he finally gets some much-needed sleep.

"You okay?" He gives me a look of concern, probably assuming that whatever expression I have is from the girl that just died. I work to give a convincing smile, feeling like my cheeks are heavy and unfamiliar.

"Fine. I just need some rest, too." I assure him, and this time he nods. He lays down on some open soil across from me while I lay back on my side. I attempt once more to fall asleep. It's difficult, but somehow the hazy summer heat and the relentless hum of the cicadas help me drift off.

My dreams don't make too much sense to me, but they're extremely vivid. I'm surrounded by people screaming at me to help them, waving their arms, and trying to clutch onto any part of me that they can grasp. I try to push them away, but every hand that slides off me is replaced by several more, gripping my arms and legs for solace. Their touch stings my skin, their shrill begging clouds my ears, and there are so many of them I can hardly focus on a single face for too long. None of them I recognize until a face full of freckles stands out. Alfie.

People are reaching for him too, clawing at him like they haven't eaten in days and he's the last piece of food on earth. They shout for him to save them, and he looks just as helpless as I feel. When our eyes meet, we make our way toward each other as if to find some relief, knowing the other is suffering the same way. Pushing through the crowd, we finally meet.

"What are we supposed to do?" He yells over their cries.

"I don't know," I yell back. Looking over at him, I spot Rebecca, dealing with what seems like a hundred more people, and I immediately think about Elliot, Molly, and Tyler suffering the same fate nearby.

"We need Garret. They need Garret. We're not what they think we are. We can't help them like they want us to." Alfie is panicking, and he looks at me in horror. The hands of the people in my dreams now feel like talons that are ripping my skin off. I wake up to the sound of my own screaming in my ears.

As I calm my breathing down, I'm thankful that my screams were only in my mind and not out loud. I can hear Tyler snoring, and the sun is almost set, giving everything an orange glow. The others are a few feet away from us now, and I can see Elliot looking at the notebook. Alfie is attempting to cheer Brianna and Rebecca up by making various facial expressions, each more ridiculous than the previous one. Only the distant howl of a darthra brings us all back to reality as we look at each other in a panic.

"They're probably snacking on those bodies," Damien says, and judging by the direction the sound came from, I think he's right. I shove any disturbing imagery out of my mind.

"We should spend the night in the trees. We'll be safer up there and able to shoot 'em down if we need to." Tyler suggests as he stands up, fully awake. A few of the others nod.

"But what if we doze off and fall?" Grace asks, glancing up warily at the trees. I see her point. We have nothing to tie ourselves to the branches with.

"Anyone that needs to sleep should take the risk and stay on the ground. Those of us in the trees will stay awake and guard." Brianna answers in a final tone, beginning to climb the tree nearest to her. I can't think of the last time I saw her sleep, but I don't dare argue with her. I begin to climb the tree I was just resting on, but I can't quite seem to find the right footing.

"I got you," I hear Olivia's voice before I see her, and the next thing I know, she's holding my feet up with ease, letting me get a grip. Taking out one of her knives, she embeds it further up in the bark of the tree, and I use that as a thin but helpful stepping stone to finally get me up to where there are branches I can grab onto.

When I'm nearly at a branch sturdy enough to be my resting place for the night, I lose my footing and almost go crashing to the ground. If it weren't for my hands grabbing onto the branches above me with all my strength, I'd fall right onto Olivia. Squeezing my eyes shut, I refuse to look down and put myself in a panic when I realize how high up I am. My stomach is clenched in anxiety, but I take a few deep breaths and allow myself some time to recover before I pull myself up.

Once I'm resting on a branch, I stare straight ahead and let my mind wander so that I don't think about how far I am from the ground below me. There's so much to think about. . .so much to worry about. . .but I focus on my family as I hear Olivia settle onto a branch below me.

Within walking distance is the mothership. The place the rebels have been searching for since this war began. The place where my father is. Walk in the opposite direction and I'll eventually find the Reserve, a place where I thought my mother and sisters were safe, but now it's clear that's not true. And in the morning, Cole will be here, and I'll have to try to make sense of everything again. My body has that anxious gut feeling I felt moments ago, only it's not fading this time. I can't gain my footing.

Who do I put first? My father, because he's closest, and risked his life to give us lives free of alien control? Or my mother, because she took care of me every day without fail after he left so suddenly. Or Mary, because without her, my incompetent self would have never been able to escape. Or Annie, because she's too young to deserve any of this, and I wouldn't have found so many reasons to smile behind those walls if it weren't for her. I want to save them all, but can I? If all of them were right in front of me and I could only choose one, would I be able to choose? Or would I freeze and lose them all?

I let these thoughts consume me as the sun sets and then rises again. Intentionally, I refrain from thinking about anything else because I know I would just drive myself further into paranoia. Focus on one thing at a time. That's all I can do. Feeling hunger gnaw at my stomach, I carefully dig out what seems to be my last can of food from my backpack, making sure I don't drop anything from my place on the branch. I eat beans for what seems like the millionth time but may be my last, looking out at the other trees to keep myself from looking down.

Elliot and Tyler are visible a few trees down from me, but even as the sun continues to rise, they're all I can spot. Both of them still have their eyes peeled toward the direction of the single howl we heard earlier, although I can make out that they're talking to each other quietly. I feel a pang in my heart, wondering again if they're thinking about leaving.

FIFTY-SEVEN

By the time I finish my food, everyone's beginning to climb down from their trees and coming into view. I make my way down very slowly, grateful for Olivia's soft words of encouragement. Once my feet are on the ground, I make my way over to Elliot and Tyler, trying not to feel angry or hurt.

"If you guys are thinking about leaving, at least say goodbye to all of us," I murmur, noting that they don't even look surprised and they aren't trying to deny it. I remind myself that they've been through a lot too and are free to make their own decisions. The fate of Elliot's family is unknown after what happened in the Reserve, just like my mom and sisters. And Tyler hasn't seen his family since the invasion started. Nothing really binds them to stay here, not like my dad binds me.

"I don't think we're leaving. Not yet, anyway." Elliot glances at Tyler.

"But you want to," I state, and they both nod.

"I really don't trust Cole. I don't like the sound of this." Elliot says.

"I want to trust him, so I would stay, but if Elliot leaves, I don't want him to be alone. I would be willing to go with him if he didn't want to stay." Tyler tells me, looking at me like he did when I confronted him about leaving me the first time. But this isn't about me.

"What would you do if you left?" I work to keep my voice down when I notice Rebecca looking at us curiously as the others scrounge up whatever food and water they have.

"Find my family," Elliot answers automatically, but Tyler stays quiet. I thought Tyler was the kind to always stay and fight, and would never stop fighting. But I guess his friendship with Elliot is stronger than I ever bothered to notice. Maybe he would work with Elliot in hopes of finding his own family as well, and maybe then he would try to keep fighting in the war somehow. Or maybe he would just be content with just trying to survive after already fighting so much. It's not like the rebels have an army at this point, anyway.

"I wouldn't blame you for leaving," I tell them. They know I wouldn't leave now that I've found my dad. If I still didn't know he was alive, I might have really considered going with them just to get back to my mother and sisters. But now we all know that if they leave, I'll stay, and we may never see each other again.

"If we do leave, we'll be sure to say goodbye. To everyone." Tyler says, and now I know that if they decide to leave, they don't plan on going until everyone, including Cole, is here. They have more time to decide than I thought. I give them a nod and join the rest of the rebels, sitting next to Olivia, who is busy eating what looks like stale crackers. She doesn't seem to notice I'm there, her mind occupied somewhere else.

"I hope you don't think either of us really wants to leave you guys," Elliot says quietly as he sits next to me. Startled, I look at him silently and wait for him to continue. He leans in as if to prevent Olivia or anyone else from hearing. "I know you may feel like you don't fit in with us as much because we've all been together, and you just joined us, but after everything happened at the Reserve, we were all looking for you. I caught up with Tyler and Molly, and we kept going around that area by the house looking for everyone, including you."

"He told me that." My voice is a whisper.

"When we decided to just go to the next base and hope that you and the others were there, he still wanted to look for you. He didn't want us to stop to sleep or eat until we either found you or got to the base. The guilt was eating him up, I'm sure. He kept talking about how he shouldn't have abandoned you like that and wasn't thinking properly. But even if it doesn't seem like it, he cares about you, too. And so does Molly. I heard she gave you a hard time that day, but she had no complaint about looking for you, even when we had no idea where her mom was. She wanted you to be alive just as much as the rest of us did."

I can't seem to find any words to respond with, but luckily I don't have to. Damien alerts us of movement in the woods, and by the time we raise our weapons, we can see that it's the rest of the rebels. Angie, Marcus, and Molly, led by Cole. My father isn't there, and even though my stomach sinks, I find that I'm not surprised. I march up to Molly and hug her, feeling her give me a hesitant pat on the back.

"Alright, Swan Queen," she lets out a shaky laugh. "Don't make me cry. I missed you too." We grin at each other before she's engulfed in Elliot's arms. I hug Angie and give Marcus a friendly nod, still feeling a bit of guilt for putting blame on him as well as Elliot. Everyone is talking and catching up as I make my way toward Cole.

"Do you have any idea what's going on in the Reserve?" I ask him, hoping he has even the slightest update to calm my scattered mind. He frowns, his eyes struggling to meet mine.

"Well, a lot of things are changing there. There's public punishment for breaking the rules. Even taking extra food will get you a public beating along with a meal reduction. No one has free time anymore, and any deviations from your schedule will result in a public whipping. And now, if you are caught trying to escape, you aren't detained. You're executed in front of everyone."

What he says shouldn't be shocking to me, considering everyone always imagined them resorting to worse punishments if things got out of hand, but imagining all those people being beaten or killed is causing my breathing to become shaky. The Reserve is no longer a vision of a controlled sanctuary. It's fully become what it always felt like: a prison.

"So people have been trying to leave, I assume," I try to stabilize my voice.

"Yes, some of them have. A lot of people were motivated by you guys, but there are also plenty of people who hate you for making things worse."

So not everyone left the Reserve arm-in-arm, excited for a shift in momentum in this war. The rebels are divided, the outsiders are divided, and now, so are the people of the Reserve. And, as it seems, so are the Émigrés.

"How many people have been executed so far?" I dare to ask.

"19," He replies grimly. "All of them had been trying to escape and got caught."

I feel an all too familiar pang of guilt, followed by an equally familiar wave of sadness that makes me feel utterly cold even in the summer heat.

"The numbers have tapered off over the past couple of days, though. People have seen enough to not want to attempt to escape anymore." He continues as if that would comfort me. Not many wanted to escape to begin with, seeing as how we were given food, water, and shelter in exchange for simple labor. But now that people want to escape the place that has now revealed itself as a true nightmare, they're trapped.

"Has anyone managed to escape lately?" Rebecca's voice interrupts us, and only then do I notice everyone has stopped interacting with each other and is focused on us.

"No," Cole replies. "None have been reported, anyway. They've moved the majority of troops from what you call the Divide and now have them patrolling outside the walls. It makes them more vulnerable, but so far it's been pretty effective. They're doing anything they can to maintain order now that your visit destroyed it."

"Why not just use the dogs?" Tyler grits his teeth, and I'm reminded of his anger that the Emigres used beasts instead of soldiers to do their dirty work.

"They can be hard to control sometimes, especially when they're starving, and usually they're starved intentionally to make them more lethal when they're needed. It's easiest to just use them as a last resort."

"But our families. . .." Elliot speaks up, looking like he's trying to maintain his emotions. "They're okay, right?"

Cole's eyes go distant as he looks away from us again, and my heart starts to break. I should have known that after we were discovered and got away, our families would be the first to suffer. I just didn't want to believe it, wanting to control what little hope and sanity I have.

"That's something I want to talk to you all about," He says. "They've been rounded up and transported to our main ship. I've tried everything I can think of to get a hold of them and protect them. Please understand that. But I still don't have as much control as I would like."

"So, what's happening to them now?" I demand, the memory of that large ship hovering just overhead when I was looking for Damien and Grace still fresh in my mind. My mother, Annie, Mary were in there. And I just watched it go by. Cole manages to meet my gaze, and for a split second, it looks like his eyes are filling with tears.

"They're in the process of being brainwashed. Their memories are being searched in order to gather as much information about you as possible. If it all goes well, in a few weeks, my people will know as much as they can, and your families won't remember you at all."

FIFTY-EIGHT

My legs tremble, and everything in my field of vision suddenly gets unnaturally brighter. The sound of the birds and cicadas becomes muffled. The nerves in my body feel like ice, and the pit of my stomach feels exactly like I've just launched myself off a cliff. People are dying every day because of our actions. Because of things I did or took part in. Lives extinguished. Parents, children, friends, and lovers.

"What should we do?" Alfie voices my thoughts, his face grave.

"I don't think we can stop any of this until the Émigrés get what they want and we're all dead," Damien says, and some of the others nod.

"He's right," Brianna steps forward. "But we're not planning on dying. Not yet." She looks at Cole, giving an expression that shows death is not an option for us even if it may help calm things down in the Reserve. The rebels will die to save everyone, not appease our enemies.

"We should rescue our families, though," Elliot says quietly, seeming to be a thousand miles away as he stares at the ground. "We can't just let them stay there and get their minds erased."

"And I assume we have to be the ones to get them out because if you tried, you could blow your cover." I speak up to Cole, trying not to glare. I understand his side, but I'd be lying if I said I had complete trust in him. He nods.

"Pardon me for saying this, as I know you won't like it, but I really don't think you guys should do this. It's too risky." He says.

"Everything we do is risky," Rebecca mutters, looking like she's trying to refrain from rolling her eyes. "We know what we're getting into."

"The first line of defense is darthra. I know you think you can handle them because you have handled them so far, but one wrong move and you're going to at least lose a limb. Then you're going to have to get past guards. They will either be the most elite of our people or humans that we have brainwashed into our own soldiers and have deemed disposable. Maybe you get lucky and survive the guards, but then in order to even get within 20 feet of the ship in the open area it's in, you're going to have to look like you belong there. Otherwise, you will be shot down immediately. There is no sneaking on. And even then, once you make it to the doors, they require a retina scan to open."

"You're making it sound impossible, but you said that we shouldn't, not that we couldn't," Elliot points out. "We understand that if you interfere too much, you'll leave an obvious mark that traces back to you, and that's the end of it. But if you can tell us how to get there ourselves, we won't need your weapons or exclusive knowledge."

"Wouldn't ambushing some guards and taking their uniforms be a start?" Tyler asks. I can see Cole's frustration growing as some of us start to vocalize agreement.

"Listen!" He interrupts us. "If you get caught, I don't think you understand what they'll do to you. They know who you are. They know how you've influenced your people and how much trouble you've caused already. My mother knows every detail of every face that invaded the Reserve, as well as those involved with them, so I won't be able to save you from your fate. You won't have a long life as our prisoner, and you won't be granted an easy death. You will be tortured relentlessly, to the point where you will beg for death because that is the only thing that would please my mother, however minor you thought your actions and their effects were. After that, you will be used in whatever way will affect your species the most, and my guess is that you will become brainwashed allies to calm all sides. Is that what you're willing to risk?"

A silence falls over us, but only for a moment. Angie clears her throat.

"I think most of us feel that our people are worth the risk. Especially those of us who have family on that ship." She looks briefly at Elliot and me, but at the same time, she eyes all of us with concern, a motherly look taking over her features. She may want to protect us, but she holds her tongue.

"Anyone not wanting to take part in this mission?" Marcus asks the group, and the fierce determination in his eyes tells me that he was never complacent with being the only one who got away from that ship, even if my father and the other men ended up safe in some way. No one opposes.

"I still don't think this is a good idea, but I know I can't stop you. So I promise I'll help you all. As much as I can." Cole offers with a sigh, gazing at us as though his last hope is slipping away.

The sound of a hover alarms us, but only for a second. Cole tells us it's Kira and we see for ourselves. Only now do I actually begin to wonder what she's been up to all this time, and since this is the first time I've seen her since knowing she's an Émigré, I feel some anger rising up in me knowing what she's done. Jacob's blood is on her hands as much as I felt like it was on mine in my grief. Before I can even think to question her, though, she launches into an announcement for all of us.

"I went to check on the second base after the outsider attack," she informs everyone, her gaze firm. "The outsiders were not successful in their takeover. A lot of them managed to escape, but a good number of them were killed."

It wasn't a takeover, I think to myself. They just wanted food and supplies. And weapons. Not the base itself. I think about Leah and Kieran, and as much as they confuse me, I hope like hell they survived.

"Interestingly enough, some outsiders managed to kill off a handful of rebels." Kira continues, and I see Olivia's face fall out of the corner of my eye. "And what surprised me the most was that it looks like they actually captured someone. They took a hostage." This causes the group to look at each other in confusion and shock.

"Who was it? Was it Ralph?" Damien demands.

"I don't know. Probably. I don't remember anyone's names very well. . .especially since I was barely there. The name started with an R." Kira replies. "I think they were hoping that some rebels would go to rescue him, but no one has left the base and it doesn't look like anyone plans to."

"That can't be Ralph, then," Olivia speaks up. "If he were taken, nearly the whole base would want to leave to get him back. Was it a young guy?"

"Oh, yes. It wasn't the leader of the base if that's what you mean." Kira answers. Olivia's eyes shift to mine.

"It has to be-"

"Ross," I finish for her, my voice flat. I'm silent for a moment, although it feels like an hour passes with everyone's eyes on me. "What are they doing to him?"

"Well, all they seem to want to do is beat him. Repeatedly. Sun up to sundown." Her facial expression doesn't change, but I can tell she expects mine to change. And it does. This is Callie's brother.

"He deserves it for what he did," Tyler growls, his gaze trained on the dirt below us.

"What he tried to do." I correct him, and his eyes snap up to meet mine and he shakes his head, looking at the spot on my forehead that Ross's fist connected with. I'd almost forgotten about my bruises that should be fading, but it doesn't change my stance. "I want to rescue him."

"Rachel," Elliot's voice is low, angry. "He tried to kill you. If Ralph didn't hang you, Ross would have killed you himself. I heard him say it."

"It doesn't matter whether he wants to kill me or not. If I don't convince them to let him go, they're probably going to kill him. Especially if no one from the base comes to his rescue." I say simply. I can't let him die, just like he initially didn't want to hurt me. Because if anything happens to either of us, it hurts Callie. Granted, she may not even be alive anymore, and it may be childish regardless to want to do this for her, but I know I have to do it. If he dies and I could have been able to prevent it, how will I be able to face her if that day comes? Better yet, how could I face myself?

"Well, I'm not letting you go alone," Tyler's voice is calm despite the fact that I can see the frustration on his face.

"I second that," Olivia says, nodding at me.

"What about rescuing our families? We don't have any time to waste if we want their memories to be intact!" Elliot looks at us in disbelief.

"We have to scope the area surrounding the mothership first," Brianna reminds us. "We can't let them think we have an inside man. That'll take some time, but even though it's necessary, not all of us need to do it." Her words settle on us, and it's clear we have to make a choice. Some of us will stay behind, and some of us will go. Preferably, the majority will stay.

"This can work," Cole agrees. "Kira knows where they are-"

"Somewhat," Kira interrupts.

"She can get you there quickly. All you have to do is convince them to let him go."

"Which won't be easy." Elliot points out.

"But my guess is the two outsiders Rachel knows saw what he did to her. They want him to make him pay for what he did. I remember the boy saying he saw her about to be hung. He had to have seen everything and singled Ross out when he got the chance." Tyler tells us, and I realize he's probably right. No other outsider in that group would, to my knowledge, even think of grabbing someone like Ross. "If she's with us and she tells them to let him go and give him to us, they might listen. It's the best chance we have."

"This sounds great and all," Damien drones sarcastically, sauntering forward until he's in the middle of the group. "But why does this kid mean risking our lives? What benefit does he bring to us?"

"Not much," Olivia says bluntly, chuckling.

"He might not bring much value to us, but that group of outsiders can. And now we know where they are." Brianna walks to Damien's side. "If we can get an outsider group to join us, we can increase our numbers."

"It's not like they'll help us on our upcoming mission." Damien counters.

"I think it might be worth it in the long run," Brianna says, and as Damien seems to ponder it, he relaxes a little. If we survive the mothership mission and have an outsider group with us, we have the start of an army again. A start at actually winning this war.

"Who's all going then?" Damien looks at everyone.

"I am," Tyler says, meeting my gaze and nodding at me.

"So am I," Olivia stands next to me.

"I'll go as well," Brianna joins us.

"Me too," Damien tells the group, giving us a look that dares us to oppose him as Brianna raises a brow in surprise. When silence follows, he adds, "Anyone else?"

"I would love to help, but my family is on that ship." Rebecca looks almost guilty as she speaks to me, and I quickly work to give her a reassuring smile to let her know I understand. To no surprise, Alfie will stay with her.

"I'm staying. I need to do everything I can to get our people out." Marcus says, and his eyes shift to mine with an expression I read as a promise to get my father back.

"I'm also going to stay." Angie turns to Molly. "You can go with them if you'd like." She tells her, even though her face betrays her strong voice and her worry is clear.

"I'm staying with you." Molly shakes her head.

"I want to get more involved, but confronting outsiders isn't how I want to start. I want to help with the mothership. I'm sorry." Grace says mainly to Damien, who shows his understanding by kissing her lightly on the forehead.

"Be safe," He tells her.

"You too," she says to all of us, giving us one last warm smile.

"I'm staying as well. Good luck." Elliot says, hugging each of us. The others follow his lead, saying goodbye before separating into our two groups so we can start putting plans into action.

My group sets out immediately to ensure most of our journey has the advantage of daylight. We walk at a quick and steady pace, with Kira as our lead. She doesn't speak, but most of us don't either until we decide it's time to take a break for food. I take the time to thank everyone for coming with me, and as I take a seat next to Tyler, I realize they all probably came for different reasons, but I don't know his reason. And I want to know it. Maybe he just likes to keep up the partner system, but I'm still curious.

"So, why'd you come? Did you think I couldn't handle the outsiders myself?" I give him a wry smile as Kira hands each of us a large packet of nuts and dried fruit that I recognize from the Reserve. She must have snagged some when she went back to the mothership, knowing we were low on food now that we're no longer on a base.

"Allergic to almonds?" She asks us quietly. When we shake our heads no, she moves on. Tyler gives me a small smile in return before answering me.

"I wanted to come because I want you to know that you have my support, and also for myself." His confession surprises me to the point where I stay silent as he takes a deep breath before continuing. "Last time, even though I forced us to go our separate ways, it drove me crazy not knowing if you were okay and knowing that I made a stupid choice. I still feel like I need to make up for abandoning you. "

"So. . ." I begin, unsure how to phrase what I'm thinking. "You didn't just want to come because you were afraid something would happen to me?"

"No, I have a feeling at least the boy and the girl will try to keep things peaceful. It's just that I haven't been fair to you. I mean, yeah, I went to the Divide with you because I was afraid something would happen to you. But I'm not now."

"Because you trust Kieran and Leah?" My voice has some mild disbelief as I finally start to eat.

"No, because I trust you." His eyes refuse to waver from mine, and I feel myself start to relax, knowing that he's being sincere. "You can handle things yourself. I sometimes need to be reminded of that, but you never fail to remind me."

"You don't need to make up for abandoning me," I tell him, smiling without thinking about it now.

"Yeah, I feel like I do. You let me know how much it hurt you and angered you. The least I can do is try to be better. To you." He starts fiddling with the laces of his boots, no longer looking at me.

"I understand why you did it, as much as it frustrated me. If we were in a situation right now where I thought that leaving you would save you, I would probably do the same thing. Even if it was another rebel or my family, I can imagine at least thinking about doing it." I admit.

"And I understand why you were mad. I didn't even give you a choice, and I was harsh about it. I know our emotions were running high and on top of that, we didn't have much time and I was also scared. But I could have handled it better. I'm sorry." He stops to retie his boots, then tosses back a handful of almonds. As he chews, still staring at his boots, I speak up again.

"It's okay. I think we both need to work on communicating better." I say, finishing off my almonds and dried cranberries. As he nods, the rest of the group gets ready to set off again. I've barely swallowed my last bite when we start walking.

FIFTY-NINE

The sun is starting to set when we see our first signs of other people near here. Clean, empty cans are carelessly tossed around and laughter can be heard up ahead. We slow our walk even more, keeping our eyes and ears alert.

"These weren't here before," Kira whispers. "I'm almost positive whoever's up there isn't the group we're looking for. This area isn't right, and I don't think the outsiders would move from where they were so soon."

"We should check anyway, just to be sure," Brianna says under her breath, and with Kira leading again, we slowly move forward. Using the trees as our cover, we come across a group passing around water and more canned food. They've got a fire going, and what looks like deer meat roasting over it. Closer up ahead there seem to be two men guarding the place, so Damien crouches down lower and we do the same. I look around carefully, but I don't recognize a single face.

"This isn't them," I murmur.

"Agreed," says Kira, cautiously starting to slink back in retreat.

"Wait!" Damien hisses almost too loudly, causing Olivia to instinctively elbow him in the side. They glare at one another before he continues. "That locket. See the locket that girl is holding?" I follow his gaze and spot a woman who looks to be in her 30s, twirling a shiny golden locket around her fingers.

"What about it?" Brianna urges.

"The girl. The blonde one who died. She had a notebook full of pictures. I don't know if any of you looked at all of them, but I did. She was in several of them, and she was wearing that locket." Damien's words send a chill straight up my spine. These are the people who attacked the girl and everyone she was with, stealing their supplies and whatever else they wanted. Anger builds up to edge out the shock as I watch the woman laugh as a man with a snake tattoo running down his arm whispers something in her ear.

"We can't go after them," Olivia says simply, turning around.

"Why not? They killed those people!" Damien's voice gets too loud again and Olivia gives him a look that could set the whole woods ablaze.

"Look at them! We're clearly outnumbered, even if we do have guns. And this is a group that killed an entire camp, for whatever reason they saw fit. They're obviously skilled as well as cold-blooded. We could lose some of our own, and then what? This isn't what we came here to do." Olivia makes her way back with Kira.

"So we're just going to let them go? Give them the opportunity to kill others?" Damien growls, following her.

"For now. Be angry all you want, but think logically, too. Otherwise, you might not make it back to that girl of yours. And if that thought doesn't bother you, think about how much you could put her in danger." Olivia says in a final tone. Damien looks at her as though ice-cold water has been splashed on his face. Before he can explode in anger, Brianna puts a hand on his shoulder.

"She's right," she says, urging us away. "It's too much of a risk. We have to move on. But remember what you can so that if we come across them again, we can deal with them properly."

As we discretely make our way back out, I try to keep a mental image fresh. The way the guards looked. The way the woman looked. And the man that she was with. Vaguely, I remember the facial features of the others. I didn't catch much else that would stick out to help me recognize them later, but I may have seen enough.

We continue our journey with a tense atmosphere, even when night falls and cloaks us in darkness. By the time I ask to call it a night, Kira says we're almost there. Probably 10 more minutes pass when we can see camp guards up ahead. When Kira nods at me, I motion for everyone to put away their weapons and hold up their hands. Kira hangs back, alien weapon at the ready, hoping to remain unseen as the rest of us move forward. I stay toward the front so that the outsiders see me first, but Tyler and Olivia are quick to take either side of me.

It doesn't take long before the guards spot us. They scream for us to stop, and I can make out their crossbows pointed our way. I hold up my hands higher, my heart thudding in my ears as I try to find my voice. They march forward with no reason to spare us, and any minute they'll see we aren't one of them. I swallow hard, my stomach clenching.

"We mean you no harm!" My voice shakes as I call out. "We just want to speak with Kieran and Leah." I mentally curse myself for not knowing their last names. Even if they're here, these guards may not know them by name.

The faces of the guards become clearer as they move closer. I don't recognize either of the three that are now surrounding us, crossbows still raised. I suddenly remember Kieran telling me that if I ever ran into an outsider, to tell them I'm from the Riverbank camp.

"We're from-"

"Silence!" The guard in the middle shushes me. "All weapons on the ground. Now!" We do as we're told, and I let go of my precious gun. I don't even attempt to keep my knife, wanting them to know they can trust me. The middle guard comes forward and pats us down for any other weapons, and I'm thankful none of the others tried to sneak anything either. I barely breathe as I wait for him to decide what to do with us. The other guards still hold their crossbows firmly, and from what happened at the Peterson base, I wouldn't be surprised if there were dozens more guards up in the trees or behind the trees out of our view. He looks at me, his eyes suspicious and harsh. I try not to appear afraid or confrontational, knowing either could land an arrow through my skull. "Come with me." He says in an authoritative tone after what seemed like an hour of silence, and I have to refrain from loudly letting out the breath I'd been holding.

As we walk, tents and makeshift shacks come into view, as do people. Men, women, and children of all ages stare at us blankly as we pass. Clothes dark and dirty. Faces grave and malnourished. Small campfires here and there emphasize their hollow eyes. I search for Leah and Kieran among all of those people outside, but don't see them. The only thing that makes me think I'm in the right place is the familiar scent of pond water and smoke I caught on the gag Leah used on me.

The guard continues to lead us and I realize I still feel on edge. I look to my right, where Tyler once stood, to try to find some comfort. He's no longer there, but before I can turn around to see him, something in the darkness ahead catches my eye. It's a long pole, making me think it could have been a flagpole once. Someone is tied up on it, and in the faint light from a distant campfire, I can see their skin dark with blood. The person groans weakly in pain, and a lump catches in my throat. The voice and the curly hair are all I need to know that Kira was right. It's Ross, looking worse than I ever could have prepared myself for.

SIXTY

A part of me agrees with Tyler and feels like Ross deserves whatever he gets. But another part of me knows this isn't right, and I have to stop it. Especially if I was the cause. He may have caused a lot of trouble for me, but he's still a human. I can at least ensure his numbered days aren't torturous.

The guards lead us to an area of wooden cabins, and I can tell right away that pre-invasion, this was a campground. We step up to the door of the largest cabin before the middle guard stops us and demands that we wait. While he goes inside, the other two guards keep us company. I turn back to the others, wondering if there is anything I can say. We'll be alright? I'm sorry for dragging you into this?

Olivia comes forward, smiling softly at me, her dark eyes doing their best to mask whatever emotions she feels. When she lifts her hands toward my face, I reflexively flinch away. But to my surprise, she just gently slides her fingers through my ponytail until a pink ribbon is in her hands. The pink ribbon. The gift from Ava I had almost completely forgotten about after encountering the darthra again. I could have lost it then. It's a miracle I didn't. My heart lifts at my joyful memories of her, and everything that a simple ribbon means to me, even if I managed to forget it.

As Olivia redoes my mess of a ponytail, I wonder if she can tell that I feel that way based on the strangely happy expression I know I must have. She ties the ribbon back in my hair, making sure it's secure, before smiling again and stepping away. No words pass between either of us. But she doesn't need to say a thing for me to understand. She came to support me, just as Tyler did. I'm sure she also wanted to come because she knows Ross and figured she could help, but I'm glad there's more than that.

"We can't lie," Brianna says, breaking the silence. When we look at her, her eyes demand that we follow her words. "If we want them to join forces with us, we have to tell them the truth. It's never going to work if we lie. If we don't tell them the truth and they join us based on that, they'll just find out the truth eventually and things will get worse."

"You're right," Tyler says, and we all silently agree. They may kill us when they find out that we're rebels, but they'll definitely kill us if we lie and they find out.

The guard comes back out, telling us to follow him inside. As he escorts us, a whole dining hall comes into view. Tables and chairs stretch out everywhere across the large, open room. Flags and maps hang on the walls. But the invasion has left its mark as well. In the candlelight, I can just make out the mud sealing the cracks in the walls, and dark stains of what looks like blood under my feet. The reality of where I am fully hits me, and as every muscle in my body tenses, I clench and unclench my fists.

Two people come out of a door at the opposite end of the room, and as they come closer, I recognize one of them. The woman with the graying hair who all those outsiders perched in the trees listened to. Her cold eyes meet mine, and for a second it looks like she starts to smile. But it's not a welcoming expression. It's amusement.

"Hello," the man next to her greets us confidently. "I'm Patrick, and this is my wife, Katherine. We run this camp of survivors. It's my understanding that you came to speak to someone?" The brief moment of silence before I speak only heightens my nerves and adrenaline, especially as I can feel the eyes of the other rebels on me.

"Yes. We came to speak to Kieran and Leah. I'm sorry I don't know their last names." I try to keep my voice steady and clear.

"Why do you want to speak to them?" The woman, Katherine, demands. Her face says what her mouth doesn't. She wants to know how I know them. Because when she last saw me with Kieran, we had to act as strangers. Should I say how? Should I lie?

"Because you have someone. . .my cousin. . ." I test the words out, although they're foul on my tongue. "Your people took him and we want him back." I know we agreed it's best not to lie, but I think I should at least offer up a summarized version of why I want Ross back.

"I thought you weren't rebels." Katherine's voice is accusatory, her smile widening. "The boy we have is a rebel. Perhaps you're mistaken." My heartbeat thuds in my ears. None of the other rebels can come to my aid, and knowing that makes me panic. I try not to start a web of lies, but I feel like prey helplessly backed into a corner by an unrelenting, hungry huntress. Lying feels like it's the easy way out, but I have to remind myself it's not worth the cost.

"We are rebels. But we're not associated with the base you attacked. Yes, we have a target on our backs, but we're not your enemies." I tell her. The back doors swing open again and I almost jump in shock.

"I told you they're not," I hear Kieran's voice before he comes into view, and my heart immediately relaxes when he and Leah march into the room.

"Why are you here?" Patrick confronts them, annoyed.

"Word gets around. And when they mentioned a girl with a pink ribbon, we had a faint idea we might know her." Leah smirks at me. I have to be thankful for their observance. Or at least Kieran's. I never had a ribbon when we met, but I did when Kieran saw me again. It must have stuck out just enough to make him remember it.

"As I was saying," Kieran commands the attention of the room again, and I'm surprised a boy so quiet can defend so relentlessly using only his words. I can only imagine it would have something to do with Leah. "They're not our enemies. I saw the rebel boy about to hang them. For stealing. They didn't belong in that camp."

"Why does he want you dead if you're family? And why do you want him back if he wants you dead?" Katherine is speaking to me again.

"He and I never got along. But family is important to me, and when I was lucky enough to find him, I wanted him alive even if he wanted me dead." More lies.

"I see. . ." She narrows her eyes at me. "What are you planning on offering up in exchange?" I don't have a lie on the tip of my tongue for that. When she notices my hesitation, she speaks up again. "He's a rebel. The only reason he's here, and not dead, is to see if we can get anything in exchange for his life. What can you give to us?"

"They have weapons. Guns, with plenty of bullets in them." The main guard tells her.

"No," Damien says immediately. "We're not giving those up." I nod in agreement. Without my gun, my chances of survival decrease drastically. I haven't built up enough strength and skill to last without it yet.

"What else can you offer, then?" Something about the look in Katherine's eyes tells me even if they don't give up Ross, we might not be leaving here with our weapons if we want to stay alive.

SIXTY-ONE

"Knowledge." Brianna comes forward. "There are alien dogs lurking in the woods, probably closer than you would like."

"Yes, we've heard about them," Patrick looks over at Kieran and Leah.

"We know the best way to kill them quickly." She continues. Patrick and Katherine's expressions don't change, so Olivia gives it a try.

"Winter will also be here quicker than you know. I'm the only one in this group from that base you attacked. I can get back in and get you anything you need."

"Tempting," Says Katherine, but she's still not convinced. Of course, she isn't. If Olivia says she can sneak in, what's preventing one of her people from just doing the same on their own? Olivia knows the place better than they do, but they don't trust us enough to do a job they can do themselves. Tyler steps up beside me, clearing his throat.

"The alien ship is also only a few hours from here. Recently, when we first found the ship, we also found a dead Émigré. Mostly eaten by one of their own dogs. But we found a spray and a paste, and after testing it out, we discovered that they disinfect wounds and heal them." He's found a lie to say as well. Dropping the bomb that we have potential alien allies so soon could cause them to panic. Or assume that everything we've told them was made up to get what we want. But the medicine alone might be enough to win them over.

"Heal?" Katherine sounds doubtful.

"Any of you have a knife?" Tyler asks them.

"I do." Leah takes hers out to prove it. "Why?"

"Cut my hand." He tells her.

"What? No! I'm not," she starts to protest, but I interrupt her.

"Leah, do it. Please." I say. She gazes at me with confusion, and it takes a while before she finally agrees. Taking a step forward, she waits as Tyler extends his left hand, palm up. Placing her left hand on the back of his hand to steady it, she looks into his eyes as if to silently ask if he's sure about this. Having spent probably most of the post-invasion out here, she knows that any cut risks infection, and infection leads to death. When he nods, she readies her knife.

"I won't cut deep," she promises, sounding much different from the girl who attacked me and held the blade of her knife against my throat.

"It doesn't matter," He assures her, then smiles. "Cut as deep as you want if that's what makes you feel better. Just don't sever any arteries, okay?"

"Okay," she smiles back. Then, as quickly and lightly as she can probably manage, she slices open the skin of his palm. She winces, as do I, but when all Tyler does is close his eyes, exhale, and open them, we relax. He's felt much worse pain. . .just days ago, in fact.

Without wasting time, he grabs the spray and applies it to the wound, inhaling sharply at the sting it must give. Then he applies the paste. I can barely smell it with a wound this small, and Tyler doesn't appear to feel much pain at all this time. When he rubs it away, all that's left is a scab that looks nearly healed. I watch as the outsider's eyes open wide in amazement. This is what our trade will be. Medicine in exchange for Ross.

Katherine and Patrick dismiss me to retrieve Ross. Most of the rebels go with me, although Brianna and Damien stay behind to continue negotiations. About joining forces, I assume. On that topic, I feel better leaving them to it. Katherine and Patrick would be more likely to listen to some of the older rebels than someone who still looks like a child. And I still don't sound as confident as I would like, nor do I always know what to say.

Leah and Kieran run off to bring back wet rags to wipe off Ross's blood. When I reach him, that's exactly what I start to do. He begins to come to life under my hands, moaning in pain every so often. By the time I finish gently wiping away the blood and dirt, it looks like most of the damage is bruises, and some small, scattered cuts that have already scabbed over. They don't look infected, so there's some relief in that.

Leah hands Olivia her knife so that she can begin cutting Ross down. I take this time to get out my water bottle and offer Ross a drink, knowing that if they were angry enough to torture, they'd be angry enough to deprive him as well. He looks into my eyes and I can't tell what he's thinking, but when he takes a sip of water, he spits it right back out at my face. Olivia is in front of me instantly, pointing the knife at him in warning as he laughs weakly.

"Who died and made you a leader?" He manages to say to me, grinning at the sight of us. Olivia with her knife, Tyler partially shielding me with a hand over where his gun once was, Leah and Kieran holding Ross back aggressively.

"What are you talking about?" I dare to ask. There's no leader when it comes to our group. And if there is, it certainly isn't me. The fury that they all direct at Ross is clear, but they're not looking to me to lead them. Not like some of the people in the Reserve are. "I'm not a leader." At least I can say that with certainty.

"That's not what it looks like to me." His mischievous grin is back, and all I can do is shake my head. He's been through a lot, so it's understandable that he'd say things that make no sense.

"This is a shitty way to treat the person who came all the way here to save you," Tyler mutters, glaring so harshly even I can't look at him for too long. "She risked her life for you."

"I didn't ask to be saved. Maybe I don't even want to be saved." Ross chuckles.

"You sure about that?" Leah snarls, yanking his hair back until he hisses in pain.

"Fine!" He's now able to make his voice loud. "Let me go if that's what you want."

When I nod, Kieran and Leah go back to untying him. Olivia keeps the knife up just in case. Ross staggers forward when the rope finally breaks, but Tyler quickly backs him against the pole again before he can even think about pulling a stunt on us. With quick fingers, Leah takes the rope and reties his hands again so that we can have better control over him when we leave.

"I'm going to stay here," Brianna says when she reaches us. "I'd like to help strengthen the alliance. And further their trust in us."

"I'm staying as well." Damien stands beside her. "I'd feel better if she wasn't alone."

"What about Grace?" I blurt out. I expect him to make a snide comment, but he just frowns, sadness drowning his eyes.

"Tell her she's free to join me here if she wants. But if she doesn't, I understand. And I love her." When I shake my head in promise, he walks away. Brianna hugs us all goodbye and follows him. I still can't help but feel anxious, wondering if they'll really be safe here.

"Promise me you won't let anything happen to them." I turn to Kieran and Leah.

"Of course," Leah assures me. Looking at them both, I see the trust and compassion they have for me. It doesn't make sense.

"Why did you do this? Why take him?" My voice gets quieter unintentionally.

"He represented something we hate about certain rebels. And even other survivors. Killing and hurting in self-defense, or for survival, we understand. But senseless violence we don't. And we owed you." Kieran says simply. I'm thankful Ross didn't seem to hear that. His actions weren't completely without purpose. We were suspected of being traitors and of working with the aliens. And now, after coming to my aid again tonight, I'm the one who owes them.

"There's a group of survivors out there who seem to be killing people for no reason other than to take their stuff," my voice gets low in warning. "Please keep an eye out."

"Thank you," Leah says, and when she hugs me goodbye, she doesn't squeeze me to death like she did last time.

"I'll try to find more of the medicine and bring some just for you and your family when I can," I promise. Kieran echoes her gratitude, and to my surprise, he hugs me briefly as well.

"A lot of people give rebels a bad name. But I think you guys might change that." He smiles at us for a split second, and with that, the two siblings go back to wherever it is they live.

The guards come back and escort us out of the camp, leading us back to our weapons. With crossbows raised as a precaution, they let us go. Once we've walked far enough that we can see Kira stand up from her hiding spot, I breathe a sigh of relief.

"Where are you taking me?" Ross asks no one in particular. Nobody bothers to answer him. Tyler is practically dragging Ross along, and I'm about to offer help, but it looks like he doesn't need it. He holds Ross firmly and securely by the shoulders, and Ross still seems too weak to fight back. "Why did you save me, anyway?" He demands of me.

"For Callie," I say easily, avoiding his angry gaze.

"Well," He sneers. "If she's dead, then this is all for nothing."

That earns him a shove from Tyler, but his words have already impacted me. I've wasted everyone's time, made them risk their lives because my conscious couldn't handle the thought of me letting Ross die. Maybe we did gain a group of outsiders, but we were never guaranteed that.

We finally stop to rest for the night. In the darkness, Ross can't see the color of Kira's eyes, so that allows us to try to get some sleep without having to hear him freaking out and asking questions. Tyler suggests I sleep in the trees in case Ross manages to escape and tries to kill me again, and Olivia even offers me the extra rope she grabbed so I can tie myself in, but to his frustration, I decline.

Instead, I have Olivia use the rope to tie Ross to the trunk of the nearest tree. I don't think he'll try anything when he's in this state, but if he does, I have my gun and my knife. To ease his mind, Tyler has the rest of us sleep a few feet away and lies down between Ross and me. As much as I know he wants to stay up and guard, these past few days have taken their toll, and in minutes, I can hear his snores. I begin to drift off as well when Kira and Olivia offer to take turns guarding.

My body is exhausted, but sleep doesn't come easy. Curled up into a ball with my head resting on my pack, I'm not too cold and I'm fairly comfortable, but my mind is keeping me awake. It keeps spinning, thinking about a potential peace with the outsiders, about the mission to the mothership, the status of my family, and whether Callie is alive. These thoughts keep me restless. I'm just starting to envision being reunited with my family to calm my mind when the sound of Tyler gasping awake snaps my eyes open.

"Rachel!" He whispers, his voice full of panic. My heart lurches at the sound. It's clear he's had another nightmare, but this one must be a little different.

"I'm here! What's wrong?" I whisper back, and as my eyes adjust, I can see the fear in his as he looks at me. He surges toward me and cups my face in his shaking hands, forcing me to be fully awake as he inspects me like I've suddenly developed violet eyes overnight. Despite his urgency, his touch is gentle, and he seems to be slowly realizing that whatever his mind came up with wasn't real.

"Where's Ross?" He works to keep his voice down, wildly looking around. When his hands let go of me, the night air feels icy on my cheeks.

"Still here, you moron," Ross mumbles from his spot over at the tree.

"Everything okay?" Olivia asks quietly, even though I can barely see her.

"Yeah," Tyler waves her off, slowing down his breathing. When he looks at me again, I can only imagine he dreamed about Ross trying to kill me, just as he feared.

"I'm okay," I assure him, making my voice soft and understanding. He nods, squeezing his eyes shut for a moment before opening them again.

"Of course. I . . . I'm sorry." He shakes his head, forcing out a chuckle.

"Don't be," I say. "We all have really bad nightmares every so often. It happens."

"I know. I just didn't mean to wake you. Or scare you."

"I hadn't fully fallen asleep yet. And I've experienced scarier things." I shoot him a grin, and he manages to smile back. "Do you want to talk about it?" Knowing how often I'd vented to him, nightmare or not, I can at least try to reciprocate.

"There's not much to say," He sighs before lowering his voice, so only I have a chance of listening. "I dreamed that I had fallen asleep, and Ross stole one of Olivia's knives and cut himself loose, then stabbed you and ran off before I could do anything. It was very realistic." The look in his eyes as he stares at the dirt urges me forward and I take his hand in mine, basking in the warmth and comfort it gives me and hoping I offer the same.

"Well, I'm perfectly fine," I promise him. "And you should have realized it was a dream. Nobody on this earth could ever sneak past you, even if you were dead asleep." My joke earns a laugh out of him that he tries to keep quiet. It's true, though. I remember sneaking out to the cornfield after Kira when he was still snoring, only to find him right behind me. Weirdly enough, it almost feels like that happened years ago. So much has changed since then.

"You should get some rest. I've barely seen you sleep." He murmurs, the concerned expression back.

"Same to you. If it helps, I can sleep here." I pat the ground next to him, moving my bag over.

"Are you sure?" He asks.

"Yes," I know all he wants is to protect all of us. And he keeps thinking he's failed, with Liesel, Jacob, Abe, Garret. And who knows how many more gone from his life? But if I can lessen the paranoia even for a night, I'll do what it takes. Now that I think about it, I haven't spent much time this close to him. And I'll be this way until the sun rises. My smile is shy this time, and I'm hoping that in the darkness he can't see the blush on my cheeks.

"Thank you," He smiles again, and I start to relax.

Laying on my side, my head on my pack and facing away from Tyler, I hear him settle in beside me. He's careful to leave enough space so that we don't touch, although the warmth of his body fends off the chill of the night. As I close my eyes and start to fall asleep, I feel his arm wrap protectively around me, as if to assure him that I'm still there. My hand brushes along his arm, and I let it linger. It's my way of saying that yes, I am still here. And I'm not leaving you anytime soon.

SIXTY-TWO

I'M NOT USED TO SLEEPING SO CLOSE TO SOMEONE ELSE. THERE were a few nights in the Reserve where a storm or a nightmare would scare Annie, and she would sometimes cuddle into my bed. But most of those nights, she chose our mother or Mary to bring her comfort. It takes me a while to fall asleep with the weight of his arm and the presence of his body, but eventually, the rhythmic sound of his light snores does me in.

When I do wake up, the sun has already risen and is almost directly overhead. Tyler is still asleep, so I get up slowly and carefully in an effort to not disturb him. I slide away from his arm, taking in the sight of him in peaceful slumber. No lines of worry on his forehead, no frown on his lips. I'd never taken the time to notice back when we shared a room, but he's proof that people really do look younger when they're vulnerable in sleep.

You care too much, the sound of my own voice in my head snaps my gaze away from him. My heart starts to ache with sadness. A few days from now, we'll be embarking on the most important, most dangerous mission we've ever gone on. I may die, and what's worse is I may survive only to lose one or more of the rebels that I've come to care for, or I may not be able to rescue my family. I have to prepare myself for the worst and hope for the best. No mission we've gone on has ever guaranteed success.

Kira looks at me as she guards and everyone else continues to sleep. Her purple eyes still give me a sense of unease as they glint in the sun, and it's like she's silently asking me if it's time to wake everyone up. I shake my head no. Tyler and Olivia deserve as much sleep as they can manage, and we all know it will take a while for Ross to recover.

Getting out more packets of food from her bag, Kira holds one up for me to take. As quietly as I can manage, I walk over to her. Grabbing my food, I whisper my thanks, but I can already hear Tyler waking up. I don't know if it was the absence of my presence or the sound of my footsteps that woke him, but I can't hide my smile as I grab a pack for him too and head over.

"See, I told you nothing can get by you even when you're asleep," I say, handing him a packet.

"Maybe you just need to work on being quieter." He smirks back, yawning freely.

"I'm being as quiet as I can!" I protest. "You're the one with supersonic hearing."

"I'd say that's the opposite of a problem." He tears open the packet and inspects the inside. "Peanuts and. . .jerky?" Popping a reddish brown cube into his mouth, he chews it thoughtfully before frowning as he recognizes the taste. "Dried darthra meat."

"We can't let anything go to waste," Kira calls over. I can see that Olivia is awake now too, and Ross is just starting to open his eyes. Before I can explain anything to him, Kira grabs a cloth from her pack and gags him with it, and I can hear her telling him to keep quiet as she explains who she is. Surprisingly, he doesn't scream or thrash around, just gazes at her in utter horror.

"What do you think he meant?" I start to ask, looking back at Tyler. "When he said I was a leader?"

There's a long pause as he thinks it over, shoving some peanuts into his mouth and chewing them with a focused expression.

"Well," He forces down another meat cube, and I try to do the same. It's so pungent I almost gag, thankful I never tried it earlier when Damien attempted to cook it. "Just looking at things from his point of view, you had a rebel from his base, a rebel from your base, and the two outsiders who tortured him all protecting you and listening to you. It's not such a far-off conclusion to make."

"Yeah, that's where I figured his mind was going, but I'm not a leader," I laugh awkwardly.

"Maybe not yet. But you're the only person I know who has rebels, outsiders, and people in the Reserve who respect you."

"I lack pretty much everything it takes to be a good leader, though," I can feel my frustration building. "I don't command the room like you or Brianna. And I'm not a hero in battle like Garret was." At the mention of Garret's name, we're both silent for a moment. I clear my throat. "I don't know why the people in the Reserve would look to me."

"So let's say you're not a leader. And you don't become one. You could still be a unifier. You can be the one factor that brings everyone together. You're already off to a good start." He looks at me, momentarily forgetting his food.

"A unifier. . ." I test the word out. It sounds better than leading. I still feel too young, too inexperienced, and too emotion-driven to lead well. Garret could have done all of this. He could have been the leader and the hero everyone wanted. But he's not here, and with him gone, there's an opportunity for me and others around me to step up. And we have to because if we don't, no one else will. No one else has gotten the opportunities we have.

"People see something in you, and I don't think you realize that," Tyler tells me. "It's understandable. Most of us don't know what it is about us that stands out to others or could have an impact. But you've got this. . .spirit. People look at you and they know you won't give up, and they know you care for them, and you have this passion that either matches their own or represents what they wish they had. They can see it. That's why the Reserve looks to you, and why those outsiders did what they did for you."

"You really think that?" I find my mood increasing dramatically. Even if he's not right, it's a good way of thinking about it all. He hasn't stated anything remarkably special. Any decent human being could have the traits he just described. But the fact that I've supposedly displayed them could be the main reason why things are the way they are right now. I start shoving the rest of the food in my mouth when I notice Olivia and Kira packing up.

"I do," Tyler confirms, getting his stuff together and throwing on his backpack.

"Well thank you," I grab my stuff as well as he takes hold of a still petrified-looking Ross.

"Hey, you asked, I answered," He says.

"So if I'm a unifier, what does that make you?" I ask, just out of curiosity. There's no question that he has the potential to be a great rebel leader. Or someone for the humans in the Reserve to look up to. Unfortunately, to our knowledge, he's not painted anywhere, and the rebels still have no official leader. But maybe, for now, that's a good thing. A smaller target on his back and less pressure weighing him down.

"Whatever people want me to be, I guess," He shrugs. "I'd say I'm still just a soldier." His words take me back to his alcohol-infused rant about being nothing but a soldier of the Earth, and I frown. Would the world really be so cruel as to kill any of the rebels off in battle and let their names be forgotten, even after all they've done? At least Garret was as close to a public figure as anyone could get. But if Tyler or Brianna or Elliot or anyone else involved with us were to die, no one outside of us would remember them. I realize now that if I want their legacy to go beyond their deaths, it's up to me to do it somehow, as long as I'm still alive.

We start off our journey back to the rebels, the sun hot overhead, although the air is starting to feel cooler. I even notice the leaves on the trees starting to change color, proof of Olivia's warning to the rebels that winter will come sooner than we'd like. Frigid temperatures, snow piling past our ankles, the flakes swirling in the wind and hindering our vison. No matter how positive any of us are, the season is deadly with the world in the state that it is now.

Winter outside the Reserve and in the Ruins is something I don't yet know how to handle. In the Reserve, we had space heaters in our homes and at our jobs, warm showers to look forward to after a long day, and piping hot soup and other warm meals to fill our bellies. It was as difficult to deal with the cold as it was before the invasion. Now, even though I never intended to be outside the walls this long, I'm going to have to learn how to adapt without even minimal luxuries.

"Keep a lookout for those other outsiders," Olivia reminds us quietly, snapping me back to the warmer present. I watch as she begins talking to Kira in a low voice, still scanning the woods. Most of her words are too quiet for me to hear, but I pick up just enough to figure out that she's asking Kira a favor. If Kira ever decides to scope out the Peterson base again, Olivia wants to go with her so that she can check on her family. Thankfully, Kira seems to be okay with that idea.

"So, Kira," Tyler speaks up when she appears to be done talking to Olivia. I glance up at him to see that he's suddenly gotten angry. His eyes show his fury, even though his voice has a forced nonchalance. "Did you know that Jacob was killed in the Reserve?"

"Yes." Kira looks back at Tyler cautiously.

"Because you decided to snitch." His voice gets colder, and I can tell this anger has festered in him since the day Cole told us everything. He may have tried to keep it under control, but something set it off. Maybe it was the whole situation with Ross, or maybe it was because he was watching her with Olivia, noticing that we all still accepted her as one of us. Like what she did was okay, forgiven, insignificant.

"I know. I made a mistake, and I'm truly sorry." Kira stops

walking to look up at Tyler, her normally icy eyes filling with tears. As Tyler halts, shoving Ross to the ground, his frustration doesn't fade.

"You and your brother say that you want us all alive. Did it slip your mind that if we got caught they would execute us?" He demands.

"No," Kira insists, trying her hardest to stay composed. "They... I didn't think they would execute you, but I considered it. Why do you think you all got out so easily? With barely any injuries or fatalities? You were completely surrounded. Yet they didn't search you to take your weapons before they lined you up, correct?"

Tyler freezes, his eyes shifting to mine as realization dawns on us. He's looking to me for confirmation of what he already knows to be true.

"They didn't," my voice is a whisper.

SIXTY-THREE

"For a while now, Cole and I have been trying to get our Kofali allies positions as guards in the Reserve, so that we can eventually free the humans there. It's been a slow process, so unfortunately not many of them were guarding when you decided to go in. But it was enough that I knew if anything went wrong and they tried to execute you, our allies could help you escape." Kira explains.

"Letting us keep our weapons doesn't guarantee we survive." Tyler hisses, knowing that Émigré weapons have always been stronger.

"And that's why they did more than just that. They would fire at you, but intentionally miss, letting you go free and possibly taking the attention of other guards off of you. And if you were close enough to a Kofali, and they knew they could get away with shooting the Kofali instead, they took it. All of them had been trained well enough to be capable of that. They couldn't outright rebel without ruining everything, so they did what they could even if to you it seems it wasn't enough." Her voice has a final tone to it as if we could either believe her or not believe her, but her intention was to help us as much as she could without destroying everything she and her brother were working for. It has some sense to it, but my anger and sadness are still there, and I can tell it's the same for Tyler.

"What about the darthra? Our chances of survival were pretty damn slim when your people decided to let them out." Tyler counters.

"I didn't know they would send them. I didn't know so many of the other humans would try to help you. My people were trying to maintain order and darthra were a last resort. If they're starved, they don't just eat humans. They eat my people too." The stress in Kira's voice is palpable. It makes me want to believe her, but even if she's sincere, her mistakes are costing us.

"If you didn't say anything, we could have made it. Maybe you didn't think so, but I know we could have." Tyler says exactly what I wanted to tell Cole.

"I didn't want to take that risk." She retorts firmly. A tense silence falls over us, thickening the air with stress. I can't think of anything to say to break it, and even Ross appears speechless for once. It almost seems like we're going to stand here for the rest of the day staring each other down until we hear a familiar voice calling out to us. I want to curse myself for being distracted enough to allow us to be vulnerable to an ambush, but Brianna's voice says each of our names and I know not to worry this time.

Brianna comes running into view, flanked by Damien and, even more surprisingly, Kieran and Leah.

"Thank God, we finally found you guys!" Leah exclaims, beaming at us. "Been wandering this damn woods for ages." Oblivious to our confusion, her eyes widen as she takes in Kira's violet irises. "Holy shit! I mean, Brianna said you guys had some aliens on your side and all, but I've never seen their eyes in person before. Shit!" She walks toward Kira, holding up her arms as if to take her face in her hands before Kieran elbows her back into reality.

"Chill out, Leah," He mumbles under his breath, but his gaze is fixed on Kira as well. In the sunlight, I can see his face go pale.

"What are you guys doing here?" I finally blurt out.

"We told Katherine and Patrick about our mission to the mothership, and they insisted we help you guys and then report back to them if we survive," Damien explains.

"And we begged our parents to let us go with them." Leah practically singsongs. "Didn't take much convincing, though. They always seem to be thrilled when we're out of their way." That doesn't surprise me. Who knows how many times Kieran and Leah went out looking for other humans to scavenge off of?

"We thought about it," Kieran adds on. "And we decided that with everything just getting worse in the Ruins, we want to help end the war."

"What about the alliance?" I ask.

"We're good. They seem okay with joining us as long as we survive this mission." Damien assures us.

"They feel the same way we do." Leah nods. "We've been in hell too long."

"Are you rested enough? Because we should keep moving." Tyler voices his concern to all of them, but there's still an edge in his voice. Brianna picks up on it, glancing quickly at each of us as if to figure out what happened. Even Leah seems to notice something's amiss, quieting down immediately.

"We're fine," Brianna says evenly. "Let's go."

Kieran gives Tyler a break and takes over the task of dragging Ross along. We continue the rest of the trek without speaking, not even stopping to eat until Kira leads us back to the rest of the rebels. The sun is setting now, and my stomach grumbles as if to remind me I haven't eaten since this morning. When Cole hands me another one of those food packs, I eagerly dig in.

"Dried strawberries, raspberries, almonds, and peanuts," I tell Tyler as I grab him a pack and toss it over.

"A true feast." He remarks, plopping down by the fire that Alfie and Rebecca have just gotten going. I take a seat next to him, eating slowly so that I can savor every bit.

"I always picked this one for breakfast in the Reserve," I say, almost remembering life back there fondly. Almost.

"Me too!" Alfie grins at me from across the fire.

"Not me." Rebecca shakes her head. "Fresh fruit all the way. I helped grow it, so it's only fair that I get to eat it!"

"Hey, I worked in the greenhouse too," I tell her, perking up. "Although my family was on the vegetable side, so that's probably why I don't remember seeing you."

"There are so many people in there, I'm not surprised we never crossed paths," Rebecca admits.

"Yeah, I was one of the unlucky ones. Got the job of carrying shit from the incoming ships to the main supply building. Never saw Rebecca at all except for lunch break, since we had the same time off." Alfie grumbled.

"Sounds like a blast in there." Tyler fights off a smile, and Alfie playfully tosses an almond at him. He probably meant to hit Tyler in the face, but he gave it enough arc to get over the fire that Tyler happily catches in his mouth. "What's the plan, El?" He asks Elliot when he comes over, sitting next to Rebecca. Kieran and Leah join us seconds later, sitting a few feet to my left.

"We leave in two days," He responds, pausing a moment as the anxiety sets in. "As Cole said, the first line of defense is darthra. They typically sleep during the day, which is why Marcus never came across them. Unfortunately, we'll need to go at night to give us more cover, so we'll need to be on the lookout for them. We observed the guards from the trees, and we agreed that Tyler's strategy of ambushing them and taking their uniforms would be best. We could see, even from a distance, that the ships had laser guns perched atop them. Snipers."

"Wait, ships? As in more than one?" Olivia interrupts as she joins us.

"Yes. We realized that there is definitely the main ship, which is the famous one we saw on TV. But there are also two other large ships. One seems to contain the smaller patrol ships and supplies, like extra weapons and hovers. Things like that. The other looks like it has prisoners. Cole confirmed this, saying the one that holds human prisoners used to contain the darthra and any criminals or extremely low-class citizens."

"Makes sense," Tyler speaks up. "That would allow the main ship to have less weight, making it easier to fly. Anything they could afford to lose, they put in other ships."

"Exactly." Elliot nods. The ship containing the prisoners has to be the one I saw flying over the neighborhood when I was with Olivia. It was huge, and like Cole said, our families were taken from the Reserve and transported to the main ship. "He also confirmed what I suspected. Many lower-class citizens and criminals weren't happy about being on a separate ship. Because of that, a good number of them are on Cole's side, which means they're also supposedly on ours. A lot of the ones on our side have trained to become guards or work in security, so we can use them to our advantage."

"So, we just get past the darthra, ambush guards to get their uniforms, make our way to the doors, and just wait for one of them to let us in?" Tyler's voice holds the doubt we all surely feel.

"It's the best we've got." He sighs. We sit quietly and let the plan sink in. Doubts start to trickle into my brain. How can this work? How many of us will die? Will any of us make it in?

"What if we get caught?" I say, one of the doubts swirling in my head. "If they search our memories, they'll know Cole and Kira have helped us."

"I talked to Cole about this," Rebecca speaks up. "If we get captured, like he told us before, he won't be able to prevent us from being tortured. But he does have one Émigré on his side that has access to the room where they do the brainwashing and is authorized to do the procedure. It's how they saved your dad and the other rebels. That's the problem, though. It's just one ally. If they take us to any of the other rooms, we're screwed. So we have to have a backup plan."

"What are you saying?" Tyler demands, but by his expression, he seems to already know. Rebecca pauses to take a deep breath, her eyes shiny with unshed tears.

"We'll do this mission in pairs, just like always. If one of us. . .if one of us is captured, the partner should kill them before they get taken in. They can't view the memories of the dead. And they won't be able to make us brainwashed puppets either."

"What if we both get captured?" I ask, my voice is barely audible.

"You have to fight back." Elliot answers. "Fight back to the point where you're either free or they have no choice but to kill you."

"The problem is the darts," Tyler mutters. "If we get hit and go down, there's nothing we can do." I can't help but imagine sinking under the pull of whatever chemical is in the darts. No matter how much I fight it, I know that it only takes seconds before my body goes limp and my eyes slip shut. "Isn't there some kind of Émigré poison we could take? Something that could kill us off before the darts take effect?" He thinks out loud.

"I talked to Cole about this as well." Elliot answers. "They do have something, but if we took it, it would be detected in our systems and the only explanation would be that we got it from them. We're high-profile enough where they want us alive and if we died from anything other than a darthra or a laser beam, they'd want to run tests to find out why."

"So, that's it then? If we can't make it past the guards, it's either get captured and risk revealing everything or die?" My voice falls flat. They all nod solemnly, their eyes distant and melancholic. All of us go silent as the weight of the mission fully sinks in. We could just decide not to go on the mission. . .to not take any of these risks. . .but to do that means our families lose their memories of us. And not only that, if we continue to fight back, as long as our families are in Émigré control, they could be killed. Maybe it's selfish to risk our alliance and the chance at getting our planet back just to save our families. It's just that at least for me I'd rather be dead than lose them.

"Is that what you want?" Tyler whispers as I snap back to the present moment. Everyone is murmuring amongst themselves now as the rest of the rebels join us by the fire.

"What do you mean?" I ask in confusion.

"If you get captured, do you want me to shoot?" His voice is surprisingly calm, like he was asking if I wanted canned food or squirrel meat. Yet his eyes show every ounce of sadness and fear that his face doesn't.

"I mean. . .I don't really have a choice, do I?" My voice is practically a squeak.

"You do with me. If you don't want me to shoot, I won't." He assures me, his gaze never wavering. I swallow hard, suddenly realizing my mortality. How I breathe through my nose and inhale the scent of the fire and the trees, how my palms are sweating, and how often I blink. In an instant, my life could be taken, and all my movements and thoughts would cease.

"It has to be done. So if the situation calls for it, do it." I choke out, watching pain take over his features as he shifts his eyes from me to the fire. He nods once, and then both of us are quiet for a while. When he speaks again, all emotion is detached from his voice.

"When the time comes, if the situation calls for it, don't hesitate." Tyler keeps his focus trained on the flames. "Promise me you won't hesitate." I know what he wants without any elaboration. He made up his mind right away, sticking to the stereotypical rebel beliefs. Never surrender, fight or die. He accepts death. In fact, he has accepted it for a long time. There's only one problem, and he knows it. Will I be able to pull the trigger?

"I promise." I sound a lot more broken than I intend, and the tears spilling down my cheeks come as a shock to me. When I stand on shaky legs, I attempt to clear my head, to no avail. Dread seeps into me like poison, tainting my thoughts. It's not just Tyler that I may have to pull the trigger on. It's every rebel who decides to go with us. It's not even about mustering the strength to gun down a potential human enemy anymore. It's about killing people I care about for the sake of winning a war. They may die by my own hand if I am capable of managing it in the heat of battle. Just the idea makes me feel cold and suffocated.

I stumble through the woods, tears blinding my vision. My emotions are running so high that my ears ring and I'm not sure if anyone is bothering to try to stop me from wandering in darthra-infested territory alone. As I make my way further, though, it's clear they've let me go. Either they're too preoccupied or too understanding. But the solitude makes the sobs come out easily.

I collapse on the soil, my crying wracking my body so much that I can barely breathe. Two days left where my survival is somewhat of a guarantee. Two days left where the rebels are also sure to survive. Two days where I don't have to aim a gun at them. Two days.

My family. In two days, I could see them. I could save them. If we succeed, this is the first step toward a nightmare-free Earth. No more darthra to terrorize me, or outsiders itching to kill innocents. A world free of Émigré control, with my family at my side. That's what I have to hold on to. Regardless of what tries to drag me down and destroy me, I have to hold on to this one hope. Grit my teeth, pull through, and fight back because I am a Collins. A rebel. My fight isn't over, it's just begun.

SIXTY-FOUR

WHEN I GET BACK TO THE FIRE, COLE IS THERE. HE'S NAMING
off a list of Émigrés we can trust. Aiira, Ticon, Razec, Errud, Verno.
They all sound too foreign for me to remember in the heat of a
mission, so I take to repeating them in my head. When we get to the
doors of the prison ship, we should be let in by one of them right
away. They'll know it's us, because soldiers rarely come in, especially
at night. They also know our faces and names and should be able to
pinpoint the location where our families are being held. All we have
to do is tell them we were sent by Kovet and Kaihri.

The sun sets and we decide to rest for the night. It's unseasonably
colder than it's ever been. Cole suggests we build a fire with the wood
he provided and promises to be a vigilant guard in the trees. But only
when Brianna decides to go up with him does everyone seem okay
with the idea. We gather around the flames, soaking in their warmth.
One by one, the other rebels drift off to sleep. The thought of Cole
being on our side with the weapons we have must be putting them at
ease, if only for a moment. Yet once again, I can't sleep.

I stare into the fire, swallowed whole by the terrifying images that
haunt me as they dance around my eyes again, like they do every

night. Jacob. The men in the Reserve. The couple I shot. The man Ross shot. The man Tyler shot. Tyler's arm and leg gashed, blood everywhere, and a dead look in his eyes. How pale Garrett was the last time I saw him. How the blonde-haired girl looked when her eyes glazed over. I was definitely not cut out for any of this, yet here I am. And now I'm partly responsible for more deaths.

The fire cracks like the snap of a whip, sending my heart into overdrive, thudding in my ears. My hands automatically go to my gun, although I look up to see no danger. Only Rebecca's eyes, bright green orbs glowing from the fire, staring back at me. Her hands are clenched tightly around a knife, Alfie's knife I recognize. As our bodies start to calm down, we look at each other with understanding.

"Never gets easier, does it?" I murmur to break the silence that feels like it's suffocating me.

"We can't help it." She attempts to smile back. It feels like it takes me hours to finally fall asleep.

The next two days go by in a blur too quick for my liking. I train, but not with my gun, since the number of bullets we have left is limited. Instead, I carve a target into a wide tree trunk with the help of Molly and practice throwing my knife beyond the point of my arms aching. Sometimes other rebels practice with me or after me, but we don't talk to one another. Conversations feel forced and pointless unless we discuss the mission.

I do everything I can to keep myself distracted from the negative thoughts that pull me under waves of sadness. Instead, I try to keep focused on what will keep me alive. Due to the countless amount of times I've done that in the past few months, I'm actually able to get some sleep both nights. Nightmares are still frequent, but I get enough rest.

The morning of the mission goes by with little discussion, as expected. Cole takes off to inform the Émigrés that we have yet to be found. The afternoon is spent getting ready. Then we head out just before sundown. We have a long walk ahead of us, and we need to be on the lookout for darthra, but nobody talks much to pass the time.

Just hushed conversations now and then. As I glance over at everyone's blank expressions, I note we look like a brainwashed army ourselves.

We stop for our first and only break, and oddly enough, the open area is right next to a cemetery. Tyler immediately wanders off to check it out while the rest of us give our legs some down time. As I watch him, I think he's trying to make sure the area is clear. Yet when he kneels next to a headstone, I notice him scribbling in his notebook. When I squint, I can barely make out the writing carved into it that he seems to be copying down.

"Prepare for death and follow me."

Those words feel comforting somehow as we get ready to embark again. Olivia, Grace, Kira, and Ross all stay behind so that we have somewhere to retreat back to if needed. Leah is eager to go with the rest of us, but Kieran is quick to hold her back. As calm as he can, he reminds her that neither of them have guns or know what they're looking for. In fact, none of them have guns, but Kira has her weapon, which is sure to keep them all safe.

Just the sight of an Émigré gun reminds me of something. Elliot can use those weapons. For reasons we still don't know. Has he figured it out yet?

"Hey," I make my way over to Elliot, keeping my voice low so no one else can fully hear. "Smile like I'm trying to cheer you up."

"What is it?" He asks, doing as I say. I plaster a smile on my face as well.

"Did you ever ask them why you were able to use the gun?"

"No," His eyes harden, although he tries to keep a small smile. "I still don't trust them enough. If there's one thing that gives me. . .us. . .an advantage over them, I'll keep it to myself." He walks ahead of me with a forced pat on the shoulder, signaling the end of our conversation.

We all continue to walk in silence, ears aching for the slightest sound of a darthra. Any minute now, we'll be entering their exclusive territory. Once we do, it'll be almost impossible to turn back. It seems like only seconds pass by when we start to split up into pairs. The hope is that we'll cover more ground, and we only need one pair to succeed.

The sun has completely set as Tyler and I walk alone. There's so much fear festering within me that I'm sweating despite the chilly air. Every part of me is hyper-alert, no matter how much time passes. When a low growl rings through the woods, my heart almost stops.

Tyler meets my eyes, but we keep walking. The growl was distant. Probably a few miles out. Regardless, it means the darthra are awake and alert. And someone or something has mistakenly crossed the path of one. I try to slow my erratic breathing and pounding heart as we pick up the pace. Four steps later, a scream pierces the air.

"Molly," I whisper. The scream indicated that she was most likely startled, but I can hear the beast vocally coming to life. The sound of a bullet follows before Tyler has a chance to reply. Vicious barks begin to mix with the sound of gunfire as I look at him in a panic. His eyes are wild and afraid, his muscles tense like he's ready to bolt. Molly's cries of obvious pain can still be heard as I grab his shoulder. "We can't go after them,"

"What?" He looks as though he's just realized I'm here. Emotions are clouding over him. Like they did for both of us in the Reserve when the laser sliced through Jacob's skull. I need him to keep me grounded. If he loses it, I will too.

"We have to keep going." My voice is firm, my grip tight like a vice. Elliot is yelling something now. Something I can't understand with the distance between us and the other sounds thrashing through the woods to fight for my attention. But the sound of him alone causes my eyes to water. Finally, Tyler nods, and we break out into a run. More than anything, I want to go back. Find them, fight alongside them, rescue them if they need it. With a heavy heart, I can only hope the continuous gunfire means they'll be okay. I hate myself already.

The two of us only start to slow down when we can barely hear the gunfire and the roars of the beasts. Next line of defense is guards, and we'll need to find some to ambush. Tyler wordlessly points up a nearby tree, indicating we should climb up and scope things out. I let him go first, since he's capable of getting higher. When I follow, it feels like it takes me hours to struggle up the trunk. Sitting on a thick branch is my first chance to let out a long exhale. Even still, my brain seems to be imagining the worst for Molly and Elliot. Are any of the others coming to their aid? Or have they all left them to their own devices. . .abandoned them, like we did?

I remind myself to think only positive thoughts as I look out ahead. I don't see much, except for a random parking lot with some cars still there. We must be in a park or something like that.

"The ship's not too far away." Tyler murmurs above me.

"See any guards?" I ask.

"None close by," He sighs. "And they don't look like they're planning on coming near us anytime soon. I think we're gonna have to lure them over."

"How?"

"Not sure yet. I don't want to waste any bullets."

"There's some cars to our right. Maybe we can find something." I suggest. When he voices agreement, we climb down and head over. Most of the cars have broken windows or doors that are already wide open. A rotting skeleton lays by the first car, a four-door that looks gray in the dark of night. I try not to think about the human remains as I search the car for anything useful, hearing Tyler walk to the other end of the lot.

"What do you think we should look for?" I inquire before he's too far away.

"Car keys, lighters, an air horn would be nice."

That gets a small laugh out of me when I get to work. All I find are chip bags and pop cans. No keys. Moving on to a large van, I'm impatient as I search from top to bottom. Of course, there's nothing but gas receipts. Two years into the invasion leaves little to scavenge. Common sense. I'm just about to give up looking through a rusted pickup when my hands slip across something between the seat cushions in the backseat. I unearth something that can finally get us somewhere.

A pack of matches.

The gears in my brain spin furiously as I try to hatch a plan. Matches. Cars. Gasoline. Fire. Explosion. Skimming through the van again, my eyes scan for a single pesky gas receipt. I know I just saw some. Opening the console, I see several and pluck out the most recent. I call Tyler over, holding up the thin pack of matches.

"When was the invasion?" I demand.

"The date? June 5th, 2036." He looks unsure of what I'm trying to do until I speak again.

"This van should have almost a full tank." I raise a brow, and he nods. For a split second, it almost looks like he's about to smirk.

"Be quick," He pats my shoulder.

"You don't want to do it?"

"I trust you." With that, he goes off to take cover.

I open the driver's side door and pull the lever under the seat that opens the door to the gas cap. Opening the gas cap, Elliot and Molly's screams replay in my mind as the scent of gasoline starts to fill my nose. If I can succeed, Elliot and Molly can be safe as long as they're still alive. They ARE still alive. And I can save my family. I can do this. Lighting a match, I toss it in and sprint off as fast as my legs can carry me. I'm almost in the clear when I think someone calls my name.

The explosion isn't as loud as I had hoped, but it still sends a jolt through my body. Even as far away as I managed to run, I can feel the heat from the flames. I had intended to keep running, but the sound of my name tempts me to turn around. When I do, I see Alfie on his knees, clutching his ears. My legs urge me to catapult toward him, yet the terror shaking through me keeps me still.

What have I done?

What have I done?

He stumbles forward. His eyes are unstable as they scan the darkness until they find me. I finally make my way toward him as he squints at me, a grunt of pain slipping past his lips. He seems dazed, but more than that. He seems injured.

"Are you okay?" I ask, my eyes searching for any form of injury and finding none. Although I notice that the tips of his hair that used to stick up have been singed off.

"What?" He yells way too loud as he removes his hands from his ears. My eyes must show my alarm because he looks at me in confusion. "I can't. . ..my ears are ringing. . ..it's hard to. . ."

"I said are you okay?" I repeat myself louder, closer to his ears.

"I think so." His voice is still too loud. We're going to draw attention to ourselves. "It's just my ears." I hold a finger to my lips. Realization creeps across his features. "Oh, God. . ." He says quietly.

"What's happened?" Tyler is by our side as the flames rage on.

"Alfie got caught up in the explosion," I explain.

"I didn't know what you were doing," Alfie says. He's trying to be quieter, but it's not enough. "I saw you and was just going to meet up with you. I didn't know. I'm sorry."

"Where's Rebecca?" Tyler catches on, speaking up so that Alfie can hear.

"Up in the trees. I'm sure she saw everything." He answers.

"Go back to her, let her help you," Tyler commands, and Alfie nods as he takes off.

Everything is starting to fall apart, and just when I think it can't get any worse, I spot flashes of white in the woods. Émigré soldiers. Without even thinking, I start to go after Alfie, but Tyler drags me away.

"We have to keep going," He reminds me, his voice breaking at the end. I reluctantly go with him, using legs that no longer feel like my own.

"He won't be able to hear them," I protest as he yanks me behind a tree and holds me against him.

The soldiers will be led straight to him. I'm sure they heard us, along with the explosion. As I peek around the tree, I see that it's only two soldiers. But I know even if they only sent two to check things out, more will arrive in seconds, especially if they know there are humans here.

"We have to get our people back. Only one of us has to succeed." Tyler's voice is desperate, like he's on the verge of losing it and is trying to keep himself sane. When did we ever operate this way? When did it become more important to succeed than to save our friends?

SIXTY-FIVE

My heart clenches as everything seems to unfold in slow motion. The soldiers spot Alfie and fire their guns before he sees them. It's not lasers that burst out from the guns, so it has to be darts. Alfie goes down as the soldiers close in on him. This is where our pact applies. I have the perfect opportunity, even if he's a little too far away. This is where we have to shoot him. But I don't do that. And neither does Tyler.

"Ambush," He whispers, and we take off. We are so quiet and so quick that the fury I feel seems louder than anything else. I approach the smallest of the two soldiers. For a brief moment, I'm reminded that they could be human and I shouldn't go for the kill. Their helmets must make it harder to hear because we're practically on top of them before they start to whip around. But it's too late.

I tackle the smaller soldier, wrestling their gun away. They retaliate, elbowing me hard in the stomach. As pain blossoms up my abdomen, I work to pin them down despite my tiny frame. This soldier is almost as small as me, so I'm able to work on finding a way to get the helmet off. I can hear Tyler and the other soldier scuffling around as I fumble with the helmet, finally getting it to release. Long, red hair spills out. I flip the soldier over to find myself staring into the eyes of my only friend from the Reserve.

Tina. Of course it's her. She didn't run away from the Reserve. She was brainwashed into becoming a soldier. Memories flash past my eyes, hitting my heart like a bullet each time. Making snicker-doodle cookies after work. Playing hopscotch with Annie after saving enough points for some chalk.

Humans are brainwashed into our own soldiers and deemed disposable, Cole's voice rings in my ears. Tina looks at me and recognition flashes in her eyes. Hope springs alive within me. Maybe they didn't erase her memories of me. But it doesn't take long for her expression to morph into hatred, and she bites my arm hard enough to draw blood. I unintentionally release her. My hesitation gives her all the time she needs. She tackles me back, bringing her knee up to my chin so hard I see stars as my teeth crash together. I think I hear the firing of a gun, but either way, Tina is still fighting back and has the upper hand.

"Tina," I choke out, but all that gets me is a brief look of confusion and a hard blow across the face that rivals what her brother did to me. Her nails scrape across my cheek, which begins to sting.

I have to find it within me to hurt my best friend. To kill her if it means I stay alive. The problem is, I don't want her dead. It's not her fault she's brainwashed. I wrestle her back, determined to grab hold of her gun and knock her out with it. She's having none of it, punching me in the stomach to make me lose my breath and let her go. Each blow sends jittery shocks of pain surging through my body. The hatred is clear, but she can't kill me. The Émigrés want me alive, and I can use that to my advantage.

If I could just get up.

My head is spinning. I'm struggling to get air in my lungs. Tina grabs her gun, ready to dart me when Tyler comes out of nowhere and tackles her to the ground. The gun slams against the Earth at an awkward angle. As the tip raises upward, something clicks and it fires a laser instead of a dart. I try to hurl myself out of the way, but the blue beam still surges across my right leg.

I cry out in agony. My knee and calf feel like they're on fire, and when I look down, I can see parts of my pants burned off, and bloody skin exposed. Looking back up at Tina, I see Tyler get his gun ready to shoot.

"Don't!" I scream, my voice cracking in pain. "I know her." Tyler wastes no time pinning her down, and whipping out a needle I've never seen, he injects it into her. Her eyes slip shut, and he makes his way toward me.

"How bad is it?" He kneels beside me, his eyes pained.

"Bad," I choke out, struggling to get up. He helps me stand. Yet even with adrenaline pumping through me like liquid fire, it hurts to move my right leg.

"You knew her?" He asks. I nod.

"Tina, she was in the Reserve with me." I feel a whimper of pain coming and I fight to hold it back. Attempting to pull myself together, I clear my throat and speak. "Where did you get the needle?"

"In the other guy's armor. Looks like there's two in each armor vest. I don't think you were there when Cole explained. It's the same stuff as the darts. Don't worry, she's still breathing."

"Did you shoot him?"

"Yes, he wasn't human,"

"What if the darthra get to her?" Tears spill out of my eyes.

"They won't. We're too close to the ship. They avoid it because of the sniper guns." He reminds me.

"Alfie. . ."

"We have to leave them. Do you want me to take you back?"

"No!" I yell, forcing myself to stand on my own. "I can keep going." Hobbling over to Tina, I rip off her armor and try not to look at her face.

"Are you sure?" The concern in his voice is so strong that I find myself getting irritated.

"My injury can get us in if no one opens the door for us." I snap, and as I put on the pants, I hiss as the fabric runs over my wound. Blood immediately soaks through any part of the right leg that is white fabric instead of armor. I put on the rest of the armor, hearing Tyler doing the same. Yanking on the helmet, I walk toward him as best I can, trying not to think of the pain. Once his helmet is on, he helps me drag Alfie and Tina behind the trees, where I can only hope they won't be found. That hope lasts about three seconds, though, because I can hear more soldiers coming even with my helmet making everything sound muffled. They're yelling to communicate and will find my friends before I even get to the ship. But we take off anyway, desperately trying to complete the mission.

Once we get to the clearing where the mothership is, its size still baffles me. I knew it would be huge, but it nearly seems too big to fly. Tyler leads me over to the smaller ship that we know to be the prison ship. Each step brings another wave of pain and anxiety. I feel like every soldier that passes is eyeing us suspiciously through their helmets, and every sniper laser gun is trained on us. Somehow, we get to the doors without any problems. Luck seems to finally be on our side when the doors open as a wave of soldiers passes behind us.

"Where the hell are you going?" One of the soldiers demands as they pass. The voice suggests another brainwashed human.

"She's hurt." Tyler answers. At this point, the pain is really getting to me, and he has to practically hold me up. My vision seems to be blurring a little. How much blood have I lost already?

"The medic station is in Ship 1, idiot!" The soldier yells back. I feel hands starting to grab me.

"They are with me." A voice says. In front of me, I can see a pair of violet eyes belonging to a figure outlined by the light of the prison ship.

"What for?" The soldier sounds confused. I don't dare turn around.

"I can heal minor injuries. We do not want her crowding up the medic station. Must I remind you of what you learned in your training?" The Émigré stares the soldier down, and I get my eyes to focus on her. Dark red hair. Sharp cheekbones and jaw. Nearly as tall as Tyler. She opened the door for us, so she must be on our side. I hope.

"You can be treated for minor injuries on any ship," the soldier recites with a sigh. Finally, I can hear him take off, muttering something about how my injury doesn't look minor. That seems to intensify the pain I feel. I don't even want to know how bad my wound looks if it feels this terrible.

"Come with me," she gazes at us with suspicion and what looks like pity as she guides us inside. The doors shut behind us and I try to get my eyes to focus on the interior. The blinding white lights overhead are painful. Walking swiftly, the Émigré leads us into the first door on the right. Once that door is closed behind us as well, she whips out a smaller laser gun and aims it at us.

"Helmets off, weapons on the ground," she commands as I take in the room. It looks like a small storage room, with mechanical silver parts and slick purple boxes everywhere. I do as she asks, eyes scanning for the nearest door, just in case she isn't on our side. "Rachel and Tyler." the corners of her mouth curve upward as she gets a look at our faces.

"Sent by Kovet and Kaihri," Tyler says, and she lowers her weapon.

"I am Razec. That seems . . . unpleasant." She stares down at my leg, and I do the same. Bright red blood is collecting onto the pristine white floor.

"Could you get her something to heal it? And then get Cole. . .Kovet to take her somewhere safe?" Tyler asks. Razec nods.

"Stay inside." She dashes out before I can even say a word.

"Take me somewhere? I'm not going anywhere!" I protest. Tyler looks at me with sadness, and I try to stand up straighter, although it causes me pain.

"You can barely walk." He states.

"Neither could you, but Émigré medicine healed you just fine." I retort.

"Rachel, I know you want to do this. I know, believe me. But let me finish this. You've done so much, risked so much. All I have to do is this one last thing. If you weren't hurt, I know you could do it."

"Don't do this," My voice is harsh, my gaze like daggers.

"We don't have much time! You know they've found Alfie. And Rebecca, too, I'm sure. There's no way, not in a million years, that they would think those two got this far on their own. That there's no one else with them. And you saw how the soldiers recognized us. They'll recognize them too and know to expect the whole group. Plus, it takes time to heal. And even when you do, you wanna waste time and find another thing of armor? One that's not suspiciously covered in blood? Or were you planning on waltzing around like that?" He's adamant, and I know his stance won't change. Once again, he's already made up his mind.

"You don't even know what my family looks like."

"I know your dad. I saw your mom and little sister at the Reserve."

"You've never seen Mary."

"I'm sure your parents will help me find her if she's not with them."

"Then why do this? Why not let me help?" My voice is rising and I step forward without thinking. A jolt of pain shoots up my leg again, making me gasp.

"You've always told me you do what you do for your family. I want to make sure you're reunited safely with them. Rachel, please, you know I have nothing to gain from this. I'm doing this for the rest of you. Let me make it up to you, especially. Please! I've screwed up. And I ignored the fact that all you wanted was your family. Let me make sure you get them back." His firm gaze makes his words seem sincere, but that can't be it. If it is, it can't be the only factor driving him.

"Your family," the lightbulb goes off in my brain. "You think you'll find them here? Just because I saw Tina."

"No," He begins, but I don't let him finish.

"See, I knew you were selfish! This is just like the-" An alarm like the one we heard in the Reserve starts blaring. Bright orange lights on the back wall begin to flash in warning. A soothing, robotic female voice begins speaking in a language I can't understand. When Tyler's eyes meet mine, they show panic, but also like he's deep in thought. Brain in overdrive. Coming up with a plan. He's right, we don't have much time, but before I can reason with him, he strides forward. Clutching my face in his hands, he crashes his lips to mine.

Disbelief. Confusion. Anger. A wave of emotions floods through me as my brain tries to process what's happening. Blood rushes to my cheeks, and I forget the searing pain in my leg. He's kissing me . . . but why? Is this his form of goodbye? No. Tyler's not one for intimacy. He may be hoping something like this would change my mind. But what he wants for certain is to distract me. Probably until Razec gets back.

I remember all the boxes behind him. Purple and shiny, with sharp edges. If I can pull him to me, disguise it as an act of passion, and push him away, maybe I can break free. My arms are just wrapping around his shoulders when I feel a familiar prick in my neck. I freeze as my blood runs cold.

The needle. He's just used his last needle. On me.

I grip his shoulders so tightly that it takes a few seconds for the Émigré drug to kick in. It almost seems like his eyes are filling with tears. The oceanic blue depths are on the verge of overflowing. But instead of extinguishing the anger in me, it fuels it to rage on.

"How. . ." Conveniently, whatever that drug is, starts to take effect as my legs begin to give out. "How could you?" I force myself to complete my sentence with as much venom as I can muster. With the last of my remaining arm's strength, I try to shove him away, but it's no use. He takes me in his arms and cradles me to keep me from falling. My eyes start to feel heavy as my body goes limp.

FIGHT, I scream in my own head, my voice rattling around in my brain. FIGHT BACK.

"I'm sorry," He whispers, and I want to slap him across the face.

"No," I mumble to myself and to him. I fight to keep my eyes open, but to no avail. They close for good against my will.

"I'm sorry, Rachel," His voice sounds thousands of miles away in the darkness. Seconds later, there's only silence.

SIXTY-SIX

The needle seems to pack a bigger punch than the darts, because this time, I have dreams in my drug-induced sleep. All of us rebels run off to the lake for a day of fun. Some go down to the shore to swim, but of course, others want to cliff dive. Tyler makes a big show of grabbing me and acting like he's going to jump off the edge with me in his arms, but all it takes is one panicked yelp to get him to let me go and jump without me. If only he was that understanding with me in reality.

It's Rebecca that takes my hand and leads me to the cliff. She asks if I want to jump with her, and I find myself nodding. Standing at the edge, I can see the dark water swirling at the bottom. It sort of looks like under the surface is a deep pit that goes down so far it's almost black in color. Tyler hasn't surfaced. In fact, I see none of the rebels in the water anymore. A new kind of fear, not related to heights, starts to seep in.

"Go," Rebecca says, and we launch off. Immediately, the distance between us and the water doubles. Our speed increases until I can no longer hold her hand. When I look over to her, she's disappeared. I'm falling for what feels like hours, the wind whipping harshly around me. It almost sounds like people screaming. No, it is people screaming. My mom. My dad. Callie. Every single rebel.

When I finally hit the water, iciness envelopes me and everything is dark and quiet again. It truly feels like I can't breathe. Invisible tentacles seem to be dragging me deeper no matter how much I fight it. I try to scream, but no sound comes out of my mouth. My heart is slamming against my chest. Just when it feels like there's no more air in my lungs, I wake up with a jolt.

I attempt to figure out where I am as fast as I can. I'm alone on a battered mattress, surrounded by wooden walls. The cracks are sealed with mud. Despite the eucalyptus smell of healing paste on my leg, the sheets and whatever oversized shirt was put on me smell like smoke and pond water. The outsider camp. That must be where I am. As if to confirm my theory, I can hear Leah talking outside the door.

"Why do you guys call it the Divide anyway? Sounds pretty lame if you ask me."

"Well, what do you want us to call it?" Damien's voice snaps. "Something like 'that place where all the buildings went boom'? Doesn't roll off the tongue as easily."

"How about just call it whatever city it was before?"

"It's a LINE of CITIES. Plural. God, why does it even matter to you?"

I walk at a slow pace towards the door, surprised at how painless it is. It feels like I was never injured, although the nasty scab running up my leg is proof that I was. With caution, I open the door. For a quick second, I think I may still be dreaming.

"Sleeping beauty awakens!" Leah shouts loud enough for me to wince, and it's clear I'm back in reality. Damien looks at me with what I can only guess is sadness. I look around for the others frantically but see no one in this tiny version of a living room.

"Where's. . ." I don't even know where to begin. "How. . .did I get here?"

"From what I was told, Cole brought you back." Leah answers.

"Where's Tyler?" My foggy brain decides to ask about the last person I saw.

"Let me put it this way, do you want the good news first or the bad news?" She keeps her voice light.

"Is he not here?" I can feel my face going pale. Leah frowns.

"Okay, I guess you want the bad news first. He didn't make it back. Well, I mean, he's alive. Just not. . .here." She attempts to explain.

"The Émigrés got him," Damien says as Leah nods. When it seems like Damien will take over getting me up to speed, she dashes out of the cabin. "But he managed to get most of your family."

"Most?" I sputter as I try to imagine what's happening to Tyler. Cole told us that torture awaits us when we get captured. Torture so severe we'll wish we were dead. I may be angry at him for what he did, but I wouldn't wish that fate on any of us.

The door opens and Leah strides in, flanked by my mother and father. I run toward them automatically, breaking down when they take me in their arms. As quick as I can manage, I stifle my tears and look up at them.

"Annie?" I dare to ask.

"She's sleeping. It's late." My mother answers calmly. I recognize her tone. The same one she used with me in the Reserve. With that, I don't even have to ask, but I do anyway.

"Mary?"

"She was kept separate from us. In a separate room, or something. I thought it was just because they had transferred her there before us, and they would put her in with us later. But they never did. We asked around the prison cells, and they all said she had been moved a few days before we arrived." My mother's voice cracks a little at the end, and my father wraps an arm around her. I take her hand, noticing how bad it's shaking. I'm sure she's come to the same conclusion as me. That if Mary is alive, she has already been brainwashed.

"Tyler went after her." My father continues. "We didn't have much information, and that was the problem. He must have gotten caught while trying to find her."

"Does . . . does Cole have any idea where she is?" I try to speak clearly.

"He's looking into it. I had no idea she was on the main ship. It's so huge. There are so many people. I wish I could have. . ." He trails off, his eyes beginning to glisten with unshed tears. I hug him again.

"You should rest," my mother suggests as I let go. "We all should." She kisses me on the forehead before embracing me once more. When she finally releases me, my parents walk out the door. Only then do I notice the sun has already risen. At least 8 hours have passed since I was on the prison ship.

The door bursts open again, and Kira and Rebecca walk in. I breathe an audible sigh of relief at the sight of Rebecca, and I'm about to ask where Alfie is when I see the fire in her eyes. She strides toward me without hesitation. Before I can even open my mouth, I feel a slap across my face that alights every nerve in my body. Both of us are quiet for a moment as the pain intensifies on my cheek.

"I was going to go help Elliot and Molly," she begins, her voice frighteningly low. "I thought everything would be fine. You know, because Alfie saw you and Tyler. He would be with you guys. Not alone. But no, I've barely taken two steps when I hear an explosion. I turn around and haul back just in time to see Alfie running in my direction. I think, oh great, he wasn't hurt! But then I see the soldiers. And then he goes down. And it takes everything in me not to scream. And what do I see? You and Tyler abandoning him. I guess I should thank you for not shooting him like we agreed, right? I couldn't even shoot him myself! But to see you leave him like that. . .you're lucky Marcus found me and dragged me all the way back to Kira."

Her words come out so fast and fierce that my heart sinks rapidly. It's like a rope is tied around my neck, and each sentence makes it tighter and tighter.

"I kept thinking about that explosion. You two did it, didn't you?

Didn't you?" She's yelling now, and Damien steps forward to hold her back. I can only nod.

"I can't believe I'm saying this." She smiles in a way that sends a chill down my spine as she wipes away her tears. "And I'll probably take it back. But I hope they wipe away every single one of Tyler's memories of you. Because I know they'll wipe every memory of Alfie's that involves me. It'll make things almost even. Almost fair. At least to me. It still won't fully compare, though. You can't fathom what it's like to know the one you love is going to forget you and there's nothing you can do."

Rebecca stomps back out, and I know I deserved more backlash than that. She's right about that. We abandoned Alfie. Even though it was agreed to, it's still not going to hurt her any less. I should have told Tyler to take Alfie back and walked to the ships on my own. Even with my injury, I still could have probably managed to get to the doors. If I didn't, at least Alfie would have been safe. But all of that is in the past. It doesn't matter now.

She is wrong about one thing, though. I love Tina, in a way. Maybe not in the same way she loves Alfie, but it's love, nonetheless. And of course, I love Mary. So the sinking, empty feeling of a loved one forgetting you is something I have started to experience. I have an idea what she feels regardless of Tyler entering the same fate.

I'm still angry at Tyler for what he did. Not only was I drugged, but he didn't give me a choice. Again. Yet he did manage to bring back the majority of my family, like he promised. I'm thankful for that. It's hard to fully understand what I feel or to know how I would react if he was still here. I do know that I feel hollow without him.

"Who else is captured? And is anyone dead?" I demand from Kira.

"Molly got taken. Angie was killed." She answers quietly. I take a deep, shaky breath before continuing.

"Are any of them going to keep their memories?"

"Molly is the only one we have control over because she's been hurt badly. We're still working on healing her."

"So Alfie and Tyler will both lose their memories," I state unemotionally.

"Yes," she whispers.

"What happens to you and your brother, then?"

"I don't know yet. We're hoping to try to free them before they get taken in for the procedure. They're being tortured until a room opens up, but they're high profile enough that it won't take long to get them a room. I'm hoping that if we can't get them out before that, we can intercept the memories before they're observed."

"Great," my voice is flat. "Where's Elliot?"

"In the room next to yours." Damien answers. I nearly break out into a sprint before Kira stops me.

"Wait! Cole gave this to me to give to you." She pulls a familiar black notebook out of her own white messenger bag. "He said Tyler wanted you to have it."

Tears fill my eyes faster than I can handle. They spill out onto the notebook as I clutch it with trembling hands. He knew there was a chance he wouldn't make it, so he thought ahead. And now he really is gone, in a way. Gone from us, at least.

SIXTY-SEVEN

I don't want to break down. Not yet. So I go to the room I've now claimed as my own and place the notebook on the mattress without looking at it. Going down the hallway, I knock on the door of Elliot's room. When there's no response, I gently open it. The room is dark, but from some kind of light, I can see enough. He's sitting on the floor, his back to me.

"Elliot," I can't seem to speak with even an ounce of fake happiness. He doesn't turn around. A plate of food lies untouched beside him. Something is beeping softly, but I don't know if that's just in my head as well.

"I couldn't save her," He chokes out. I immediately go to him and wrap him in my arms. "I kept missing when I shot. It was so dark. . .so hard to see them. Angie and Marcus had to intervene. Angie didn't make it." He's crying into my shoulder now. "Molly got her hand bitten off. She tried to run to divert the darthra from Angie, but when I finally went to look for her, I heard the soldiers take her. I had to go back with Marcus and Rebecca. I couldn't keep going. Not after that." His sobs intensify. "I'm a coward. A failure."

"Shh, I'm here," I murmur, rubbing his back the way my mother used to with me. His hands clutch me as if trying to find solace. As he moves, something clatters to the ground, and I pull away from him slightly to take a look. It's like a tiny computer tablet, screen glowing brightly in the darkness. I can hear it beep again.

"What is this?" I let Elliot go to pick it up.

"It's Kira's." He attempts to compose himself. "It lets her keep in touch with the ship. I. . .was looking to see if there was security footage of the prison rooms where they're being held. Just so that I know they're still alive."

Looking down at the screen, I can see Alfie, dressed in white with dark purple bruises already decorating his face and arms. He's in a tiny, all-white room with no windows, sitting in the center with his eyes staring blankly ahead. The room is no bigger than a tiny bathroom, with no bed or shower or anything. Only what looks like a silver toilet in the left corner. And a drain in the center of the room. Even with him sitting so far away from the camera, the image is so clear that I can see him shivering. Just this sight alone makes me feel like the air around me just got heavier like I'm being shrouded in guilt, fear, and sadness. I sit watching him without a sound, wondering if there was any way that I could reach out to him. Comfort him. Apologize over and over.

"What's with the beeping?" I ask when I hear it again.

"They do it every few minutes. My guess is to keep them from sleeping." Elliot's voice is shaking again. I barely have time to process this before he continues. "I should be the one to tell you this. So that you don't notice it later and come asking. My parents are dead."

"What?" I gasp, nearly dropping the tablet. "Did they not make it out of the prison alive?" Elliot begins shaking his head back and forth as tears spill down his cheeks.

"They weren't even in the prison when Tyler got there. Your family told me they were killed not long after they arrived on the ship. They originally thought my family had been moved to somewhere else, just like Mary. But they heard some human guards talking."

I hold him to me again as I try to think about what Elliot's parents could have possibly done to warrant their executions. Everyone else seemed to be scheduled for brainwashing without question. No reason to be killed if they could be used. What made his parents so different? What had they done? And does that mean Mary's dead, too?

All of a sudden, I can hear a faint scream coming from the video. The hairs on the back of my neck stand up. I think I recognize the voice. When Alfie perks up and buries his face in his hands, I'm certain as to who the blood-chilling screams belong to. Tyler.

"What's going on? How do I look into his feed? What's happening to him?" The questions frantically spill out of my mouth.

"It's better if you don't look." He insists, taking the tablet from my hands.

"Why? Let me see!" I attempt to take it back, but he holds it away. On the screen, I can see Alfie rocking back and forth as the screams continue.

"I already saw them do it to Alfie. Didn't you see how he looked?" The bruises, the shivering. That doesn't tell me anything. "They fill the room with water. Completely. Which means he has nowhere to go and is eventually submerged. He doesn't have anywhere to get air."

The memory of Tyler and me standing at the edge of the cliff hits me hard enough that it feels like my breath is knocked out of me. His fear of drowning. The only fear he had clearly communicated to me. The one that may very well be the most severe. Every ounce of anger I feel at him fully fades away. In seconds, I'm nothing but completely, deeply terrified for him.

"As he's trying to stay alive and not panic, I'm sure they're monitoring his heart rate. Once enough time has passed, they drain the room. Then the electrocution begins." Elliot continues.

"Electrocution?" I repeat dumbly.

"I thought the silver things on their wrists were shackles. But it's what the Émigrés are electrocuting them with." It's what Tyler is experiencing as we speak. Although I'm thankful that Elliot has turned off the tablet, my fists are clenched, and I shut my eyes.

My hatred toward the Émigrés stirs up again. They aren't doing this for information. Or to avenge deaths of their own. They're doing this because it makes them feel better. It amuses them to torture those who made them look like fools. This is all part of the fun.

"Annie wants to see you," my mother's voice says from the doorway, causing both Elliot and me to flinch. I turn and give her a nod, standing on my feet and extending a hand to Elliot. He takes it and I firmly pull him up.

"We can't let them win," I mutter, gritting my teeth.

"We won't." His voice is stronger now. His fury matches mine.

Both of us walk together behind my parents. I've only taken a few steps outside when Leah stops us.

"You didn't give me a chance to tell you the good news. I'm sure all you've heard is the bad stuff." She offers me a gentle smile.

"I wouldn't call it good news," Damien scoffs as he walks by us. Toward Grace, I assume. Which reminds me. . .

"Everyone you stayed back with is okay, right?" I ask.

"Well. . .don't hate me. . .but Ross escaped. He didn't hurt anyone, I swear. We were all just so tired. He said he had to take a piss. Kieran untied him. He said he wanted some privacy and took off."

"His choice," I mutter, and I realize I don't care. Everything I had done for him was because I knew it was what Callie would want if she were alive. At this point, she might as well be dead. My actions don't matter, because to her I'm just another enemy.

"The GOOD news, at least to me, is what Brianna did," Leah starts. "The Reserve apparently has nightly broadcasts. Like the news. Do you remember those?"

"Yes." I nod. We were all forced to watch before curfew. It was at the end of my shift, as well as the beginning of other people's shifts, depending on their job. But every night, we had to tune in to these massive screens surrounding the main building. I barely paid attention because almost every report was the same. Something about the amount of food grown that day in each Reserve worldwide. Snippets about the Kofali working on better housing for the humans. Longer break times are in consideration. Another human was cured of cancer by the Kofali in the medic station. It only took about a week before I'd had enough of them smugly patting themselves on the back, trying to make us think they were helping us. That they were inherently good.

"Well, she and Damien found the newsroom by accident. It was in the prison ship."

"They interrupted the broadcast?" Elliot jumps ahead, pulling out the tablet and tapping the screen. "I know there's a section where broadcasts are stored. Let me just find it."

"Here," Leah grabs the tablet, taps it a few times, and hands it back. I stare at the screen, watching the Kofali news anchor talking about the importance of human cooperation with the Kofali guards in the Reserve and the dangers of attempting to survive outside. I can only imagine how many nights she has talked about this since our incident at the Reserve. Looking closer, I watch as her violet eyes gaze back at us unemotionally. Her tone is as professional as always.

When she starts to talk about the amount of each fruit and vegetable grown that day, things start to change. The door bursts open, obviously unlocked and unguarded. They had no reason to think anyone who could get into that ship would want to go into a newsroom. The anchor is startled. Looking back to see only two armored, helmeted soldiers, she starts to relax. She thinks nothing of it. Maybe assumes it's a precaution. Which allows for one of them to step forward and slam their silver gun down on her head.

She crumples onto the control table as the soldier takes off their helmet. It's Brianna, who gazes at the camera with eyes full of determination. Knowing she only has a few moments before she's cut off from the air, she speaks fast but with vigor.

"Humans of the Reserve, this is one of the rebels of the Ruins. I am here to tell you that, yes, it is possible to fight back. These aliens, whether you know them as Kofali or Émigrés, are not immortal. We can still win this. A day will come when the rebels will liberate you from the Reserve and take back the Earth from these monsters. Be ready for that day."

The message is simple and clear. With that, she puts on the helmet to make her escape with Damien.

"This was broadcast to the Reserve? Everyone saw it?" Elliot inquires.

"Not just to one. To ALL of them." Leah says with excitement. "All over the world!"

My heart leaps, and for the first time since I woke up, I'm thrilled. I understand why Damien is a little unhappy with this. The target on our backs keeps getting bigger and bigger, and he hates it. But this is what the people of the Reserve have been looking for. Someone to put their faith in. They tried to put it in Garret, but he's gone. Alfie is too, in a way. He and I are too young and too broken to properly take on the role Garret left behind. But Brianna is perfect. People will rally around her.

As quick as the lighting of a match, my role in this war becomes clearer. Tyler was right. I may not be a leader, a savior, or a symbol. But I can unify the rest of us in the Ruins. As Katherine and Patrick come out of the main building to greet me, I feel more certain. Even they look at me differently now. Genuine smiles, waiting to hear what I have to say. I haven't done much, but I'm in the position to do more. And Brianna has set things in motion.

Annie dashes out and leaps into my arms, and as I hold her close, I know what I have to do. This war is my fight, too. I have almost all of my family back, just like I wanted. Yet I'm not done. Even if I had Mary back, even if we all tried to survive on our own as a family, we wouldn't be safe. Not until this war is over. And I can help end it. I know that I can fight back, I will fight back, and I want to fight back, making this world safe again for my family and everyone else.

However insignificant the enemy finds my voice or my presence, they will know that every time they try to break me down piece by piece, they carve me into a warrior. A restless, furious warrior made up of every man, woman, and child they so heartlessly murdered. The hearts of the slain beat in mine. The hearts of those waiting to be free beat with mine. Their blood pumps through my veins. They ignite a fire in me that will push me through even the darkest of times and will refuse to ever be put out.

I am a warrior of the earth. And I will not stop until this planet is ours again.

--- END ---

AUTHOR'S NOTE

Dear reader,

Thank you so much for taking the time to read my debut novel. This book took me years to write, edit, and finally have the courage to publish.

It would mean the world to me if you left a review on Amazon. Every review helps to get my book out there for more people to read, and keeps me writing more books.

Thank you!

ACKNOWLEDGMENTS

I want to thank all of the people who made this book possible, because without you, I would have never published this. First, thank you to all my alpha readers: Michelle Teng, Jacob Bishop, Kirsten Bautista, and everyone on Wattpad. Your support and encouragement kept me going even when I wanted to give up.

Thank you to my beta readers, Fanna S, Drew J, and Maddie D. This book changed and improved so much due to your feedback.

And finally, thank you to Deranged Doctor Designs for the amazing cover. Your team brought my book to life.

ABOUT THE AUTHOR

 Elle Nolan is an emerging author of science fiction novels. She started writing poetry in grade school, and after being encouraged by a teacher, she joined a short story writing club. She went from writing novels in her diaries, then her school notebooks, and eventually her college laptop. After many long days and nights of writing and way too much procrastination, she finally got the courage to edit and publish her work.

Writing stories has always been the thing that made her the happiest. When she isn't writing, she enjoys hiking, cooking new recipes, and spending time with animals.

Learn more at ellenolanauthor.com

9 7 9 8 9 8 7 2 4 0 1 0 6